DOUBLE ALCHEMY

Susan Mac Nicol

Copyright 2014 Susan Elaine Mac Nicol

THE WORLD IN SHADOW

In modern London there lurks a warlock, Quinn Fairmont. Dangerous, powerful, tortured, sharing his body with the soul of an ancient Welsh sorcerer, Quinn is never alone—and never wholly himself. He fights against all those who would exploit his kind. He takes pleasure where he can find it.

In the forest of Hampstead Heath, Quinn's hometown, Cade Mairston appears to him like a waking dream. Lithe, lean and silver-eyed, he evokes feelings in Quinn unlike any other: lust with true affection, immediate and shocking. Cade is clearly more than he seems. And yet, if a man of the world, Cade is innocent. He knows nothing of warlocks, witchfinders or Withinners. He knows nothing of what he is, what he might be, or what he might *feel*. For him, the story is just beginning. Magyck, peril and passion await.

DOUBLE ALCHEMY

Susan Mac Nicol

www.BOROUGHSPUBLISHINGGROUP.com

PUBLISHER'S NOTE: This is a work of fiction. Names, characters, places and incidents either are the product of the author's imagination or are used fictitiously. Any resemblance to actual events, locales, business establishments or persons, living or dead, is coincidental. Boroughs Publishing Group does not have any control over and does not assume responsibility for author or third-party websites, blogs or critiques or their content.

DOUBLE ALCHEMY
Copyright © 2014 Susan Elaine Mac Nicol

All rights reserved. Unless specifically noted, no part of this publication may be reproduced, scanned, stored in a retrieval system or transmitted in any form or by any means, electronic, mechanical, photocopying, recording, or otherwise, known or hereinafter invented, without the express written permission of Boroughs Publishing Group. The scanning, uploading and distribution of this book via the Internet or by any other means without the permission of Boroughs Publishing Group is illegal and punishable by law. Participation in the piracy of copyrighted materials violates the author's rights.

Digital edition created by Maureen Cutajar
www.gopublished.com

ISBN 978-1-941260-04-3

As always—my family. The ones who are constantly neglected as I do things to men that are perhaps out of their understanding but they love and support me anyway.

ACKNOWLEDGMENTS

There are always so many people to thank when I produce a new book. I feel a little like one of the stars at the Oscars, standing on stage with my little piece of paper and facing out over a huge audience to say my (hopefully short) Thank Yous.

My publisher Boroughs has to be one of the first. I have an editor called Jill Limber who believes in me and is my constant nurturer in all things writing related. I have a feisty CEO called Michelle Klayman who is constantly on my case to tell me I'll get where I want to be one day and to keep writing. Then there's Chris Keeslar, Editor in Chief, who can put a cover and blurb together like nobody's business and make it look so easy. They are all so supportive and people I count as friends as well.

And then there's my readers. The people who constantly amaze me with their unswerving support and love of my stories. Without them, I'd be nowhere. They are my sanity, the ones who cheer me on and inspire me to write the next one. I love each and every one of you.

CONTENTS

Title Page

Copyright

Dedication

Acknowledgments

Chapter 1

Chapter 2

Chapter 3

Chapter 4

Chapter 5

Chapter 6

Chapter 7

Chapter 8

Chapter 9

Chapter 10

Chapter 11

Chapter 12

Chapter 13

Chapter 14

Chapter 15

Chapter 16

Chapter 17

Chapter 18

[Chapter 19](#)

[Chapter 20](#)

[Chapter 21](#)

[Chapter 22](#)

[Chapter 23](#)

[Chapter 24](#)

[Chapter 25](#)

[Chapter 26](#)

[Chapter 27](#)

[Chapter 28](#)

[Chapter 29](#)

[Chapter 30](#)

[Chapter 31](#)

[Chapter 32](#)

[Chapter 33](#)

[Chapter 34](#)

[Chapter 35](#)

[Chapter 36](#)

[Chapter 37](#)

[Chapter 38](#)

[Chapter 39](#)

[Chapter 40](#)

[Chapter 41](#)

[*Author's Note*](#)

[*Author Bio*](#)

DOUBLE ALCHEMY

I will adore my Father, My God, my strengthener,
Who infused through my head a soul to direct me.
Who has made for me in perception my seven faculties
Of fire and earth and water and air,
And mist and flowers and southerly wind.
Other senses of perception thy father formed for me.
One is to have instinct, with the second I touch,
With the third I call, with the fourth I taste,
With the fifth I see, with the sixth I hear.
With the seventh I smell.

—excerpt from the *Book of Taliesin*, "Song to the Great World"

Chapter 1

Cade Mairston looked at his watch. Seven o'clock. He heaved a sigh as he started the walk home from the gym.

Even the punishment of circuit training and swimming the pool until he could hardly breathe hadn't relaxed him completely. Today had been the day from hell at work and he was glad it was over.

Absently, he brushed dark, wavy hair from his face as he walked the route home through Hampstead Heath to Little Venice and his beloved houseboat, the *Lucky Devil*, moored on the river. He shared it with a Persian cat called Marco Polo who'd be wondering where he was.

The evening was still fairly light and Cade enjoyed the final setting rays of the sun as it disappeared behind the horizon. He quickened his step, anxious for the soft depths of his old and comfy couch.

A strange sound attracted his attention, a slight movement catching his eye through the trees. He stopped. Even though he was a muscular five-foot seven and powerfully built through years of swimming and aqua aerobics, cold fear dribbled down his spine.

Cade frowned. He wasn't usually so jumpy, but the whisper of sound he'd heard, deep and husky, sounded like the noise someone made behind you as they raised a knife, ready to strike. He shivered, risking a quick glance behind him. There was no one there.

The air was heavier now somehow, seeming to shimmer. He blinked to clear his vision then scowled at his silliness and continued walking. Then he heard the noise again, louder than before, a sort of low chant, repetitive and mesmerising. Drawn to its source like a ball bearing to a magnet, Cade moved trance-like toward the sound.

A tall, broad-shouldered figure bent low over the ground, crouching as it seemed to study something that had taken its interest. A dark cloak billowed out around the figure and Cade caught a glint of something shiny at the waist.

The figure rose from the ground as a faint mist swirled around it. He stopped chanting suddenly, raising his head to sniff the air.

Cade ducked behind a huge tree as the figure rose to his feet, looking around warily. Cade had no idea why he was hiding; it just seemed like the right thing to do.

What the fuck is wrong with me? I'm a grown man, for God's sake, not a damn sissy boy.

Yet there he stood, holding his breath. Cade's heart quickened and he couldn't help feeling that surely this strange apparition could hear the sound of his heart pounding. He swallowed, wishing he'd just continued on the path home. This felt…*dangerous*, as if it was something it shouldn't be.

He'd no desire to become the mutilated corpse of some psycho killer's next victim. The figure muttered something, a harsh, guttural sound that made Cade shiver uncontrollably. His body prickled unnaturally as if tiny ants were biting in thousands of places. Cade closed his eyes, willing the alien sensation away.

Then it was gone. The feeling dissipated, his heart slowed down and the sense of danger passed. He waited a few moments then opened his eyes.

He shouted in fright as he saw a blurred figure before him, standing about four feet away. The figure reached out an arm and made a move toward him.

Cade moved forward instinctively, ready to plant his foot in his would-be attacker's groin then punch him in the hollow of the throat just above the chest. Matt, an ex-boyfriend and a martial arts instructor, had taught him that was a good way to disable an attack.

The figure was swifter. Even as Cade struck out at the person, he moved back and to the side in a deft move, with reflexes quicker than Marco Polo's.

Cade went hurtling forward, the impetus of his intended strike making him fall, and landed ignominiously flat on his face.

As he lay there, slightly winded, an amused voice behind him said, "Very impressive. Now if you promise not to kick me in the balls whilst I help you up, I'm sure we'll both get along famously. I promise you I'm not going to hurt you. I was just wondering what you were doing hiding behind a tree. I thought you might be in trouble."

Cade sat up, tugging the grass and twigs from his hair as he looked up in frustrated 'male ego' shame at the tall figure standing before him. The stranger's face was quizzical, his broad shoulders shaking with suppressed laughter, his dark blond hair catching the straying lights of the sun.

Despite his situation, Cade appreciated the stranger's considerable assets. The blond man was indeed very palatable to the eyes. Taller than him, with lean, muscled legs and a torso that just whimpered "bite me, lick me."

Cade had no doubt that beneath the expensive dress shirt and tailored suit lurked the physique of a Greek god. At least, that was *his* fantasy. Truth be told, he felt rather foolish at his undignified tumble.

He scowled. "Who the hell are you? And where did you come from?"

The man chuckled but didn't answer his questions. "I saw you hunkered down against a tree, your eyes shut and looking as if you'd seen the hounds of hell at your heels. I thought I could help, a Sir Galahad coming to the rescue of a fair knave, perhaps?"

Cade's hackles rose at the teasing tone.

The stranger frowned as he moved forward, holding out his hand. "Perhaps if I introduced myself, we could start again. Quinn Fairmont."

He held out a hand and Cade regarded it mutinously. Finally he reached out and shook it half-heartedly and Fairmont pulled him to his feet. "Cade Mairston. And I'm no fucking knave in need of rescue."

Quinn Fairmont smiled at him, having the last word but his eyes narrowed and his nostrils flared. He held onto Cade's hand too long until finally Cade pulled it back, feeling a strange disquiet as well as a familiar sexual stirring in his groin, with his cock slowly rising, scenting a possible conquest.

He was used to getting rock hard when he saw something he liked but the speedy progression of his current hard-on surprised him. Quinn regarded him with a more intense scrutiny than before. He lifted his head, sniffing the air, the same as the figure Cade had seen earlier had done. It was a disconcerting sight, like a lion scenting its prey.

"Did you see that man in the clearing?" Cade asked him. He needed to take his mind off the turmoil in his groin and the feeling of disquiet in his belly. He blinked, trying to clear the irritating haze in the air.

Quinn frowned and turned around to peer behind him. "What man?"

"There was a man crouched down on the ground not too long ago. He was whispering." Cade's vision cleared.

Quinn Fairmont took another step back, his face set. The smile he'd been wearing had disappeared.

Quinn shook his head carefully. "I didn't see anyone. There's only me around to my knowledge."

Cade stepped forward and gestured toward where he'd seen the figure. "He was there. I saw him. Are you sure you didn't see anyone?"

Quinn's face was blank now, his eyes watchful. He seemed less composed than before. "I saw no one. Like I told you, there was no one else around when I saw you."

Cade shook his head, mystified. "He must have disappeared very quickly then. I wonder where he went to."

Quinn moved closer to Cade and once again his nostrils flared. Cade's pupils dilated. His insides churned, lust for this man rising through his body as his groin burnt with heat. He stepped back in confusion, his erection swelling most uncomfortably. He swallowed.

Quinn's nostrils flared and he narrowed his eyes. His chin lifted and he sniffed. Despite his discomfort, Cade was taken aback by the action.

"Are you sniffing *me*?" he asked acerbically.

Quinn moved back once again, his face set. "Of course I'm not sniffing you, you idiot." He had regained some of his composure. Dark brown eyes gazed into Cade's hypnotically. Quinn's aftershave—Hugo Boss of some sort, a favourite of Cade's—drifted into his nostrils. The dark blond stubble on Quinn's chin beckoned Cade to run his fingers over it as his erection threatened to push itself through the zipper of his trousers and make itself known. He was surprised the little zipper teeth hadn't taken flight with the pressure within his pants and pinged their way into the atmosphere.

He shifted, trying to ease the fullness in his groin and quash his feelings by saying impatiently, "Yes. But what are you doing in the woods anyway? I didn't see you when I walked through here."

Quinn shrugged nonchalantly but there was apparent discomfort in his body as he moved awkwardly. A quick glance at Quinn's groin told Cade the other man had a similar problem.

Fuck, what the hell is going on? This was all happening much too fast. He'd never been this turned on before.

Quinn moved further away from Cade, taking a deep, shuddering breath. His fingers curled tightly into his palms as if he were trying to hold himself back.

Cade also took a deep breath. Quinn moved slightly farther away. The intense feelings he had lessened.

Quinn's lips moved silently as if he were speaking to himself. Finally he spoke aloud.

"I live close by. I was out for a walk when I saw you. You must have missed me." Quinn smiled mockingly. "I wasn't aware I needed anyone's permission to be here."

Cade ignored his comment as he shook his head thoughtfully. "I'm sure I didn't miss you. You appeared from nowhere." It was becoming more difficult to breathe properly with each passing moment and he decided he'd had enough. He wasn't sure where these sudden feelings of utter lust for a complete stranger had come from but he didn't want to be noted in the newspapers as the Hampstead Heath "Ravager of Men."

The need to flee became paramount even as something fierce inside him beckoned him to launch himself at the other man and bite his lips with a fierce passion he'd never felt before. He quelled the impulse by clenching his hands into fists so his nails cut into the skin.

"Anyway, I have to get to the tube station. I need to get home. It's getting late and my cat will be wondering where I am." He knew he was babbling and started to turn away. "Nice meeting you, Quinn. Just don't go lurking around any other strange men. They might not be as charitable as I am."

Behind him, Quinn spoke softly. "Perhaps we'll see each other again, Cade Mairston."

Cade looked back at him. "I wouldn't count on it. I think I'll stay clear of this place for a while. It just doesn't feel quite right."

He walked away briskly, aware of Quinn's eyes on his back. Cade had a sense of losing something valuable. He chided himself for being such an arsehole over a man he'd just met, and he took out his iPod. Perhaps listening to some music would help him get over this strange desire he had to fuck the man senseless.

Despite his last words, something told him that this wouldn't be the last time he saw Quinn Fairmont.

***

Quinn Fairmont sighed, a deep shuddering breath, and watched Cade Mairston walk away.

Jesus! That had been intense. Now I have an immediate need to screw the first man or woman I came across. The aphrodisiac effect of Cade being what he is can be a bitch to control but God, it feels so good.

He passed an unsteady hand over his eyes.

Cade Mairston was no ordinary man. Quinn had known it from the minute he'd touched Cade's hand, smelt his scent and heard the rushing of his blood through his veins. Cade was Fey.

Not overtly Fey, but something resided there, buried deep down within him. Quinn didn't think Cade Mairston had any idea who or what he was.

Quinn shivered. The way Cade had crouched in a fighter's stance, fierce glare and strong body ready to do battle—he'd been inspiring. It was only due to Quinn's Warlock skills that he'd the ability to anticipate and deflect the other man's moves and not be grievously injured. Cade Mairston was a strong, agile presence and Quinn wouldn't have liked his privates to be on the receiving end of the other man's foot, which was attached to a muscled leg which he wished would wrap itself around his legs as he pounded the man's arse....

Quinn checked himself mentally.

Christ, Quinn. Get a grip! Hell, my hormones are running riot.

Thank God the man was gay. Quinn's gaydar worked very well, thank you, despite noticing the evidence of the large erection the man had sported in his trendy cream chinos for him.

What were the odds of meeting another *gay Fey*? Quinn chuckled softly. If things had turned out the other way, Quinn would have been in danger of deflowering a straight man and *that* one never worked out for the best.

Cade had looked a little rattled himself. For a moment, from the look in Cade's smouldering grey eyes, Quinn had thought *he* might be about to get savagely violated. While Quinn topped most of the time he was definitely not averse to being taken by a man like Cade. There'd been anticipation so strong for Cade to touch him, kiss him right there, that he'd lost his breath for a moment. Quinn had a really tight feeling in his boxers right now as his cock threatened to burst into song and dance a jig out of his pants.

He sighed. Best get home, have a cold shower and do whatever else was necessary to relieve the turmoil snaking through his nether regions. Cade's sexy stubble on his jawline and light silver eyes were playing havoc with Quinn's sexual urges. Next time they met—and he was sure there'd be a next time—he'd have to search his apothecary for something that would deaden the sexual attraction. If not he'd never make it through a next meeting without ripping off Cade's clothes until his need was fully satisfied for the first time. After the first time, it became more controllable. Experience had taught both he and Taliesin that.

Taliesin chuckled in his head.

Quinn, that man has done something to both of us that I have not felt in a long time. My prick is so needy I have to travel to the village to find someone to relieve this ache. My own palm and fingers are not going to soothe this beast I have between my legs.

Quinn scowled. "Best be off then, sorcerer. And spare me the gory details. Just get your rocks off and I'll do the same."

As a Warlock, Quinn had a magyckal alter ego, one he chose when he came of age and who agreed to be his "Withinner." Taliesin, a sixth-century sorcerer, was his magyckal consult until death claimed either one of them. The two men were intricately linked in time and body and shared memories, thoughts and emotions. And Taliesin was even more ruthless than Quinn himself. His Withinner resided in his time in the sixth century and Quinn in his time. It was complicated and Quinn had never analysed their relationship. It simply *was*.

Chapter 2

Cade walked onto the deck of his houseboat with a sigh of relief. He wanted nothing more than to jack off in the shower, pour himself a glass of wine, sit down with Marco Polo and mull over the events of the evening.

Cade was gobsmacked at his visceral reaction to Quinn Fairmont.

The warm sensation in his groin was still evident, his erection still throbbing and he really needed to take care of it. Granted, the man was gorgeous. A six-foot-plus bundle of broad shoulders, dark, mussed-up blond hair and deep brown eyes with a square jaw and, from what he'd fleetingly seen when he'd turned around, a tight arse that he'd love to sink his teeth into. He bet the man was hung like a horse and Cade's balls contracted in pleasure at the thought of having the man's cock inside him.

He flushed hotly, realising that in the woods Cade had really wanted to rip Quinn's clothes off and beg him to fuck him senseless. It had been too long since seeing Matt, his ex-but-still-occasional-itch-scratcher.

As he opened the wooden door to his boat, the slinky form of Marco Polo wrapped itself around his ankles as he gave the plaintive meow that meant he was hungry. Cade reached down, picking up the Persian and kissing him softly on his furry head.

"Hey, Marco. How are you doing, kitty? I suppose you're starving. Sorry, I meant to be home sooner but I got distracted by this really annoying man. Let me have a shower first because honestly, this thing in my pants won't wait. Then I'll feed you."

He walked through to the bathroom to a chorus of indignant meows from his cat. The shower was hot, fulfilling and the solitary jerk-off session was just what he needed. It didn't take long. Just a few jerks on his dick, picturing Quinn's mouth and those sultry hazel eyes, had him trembling and groaning in pleasure and release.

He finished showering, wrapped a fluffy towel around his waist, and then walked though to the galley. Marco purred, rubbing his face against Cade's ankles. He quickly filled his bowl with cat food. Marco purred his satisfaction and Cade watched as the animal ate daintily, nibbling at his food like a spoilt courtier checking that everything was just right before he put it in his mouth.

Cade poured himself a glass of red wine and sat down in his easy chair to enjoy it. It had been quite an evening to remember. He still couldn't believe that he'd missed Quinn as he was walking through the woods and that the mysterious dark figure had simply disappeared into thin air. Frowning, he set down his wine glass on the aside table and drew his laptop toward him.

Let's see if I can find anything on this Quinn Fairmont. If he stays in Hampstead Heath, he must be fairly wealthy.

Places around there started in the millions and he didn't look the sort of man who would stay just anywhere. He'd seemed very…sophisticated.

Cade plugged his name into Google and immediately found one or two hits related to a Quinn Fairmont: book collector and city philanthropist. He clicked on the entry and found what he was looking for. There was an article on the man, with a picture that was less flattering that what he looked like in person.

Quinn Fairmont: Book Collector and Philanthropist.
By Jody Cavanaugh – Book Collector Magazine

Cade snorted. Well, that was an original name for a magazine about Book Collecting.

I was fortunate enough to meet this fairly reclusive man at a recent Book Fair held in the City. Quinn Fairmont is known for his tendency to be wary of the press and shuns most of the limelight when it comes to highlighting the work he does as one of London's best-known philanthropists and generous donors to charities and other deserving causes. Mr. Fairmont's particular passion is tackling issues of cultural diversity and prejudice and racism within the city. Via his company, QuinnCo, he is actively involved in several initiatives to implement humanitarian and aid programmes, the most recent one being the programme to teach schoolchildren both cultural and religious tolerance in an effort to stem the rising hate crimes in the city. QuinnCo is a company that was started by the Fairmont family many generations ago, and it is one of the companies named most influential and successful in the prestigious Mountjoy Listing of Businesses for 2012. Yet it has remained very much a family business despite its success and Quinn Fairmont is fiercely protective of QuinnCo and its privacy.

Mr. Fairmont also owns one of the best and most exclusive collections of books of the occult and arcane magic and witchcraft in the world. Whilst he would not grant me any formal interview, I did manage to ask him what his latest passion was in his book-collecting endeavours.

He told me with a charming smile that he was currently pursuing a very rare edition of the Malleus Maleficarum, the now-infamous volume of work written in the 15th century by Heinrich Kramer and Joseph Sprenger. This work, as any renowned book collector knows, is a treatise on witchcraft, dealing with how to identify them and how to deal with witches.

There are sceptics who believe there is no volume other than those which are already held in museums and private collections. Mr. Fairmont told me with an enigmatic smile that they were wrong. He declined to comment further.

The cat leapt into his lap. "Well, that sounds like the man I met, Marco." Cade stroked his fur softly. "Telling everyone else they were wrong when they're probably right. I'm still convinced he did see that other man in the forest. He just didn't want to admit it. I wonder why? But he sounds very rich and I suppose he's doing his bit for society. I can't stand people who judge others on religious or other grounds either. So we have that in common at least."

He browsed through other articles concerning the elusive Mr. Fairmont but they didn't offer much more information about the man. He did, however, find some pictures of him with a stunningly handsome brunet man, with helpful cutlines:

The dashing Quinn Fairmont and his date, handsome Adam Carnover, at the recent Crystal Book Awards Charity Gala.

Christ, so the man was gay, thank God for that. He'd hate to have the hots for a straight man.

The second newspaper article from *Gay Living* was just as annoying;

One of London's Most Eligible and Out Gay Bachelors – Has Mr. Fairmont's title finally been usurped by the charms of Adam Carnover, one of London's most eminent fashion designers?

Cade scowled at the pictures and the gushing sentiments contained in the article that the "exquisite" Adam was indeed

Quinn Fairmont's match made in heaven and that Fairmont was seriously considering asking him to marry him.

"Just as well I didn't jump his bones in the forest, then, Marco. " Cade muttered darkly as the cat jumped down, sauntered across the floor of the lounge and disappeared onto the deck. "It looks like he's already spoken for. Plus, how could a mere anthropologist compete with the likes of that gorgeous specimen of manhood?"

He heard the note of envy in his voice at Mr. Carnover's sexy and petite frame with a body that was made for designer clothes and probably a lot more.

He closed his laptop with a sigh and looked at his watch. It was ten o'clock and he thought he may as well get to bed. He was hard again and his left hand would need all its strength tonight to release some of this remaining pent-up sexual energy he felt. Perhaps then he could get Mr. Quinn "Sir Galahad" Fairmont out of his mind.

Chapter 3

Quinn scowled as he rummaged through the giant wooden chest in his specially created basement that contained his treasured library and most of his magyckal paraphernalia, potions and spells. He'd bought this place on the heath especially because it had a huge subterranean basement, large enough for him to store everything he'd accumulated in his thirty-six years as a Warlock as well as Taliesin's possessions, accumulated over the last fifteen centuries.

It was no mean feat having the ability to store such exotic items as unicorn hair, dryad tears, kairax root and thousands of other obscure items that Taliesin bought back from his travels. Quinn applied the same method of preserving his Withinner's treasures as he did his own very precious and rare collection of books and artefacts.

The purpose-built library in the concealed basement was a hermetically sealed room, guarding against such human risks such as improper lighting, airborne pollutants, insect infestations and mould. Minimal human contact featured strongly in there too, with the only person able to enter either of the rooms being Quinn or his Withinner and then only by a retinal scan. Quinn really couldn't afford to have anyone from the outside world find his Warlock treasure trove. The need for secrecy was paramount. To reveal it could be disastrous.

He exclaimed in triumph when he found what he was looking for. He held up two small, green vials, with ruby-coloured stoppers. Quinn hadn't brought his reading glasses down to the basement so he peered at the labels a little myopically. "*Mirrabar*

Blood" read the description in Taliesin's incredibly flamboyant handwriting.

Quinn knew the Mirrabar to be a small, ice-cold-blooded being that dwelled in the fjord caves of Norway. Once Quinn ingested this, it would cool his own blood down to a point where he at least would be able to tolerate another Fey, at least for a short time. The lasting results had yet to be proven but he hoped wryly it would work long enough for him to have a part-way intelligent conversation with the delectable Cade Mairston without regressing to caveman mode.

Quinn whistled as he closed the chest and secured the room to go back upstairs. He'd put the one vial in his jacket pocket whenever he went out, just in case, and the other one could go in the bathroom cabinet in case he ever needed it.

Upstairs in his study, which spread across the second floor of his house and looked out over the heath, Quinn sat at his desk, reading glasses now on, and busied his fingers across the keyboard of his desktop. He typed in "Cade Mairston" and waited to see what came up. Hopefully he'd get lucky and find out more about him on the wonder that was Google. If not, he had other resources at his disposal to gather information. He absentmindedly pushed his glasses up his nose with his index finger as he waited. Quinn was now very careful not to use his middle finger for this purpose as he was wont to do, as the last time he'd done that, some huge fellow in the gym had taken umbrage, thinking he was pulling a rude sign at him. Quinn had managed to talk his way out of it, but it hadn't been easy.

There were no hits for "Cade Mairston" on the first page Google pulled up, so Quinn clicked NEXT. Halfway down the second page there was a reference to a "Cade Mairston – Institute of Anthropological Studies, London." There was no picture but he clicked on the entry anyway. He smiled in satisfaction as he saw a group picture appear, of some college and university professors' group. *His* Cade was smack in the middle. He frowned as he looked at the picture.

The least the photographer could have done was put him on the side of the shot.

He'd placed Cade in the middle between two very much shorter, almost dwarf-like scholarly elderly men. Cade was a few inches shorter than Quinn, a fact he rather liked, but even so his intended new lover still towered over the other two like Godzilla. A very good-looking and sexy Godzilla, but the picture layout offended Quinn's aesthetic sensibilities.

Not the most flattering shot, Cade. You deserved better than this. With that superbly sexy rough look, you should be on the cover of Adventurers Weekly.

He chuckled at this thought, quite fancying the idea of his Cade in *Indiana Jones* gear and with a whip in hand. The mere thought of a whip being wielded by Cade made his balls ache.

Quinn read the article, something to do with some study Cade had done on the culture of the Vikings in the ninth century. He smiled wickedly. He could tell him a few things about that time. He was sure Taliesin would wax lyrical about it too if he got the chance, which, God forbid, he wouldn't do. Introducing his Withinner directly to a man like Cade, a Fey, would be tantamount to putting a naked, bubble-butted twink slap-bang in the middle of a jail cell of sex-starved male prisoners. Cade would stand no chance with Taliesin's voracious appetite for both sexes, something Quinn had once shared.

Quinn wanted only Cade for his own. He wondered idly whether it was normal to be able to be envious of his Withinner.

It wasn't something they told us about in Warlock training, that's for sure.

The line between a Warlock and his Withinner was very thin and self-control was something you learnt when you were what he was. Quinn sat back in his chair, his long legs propped up on his desk as he regarded his computer screen thoughtfully. So according to this he was a cultural anthropologist. Quite a coincidence if you believed in them, which he didn't. He was also only a year younger than Quinn, at thirty-five. Quinn believed devoutly in karma, and that everything happened for a purpose and that every action you took created a consequence that then went off in its own direction, causing yet another consequence. His running into Cade in that wood had been something that was no mistake. Cade's career choice certainly fit in well with Quinn's charity and research grant work and he was sure he could wangle the anthropologist an invite to the next benefit dinner in his very full diary. He made a mental note to speak to his virtual PA, Emily, about it when she called later. If memory served him correctly, there was one next week, which would be perfect.

Cade hadn't seemed the sort for these types of dinners so he might need a bit of persuading. Quinn grinned. The money he'd inherited from his father's dynasty certainly gave him a lot of persuasive power when it came to universities and colleges and the grants and donations he made to them. He was sure he'd have no problem convincing some dean or professor at the IAS to make sure they told Cade to attend on behalf of the Institution. He was looking forward to seeing him again.

***

Cade stood back from the mirror and studied himself with narrowed eyes. He still couldn't believe that his boss, Ambrose Tickler-Brown, had insisted he attend this poxy charity dinner tonight on behalf of the IAS. Cade had argued with him until he had nothing left to say which, for him, was fairly unusual. But the

Professor's face had been implacable, strangely so for the normally self-effacing and gentle man Cade knew him to be.

"I'm sorry you don't like the idea, Cade," he'd said quietly. "But I can't make it and I really need your assistance in attending as an IAS presence. I don't ask you to do much but I'd appreciate it if you could just do this one thing for me, please." Given his reasonable words and the fact that he was right, Cade believed he'd no choice but to take up the mantle of IAS representative and attend. He and one of his friends, Donna, had been out searching for a suit to wear. Shopping was something Cade hated with a passion. Jeans, chinos and tee shirts were his mode of dress, especially in his line of work. He didn't even own any formal wear. After scouring what seemed like the whole of London, Donna had finally found Cade the suit he wore now. Even Cade had to admit it didn't look too bad. Donna had dragged him into Ted Baker's on Regent Street and insisted on buying an Italian wool jacket and pants that had cost him an arm and a leg. Cade was careful with his money, not having all that much to spare, and he tended not to splurge, but Donna had been very persuasive.

Cade had to grudgingly admit that he looked pretty good tonight in the close-fitted suit and the deep blue shirt. Not that he intended pulling anyone but he wouldn't refuse it if it came his way. He was still fantasizing about Quinn Fairmont, so anyone else would be a welcome distraction from the caramel-eyed blond man who seemed to fill his every thought lately.

He deftly fastened the cufflinks Donna had also made him buy. They were onyx and amber in a shovel-and-pick design she'd said laughingly reminded her of his profession. His gold tie clip matched in the form of a rather contemporary shovel. Cade thought it looked silly but Donna had insisted it was all very trendy.

With a deep sigh and one last stroke of Marco's furry head, he picked up his wallet and shoved it into his pocket, ruining the line of the suit in an act of rebellion. Donna had wanted him to take a man bag and he'd point blank baulked at that suggestion. He went out the door onto the deck where the taxi was waiting.

Chapter 4

Quinn Fairmont stood impatiently waiting for Cade to make his appearance at the Dorchester Hotel in London. He'd been twitchy all night and he was sure his longtime business partner, Jomo Onyango, wondered what the hell was wrong with him. Jomo had looked at him curiously more than a few times.

He saw Jomo making his way across the crowded ball room, working it in that charming way only he could do. The dapper, six-foot-four and very dark-skinned Kenyan smiled, showing white teeth as he approached Quinn.

"Quinn. You look veritably antsy tonight. What the hell is wrong with you?"

His voice was deep, the tone of his very posh English upbringing in Cambridge overlaying his African heritage as he spoke. Quinn knew more than a few women who actually swooned when Jomo talked.

Quinn grinned. "Unlike you, Jomo, I haven't got the ability to have anyone I fancy have an orgasm every time I open my mouth. Some of us actually have to go out looking for a partner. I happen to be waiting for one to arrive and he's taking his sweet time about it."

Jomo chuckled loudly, a deep belly laugh that caused said orgasmic women to turn around and flutter their eyes at him. "How can you let your date come to this party under his own steam? That's not very gentlemanly, my friend."

Quinn flushed slightly. "He's not actually my date. It's a little more complicated than that."

Jomo looked at him quizzically. "I didn't know you did complicated after Adam. I thought you were looking for a relationship with no strings?"

Quinn scowled. "I am. I will be, I mean."

Jomo regarded him curiously. "You sound very unsure. I hope you have it all figured out. Last time you went into meltdown and it was not a pretty sight."

His words belied the affection in his tone as he looked at his friend. Quinn's face darkened at the reminder of his relationship with Adam Carnover.

Jomo had no idea exactly how and why that relationship had ended and Quinn didn't want to remember either. He'd been trying to forget the whole terrible story and the disturbing events that followed.

Taliesin murmured softly.

It had to be done, Quinn. You know that as well as I do, old friend.

Quinn sighed. "I'm fine, honestly." His face brightened as he saw Cade walking into the room.

Seeing the admiring look on his face, Jomo turned around and whistled appreciatively.

"You dog! If that incredible brooding brunet is the reason you have been so fidgety tonight, I understand why. He looks strong and very sassy, I bet. He will be too much of a man for you to handle." He leered at his friend. "He could make *me* bat for the other team, Quinn."

Quinn scowled at Jomo's teasing tone. "You'd be surprised what I can handle," he murmured as he watched Cade look around uncertainly.

Believe me, if we can defeat Aethelflaed, we can manage anyone. She was one very formidable lady.

Taliesin chuckled. *She was indeed. I was lucky to get out of that encounter with my life and you with yours.*

Quinn scowled. *Stay out of my head tonight, Withinner. And I shall feel it if you lurk. I want privacy tonight so keep your counsel.*

Taliesin's silky voice was sly. *Of course, Warlock. I understand you have some base needs that need fulfilling. I shall amuse myself.*

Quinn wasn't so sure about that but Taliesin's promise was usually one you could rely on. He left Jomo and walked over to the bar. "May I have a gin and tonic please?"

Once he'd got his drink, he took out his little vial of Mirrabar blood and as surreptitiously as possible, he emptied it into the drink. The red substance swirled on top of the drink for a few second then sunk to the bottom. He raised the glass and drank it down quickly. The last time he'd taken this had been about ten years ago when he'd met a Siren. That relationship had been intense for a while but not long lasting.

The familiar burning that ensued as the liquid coursed through his body made him gasp slightly as the reaction set in, closing his eyes momentarily.

"Sir, are you okay?" The barman's voice was anxious.

Quinn opened his eyes, taking a deep breath. "Yes, thanks. I think I just downed that one too quickly. Can I have a glass of merlot now please?"

The barman looked slightly concerned at the speed at which Quinn had finished the last one but poured him another drink. Quinn smiled as he took it and walked over to where Cade stood looking around him. His eyes said he didn't really want to be here.

The lure of Cade's blood pulled Quinn to him and halfway across the room Quinn had to stop to catch a breath. Perhaps the Mirrabar blood took a little while to work because there was still a primeval urge in his loins, an uncontrollable tightness that made him feel faint with longing. His trousers seemed to have shrunk to midget size. He waited a few moments, breathing deeply and after a while he heard a faint buzzing in his ears as the antidote started to work. His body started to feel more relaxed and the fierce desire had dissipated.

Cade was scowling now, an expression which made him look fiercer than ever. Quinn chuckled softly as he approached him with the glass of red wine. Cade's eyes widened as he saw him. His high cheekbones flushed pink.

"Mr. Mairston, fancy seeing you here," Quinn drawled. He held up the glass of wine. "I imagined you to be a red wine sort of man. Was I right?"

Cade regarded him thoughtfully. "I am indeed, Mr. Fairmont." He took the glass from Quinn carefully, watching his face as he did so. "I didn't realise you would be here tonight."

"It's one of the charities I support," Quinn explained as he tried hard not to look down at the swell of the other man's obvious arousal at Quinn's nearness. Despite the contents of the vial Quinn had ingested, Cade's groin seemed to beckon him to bury his face there. He groaned inwardly.

Christ, he really needed some self-control or he was going to get his arse kicked or worse, arrested. *Doesn't this stuff work properly?*

He cleared his throat. "It's good to see you again. May I say you look very handsome? The most stunning man here tonight without a doubt. That suit is a definite wardrobe asset." He grinned wickedly.

Cade's face grew rosier, the freckles across his nose on his pale skin standing out darker. Quinn wanted to bite that rather Roman proboscis and he swallowed, moving away swiftly lest he be tempted. "Did the Institute ask you to come in Professor Tickler-

Brown's place? I heard something had happened and he couldn't make it. Bad for him, but I have to say, good for me, being able to see you again."

Cade nodded warily. "Yes, Ambrose had some sort of family emergency." He swallowed, his hands fidgeting at his side.

Quinn saw the uncertainty in Cade's eyes as he dealt with feelings for him that he couldn't explain. Confidently he moved closer to the other man, seeing his pupils dilate, hearing his quick, indrawn breath. Quinn knew he was being very unfair but this wasn't the time to be fair. This was the time to conquer.

"Would you like to go sit down somewhere?" he enquired. "Perhaps you can tell me about what you do at the Institute and we can get to know each other a little better?"

Cade nodded, his hands shaking. The red liquid he held in the glass surged gently. Quinn put his hand gently on Cade's shoulder as he guided him to the table. His hand tingled as he touched Cade, and he felt the rush of blood under Cade's skin. Taut muscle felt incredibly welcoming under Quinn's eager fingers.

Cade started and goose bumps blossomed on his bare neck. He seemed to be having trouble breathing and Quinn saw the desperate rise and fall of his muscled chest under the tailored shirt.

Cade's silver eyes regarded Quinn with confusion, his lips trembling as he sought, no doubt, to understand what was happening to him. Quinn would bet his pension (if he had one) that Cade had never felt this way before. The knowledge made Quinn heady with power. He sensed the raging desire in the other man's body for him.

He smiled in satisfaction as he moved behind Cade, inhaling his scent and his intoxicating essence. Quinn wanted to rip Cade's clothes off to reveal what he imagined was smooth, sweaty, heated skin. He wanted to run his hands through the man's wavy, silky hair and hold it in his hands as he forced him downward toward his groin and made him take his cock in that sinfully sexy mouth. He wanted to plunge into him right there and then and it took all his self control not to do any of these things.

They reached the table and Quinn pulled out a chair. Cade sat down, gazing at him wide-eyed as he took one large sip of wine, then another. Quinn watched in amusement as half of the contents of the glass disappeared. He raised an eyebrow. "Thirsty, were we? I'll get you another one."

He walked to the corner bar and ordered another glass. By the time he'd gotten back, Cade's first glass was finished. Cade took the second one from him, his face bemused.

Quinn suppressed a pang of guilt at what he was doing to Cade. He squashed it as he told himself he was a full Warlock and Cade was a very novice Fey. Quinn's needs were greater than Cade's.

"So, Cade Mairston, tell me about yourself. What do you do at the Institute?"

"I'm an anthropologist. Cultural or social, whichever one you want to use. I prefer cultural. Social sounds like I do good works at soup kitchens and I don't do that."

Cade smiled faintly, seeming to get a little more control now he was talking about work.

Quinn nodded. "You do research then, and perhaps some teaching?"

Cade nodded. "Research, helping with dissertations for anthros—what we call anthropologists still getting their degree—I occasionally deliver lectures, take some teaching classes." He shrugged. "I like to get out in the field, so I tend to apply for any projects that will get me out of the office for a while, or out the country. There's one in a couple of months' time actually that I'm going on, to Gwynedd in Wales. I'm really looking forward to some fieldwork out there. I tend to specialise in the culture of the British Isles."

Quinn smiled. "I know that area of Wales very well. I'm sure you'll enjoy it out there. As long as you don't mind the wind and the rain."

Cade shrugged again, licking wine off his mouth. Quinn's heart nearly stopped at the sight of a pink, wet tongue against full lips.

Christ, was this stuff ever going to work properly? It didn't seem to be potent at all.

He swallowed. "It must be fairly interesting work, doing what you do? It almost correlates with what I do, business-wise. My company, QuinnCo, teaches children and adults that cultural and religious differences aren't the enemy. I've seen too many instances of persecution of people for race, colour or beliefs, and it wasn't the way the world was supposed to be." Quinn's face felt stiff as many centuries of memories of Warlock and witch persecution swum hazily through his mind.

He was aware Cade watched him intently, his eyes fixed on Quinn's mouth. Quinn was finding it very hard not to reach over and take the other man's lips in a savage kiss despite the serious subject matter being discussed. The Mirrabar blood was definitely *not* the defence it was cracked up to be.

Cade nodded, his hands wrapped around his wine glass. "I read about you on the internet." He spoke huskily and flushed a little at the admission. The wine appeared to be making him a little more open and talkative.

Quinn found enough self-control to grin inwardly, flattered Cade had been interested enough to do some research on him.

Cade sipped his wine. "The work you do is very noble. It's not easy taking someone's ingrained beliefs and trying to show someone else's point of view. I imagine it takes a lot of effort and patience."

Quinn nodded. "It takes time. These children have been indoctrinated in the beliefs their parents hold. You're right. It's not easy trying to give them options in what to believe in. If they want to be open minded, not only do they have to face it for themselves, they have to argue it with their parents and family too, and that can be catastrophic sometimes. And then of course there's always the flip side that *we'll* go too far ourselves and try convince them to look at something they really don't want to consider. It's a very fine line."

Cade suddenly stood up, his face pale. "Excuse me a minute. I need to go to the men's room. Can you point me in the right direction?"

Quinn gestured toward the left. "Behind the bar in that far corner, just at the side of that large palm tree. It's over there."

Cade nodded quickly and disappeared. Quinn watched him go and leaned back in his chair. He sighed heavily. He knew he was being a real bastard doing this to him but until they'd gotten over the first hurdle, it would always be like this.

The constant sexual energy between them that would be all-consuming and quite destructive and couldn't end well. He fingered the scar on his chin reflectively as he stood up. He'd best go see how Cade was doing. He knew the first flushing of Fey attraction was intense, sometimes even damaging, and he wanted to make sure Cade was okay. He might even have to force the issue, make Cade so desirous of him that he wouldn't say no any longer.

I certainly think I might like that move too, Quinn thought in amusement.

***

In the men's room, Cade stood with wide eyes in a pale face, his trembling hands clutching the sink basin. The only other patron in the bathroom glanced at him curiously but said nothing. The stranger finished at the urinal, zipped himself up and left the room with a nod at Cade who gave a distracted half smile back. *What the hell is wrong with me? How can I feel this way about a man I've just met? It's insane. I have the boner the size of China and my arse is begging for the man to fill it. I've never felt this way before. Ever.* He could hardly be still, the sensation in his groin overpowering. Whilst Cade had been watching Quinn speak, all he could think about was biting his bottom lip and ripping that white tailored shirt off his shoulders. The attraction was so extreme he'd thought he was going to be sick. Cade leaned down, drinking some water from the tap, taking a handkerchief from his pocket and wetting it, then patting his forehead. The sensation had partly gone and he was a little more back to normal. But in Quinn Fairmont's presence, he seemed to be nothing more than a bag of screaming lust with a throbbing hard-on between his legs that he couldn't control. He took a deep breath before leaving the bathroom. He started as he saw Quinn leaning against the wall, elbows folded, a brooding look on his face, his blond hair looking as if he'd just run his fingers through it.

Christ, the man looks like pure sex on legs.

"Do you make a habit of this, Mr. Fairmont?" Cade said grimly, wanting to take some control back. "This is the second time I've found you lurking around."

Quinn smiled lazily and unpeeled himself from the wall. "You seemed a little distressed. I wanted to see you were okay. Again. I told you I have a Sir Galahad complex."

The corridor was empty of people, leaving Cade feeling exposed. He tried to move past him but Quinn blocked his way, moving closer to him than he could stand.

"I'm not some shrinking violet," Cade sneered as he tried to push past. But just the smell and the feel of the man's body as he brushed past was intoxicating and his head swum. "I'm a big boy and quite able to take care of myself."

Quinn's grin was like a hungry lion about to devour an impala that had been brought to its knees and was waiting for the inevitable. "Oh, I have no doubt about that," he smiled lazily with a quick flick of his eyes at Cade's groin.

Cade felt himself flush, knowing there was no way this irritating man could miss the bulge at his groin and his obvious—yet still perplexing—arousal. Quinn's face relaxed as he reached out and trailed a hand along Cade's arm. Even through the suit and shirt, Cade's skin prickled and grew hot with yearning.

"It's not going to go away, you know," Quinn said quietly. "These feelings you have for me."

"Feelings?" Cade's voice was choked. "This is more than just feelings. What the hell have you done to me? I've never felt like this before..." His voice trailed off as Quinn's fingers brushed his jaw. Cade could no longer speak.

Quinn's eyes mesmerised Cade as he moved closer, and both men's breathing got deeper. There was a feeling in Cade's lower stomach that he knew well, a deep, aching need that only a good, hard bout of sex could cure. Quinn reached out to caress his cheek in a surprising gesture of tenderness. Cade closed his eyes, knowing that this situation was simply ridiculous. He'd only just met the man but was still loving every touch, every whisper of contact he was initiating. Out of hazy eyes, Cade saw the deep scar on Quinn's chin and wondered for a moment where he'd gotten it.

"We need to consummate this relationship, Cade, or it'll be unbearable."

Cade had no idea what Quinn was murmuring about. All he knew was that his body was screaming for him to touch Cade any place he wanted, do anything he wished with him and he was both ashamed and elated at the same time. All reason had fled and left in its wake an absolute burning lust for this man.

"I know somewhere we can go," Quinn whispered as he pulled Cade's unresisting body along further down the corridor, away from the crowds. He opened the door to a small office, dark and smelling vaguely of cigars. He tugged Cade inside, closed the door and yanked him closer, taking his mouth in a kiss that sucked at Cade's insides and caused his cock to grow painfully harder. With his body's total blood supply currently engorging his erection, Cade thought faintly there was nothing left for the rest of his body and his heart might simply stop. Yet even with the fear he might expire from wanting, Cade kissed Quinn back, his tongue sucking his, as Quinn pushed his tongue so far down his throat, Cade thought suffocation might get him before the lack of blood to his heart.

Quinn groaned, the sound of his obvious need piercing Cade's semi-consciousness. "Christ, you taste like a man should. Spice, sweat and so fucking amazing. I knew you'd be special but I had no idea you'd taste *this* good."

Cade had no idea what made him so unique but he wasn't complaining if this was what it meant. Quinn fumbled with Cade's trousers, undoing them at the same time that Cade slid his hands over the front of Quinn's groin and heaved a shuddering breath at how ready the man was.

Quinn moaned deeply and buried his face in the side of Cade's neck as he pulled Cade's hips closer, their mutual hardness against each other making them both gasp. "God, you feel so good. It's been so long since I've had this feeling. You're incredible, you know that?"

Cade's voice was husky when he spoke. "I don't know what the hell's happening to me. I've never felt anything this intense before…"

Quinn kissed him fiercely, whispering into his mouth, "Don't fight it, just let it go and it'll all be fine. Just believe me, this was meant to be."

Cade's head swam and he had no idea how he suddenly ended up totally naked, his clothes in puddles at his feet, with Quinn busy stripping down with demonic speed to stand before him, gloriously naked too. Cade's eyes widened in both appreciation and apprehension.

Fuck, the man must have big feet. I don't know how that's ever going to fit inside me.

Cade was versatile when it came to bottoming or topping, but he preferred bottoming. There was nothing quite like having a hot, silken sheath inside you, making contact with all the right bits and feeling a man's pleasure as he thrust himself inside. And he wanted Quinn to take him that way, no mercy and as hard as he could. He thought he had Quinn's measure as a man who preferred to top.

Quinn pulled Cade over to a large leather sofa in the corner. Cade gasped as the cold leather caressed his naked back. Quinn covered Cade's body with his, kissing him as Cade moaned and writhed beneath him, the feeling of Quinn's hot, sweaty skin on his too much to bear.

Quinn's chest, covered with dark blond hair, was a tantalising pleasure trail down to his groin where his cock now lay pressed against Cade's stomach. Cade had little chest hair and the tickle of rough against his own smoothness was delicious torture.

Cade had never experienced such sensations with any man before. His whole body was on fire and the only way to put the fire out was to get this man inside him and let him pound away until he came. Cade reached down and grasped Quinn, hearing his cry of pleasure as he whispered in his ear. "I need to feel you; you need to fuck me. I can't bear this a minute longer."

Quinn chuckled wickedly. "We have to practice safe sex," he murmured, "at least until we know each other a little better."

He moved swiftly away from him. His taut buttock cheeks were a delight to behold and Cade simply lay and watched the spectacle, impatient and burning up as Quinn found his trousers and fumbled in the pocket, coming out with a silver foil packet and another one of lube. He grinned at him as he opened them both.

"Do you want to put it on or shall I?"

Cade stared at him, faint with both need and uncertainty. It seemed such an intimate action, rolling on a condom over his erection, and he shook his head. "You put it on."

He knew soon this man was going to be inside him but he thought putting on a condom was too intimate? What the hell was his rationale for that?

Quinn expertly fitted the latex sheath over his impressive, glistening cock, and was soon back above Cade as strong, muscled legs straddled Cade's sensitive body. Cade gulped at the sight of Quinn's erection jutting out from his body like the mast of a ship.

"Which way do you prefer?" Quinn murmured. "I'm easy either way."

Cade shivered at the thought of being taken *any* way by this man, a man who drove all coherent thought from his being and looked at him with eyes that blazed fiercely. Cade had never seen such hunger for him in a man's eyes before.

His answer was to pull Quinn over the top of him, watching as Quinn's lips curled in a wolfish smile. Obviously this was Quinn's preferred method from the satisfaction on his face.

"I don't even know you, so there's no way in hell I'm not watching you when we do this," Cade growled.

Letting Quinn take him from behind seemed like the ultimate in submission, and no matter how ravenous he was Cade wasn't ready for that. Not yet. He shuddered as he realised he hoped there might be a next time.

"Do you want me to prepare you?" Quinn waggled his fingers in front of Cade's face. "Or do you want to do it yourself?"

Cade's answer was to part his legs wider, bringing them up to his chest. "There's no fucking time for foreplay," he hissed as his hips surged up, brushing Quinn's groin and making him close his eyes in pleasure. "I think I said I want you inside me. Now."

Quinn's low chuckle was nearly Cade's undoing. "Quite the toppy little bottom, aren't you?" he whispered as he reached down, smearing Cade's own fluids over his cock to make entrance easier. He leaned forward and whispered into Cade's ear.

"And there's no way we're doing this dry, no matter what you say, so ready yourself." His fingers, coated with vanilla-scented lube, slid inside Cade, stretching and opening him up. Cade hissed in pleasure even as his cock throbbed with the need for release.

Quinn was breathing heavily in his ear. "Christ, you are so fucking sexy and this is torture for me too. I just want to be inside you."

"Then fucking do it already!" Cade growled in desperation. "I'm ready."

Finally, with one supple movement of his hips, Quinn slid inside Cade's eager and ready arse, the size of him making Cade cry out again in wanton delight. Quinn thrust into Cade's body with a desire borne of desperation and need. He knew exactly where to strike, his body moulding and moving against Cade's, his obvious pleasure in every thrust. Cade thought he might die from delight himself.

Christ, this is like nothing I've ever felt before.

Enveloped in warm, velvet heat; the sensation wrapped around his body, seeping into his skin. Just the feel of Quinn's skin on his and Quinn's cock inside him was enough to drive him crazy. His cock slapped against his stomach as Quinn moaned. The friction of sweaty skin against his engorged and needy member was exquisite.

Cade's vision blurred as Quinn hit his prostate again and again and he gasped, trying to draw a breath as the air in his lungs left him in pleasure. The room swam around him, seeming hazy and brighter and all the time Quinn's deep, slamming movements matched Cade's wantonly thrusting hips as they fucked, their mouths ground together as if trying to swallow each other. Cade heard heavy, indecent pants and was mortified to discover they were coming from him. Quinn's face gleamed with sweat and his tawny eyes, like molten pools of dark amber with golden flecks that blazed deep, stared into Cade's as if he was the only thing that existed in Quinn's world. Cade lost himself in those eyes, heard Quinn's own gasps and moans as he kept up his assault of Cade's body. Quinn bent his head toward him, his lips trailing along Cade's collarbone, and Cade exclaimed in pain as sharp teeth bit the skin beneath his ear. He swore Quinn growled loudly, like an animal, and then he did it again.

Time seemed to slow down and Cade heard sibilant hisses in his head as if someone was whispering in there. It was a most unnerving sound and he shook his head from side to side, willing it away. But the soft noises continued and finally he heard Quinn curse vehemently.

"Stay out of this, you horny goat bastard! This one's mine." The anger on Quinn's face did not bode well for whomever Quinn was talking to and Cade was too caught up to wonder exactly what the hell was going on and who the goat bastard might be. There was no one else in the room that he could see, *when* he could see that was.

The air shimmered before his eyes and he blinked frantically, trying to clear his senses. The atmosphere was imbued with palpable electricity and for one scared moment, Cade thought he might simply explode from the feelings invading his body. His whole being prickled, the incredible sensation of something inside him rising like a current of energy. He cried out in fear and ecstasy as he came and Quinn muffled his screams with his ravenous mouth.

Cade ejaculated with such intense pressure it actually hurt. His orgasm travelled through his body like a current being switched on. Even the roots of his hair tingled and the tips of his fingers buzzed as if he'd stuck them directly into a live wall outlet. His heart beat so strongly Cade thought dazedly it might propel itself out of his chest like an alien bursting forth. He imagined this was it was like to be fucked to death.

It wasn't such a bad way to die, in his opinion.

A grimace formed on Quinn's face as he threw his head back, the chords in his throat tensing as he climaxed, his body shuddering from top to bottom. Despite the condom, Cade felt the man's come inside him, hot, wet and a lot of it. He shot into Cade as if there was no end. If Quinn had been a wolf, Cade would have expected him to howl in triumph.

Finally, with a loud expletive, Quinn collapsed on top of Cade, the sweat on his face on Cade's cheek, the smell of him overpowering in its masculinity. Cade had no voice; he thought it might have disappeared with the copious amounts of spunk that had jetted forth from him. He wondered in confusion how it was even possible for the human body to produce such an amount. White, sticky and musky, his semen coated both men's bodies from hip to throats with a tantalising scent of musk and sex.

Christ, it was a real damn mess. The stuff could be used as wallpaper paste and would probably cover at least one wall.

They lay together like that for a while as Cade tried to find his missing speech capabilities. Quinn rolled off him finally, and lay to one side as he removed the condom. He turned over to regard Cade with a look of affection. Cade lay there, still feeling incredibly good but at the same time, feeling a wash of shame at his behaviour.

How could he have done what he'd just done? He was used to one-night stands but this? This was something else entirely. Quinn Fairmont was a stranger to him and Cade had just literally let him screw him like an animal without any reservations whatsoever. The intensity of the situation made Cade very uncomfortable.

Quinn reached over and brushed a stray lock of hair from Cade's face as he smiled down at him. "I had no idea you were so noisy. I'm surprised we've had no one running in here trying to find out what all the fuss was about. That was incredible though."

Cade was quiet as he tried to sort out his thoughts.

Quinn frowned. "Is everything all right? I didn't hurt you did I? Sorry, I sometimes get carried away in the moment."

"No, you didn't hurt me." Cade's voice was flat as he sat up and moved over to where his clothes lay on the floor. He dressed with trembling hands, struggling to button up his shirt with the shaking of his fingers.

Quinn watched him with concern. "Cade, I know you don't quite understand. I need to explain what just happened. I know it will sound crazy but I have to try…"

Cade waved a hand to stop him talking as he finished dressing and looked around for his jacket. "You don't have to explain anything. I just let a man I barely know fuck my brains out. I'm no angel but even for me this was a bit out there. I just want to get home and have a large drink." He looked at Quinn. "Did you put something *in* that drink you gave me to make me feel this way? Because I have never experienced anything that intense in my life."

Quinn's face darkened and he sat up, his face grim. "I can assure you, Cade, I really have no need to drug men to get them to sleep with me, arrogant though that may sound. I don't know how you could think I'd do something like that." He sounded angry.

Cade was too tired now to care. "Well, I'm sorry if I offended you. I had to ask."

Quinn's face softened at his confusion. "If you'd just let me try and explain—"

Cade cut him off. "Forget it, it doesn't matter. Thank you for the raunchy sex. It was very pleasurable but I have to get off." He chuckled grimly. "Although I think that ship has already sailed."

He shrugged on his dinner jacket and walked to the door. Quinn stood up, still naked, and tried to take his arm to stop him.

Cade's jaw clenched. "Quinn, I know it takes two to tango and I'm not blaming you, but I want you to just leave me the hell alone. Please."

Quinn's hand dropped and Cade felt his eyes on his back as he left the room. Once outside he took a deep breath and marched to the exit. The only thing he wanted now was to get home and try and figure out what had just happened. Something deep inside him made no sense—there was an emotional connection to the man he'd just fucked. He wouldn't call it making love; physically it had been too animalistic for that description. But it all seemed too deep for just a chance meeting in a forest and a sudden desire to jump his bones. It was as if Cade Mairston knew Quinn Fairmont better than he did and whilst it was strangely satisfying, he was also very scared.

***

Back in the office, Quinn dressed in silence as his mind raced with thoughts of how he could have handled this whole situation better. Cade was obviously upset, thinking he'd acted out of character and seeming ashamed of his behaviour. The initial attraction would at least be less intense now that they'd—what the hell had he said to him?—'consummated' their relationship, although the desires would still be strong between them. But they would at least be more controllable.

But I certainly won't rely on that Mirrabar blood again.

He wished he could have gotten the chance to explain to Cade that it hadn't been something Cade could have controlled, that he'd stood no chance against the calling of his Fey blood to Quinn. In that respect, he reflected wryly, it *was* a drug and he'd been right to think of it as such. But the thought that Cade believed Quinn could slip something into his drink still rankled and he scowled fiercely as he dressed. He had to admit the sex had been mind blowing. His body still felt the aftershocks, tingles reverberating through his skin and his blood like a serious case of pins and needles. He expected Cade was feeling it too. Taliesin had stirred in triumph the whole time he was making love to Cade, the Withinner urging him on, getting the same satisfaction he did. Quinn had tried to tell him to butt out but, he reflected wryly, Taliesin had never done what he was told. He knew Cade had heard his growled command to his Withinner to back off and no doubt that had confused him too. Both personas were very aware of each other, Taliesin lurking just below the surface. But Quinn controlled Taliesin; Quinn was the ultimate Master.

At least most of the time, he thought grimly. When Taliesin wanted something, it took all of Quinn's power to get his passionate Warlock under control.

Chapter 5

Jomo sighed in exasperation and looked across at his business partner. He and Quinn sat together in the large self-contained office at Quinn's home. The office was well kitted out, with polished wooden desks, leather chairs and various pieces of computer equipment, plasma TVs and other gadgets. The large picture windows running along the far wall afforded a magnificent view of the heath. Most of the back-office business services and office functions were outsourced as the two partners preferred to operate from Quinn's home rather than an expensive place in the city. He looked at Quinn now, head down, studiously perusing documents requesting grant money and donations. He cleared his throat but Quinn still didn't look up.

Jomo sighed again. "You can ignore me all you like, but I know something is wrong, my friend. You have been very quiet since that last dinner when you had that man in your sights. Did you manage to get his number at least?"

Quinn looked up and Jomo was taken aback by his expression. The normally uber-confident Quinn seemed almost vulnerable, a strangely haunted look in his eyes. Jomo had seen that look before on people hiding from the police in his home country.

"No. No number." Quinn said quietly. "And I'm fine. It just didn't go the way I planned, that's all." He shrugged. "Well, it did, but…" His voice trailed off.

Jomo leaned back his bulk in his chair and regarded Quinn curiously. "Where did you meet him anyway? Have you been seeing him long?"

Quinn shifted uncomfortably in his chair. "Look, no offence or anything, but can we just let the whole thing go? It just didn't work out, that's all. Plenty of other fish in the sea and all that." He returned his attention to the documents he'd been studying intently.

Jomo narrowed his eyes. He knew there was no point in prying when Quinn was in one of these moods. He could be one of the most secretive and tight-lipped people Jomo knew and no amount of threatening would budge him. "Fine. I will forget I ever saw him in that amazingly well-fitting suit, with that magnificent glower on his face and let you get on with trying to do the same thing. Not very successfully, I might add."

He chuckled as Quinn glared up at him with murderous eyes.

Jomo raised his large hands and shook his head. "Sorry. I say no more. My lips are sealed." He stood up and picked up his mug. "Would you like more coffee?"

Quinn nodded. "Yes, please. These grant documents are as dry as dust. I need something to keep me awake."

Jomo disappeared to the kitchen to pour yet another coffee from the large industrial machine Quinn had installed to keep them both sane.

***

Quinn sat back with a sigh.

God, Jomo was too perceptive. We've been friends so long, nearly fifteen years, and I tend to forget Jomo knows me so well.

Quinn was still disturbed at the way things had been left with Cade. He'd seen the expression in Cade's eyes when he'd turned to spit out his last words. It had reminded him of a cornered wolf he'd seen on the Siberian steppes. He knew he had to try seeing him again and explaining. Quinn knew where Cade worked and he was sure he could use his charm to try and convince someone at the IAS to give him Cade's address under some pretext. He'd give them a call and see what he could do. Perhaps he'd try get out there this weekend and see what the sexy Mr. Mairston was up to since he'd seen him last. Quinn sighed. He had to convince Cade that they were meant to be together. Quinn had never felt this strongly about a man before and God knew he'd had plenty of opportunity to mate with the best. But Cade Mairston was something very special. And Quinn wanted him badly.

***

Cade sat on the deck of his houseboat, enjoying the early May sunshine. He'd been swimming at the nearby pool this morning, finding solace in the steady sweeps of his arms and in the quiet solitude of being under the water. He gazed out down the river, seeing fellow houseboat mates out on their decks, pottering and enjoying the good weather. He raised his glass and took a sip of red wine, leaning back and closing his eyes while enjoying the feel of the sun on his face.

"Cade?"

The quiet voice catapulted him into alertness and he opened his eyes to see Quinn standing on the shore path, outlined against the sun. There was sudden excitement at seeing him followed by an overwhelming urge to tackle him to the ground, beat him senseless and throw him into the river.

"Quinn, I thought I told you to leave me alone. How the hell did you find out where I live?" Cade rose to his feet as anger surged through his chest. He *was* pleased to see Quinn wasn't attempting to come aboard until he was invited.

Quinn regarded him evenly. "I really need to talk to you about the other night. I know you're angry but I think I can help you with that. You need to understand where those sexual urges came from."

His gentle voice was disarming. Cade's attraction to the man had not lessened as Quinn stood in the sun, his blond hair shining and his handsome face serious. But it was nothing like the other night when they'd both been ravenous beasts.

Cade exploded in fury. "For God's sake, can you not just get it into your thick skull that it was a one-off Red Letter Day experience and it's not going to happen again? Whatever it was doesn't matter." He moved forward closer to Quinn and again his breath quickened and his legs went weak.

God, not again! This just can't be happening.

"You're wrong. It will happen again. Do I need to prove it to you?" Quinn's voice was once again hypnotic. He moved forward onto the deck of the boat and the closer he got the more the more the urges rushed through Cade's body. They might not be as intense as the other night but they were certainly a force to be reckoned with. He gasped in fear and stepped back, almost tripping over Marco Polo who was lying on the deck sunning himself. The cat gave a startled meow and fled into the cabin.

Quinn was right in front of Cade now. "You're right. The feelings you have for me aren't normal. They're brought on by something deep inside you. Something you didn't even know was there. Something that drew me to you in the first place."

Quinn's eyes were bottomless depths with wide pupils, the flaring of his nostrils betraying his own emotions as he looked at him. Cade sensed suppressed violence and Quinn's own arousal at being so near to him. He closed his eyes, desperately trying to find sense out of the craziness.

Quinn reached forward and slowly, gently, drew Cade against his chest. Cade was powerless, his hands dropping to his sides like leaden weights. All thoughts of any resistance had gone. Cade went dizzy as Quinn whispered something in his ear, something that wasn't English and sounded suspiciously like what he'd heard the dark figure in the forest utter, a harsh, guttural sound that made his head spin. Then the blackness descended and he remembered and heard no more.

**

Quinn stood in Cade's lounge, watching the still, supine man on the couch where he'd placed him after he'd put Cade to sleep. Quinn had no choice. Cade's resistance had been too strong and he'd needed a little Warlock magyck to get the job done. He was still struggling to control his own feelings. It would get easier the more they made love. Then things could be fairly normal, at least as normal as they could be for a Warlock and a Fey.

He sighed as Cade stirred. The spell Quinn had found in his library and whispered into Cade's ear would do the job for a short while and help them both hold those urges for each other at bay. Cade needed some solace; it seemed overwhelming for him. Quinn figured he'd have to do some magyck to make Cade convinced of who he was and open his eyes to who Cade himself was. He hoped it wouldn't blow his mind too much. He really wanted to get to know this man better.

Cade blinked and stared at him out of those incredible silver eyes. Quinn made no move toward him, knowing that would have been suicide. The man wouldn't be above giving him a punch or worse.

"What the hell did you do to me?" Cade looked down at himself as if he was checking he was still clothed.

Quinn grinned. "Your virtue is intact, I promise. But I imagine you're feeling a little—less intense?"

Cade's eyes narrowed. "Yes, I feel a little less agitated," he muttered.

Quinn wished he could say the same as it was taking all his considerable self-control not to ravish him again. Taliesin wasn't helping either, stirring within, his arrogant whispers telling Quinn to throw caution to the wind and have his way with Cade. He quashed that, feeling Taliesin retreat in sulky fury.

"What did you do to me? You said something." Cade stood up, frowning.

Quinn sighed. "I cast a spell on you. I thought it would calm your emotions down. It should hopefully last long enough for me to talk to you and tell you who I am and what you are."

Cade looked at him as if he were crazy and Quinn sighed. "Cade, you're an intelligent man. Surely you can see that what we have is not normal. It's magyck."

"Magyck? Bloody spells?" Cade backed away from him slowly, his eyes darting around the room as if looking for a weapon. "What the hell are you talking about?"

"You have Fey blood. I'd guess Water Sprite from your scent and your obvious love of the water. And I'm a Warlock. Some people call us male witches if you like, although we prefer Warlock. It's a bit more masculine despite what all the old legends say about it not actually being correct. I can assure you Warlock is the right expression for people like me. As for what happened the other night, your Fey blood acts as a very powerful aphrodisiac for both of us."

"A Warlock. And I'm a Sprite?" His voice was faint. Cade looked at him as if he'd just escaped from a mental institution "Quinn, I really think you should leave now. You're talking crazy and I don't do well with crazy. If you like I can call someone for you and they can take you back to the asylum you escaped from."

The attempt at humour amused Quinn and he laughed, a sudden explosive sound that make Cade look around the room even more anxiously.

"Let me show you something. Perhaps then you'll believe me." Quinn moved forward and Cade picked up a large vase sitting on the side table and held it with his arm cocked back, as if preparing to throw it.

Quinn grinned. This was fun. "That's not going to do you any good."

He closed his eyes, his lips moving in a quiet incantation. Cade gasped as the vase was slowly tugged from his grasp, softly at first then more forceful as Quinn increased the spell until the vase was pulled firmly from Cade's hands. In instinct, he reached forward to catch it as it fell. But the vase stayed in the air, hovering slowly, and as Quinn lifted his hands, his fingers motioned the vase toward him. He opened his eyes, curling his fingers, pulling the vase toward him inexorably until it rested in his hands. He smiled at the look of disbelief on Cade's face.

"See? How do you explain that? It's magyck. Something I was born to do and something which you can see because you're Fey." He motioned at the vase, "This was just a parlour trick. But you can see much more."

Cade's face was pale. "How did you do that? Are you like that magician guy from Bradford-Dynamo? He does things like that."

Quinn scowled fiercely. Being compared to a sleight-of-hand TV magician, however good he was, really insulted him. Taliesin reared in indignation at his words as well.

Show this upstart some real magyck, Quinn. Something he'll really have to believe. He's really stubborn, this one, isn't he? There was a hint of avarice in Taliesin's voice, something Quinn wasn't truly comfortable with. But he smiled wolfishly as he obeyed his Withinner.

Cade still looked at him in disbelief. Quinn moved toward him, his blood starting to sing again as his primal desires surfaced. Quinn fought them back as he reached out and took Cade's hand. Cade gazed at him, his mouth parted, as Quinn drew small circles on his rough palm, whispering the incantation. The air around them changed, becoming misty and warmer. Cade's eyes darted from side to side as the houseboat slowly disappeared to be replaced with…nothing. It was as if they were alone in a sea of mist with only the water below—deep, dark, still water that rippled and gurgled as if still lapping against the houseboat. But the boat was gone.

"Can Dynamo do that?" Quinn muttered sulkily.

Cade finally found his voice. "What the hell are you, Quinn? How can you do this?"

His voice was wondrous, not scared anymore. He was beginning to realize Quinn was telling the truth.

Quinn leaned forward and kissed Cade, feeling his lips part beneath his, hearing the sigh of his breath as he breathed into his mouth. Cade's arms wrapped around his neck, pulling him closer. Quinn felt complete, as if he'd finally found a part of himself that was lost.

The strong male body pressed against his made his desire burn like hot flames licking at his body. Quinn groaned and pulled away reluctantly. This was not what he intended, no matter how much he wanted it. He was here to try and explain things, not simply seduce Cade again. There was time enough for that. He slowed his breathing, said a few soft words and before long, the boat was back, and he and Cade were standing entwined together in the lounge once again.

Cade looked around him with a glazed expression then moved away to pick up his wine glass and the half-empty bottle. He poured a hefty dose of wine into it, which he proceeded to finish. Then he looked at Quinn. "Sorry, I'm being rude. Do you want some?"

Quinn chuckled. "I wouldn't mind some, actually. It's thirsty work, conjuring."

Cade took another glass from a cupboard and poured him wine. Quinn sipped it, relieved that the other man now appeared to be more reasonable about the whole thing.

Cade studied him for a long moment, then sat down on the sofa and patted it. "Why not sit down and tell me a bit more?" he said softly. "I'm guessing there's a lot more to tell."

Quinn chuckled softly, marvelling at the transformation from the previously aggressive and confused man to this one, who was more composed and more in control. Cade curled up on his couch, tucking lean legs beneath him and regarded him steadily.

"So tell me again what you are and how I fit into all this craziness. I can see there must be something to your story. You made my house disappear and you make me feel as horny as hell. I also feel as if I've known you much longer than I have." He looked around anxiously. "You didn't do anything to my cat, did you? Because if you did—"

Quinn laughed. "Your cat is just fine. Look, he's outside there on the deck."

He settled himself in for the tale. It was already starting to get dark outside and this could take a while. "Magyck exists. You've just seen some of it and believe me, like I said earlier, that was simply a parlour trick. The things I'm able to do go much deeper than you could ever yet imagine."

He took another sip of wine. "My family, the Fairmonts, are a very wealthy and respected Warlock family. We've been around centuries. My father was a Warlock, as was his father and so on. I can trace my ancestors back to the sixth century as things stand. We're born with the ability to do magyck. But at the age of seven, we come into our own and our powers increase." He'd tell Cade later about Taliesin and the ritual of accepting a Withinner. He wanted to keep that for last.

"When I met you on the heath the other night, I could sense, smell that you had Fey blood. It's very deep inside and you probably would never have known, had you not met me, that anything ever existed within you. The chances of meeting another Warlock or even another Fey are astronomical in a world as big as this one. There aren't a lot of us left."

His voice turned grim. "We've been hunted down, persecuted, victimised and targeted for destruction all our lives. It's how I lost my parents when I was six years old. They were both murdered and I was lucky not to be killed too."

Cade reached over and laid a hand on Quinn's, his face grave.

Quinn covered it with his other hand. "The blood that courses through your veins has a very strong pull for us both. It acts as an instant aphrodisiac and rational thought just isn't something that factors in once we're anywhere near each other. You were right when you said it was a drug. Only it's your blood that's the drug. Not anything I could have given you."

Cade flushed. "I'm sorry about that comment. It was a nasty thing to say. I was confused—"

Quinn leaned over and placed a finger on his lips. "Forget it. I might have thought the same thing had I been in your shoes. It's a very intense thing to experience and even whilst I've experienced it a few times before, it still unnerves me too."

Cade frowned and Quinn grinned. "You're not the first man or woman I've had to put to sleep. There have been a few. Of course some didn't fight the attraction. They embraced it right from the start which made it a much more pleasurable experience for us both."

He laughed at the sudden jealous expression on Cade's face, glad Cade felt strongly enough about Quinn to be that way. "Needless to say, those feelings you had the other night were for this reason. So you're not a rampant sex maniac, just a hot-blooded

Fey obeying his instincts to ravage a Warlock." He grinned, loving the bemused expression on his lover's face. Because without doubt that was what this man was going to be: his lover.

Cade shook his head in wonder. "But how did I get this way? How do I find out where it came from? I was only ten when my father died and I never knew my mother. She died in childbirth with me. My father was a merchant navy sailor; he travelled the world and I had a family friend who looked after me when he died. Sally died about ten years ago as well."

His voice was sad. Quinn thought it was tough having everyone that could tell you anything about yourself dying and no longer being able to answer any questions. He knew that feeling well.

Quinn sat back thoughtfully. "They may never have known. Sometimes whole generations can simply remain as human all their lives. It's only you meeting me that's unlocked it in you. The physical attraction is extremely fierce when you first meet. Once you've consummated the relationship for the first time, it lessens. The more you get to know each other and the more sex you have, the more you then start to make love and not just screw each other."

He laughed at the expression on Cade's face. "It's all pretty primal to start with but then that's exactly what it was the other night between us."

Cade blushed faintly and Quinn reached over to caress his jawline. "It was amazing and I'm hoping to repeat the experience soon."

Cade flushed a deeper red and Quinn chuckled. "It's very difficult for me to just sit here this way and not ravish you," he said huskily. "It's taking a lot of self-control to leave you alone. If I hadn't put that spell on you, for both of our sakes, we'd be screwing like rabbits right now." He smiled. "And we'd probably run out of condoms."

Cade swallowed as his pale eyes filled with a light Quinn recognised. The flush of sexual attraction was growing deeper. Cade's pupils dilated and Quinn wondered whether the spell was wearing off. He'd better get through this story quickly.

"As I said before, I'd say from your love of water and your scent that your Fey is a Sprite. Do you know what a Sprite is?"

Cade shook his head. "I've heard of it but not in any detail. Aren't they the seal people?" His voice sounded very dubious.

Quinn laughed. "No, those are Selkies. The ones I'm talking about are called Nix in Germany, Näck in Sweden, but they have many other names. They're shape shifters, said to be mischievous, and a little like Sirens. They played music and sang to lure people in. We have them in the British Isles as well as in other parts of the world." He laughed softly. "They were said to be beautiful young men who wore few clothes and enjoyed swimming naked." Quinn cocked an eyebrow at Cade. "I'm guessing you like skinny dipping and letting it all hang out?"

Cade scowled. "Funny man." But Quinn thought from the gleam in his eyes he wasn't far wrong in his assessment. That thought of Cade naked in the water made him harder and he shifted uncomfortably.

Cade shook his head. "I can't believe I'm sitting here having this conversation with you. Do I need to be committed for considering all this to be true? If I hadn't seen what you did to the boat, and felt this pull we have, I really couldn't take this seriously. But I experienced something inside when you were drawing those circles on my hand. It was almost primeval. As if it unlocked something different inside me." His face was white, his eyes dark in the dimming light.

Quinn's heart tugged. He nodded. "That's exactly what it was. You're not crazy; you're finding out about something ancient in yourself and being told you have a strong attraction to man you hardly know. I'd say that's very disconcerting. But you're taking it all very well now I've actually managed to get some of the story out without you ripping my throat out with your teeth."

Cade chuckled softly and the pull between them grew stronger. The spell was wearing off. It had needed a lot of Quinn's own power just to get this far and resist the attraction. He stood up to try and get some distance and quell the rising desire in his body. Cade's growing arousal was getting stronger by the minute.

"So effectively I'm a Warlock, you're a Sprite and we have this incredible attraction. That means that if we intend having a fairly normal relationship, which I'd really like, and where we don't rip each other's clothes off every time we get close to each other, we need to spend more time together. We also need to make love more so we can start to control the urges. I know it sounds like every man's lame excuse to have sex, but I'm afraid in our case, it happens to be true."

His voice trailed off as Cade stood up and moved over to him, his breathing heavier than it had been, his eyes darkened. His chest rose and fell under the tee shirt he wore, his evident need for Quinn emanating from every pore in his body.

Quinn cleared his throat. "I didn't mean we should start now, much as I'd like to. Maybe I need to allow you time to process all this information first—"

Cade growled as he pulled Quinn toward him, taking his mouth in a kiss that was neither gentlemanly nor patient. Greedy hands slid under his shirt, inflaming Quinn's skin with his touch. Quinn left all thoughts of resistance behind as he prepared to be royally screwed in the nicest possible way.

Chapter 6

They lay beside each other in Cade's bed, snuggled under the covers together. It was a large king-size bed, one they'd made the most of that evening.

Quinn turned and regarded Cade with drowsy eyes as his fingers traced soft patterns across his chest. Cade caught his breath at Quinn's lazy touch. His body was still jazzed up from their lovemaking. Quinn fingered the small metal piercing in Cade's left nipple with lazy indolence. Cade's hands caressed Quinn's stomach, lingering on an ugly, puckered three-inch scar which stretched down toward his left hip.

Hell, this man is beautiful. He's like a wild beast, all muscle and sinew. He's also scarred like one.

"You are quite the animal, Mr. Mairston," Quinn murmured. "You seem to be really getting used to this whole situation." He caressed the nipple piercing. "And this was a surprise. A really nice one I have to say. You didn't have it in the other night. And I think I explored you enough to know you don't have any more anywhere." He grinned wickedly as Cade's fingers pinched his hip.

Cade laughed softly. "I took it out for the benefit dinner. It doesn't fit well under a dress shirt. And as for all this, I don't believe it all myself. But I don't seem to have a choice. You've made that quite clear. And I have to say it's not all that much of a hardship. You're a pretty personable and sexy guy and to be honest, this just feels so right—somehow." He licked a wet tongue down Quinn's shoulder and grinned as Quinn lost his breath.

Cade murmured, "I saw you in the paper with a man called Adam Carnover."

Quinn started and looked at Cade with hooded eyes.

Cade watched his eyes. "Is he still in your life? The papers seemed to think you were getting married."

Quinn leaned over and kissed his forehead softly. "I wouldn't be here with you if I was with another man. Adam isn't in my life any longer."

"What happened?"

Quinn frowned, his face dark. "We had a difference of opinion and decided to go our separate ways."

"Was he like me, or was he normal?" Cade asked curiously, glad that the man was no longer around but still intending to find out more about their past relationship.

Quinn was still. "He was normal, nothing like you," he said shortly.

Cade could tell he really didn't want to talk about his ex. Wisely, he let it rest for the moment. "Another thing you haven't told me. Who was that man I saw in the forest that evening? Was that something to do with you?"

Quinn's eyes narrowed as if debating what to say next.

"Are you going to tell me?" Cade watched him closely. He reached down and grasped Quinn's semi-erect cock. "Or do I have to suck it out of you like I did earlier?"

Quinn gave a low laugh and sat up, the bed covers draped across his waist as he leaned back against the headboard. "As much as I find that idea very appealing, I think I need to recuperate first. I don't think I've got any moisture left in my body after that very intense blow job. But please feel free to repeat the experience in a little while."

Cade grinned and continued his lazy stroking of Quinn's cock. "So does that mean you're going to tell me then?"

Quinn shook his head in amusement. "I can't think of anything when you're doing that to me. You're damn insatiable."

Cade huffed and removed his hand, pulling back to sit up against the pillows. Quinn grinned. "Thank you. Maybe now I can think straight." He turned to plump up his pillows then sat back with a sigh. "When a Warlock is seven years old, he undergoes a ritual. It's a rite of passage where he becomes a fully 'powered up' Warlock, if you like. It's a pretty tough ritual and takes a lot of courage and a fairly high pain threshold."

"But you're only seven years old then!" Cade was aghast at the thought of a child going through something painful.

Quinn shrugged. "You grow up tough those first seven years. By the time the ritual comes around, you're ready for whatever you need to go through." He hesitated. "Each human Warlock has a magyckal counterpart. We call it our Withinner. Mine belonged to my father. His name is Taliesin." Quinn pronounced the odd name in a strange way. *Tal-yiersen.* "Taliesin is an immortal legendary sixth-century Welsh sorcerer, poet and bard. His real time is that of King Arthur and Merlin."

Cade's mouth dropped open and Quinn grinned. "I've never really known Taliesin to be much of a poet other than the occasional very inventive cursing. In more modern times, he's been the Withinner of many a famous person, including Leonardo da Vinci."

Cade shook his head slowly, still catching up with Quinn's earlier words. "He actually exists in Arthur's time? And da Vinci was a Warlock too?"

"Yes, Cade, da Vinci was a Warlock. The last person to have Taliesin as a Withinner, before my father received him, was a man called Thomas Dooley. He died of cancer in 1961 when my dad was seven years old. Dooley was a great humanitarian and even today the organisation that he founded, the Dooley Foundation, helps those less fortunate. My father was of the same ilk. I suppose you could say he was almost the Dooley of his time. He was passionate about trying to make a difference. QuinnCo, the company my dad took over from his father when he died, believes in tolerance and trying to change the world through education. QuinnCo also works with the Dooley Foundation and we hope that between us, we open people's eyes and give them choices.

Quinn frowned. "When my dad was murdered, when I was six, Taliesin had a choice. I wasn't old enough to receive him yet so he could have gone to someone else. But he chose to wait for me. When I was seven we had our ritual and now he lives alongside me in his time in the sixth century, which is where he chooses to stay as an immortal."

Cade was overwhelmed with the story he was hearing of sorcerers and immortality. He watched Quinn's face as he grew more animated about his history

"Our Withinner amplifies our magyck. I have my own magyck as Quinn Fairmont, Warlock, but with Taliesin's it's seven times more powerful. Seven is a very powerful number to any Warlock. There are portents all through history about the number. I have a certain phrase I can use to invoke him. When I do, we swap places. It's really that simple. He appears as a dark, aggressive, six-foot arrogant warrior in a cloak and I time travel back to the sixth century."

He grinned wryly. "It's a little strange landing on the shores of the Welsh coast dressed as I am. The magyck makes sure I always go back to Taliesin's cottage. Occasionally I have almost frozen to death in the midst of a really bad winter but overall it's not too bad. His place is fairly homely and I just chill out and wait. I can't afford to be seen hence the short time we trade places. We only trade places to accomplish an end so it's not too bad. We can't exist in the same place together. It's dangerous for both of us."

Cade's jaw dropped open further at this announcement.

Had he fallen into an episode of the Twilight Zone?

Quinn chuckled. "Taliesin can only go back and forth between his time and the one occupied by the Warlock he's with at the time. He can't travel through to any other period in history. I imagine this is so we don't change past events or influence history. That's forbidden in the Warlock Creed. It's a safety valve." He brushed a sweaty strand of hair from Cade's forehead and Cade's skin tingled at the touch.

"We also can't fight each other as Withinners, even though they are far more powerful. If we choose to fight another Warlock it has to be as our human self with Warlock power. We only use our Withinners to amplify our magyck. *They* generally have no fight with each other and normally won't fight each other anyway. It's the human element unfortunately that tends to be the troublesome side. Nothing in history has really changed in that way." He smiled wryly.

"What were you doing that night I saw you? " Cade asked curiously.

"Taliesin wanted to collect some special lichen in the woods. I was busy revoking him when you saw me. Sending him back to his time and bringing me forward. In certain situations he can do the same to me, say if I were injured or unconscious somewhere, he could bring me back here or to a Warlock clinic."

Cade's brow furrowed.

"Generally revoking means I control him, not the other way around. At least most of the time," Quinn said wryly. "He can be a little awkward when he wants to be."

"Do you remember what he does when he's him and vice versa?" Cade was fascinated by all this, his keen anthropological mind seeing the possibility of being able to solve many of the answers to questions he'd always had.

Quinn nodded. "We retain each other's memories but very deep down. You can imagine how it would be if in my present human form I had all of the fifteen centuries of memories of Taliesin. He's an Immortal, used to it, but my mind probably wouldn't cope. It would go into overload and drive me insane. So they're buried really deep but we can call on each other's deeper memories when we want to. It's safer that way. For me at least. And yes, we're always conscious of each other." He shrugged his shoulders apologetically. "It sounds complicated, I know."

A surge of disquiet ran through Cade. "If you invoked him, he'd remember this and everything we've done?"

Quinn nodded. "He would have been aware of it as it happened. It would be the same with me. Whilst something's actually happening, like in the here and now, both of us feel the same things at the same time. We can both choose to block each other out whenever we want. I certainly shut out his life as much as I can unless he needs me to listen or I really need to find out what's going on with him. But he tends to block me out a lot too." He shrugged. "But I'm so used to having him in my head all the time that it feels strange when he's not there." He smiled wryly. "Taliesin finds my life fascinating so he tends to eavesdrop a lot on my conversations."

Cade's face was a picture. "So when you, you know, come when we make love, he can feel it too?" He scrunched his face in a thought. "I had the feeling someone was in my head when we were"—his voice trailed off—"*together* the first time. Is that possible?"

Quinn chuckled. "Yes, it might be that you can sense or hear him when we're physically intimate. I try to keep him out of my love life, but when the passion gets loose it's pretty difficult and I sometimes let him in without realising it. He's pretty polite though and tends to give me my privacy. I have the same feelings when he's getting happy on his side, which is fairly often." He grinned. "I block it out regularly or else I'd have a permanent happy smile on my face."

Cade was dumbfounded. "That must make you both very happy, getting twice as much as usual, as two people."

Quinn laughed. "It's certainly nothing to sneeze about, I suppose. And if I get hurt, Taliesin suffers too. It doesn't work the other way around for which I'm pleased, as Taliesin tends to be a bit of a scrapper. But we also heal quickly."

"Is that how you got that scar on your chin and that one on your stomach?" Cade asked quietly.

Quinn touched the chin scar gingerly. "This one was from a Fey woman who really tried to fight the urges and came at me with a knife. She sliced my chin open. I managed to make her see sense, finally." He regarded Cade steadily. "Fey attraction is not a respecter of gender. One has to go with the flow."

Cade's breath left his body. "So you're both bisexual? Have you ever, you know, with a woman?" He waved his hand.

Quinn's face tightened. "Yes to both questions. I experience what he does; when he's making love to a woman I can feel it. But I tend to switch off as I said. And I was intimate with both sexes until about six years ago when I decided I really preferred men to women."

Cade stared at him. "I see. Wow." He was a little discomfited at Quinn's confession.

Quinn quirked an eyebrow at him. "Problem?" he enquired softly. "You don't like the fact I've been with women?"

Cade felt his face colour. "No uh, it's not a problem. Just never been with a man who's done both before."

"You always knew you were homosexual then?" Quinn trailed hands through Cade's hair and Cade wanted to purr like Marco Polo.

"Since I was twelve and got hard at the sight of the other boys in the shower. I had to try hiding it somehow because the school I went to wasn't all that conducive to gay boys." Cade would rather forget the memories he had of the boy's boarding school he'd been at, a stern, no-nonsense place that frowned on anything out of the norm. He remembered one of his fellow students being discovered jacking off to pictures of a young Tom Cruise. The poor thirteen-year-old had been ragged unmercifully, called every derogatory name that creative and cruel young boys could think of. The boy then tried to hang himself after two months of hell. Luckily someone had found him dangling from the crossbeams in the outside barn and got to him in time, but after that there was no way Cade was making his sexuality known.

"I finally come out to my guardian, Sally, when I was fourteen." She'd known something was amiss but hadn't suspected it might be that he was gay. She'd quickly moved him from St. Swinthin's School for Boys to one that was more tolerant.

Quinn leaned forward and kissed him gently. "That look on your face—it sounds like you had a bit of a rough time. I'm sorry you went through that." He frowned. "Forgive me for asking but what happened to your parents that you needed a guardian?"

Cade smiled sadly. "My birth mother, Anna, died giving birth to me. My dad looked after me." He heard the wistfulness in his voice. "My dad died at sea when I was ten. His body was never found."

Quinn reached over, his thumb stroking Cade's wrist, comforting and familiar. "Christ, Cade, honey, I'm sorry about that. It must have been quite a shock to you."

Cade nodded. "Dad had a family friend, a woman called Sally Greer. She was wonderful, really took me under her wing when he died." He still thought fondly of the steady and loving woman who'd been a mother to him in everything but biology. The old feeling of grief flared for a moment in Cade's chest. "Sally was killed in a freak accident eleven years ago when I was twenty-four. She was electrocuted when a faulty wire sparked in the kitchen." He heaved a deep breath. "I found her lying in the kitchen when I went over to visit. She hadn't been answering the phone. I knew something was wrong." He shivered as he recalled the sight. Sally had been lying on the floor, her eyes wide open and her body cold. Cade would never forget the trauma of that day. The image was seared on his memory.

Quinn pulled him into a hug. "God, Cade, that must have been dreadful. You've certainly had your share of heartbreak, baby."

Cade shrugged. "You might want to be careful getting involved with me, Quinn. I'm pretty bad luck to be around." He said the words jokingly but it wasn't the first time he'd felt the frisson of fear down his spine at the thought he might not be good karma for anyone. Everyone he loved had died.

Quinn reached over and grasped his face, taking his lips in a deep, searing kiss that left Cade once again breathless. "I'm tough; I can take it. I'm more than willing to take the chance." His arms tightened around Cade and he sank into them, feeling a sense of well being he'd not experienced before.

"You didn't tell me how you got this scar," Cade's fingers trailed down the ragged edges of Quinn's hip.

Quinn's face darkened. "It's a long story and one I'm not disposed to tell right now." Quinn's face was unreadable and Cade saw he didn't want to talk about it. He kissed it instead, trailing his tongue along the skin as Quinn sighed in pleasure at the gesture.

"Could you not use your magyck to heal it?" Cade said teasingly. "All-powerful Warlock like you?"

Quinn's eyes flickered. "I ran out of magyck on this one. It was too late to heal it by the time I was ready. So," he shrugged, "it's just part of me now."

Cade had the feeling that wasn't the real story and that Quinn was hiding something. But he thought he'd leave the subject alone right now. He had another question anyway.

"Will I ever get to meet your Withinner?" Cade looked up at him.

Quinn looked uneasy. "Maybe someday. But I think for now you should concentrate on me and learn more about the human rather than the paranormal. Little bites of the elephant, Cade."

Cade nodded. A strange expression fleeted across his lover's face, as if he were listening to something only he could hear.

Cade saw it. "Is anything wrong?"

"Hmm? No, nothing wrong. Just a little nagging voice in my head that won't leave me alone. It'll pass."

He reached out and pulled Cade closer for a kiss. Cade gave himself willingly, revelling in the feel of Quinn's hands in his hair and his lips taking his with a sense of ownership he guessed he'd better get used to. Quinn Fairmont was a man who took control of what he wanted.

Chapter 7

The following morning Cade was up at eight making breakfast in the galley when Quinn came through after showering. He reached over and kissed the back of Cade's neck, causing his skin to break out in goose bumps. Cade realized that after the numerous sessions they'd had last night, the primal urges were starting to abate, just as Quinn had promised. He was still the sexiest man Cade had ever seen, but the urge to rip his clothes off every time he laid eyes on him was lessening. He missed it a little. They'd also agreed they trusted each other enough for a no-condom policy. Cade knew he was certainly fine. He'd been clean tested a while ago and practiced safe sex since then. Though he hardly knew the man, he just knew Quinn couldn't lie to him about something as important as this.

"Nothing special for breakfast," he warned. "Just scrambled eggs on toast and coffee. I like cooking but I wasn't expecting company for breakfast."

Quinn chuckled as he sat down at the small dining room table to tuck into his breakfast. "That makes two of us. I tend to either order in or keep it simple: tuna sandwiches or omelettes." He ate his breakfast in enjoyment as Cade sat down to join him. The morning was quiet, slightly overcast, and the boat bobbed gently on the water. There was a companionable silence as they ate, interrupted only by the faint meows of Marco Polo as he roamed the room, winding himself around their feet, wanting attention.

"He's not used to company. Normally it's just me, him and either the television or my latest thesis spread all over the table."

Cade looked at Quinn enquiringly. "If you can travel back to Taliesin's time, that means you or Taliesin," he struggled to pronounce it the way Quinn had and he grinned at his attempt, "must have seen a lot of history. You'll be able to tell me about the culture and the people that lived all those years ago, won't you?"

Quinn nodded as he stuffed bagel in his mouth. "Yes, I can probably help you with research if you want. I'll need to dig down a little deep but as long it's not too often it should be okay."

"Why not often?" Cade asked curiously. "Does it give you a headache or something having to dredge up all those memories?"

Quinn stopped chewing and regarded him sombrely. "Each time I invoke Taliesin or dredge up his memories, it intensifies the Warlock in me. I become *amplified*, for want of a better word. I told you we had enemies in the past, Cade. Well, we have them in this time too. There are a lot of other Warlocks who want to possess Taliesin for themselves. And there is a way they can do it. Each time I invoke him or his past, it draws them in like vultures to carrion. I just don't need the constant pressure to be on my guard. I've done that before and it didn't turn out too well."

His voice was grim. Cade stared at him in fascination.

"As well as that there's the inevitable Witchhunters Alliance trying to destroy Warlocks and witches, and there's usually a Witchhunter that's constantly seeking us out. It's a fucking battlefield out there." He sighed and leaned back in his chair. "Have you ever heard of Matthew Hopkins?"

Cade nodded. "Yes. He was the self-styled Witchfinder General back in the seventeenth century. If I remember, he was responsible for over five hundred executions of witches in Essex, Suffolk and other eastern counties."

Quinn shook his head grimly. "You can double, even treble that number when you add the Warlock numbers to it. No one seems to know much about the persecution of them. He decimated a whole population of my kind. I lost a lot of family in his insane purging of witches. Unfortunately Hopkins is a breed of Fey too."

At Cade's gasp, Quinn nodded. "He's a Mannacrux, a sworn enemy of witches and Warlocks and one dedicated to our decimation. Hunting witches was simply a side benefit of hunting down us. Just like I have Taliesin, one of his progeny will inherit his talent and his memories. It's not the same as having a Withinner, but his descendent is imbued with his knowledge and skills and takes up the mantle of being the next Witchfinder General. There's one in every Hopkins generation and I have to be on my guard that he or she doesn't track me down."

Cade sat open-mouthed at this story. The normally affable Quinn looked magnificently dangerous as he sat there telling him about people who meant to do him harm. It was easy to believe from the set of his jaw and the fire in his eyes that this was indeed a powerful Warlock sitting before him at the breakfast table.

"If they do find you, what happens?" Cade asked. "Can they kill you?" He covered Quinn's hand with his. Quinn sat back and pushed his plate away.

"Yes. As Quinn, I can die like any human but my lifespan is more than normal. Warlocks like me have sometimes lived to be around 120 years old."

He grinned at Cade's startled gasp. "God forbid I should live that long. So I'm not immortal but Taliesin is. I heal quicker and I'm probably a lot harder to kill as Taliesin will protect me to some extent and magyck can have some effect. But I can still die like any human and one day, God willing, I'll die of old age and not by the hands of a Mannacrux or another Warlock. Then Taliesin will go onto to be with anyone else he deems worthy. It's unlikely I'll have a male heir given my predilection for men." He smiled but Cade thought he looked a little sad at that prospect. Quinn's face was grim. "Unfortunately there are very few Fairmonts left due to the purge. My father was an only child, as was I. My grandparents are both dead. There are some scattered around from before my dad's time but I don't really know who or where they are. It's an ongoing project to try finding one who can carry on the Fairmont name." He shrugged. "Or I'll need to find a surrogate mother to have my child. That's a distinct possibility and my preferred option should I find the right woman."

Cade's mouth dropped not just at the words but the arrogance in them. Quinn most certainly wouldn't let just any woman bear his child. "Really? You want to be a dad?" Truthfully, it wasn't something Cade had ever considered.

Quinn nodded. "I wouldn't mind being a father. I may have no choice in the matter." His jaw tightened. "I can't let the Fairmont bloodline die out because I'm gay. There are options. And as far as I know we've always had male heirs. It's just the way we Fairmont men make babies."

Cade was nonplussed. Quinn's words meant that perhaps one day, if they were still a couple, he might be a dad too. That thought scared him so he changed the subject. "How can another Warlock take Taliesin from you?" Cade stood up and paced around the deck. "Do they invoke him or something as well?"

Quinn shook his head. "The only way Taliesin can be commanded is if someone kills me with a dragon claw dipped in that same dragon's blood."

Cade blinked in surprise. "Dragons exist?"

Quinn looked at him in amusement. "Of course. Well, they did." He frowned. "There hasn't been a sighting of one in centuries but they existed."

Cade watched in stupefaction at this bit of information as Quinn tapped the side table with fingers like raw nervous energy. "Going back to your question about how Taliesin can be taken. The claw and blood will be immediately fatal for me and Taliesin will have no choice but to do the bidding of the person who's killed me that way. Dragon's blood alone, on a knife or something, won't make a Withinner obey another, but it will make a Warlock really suffer before he ultimately dies. Dragon's blood also counteracts any magyck we may have in us and it's really the final death knell for a Warlock." His voice grew sad. "The other way to kill a Warlock is to drip another Warlock's blood into him. An open wound works best. It has to be combined with a magyckal spell of destruction, and the blood acts like poison and is fatal. Blood-bond death doesn't work if it's done by accident, like in battle when there may be transfer of fluids, stuff like that. The spell is what gives its potency to kill. When the human Warlock dies this way, all the memories the Withinner had with him before that die too. It's as if his Withinner's mind is wiped clean like a blank slate." He stopped and took a deep breath. "It's how my parents died, by a rogue Warlock. It was one of the worst things to deal with when my father was killed that way. The fact one of our own killed them both and the fact I couldn't see anything that Taliesin might have had in his copious memory bank about my dad's memories or his life. Taliesin wasn't happy about it either. And if Taliesin himself is killed with the dragon's blood and claw, it's over. It's the only thing that can actually kill a Withinner. That's the way it works. The chances are I'd die if he did. The psychic shock would be too much for my human body to withstand."

He sounded weary. Cade walked up behind him and wrapped his arms around his shoulders, kissing the top of his head. Quinn leaned back into Cade, closing his eyes.

"Then I guess we'll have to make sure there's no one with a dragon's claw just around the corner," Cade murmured. "They'll have me to get through first. And we Sprites can be a really nasty bunch…can't we?" he said hopefully.

Quinn laughed at Cade's words. "Actually, you're pretty much a bunch made for loving, not fighting. Which is fine with me." He stood up and drew Cade into his arms, kissing him fiercely. "But no one's going to get me," he whispered into his neck when he'd finished. "You can count on me being around for a lot longer."

Cade hugged him tightly, wondering how his life could change so much for the better just by this man being in it. The transition from Cade Mairston, bachelor to Cade Mairston, Water Sprite with a Warlock in his bed had been very quick and he still couldn't quite get to grips with it.

The bond between him and Quinn was incredibly strong, with Cade feeling he'd known him forever instead of just a few meetings in the last three weeks. Quinn had said it was the Fey blood. Centuries of attraction between their different races were embedded in their genetic makeup, making each of them more aware of the other than in a normal relationship.

Cade didn't care. Quinn was the one he'd been waiting for his whole life. And he knew he would do anything to protect Quinn and their relationship.

Chapter 8

The next few weeks passed in a blur for Cade as he got used to the idea of having a permanent man in his bed, one who was not like any other man he'd ever met. Quinn Fairmont was sexy, fiercely intelligent, deeply mysterious, extremely private and arrogant. Cade's male ego baulked at Quinn's dominant approach to their developing relationship. Cade found himself being told in no uncertain terms that they were "going out" and Quinn would be picking him up, or that he was coming around and most often than not, brought dinner with him from a local take away, normally accompanied by a very good bottle of red wine. Thai food appeared to be one of his favourites. Cade thought wryly it was just as well he liked it too, or he'd be permanently starving.

Whilst he was enjoying the attention Quinn was giving him, attention that left him permanently breathless when Quinn was near and in a state of constant arousal despite him saying things would soon "calm down," Cade's rebellious and independent streak was rising to the fore. Quinn also let nothing personal about himself pass his very kissable lips. Even after three weeks of seeing each other constantly, he was a closed book. Other than his business life, his explanation of his state of being as a Warlock and his company, QuinnCo, Cade knew absolutely nothing more about him than when he'd first met him.

Quinn was evasive to the core, deflecting any personal questions by either changing the subject adroitly or initiating erotic and passionate sex, which blew Cade's mind and made him forget what he'd asked in the first place. Cade had even wondered suspiciously if he was doing some sort of magyck to *make* him forget.

"I can't help it you're easily distracted by my body," Quinn had grinned at his exasperated expression even as his lips trailed down Cade's chest and bit the nipples that hardened whenever Quinn was around. Cade's nipple piercing had never received so much loving attention. "Are you not enjoying my ravenous appetite for you and the mind-blowing sex then?" he'd murmured silkily. "You can have more time to talk, but I can't promise I'll be able to answer. I might have my mouth full. It could turn out to be a pretty one-sided affair."

Quinn had just managed to catch Cade's hand as it rose to punch him aside his head, and he'd given a deep, satisfied laugh. Those two actions alone had led to a tussle on the couch, which had again led to sex. Cade just couldn't win with the man. He watched Quinn now as he lay lazily on the couch in the cabin, his dark blond hair tousled and untidy from their previous lovemaking, his eyes closed as he lay back with his hands tucked behind his head. His checked shirt was open and Cade saw the rise and fall of his chest as he breathed, the golden hair covering it and the strong muscles of his stomach. His jeans zip was still half down and Cade could see the line of hair that led down into his groin, a place he'd put his mouth only an hour before.

"Do you like what you see?" Quinn murmured softly, a slight smile on his face. "I can feel your stare burning through my trousers from here."

"Jesus, get over yourself! You're such an arrogant sod." Cade's face flushed at being caught out ogling and he glared at Quinn angrily.

Quinn chuckled and opened his eyes, watching his face intently. "You were looking. Admit it." He had a distinctly smug and self-satisfied tone, causing Cade to shake his head in frustration.

"Christ, I think you're the most annoying man I've ever met," he muttered.

Quinn grinned as he sat up, zipping himself up and starting to button his shirt. "I'm also the only Warlock you've ever met. How do you know we're all not all arrogant tossers?" He raised one sexy eyebrow and the sight made Cade turn away and swallow.

"No, I think it's safe to say this attitude is all Quinn Fairmont." Cade scowled as he watched his lover get up off the couch in a lithe movement and reach over for the bottle of wine on the table. Quinn looked at him enquiringly and Cade shook his head.

Quinn shrugged and poured himself a healthy glass. "What is it that annoys you about me?" he enquired as he sipped his wine. "Go on, tell me. I promise I'll listen."

Cade noted dryly he didn't promise to change anything, a typical Quinn cop out. Give nothing more than what was needed. He did think he was being a heel though. He was about to complain about a man who treated him like a king, was without doubt the best lover he'd ever had and spared no expense to entertain him. Quinn was intelligent, fun and made him laugh.

Cade shrugged, feeling a little mean. "You never talk about yourself. And you assume that when you want to do something, I do too. I'm also getting a bit tired of takeaway Thai food. Perhaps we could try something else some time. Indian, maybe? Or I can cook. I'm pretty good at it if I may say so." He sat down next to Quinn on the couch.

Cade saw Quinn's grimace of distaste and hoped it was at the mention of the Indian and not his cooking skills.

Quinn acknowledged his words with a gracious nod of his head. "Fine, Chinese next time. And I had no idea you liked cooking so by all means, feel free to do that. I'm afraid my culinary skills are non-existent so I can't return the favour. But I'm sure I can think of something else I'm good at to say thank you." He raised one sardonic, golden-hued eyebrow. "And if you tell me what it is you want to do next time, we can do that. All you have to do is tell me. But half the time you don't really seem to mind what I have planned so I go with the flow." He leaned across and kissed Cade, his lips tasting of wine. "I'm yours to command. I live to please you."

His words, whilst joking, had the ring of truth and Cade immediately felt churlish at his complaining. He kissed Quinn back, tongue slipping into his mouth, and Quinn growled as he pulled them together, his hardness pressing into the taut skin of Cade's stomach. As Quinn pushed him back against the couch, his intentions clear, Cade prepared to be taken again. It was only later than night that he realised that once again Quinn had deftly sidestepped the comment he'd made about him not telling him anything more about himself.

Chapter 9

Jeremy Payton heaved his stocky, short fifteen-year-old body out of the roller coaster seat with a swagger that said it hadn't really done anything for him. His sulky face was set in a slight snarl as he turned to his friend with a sneer.

"I think I should ask for my money back. That was a shite bloody ride." He looked around him, his slate-green eyes looking hungry for a fight. "Where's that tosser then? Let me at him. He needs to give me my fucking three quid back."

Slightly scared, Kyle Loggins looked at his friend. "Let's just go, Jer. I don't need any trouble. The Old Bill has already given me one warning. I don't need another."

Jeremy scoffed. "You're just a pussy, Kyle." But he grinned and made his way away from the roller coaster.

Kyle sighed in relief as he followed his friend. Jeremy was always looking for a fight and he tended to be a very dirty fighter. The two youngsters walked through the fairground in Clapham Common. The fairground was packed and the two boys were able to lift a variety of wallets and other items as they meandered through the crowds.

Jeremy had an ulterior motive for coming to places where people congregated and the mass of humanity was at its highest. As the youngest Witchfinder General so far in history, Jeremy's talents at spotting witches was at its peak. In his book, Warlocks and witches were all the same. He made no distinction. They were all dirty bastards and bitches. Once he'd found them, he took great delight in finding new and inventive ways to destroy them. His biggest advantage was that no one suspected a teenage boy of being dangerous and life threatening, a fact he used to his gain without fail.

He'd picked up the scent of a Warlock, a young one, probably about twenty years old. Jeremy stopped, sniffing the air carefully, trying to determine where it was coming from. He patted his anorak, finding comfort in the fact that his centuries-old stag-hunting dagger with its special Witchfinder properties was still firmly hidden in its depths.

He looked at Kyle. "You keep seeing what you can pick up. I've got some business to do. I'll be back later."

Kyle sighed. He was used to Jeremy going off to do "his business," whatever that was. He nodded resignedly and watched as his friend disappeared into the crowd. He didn't want to follow, didn't want to know what Jeremy did. He just knew it was better if he didn't.

Jeremy hunted, navigating his way around the people, following the scent that so attracted him. He finally found himself in front of the Haunted House, watching as the rail cars filled with people trundled in and out of the entrance, screaming kids and teenagers alike giggling and clutching each other in the throes of simulated terror.

Jeremy's eyes were flat as he watched one couple enter the ride, a young man and a girl, huddled together, with the young man's arm around her shoulders protectively.

Jeremy sniffed the air and grinned nastily. Time for a little bit of terror of his own. He slipped past the harried custodian of the ride using a masking spell he'd perfected, and he headed into the dark dungeon depths of the fair attraction.

Once inside, he could see perfectly, his vision adjusting to the darkness within. Like a shadow, Jeremy flitted his way toward the far corner of the ride, where he expected the rail car containing the young couple to be in the next few minutes. He took the dagger out of his coat and stood there silently, slowing his breathing down. He knew the young Warlock would detect him, but he hoped that the surprise and the hidden advantage he had might slow him down, enough that Jeremy could slit the Warlock's throat with the dagger. He heard the steady rumble of the car as it approached and readied himself. He became acutely aware of the rising suspicion of the Warlock as the car drew nearer and heard the man whisper, "Irene, get down, stay down and don't move."

Jeremy grinned wolfishly, his teeth showing white in the dark of the funhouse. This was the part he enjoyed the most. The part where it was just him and the bastard witch. The one that pitted them against each other, hopefully ending up with the witch's blood spilling warm, the metallic tang in his nostrils. He sensed the Warlock's presence in front of him before he even saw him.

The lemony scent offended his nose and he grimaced. This Warlock was young but obviously had the benefit of a Withinner, one who was infinitely older and more experienced. Jeremy wasn't interested in the Withinner. They were too difficult to kill and he hadn't got the patience. It could just go back to wherever it came from and find another human to nest in. He just wanted the man himself dead and rotting like the witch he was.

Jeremy stepped forward as the Warlock said something under his breath, a soft breathless whisper that was probably some sort of protection spell. Jeremy grinned. It wouldn't help him. Jeremy held his dagger in front of him, ready to strike with its special tip of cadmium, something he'd been given by a "friend." Cadmium had a very negative effect on Warlocks and their shields, penetrating any barrier the Warlocks might build.

He heard the man not more than two feet from where he stood. Jeremy took the offensive and lunged forward suddenly with his dagger, feeling it strike something, give, and then continue through. The Warlock moved swiftly, dodging to one side but Jeremy could already smell that his dagger had made contact with the skin. He heard the Warlock's hiss of pain as the poison rushed through his system, immobilising him enough to allow Jeremy to take his final blow. Jeremy smiled.

Funny how these witch chaps always though their fancy spells could protect them from me when all they need is a simply physical act of getting the cadmium into their bloodstream. They overcomplicate things. With them everything is meta-physical. They never seemed to expect a human act of aggression like a simple stabbing. He hoped the other event he'd organised for tonight had the same success.

The young Warlock fell to the ground, a slight froth at the corner of his mouth as the cadmium did its work. Jeremy smiled at the man as he lay there, unable to move, temporarily paralysed. He leaned over the witch, his face curious as he observed the man's eyes. He liked to look in their eyes as he killed them. He raised his dagger and with one swift movement he drew it across the young man's throat, feeling the blood gush out, warm and sticky.

The Warlock gave a final gasp and a tremor of pleasure went through Jeremy's body as the man died. He stood there for a moment, enjoying the sensation, and then slowly wiped his blade on the man's shirt. He didn't stick around to see the man's Withinner drift gently to the surface and disappear in a veil of white mist. Instead, Jeremy tucked the dagger back into his anorak and slipped out of the funhouse as quietly as he'd entered.

Chapter 10

Quinn sat in his study with Jomo when the young Warlock took his final breath. Bile rose in Quinn's throat and knowing what it meant, he pushed his chair back from his desk, stood up and rushed blindly to the bathroom.

Jomo exclaimed behind him. "Quinn! Are you having another one of your panic attacks? Do you need any help?"

Quinn leaned over the toilet, retching nonstop, watching with alarm as small puddles of blood-stained mucous made scarlet splashes down the toilet bowl. He sank down to sit alongside the porcelain vessel, his hands trembling, his eyes haunted and filled with hot tears. This reaction meant the heralding of another Warlock's death and the grief in him was deep. Taliesin raged inside him, the Withinner's fury and grief adding to his own.

This was the worst attack Quinn had ever had. He took a few deep breaths as he tried to control the rising clamour in his chest. Finally he was able to stand up and wash his mouth out, seeing the paler streaks of blood now washing down into the basin. He flushed the toilet and rinsed out the basin. If Jomo saw any blood, he'd be rushing him off to the ER tout-suite.

When he went out, Jomo was standing there, his face filled with concern. "Christ, Quinn. You look terrible. You're as white as spoilt milk. We should get you to a doctor."

Quinn had told Jomo he suffered from occasional panic attacks. It was the only way to explain to his friend these occasional episodes. He didn't think Jomo believed the story.

"I'm fine now," he whispered huskily, his throat still sore from retching. "Nothing to worry about. It's over."

"You really look bad. I'm worried about you. You have to promise me you'll go the doctor and get yourself checked again."

Quinn nodded. "I will, I promise." He smiled wanly. "Please don't tell Cade about this if he calls. I haven't told him about them. I'd rather keep it between us if you don't mind." The two men had not yet met but Quinn knew they spoke on the telephone occasionally when Cade called the house.

Jomo frowned. "I don't like lying to Cade; he's a good man. All I can promise is that I won't tell him directly. But if ever he asks me anything about it, I won't lie."

Quinn nodded. "Fair enough. I respect that."

He sat back down in his chair and turned his attention back to the document he'd been reading. But his mind reeled at what had just happened.

What the hell had all that been about? He'd never vomited blood before, normally it was just bile. As Grand Master, he felt it when one of his own was killed, but the depth of reaction depended on how close the killing was. The fact that this one was so violent a reaction, it must mean that the Witchfinder General himself had done the killing. It was the only explanation. It also meant he was very close. But no matter where the death occurred, there was always something, even if it was simply an unpleasant feeling or twinge.

Quinn looked up at his computer screen as an animated book flew across, telling him email had arrived. As he reached for his mouse to open the mail, his blood froze. The digital clock on his desktop showed *21 June 14.32 pm.*

Today was the Summer Solstice. It was Litha or a Lesser Sabbat in the witch's calendar and one where later he'd be invoking Taliesin to gather specific herbs and plants like calendula, which were more potent on this day. This must also be the reason this attack had been so virulent. He was still ill and shaken from the intensity. He was aware Jomo was watching him carefully and he looked up, trying to smile.

"I'm not an invalid so you can stop looking at me as if I'm going to keel over and die."

Jomo scowled, his dark brow furrowed. "I remember the last time this happened when I was around you. It was when Adam left you. I still don't know the full story behind that and I still don't know where the hell he went, but you were very sick then too."

Quinn's heart beat faster and his throat dried up. He didn't need reminders of that in his present precarious state. "That was nine months ago and it was a very different situation. And I've told you—Adam decided to go live with that campy Italian count in Tuscany somewhere. He's probably married to the guy by now." He mentally crossed his fingers at these last comments.

Jomo didn't look convinced. "That's a maybe. But I'm keeping an eye on you, my friend. And if things get worse I will tell Cade. That man will make sure you do what you're told."

He grinned and Quinn returned the gesture. "Have no doubt about that. He can be damn scary." His tone was affectionate.

Jomo chuckled. "He's been very good for you. This man makes you smile and you've been happier with him than you ever were with Adam. I am glad the man with the brooding face returned."

Quinn smiled. He was very glad too and talking about Cade's face, he had a burning desire to get to his place and make sure his mouth was put to good use, up close and personal.

***

Cade was busy preparing pasta when Quinn arrived at the houseboat later than evening. He smiled at seeing him as he entered. But Quinn's face was shadowed, his eyes haunted.

Cade had a bad feeling. "Something's wrong."

Quinn sighed. "A Warlock was killed today. I feel it when it happens to one of our own. This was particularly unpleasant given the day it is today: the twenty-first of June. It's a Lesser Sabbat in the witchy Warlock calendar."

Cade took a deep breath. "You can actually feel when one of you dies?"

Quinn nodded tightly. "Occupational hazard that goes with the top job. It's not the most pleasant of feelings to deal with. It's been a while since I've been this bad."

Cade wondered what "job" Quinn was alluding to. He was about to ask when Quinn's mobile rang and he pulled it out of his pocket. Cade saw his lover's face change to an expression of fierce determination.

"Percy. I thought you might be calling. What have you got to tell me?"

Quinn's voice was authoritative and commanding. He listened, his eyes narrowed. "That's too close. We need to find this bastard; I want his fucking head. This was a very bad one."

Cade was taken aback at the vehemence of his tone. Quinn's face was implacable as he paced up and down the lounge. "I don't care what you need to do. Send me all the details and I'll do a little investigating myself." He frowned at something the voice said. "Cadmium? That's a new one. How come we haven't seen this before?" He listened to the voice and then exploded in temper. "Christ almighty, how many more inventive ways can these bastards find to kill one of us? Send out a general warning to everyone. Tell them what it does and that they need to be careful. And send me the details of Ross's family. I want to pay them a personal visit and give them my condolences. I want to tell them myself that we'll catch this animal and make him pay for what he did."

His voice was steely and Cade saw the powerful Warlock coming to the fore. "And let me know if you get any other information that may help us track this bastard down. I want to be kept up to date on everything. And I mean everything. Thanks, Percy." Quinn cut the call and stared at Cade in frustration.

Cade stared back and asked evenly, "Who's Percy?"

Quinn heaved a deep, shuddering breath. "Percy is my Marshall in the Warlock Consortium."

Cade stared at him in surprise and Quinn grinned. "I have the dubious honour to be the Grand Master of the Consortium. As a Fairmont and one of the most powerful Warlock families, we get to be voted into power by the Council. Effectively every Warlock in the world is under my command."

Cade stared at him open-mouthed. He'd wanted Quinn to open up to him but he'd never expected to hear something like this. "Jesus. You're like the king of the Warlocks?"

Quinn chuckled at his obvious awe. "If you want to put it that way. Why, does it turn you on?"

Cade nodded, stunned by the information. "Absolutely. I'm fucking a royal personage. But how does it work? You can't be responsible for all of them surely?"

Quinn nodded. "Ultimately, I am. But we have various Chapters throughout the world that manage their own countries and report into me. I have a fairly large management team as you'd expect. Percy tells me what I need to know from each of them and keeps me informed. I trust him with my life and there are not a lot of men or women I can say that about." He raised an eyebrow.

Despite his obvious stress, Cade could see that something he'd said was still on Quinn's mind as he spoke again. "So you like the idea of bedding a king then? That whole thought gives me a great idea for a role play. You can be my serf and I can tell you what to do."

"You mean like normal then," Cade murmured drily. "Because between you and me, I don't really see any difference in *that* scenario to what we have now." He laughed softly at Quinn's glower and moved forward to wrap his arms around Quinn's neck and press his groin to his. The rising desire in Quinn's body made him grin as he slid his hands inside his shirt, feeling the soft puckered scar on his hip as he did so. He wanted to take Quinn's mind off the horrible news he'd just gotten.

Quinn groaned. "God, Cade, you drive me crazy. I just can't get enough of you. I'm beginning to think these stories about the attraction getting easier to manage are all lies."

Cade chuckled, his breath deepening as he nibbled Quinn's ear. "I didn't realise I was making love to a king all these weeks. I guess that sort of makes me your queen then, doesn't it? "He laughed out loud at the put-out expression on Quinn's face as he teased him. "I can be camp if you like, to be more in keeping with that." He affected a feminine sweep of his hip against Quinn's and fluttered his eyelashes. Quinn growled and shut him up by sealing his mouth with his lips as his tongue thrust aggressively into Cade's mouth. Cade began to pull Quinn's shirt out of his trousers and as he reached down to palm his groin, Quinn took a deep, shuddering breath and almost collapsed against him.

"Why, Mr, Fairmont," Cade simpered, still teasing, "I didn't think my touch warranted *such* a reaction—" He stopped and regarded him worriedly.

That hadn't been Quinn swooning at his touch, in jest or not.

"Quinn, what's wrong?" Cade drew back and drew a sharp breath seeing his lover's grey face.

Quinn seemed to be struggling to breathe. He reeled away from Cade and swiftly rushed to the bathroom.

Cade heard the sound of vomiting. Scared, he walked quickly to the small bathroom and saw Quinn hunched over the toilet bowl, retching up what looked bile and blood.

Cade's stomach churned as he watched him. "Quinn, that looks really bad, bringing blood up like that. It's not normal. Maybe we should get you to a doctor…" he said tremulously.

Quinn waved at him. "I'll be fine. Just let me get over it."

When Quinn finally stopped and sat back against the wall, grey faced, Cade silently handed him tissue paper.

Quinn wiped his mouth as he looked at him with fear in his eyes. "There've been more killings, I can feel it. More than one. Jesus, what the hell is going on today?"

He stood up, flushed the toilet and washed his face, rinsing his mouth out with water and a bit of toothpaste before he turned to look at Cade again.

Quinn closed his eyes wearily. "I need to call Percy again."

As he said the words, his mobile rang.

He looked at it in dread and answered. "Percy?" His face whitened further as he listened to what was being said.

Cade watched in concern at the stricken look on his face.

"When did this happen?" Quinn said tersely. He closed his eyes in pain and swallowed. "I'll be there in a while. Wait for me." He put his phone back in his trouser pocket with slightly trembling hands and zipped himself up.

Cade took his hands fiercely. They were ice cold. "What's happened?"

Quinn stared at him with haunted eyes. "One of the Scottish Chapters has been attacked. There was a Litha ceremony at one of the consecrated grounds. A renegade Warlock attacked the congregation. One of us, Cade. I have three dead Warlocks and a lot of injured. They got the renegade though. I need to get up there. I need to deal with him."

"Do you need me to take you to the airport?"

Quinn shook his head tiredly. "I don't need an aeroplane, I have Taliesin. He can get me there faster than anyone. Instantaneous time-travel, remember? He can do it in real time. It's just the future we can't travel to." He frowned. "But it means I need to invoke him and I don't want to do that here. If anyone picks that scent up, they'll see where the signature came from and that could put you in danger. They may come here looking for me. I need to get somewhere else where I won't cause you any trouble." He reached over and kissed Cade briefly then picked up his jacket. "I'll walk a while, get away from here and then do it. I'll try get back later but I can't promise. I'm not sure how long this mess will take to clear up."

He disappeared into the cool night air, leaving Cade standing behind in helplessness. His Warlock king's face had been implacable and Cade pitied the renegade Warlock in captivity. He had a feeling there would be no mercy shown by this Grand Master.

Chapter 11

Quinn walked for about half a mile down the road, along the canal walk. He found a short path that led into some fairly dense foliage and walked down it. There was no one around. He took a deep breath and held his hands up as if playing patty cake with an invisible friend.

He chanted quietly over and over again, "*Taliesin, yn dod allan.* Taliesin, come out."

The air around him grew still as Taliesin made his entrance. There was no flash of light, no significant change in anything obvious. One minute, Quinn was there and seconds later he was gone. In his place stood a tall, cloaked figure, staff in hand, head bowed as he grew aware of his surroundings. Slowly his head rose, his dark eyes glittering in the soft light of the street lamp above, his dark face with its strong, chiselled features and cruel mouth observing his surroundings. Dark ringlets surrounded his head, shoulder-length curls that sprung to life as he moved. He lifted his head and smelt the air, satisfied that no one was around.

"I feel it too, Quinn," Taliesin muttered. "Something is wrong in the city tonight. The Witchfinder General has made his entrance and we need to find him. But first things first. We have an enemy to deal with. One of our own that needs putting down like a rabid dog. I only hope you will let me help you."

Taliesin grinned, his teeth white in his dark face. "It's been a while since I had any fun with a traitor and I could do with honing my cutting skills. And once we have taken care of business, perhaps you will let me meet that lusty young man you've been spending so much time with. It's been a while since I had any of that too."

He grinned wickedly at Quinn's unequivocal response. "Quinn, Quinn, allow me a little bit of fun. You seem to have been having enough of your own from what I could feel."

Taliesin raised his staff, making a circular motion with it as he closed his eyes, visualising where he needed to be. With a quiet sigh, the air around him seemed to part, and the Withinner stepped through as the air closed ranks behind him. The clearing was quiet, with no evidence that anyone had ever been there. Taliesin arrived in the old Crombie Country Park in the county of Angus in Scotland split seconds after leaving Little Venice. He stood for a minute to get his bearings. Around him people moved slowly and tiredly around the far end of the park, where the revellers had been holding their reverence ceremony.

Taliesin smelt the blood in the air, the electricity left behind by the Warlock battle prickling his skin, and he heard the moans and groans of the injured as they lay on the field. Taliesin knew the area would be hidden from non-Warlocks and witches, protected by magyck so that outsiders couldn't see beyond the dome-shaped sphere that locked them out. Quinn was trying to revoke him and he scowled, fighting the change. Quinn's anger at his rebellion coursed through his body in fierce waves but still Taliesin fought it. He wanted a piece of this scourge they called a renegade. But Quinn's desire was too strong and finally, with very bad grace, Taliesin gave in. In seconds, Quinn stood there, his chest heaving from the battle to revoke his Withinner. His face was thunderous.

That bastard Taliesin was becoming impossible! It was becoming more and more difficult to revoke him when his blood was up. And the comment about Cade still irked as well.

Quinn turned as his Marshall, Percy Ballantyne, approached him.

Percy's face was grave, his short, rotund frame set with grief. "Quinn, I'm glad you're here. It's a nightmare. The renegade has been bound and taken to the Lodge. He's awaiting you there. Magnus is with him so he won't be going anywhere." He chuckled grimly.

Magnus Onnarsson was a giant of a Warlock, almost seven feet tall and as wide as a barn. He was known for having one of the most explosive tempers and the renegade would do well to stay out of his way completely.

Quinn nodded. "I'll get over there now. How are the injured doing?"

"We have a lot of healers here tonight. They're doing what they can but we still lost three. Seamus Tully, Henry Dowager and Colin MacTyre."

Quinn closed his eyes in despair at the names. He knew each one of these men personally.

"They fought well but this renegade had something we weren't prepared for. He had cadmium on his blade. The same thing that weakened young Ross and got through his shield. I have a feeling there's a connection somewhere. Ross's killing and these new ones are related. I can feel it."

Quinn nodded. "Find me someone who can tell me more about this cadmium and why it affects us the way it does. I also want to know how we can protect ourselves against it. I'm going to question this renegade, find out why he turned against his own and where he got this cadmium idea from. Perhaps it may give us a link back to the Witchfinder. I still believe he or she is behind all today's events."

He turned and made his way over to the Lodge, the mystical building created by members of the Warlock Circle whenever it needed a base of operations. It was within the dome and invisible to the outside world. The magnificent pillars of the Lodge building shimmered in the cool night air as Quinn entered and nodded at the people milling around its entrance hall. They nodded and made way in deference to him as he made his way to the self-contained area at the rear where he knew the renegade was being held.

Magnus Onnarsson grinned at him as he approached. "Mr. Quinn. I've kept him on ice for you. I'm more than happy to come in and assist you if you like. I can rip his arms off whilst you mess with his chest in that way you do."

Quinn smiled slightly. "It's an admirable offer, Magnus, but let me have him alone for a while. I need some answers first."

He walked into the enclosure, protected by strong magyck to contain this renegade Warlock. The man, red-haired and slim, shorter than Quinn by several inches, was pinned against the far wall by gleaming shackles. Magnus had done a good job of trussing his victim like a bird held together with string ready for the oven.

The magyck shackles would withhold his own powers and render him virtually all human. Taliesin stirred inside Quinn, urging him to let him out so he could play too. Quinn ignored it for the time being and approached the man pinned against the wall. He smelt of fear and had panic in his eyes. Quinn snarled in satisfaction. He had three good men dead outside and was giving this man no quarter.

"I know you." Quinn regarded the trussed victim with flat, darkened eyes. "You're Jimmy Christie. We've met before. Do you know why I'm here?"

He reached out and placed a hand, shining with blue light, against the man's chest. Jimmy struggled in terror and heaved a sigh of both pain and fear as the energy Quinn generated got more intense.

"I want to know why you did this and who put you up to it." Quinn increased the pressure, seeing his captive struggling to breathe. The heat from Quinn's hand scorched his shirt and the smell of burnt skin invaded the air.

"You know how this works. Eventually my hand will burn its way right through to your backbone and it will be the most intense pain you've ever experienced." Quinn's voice was conversational. "You can stop me any time by telling me what I want to know. I know you might have coveted another's Withinner but I didn't find any dragon's claws among your paltry possessions so I'm not sure that was the intention. Your intention was just to kill your own kind, wasn't it, Jimmy?"

Quinn's voice was hypnotic. Jimmy's eyes widened with pain. "We're almost past the point of no return, Jimbo. You might want to decide fairly quickly which side you're actually on."

Jimmy tried to say something and Quinn released the pressure on his chest. Drool dripped from Jimmy's mouth. "He promised me a lot of money if I did it. He said I'd be rich, all I had to do was get here and kill as many as I could." His voice was hoarse from pain.

Fury leapt in Quinn's chest. "Money to kill your own kind, Jimmy? That doesn't say much about you as a man, does it? Who was this mysterious man who promised you money?"

Jimmy's eyes were panicked. "He'll kill me. He's a merciless little git. I can't tell you."

He screamed as Quinn pressed his hand against his chest once again. Quinn's eyes were merciless themselves. "If you don't tell me, Jimmy, you'll die anyway. You may at least try your luck with me."

Jimmy was sobbing now, his face slack with pain. Drool ran down his chin onto Quinn's hand below.

Quinn was disgusted at having the man's fluids all over him. He was also losing patience. With a quick twist of his hand on Jimmy's chest, he intensified the energy burn and the man screamed loudly, a horrible sound that reverberated through the room.

"Last chance, Jimmy," Quinn snarled. "I have better things to do. Who is this man who promised you money?"

Jimmy tried to speak. "Not man. Boy." His voice wheezed in agony.

Quinn was so taken aback by these words he lifted his hand off the man's chest, wondering if he'd heard correctly. "A boy? What do you mean, a boy?"

"He was a lad, about fifteen years old. He gave me a vial of that stuff, told me to put it on my dagger and make sure I got it on the skin. He said it would make them weak and then I could stab them through the heart. He said to make sure I got the heart or slit the throat."

Jimmy was crying now, tears falling down his cheeks, snot running out of his nose and dribbling into his mouth.

"Where did you meet this boy?" Quinn's blood chilled.

"Clapham Common. At the fair. He was there with his friend. A little tosser called Kyle, about fifteen years old, dirty brown hair."

"What's this boy's name? The one who gave you the vial?"

Jimmy shook his head as he blubbered. "I don't know. I only heard him call the other boy Kyle. I never got *his* name. I swear. That's the truth, I swear."

Quinn nodded. He sensed the man told the truth. He leaned in, close to Jimmy and whispered in his ear. "You don't deserve your Withinner, Jimmy. He needs to move on to someone more worthy. You won't need him where you're going."

Quinn stepped back and with a ferocious snarl, his hand connected with Jimmy's chest. The man's eyes widened and the energy surge Quinn had sent his way stopped his heart. Quinn watched the man's face slacken and his head dropped onto his chest. Jimmy was dead, the smell of ozone in the room overpowering. As Quinn watched, the Withinner slowly formed beside Jimmy's body. He was a short, blond man, who looked at Quinn with pain and grief etched on his face.

"I understand you had to do what you did," The Withinner said quietly. "He sinned against his own kind and he paid the price. Jimmy was weak. I'm sorry I couldn't stop him. I tried."

Quinn nodded. "I'm sure you did. I'm sorry it ended this way. Go in peace, my friend."

He watched the Withinner slowly fade from sight. Quinn was drained. The power he'd needed to conduct his interrogation and finally put Jimmy out of his misery had been intense.

Taliesin's approval at his decision to kill the man echoed inside and he sighed heavily. Yet another death on his conscience. But he wasn't prepared to let Jimmy get away with what he'd done. At least it had been swift for him at the end.

Quinn sensed someone behind him and turned to see Magnus. He motioned to the body. "Get rid of him for me, I got what I needed. We have a lot to do to clean up his mess, not least of which is finding this person who hired him. I'll get started on that when I get home. I have a starting point and a name. That should help me."

Magnus nodded. "I'll do that, Mr. Quinn. Can I get you anything, Sir? A whisky perhaps? You look a little pale."

Quinn regarded the man fondly. "No thanks, I want to see how the wounded are doing and have a word with Percy. Then I'll get home."

He patted the man on his back as he left, a back like a steel container. He saw Percy outside. "I have a couple of leads from Jimmy Christie. I'll follow them up personally. How are the people who were hurt?"

Percy nodded. "They're all fine. The bodies have been taken to the Lodge. They'll be buried in due course with the usual ceremony. I'll make sure you know when that is. I know you'll want to be there." He looked at Quinn, a frown on his face. "You killed Jimmy then."

It wasn't a question, simply a statement of fact.

Quinn nodded. "I needed to make an example and Jimmy was it. We've had four deaths in one day. I need to warn whoever's planning all this mayhem we're not going to take it gently." His face was grim. "And I still want that information on the cadmium. How's that going?"

"I've got someone who'll come and see you when you're home. Her name is Mary Hawthorne. She'll find you. She says she might be able to help you."

"She's a witch?" Quinn watched him quizzically.

Percy nodded. "Yes. A very good one, from all accounts. She's young too. Powerful alchemy skills, one of the best. Perhaps she can help us with this cadmium problem."

Quinn nodded. "Thanks, I'm going to get home now. Keep in touch, will you? Let me know if you hear anything about anything." He turned and strode off to the edge of the dome. He stood, looking back at the activity and sighed. Time to summon the Withinner. He hoped this time he wouldn't have as much trouble revoking him when he got home. Taliesin's urge to meet Cade was starting to get a little obsessive and if he was honest with himself, Quinn was a little worried that one day he might not be able to stop him.

Chapter 12

Cade sat in the lounge on the boat, perusing the last version of his latest dissertation. His envisaged trip to Gwynedd had been postponed due to a funding problem. Once this latest paper was out of the way, Cade would have at least six months before having to do anything else. Hopefully he could concentrate on teaching and lectures, something he was looking forward to. The change in schedule would also give him more time to be with Quinn, who looked as if he needed someone at the moment. His latest admission as to who he was had certainly thrown Cade. Quinn was turning out to be a very complex character and Cade wondered what the hell he'd gotten himself into.

Cade heard someone on the deck and stood up, smiling. He'd been expecting Quinn and he wasn't prepared for a tall, dark and brooding stranger wrapped in a cloak, carrying a large wooden staff. The man's hair fell in thick swaths around his swarthy face. He stood in the doorway and regarded him with a wicked glint in his dark eyes and a very cocksure smile on his face.

"Cade." His voice was deep, with a slight accent. "It's very nice to meet you at last. Quinn has done the devil of a job keeping you from me. I can see why. You are quite comely."

The dark stranger moved forward and desire coursed through Cade's body. He hardened instantly and had to reach out a hand to steady himself from suddenly trembling legs. At hearing more words, Cade thought the man's accent was Welsh.

The dark man bowed down and chuckled wickedly. "Let me introduce myself. I am Taliesin."

Cade swallowed. Overwhelming desire surged through him, heating his skin and causing it to prickle and tingle like a million miniature laser beams were invading his body.

Taliesin extended his hand. Cade took it hypnotically. Taliesin held it, his thumb slowly circling his palm. Extreme heat flooded Cade's being and he gasped, his extremities growing hotter and getting too large for his trousers.

The other man laughed. "Quinn was certainly right in keeping you for himself. The urges are very strong between us." He licked his lips as he watched Cade's face, studying his mouth with an intensity that made him weak.

"Taliesin. Where's Quinn?" Cade managed to whisper finally, his mouth dry, his groin so hot he thought he might combust.

Taliesin smiled. "He's trying very hard not to burst a blood vessel at the moment. As is Draigh." Cade wondered faintly who Draigh was. "I probably don't have long and there'll be the devil to pay when Quinn does make it back." He chuckled again. "But I had to see what awaits me. I think it will be worth the wait."

Taliesin's face twisted in pain and he grimaced. "Quinn is very upset," he said softly. "He's had a very rough night, so I suppose I should go. He deserves some peace. But first I think I need to claim a little prize for my willingness to disobey him. I may at least have something to remember of my own instead of experiencing it all second hand."

He pulled Cade close to him and took his mouth in a kiss that felt like it sucked the very life out of him. Taliesin's warm tongue entwined with his as he devoured his mouth. The dark man's hands gripped his arse, pulling him against his groin and Cade gasped at the hardened feel of the man.

Christ, he was built like a fucking bull! How the hell could he refuse such a gift?

Because Cade had no doubts that he'd allow this man to do anything he wanted to him.

Coherent thought faded from his brain as he moaned and pressed himself against the magnetism of the man holding him in a tight grip. Cade's own cock wanted to explode. He thought he heard the pop as his inner flesh fought free of the skin that encased it and wondered vaguely why it didn't hurt more.

Cade groaned loudly as he came in his pants, the warmth of his ejaculate flooding his groin like heated treacle.

Taliesin's eyes were dark and smouldering as he released Cade with a smirk. Cade closed his eyes, feeling faint at the incredible sensations still surging through his body. This was even more intense that what he'd experienced with Quinn the first time they'd made love. Cade tried hard to quell the emotions inside that Taliesin's kiss had wrought, a sense of guilt flooding his body at his still-clammy semen coating his groin. Despite his orgasm, his body still burnt with lust. All he wanted to do was drag this man close to him and let him pound away at his arse until he was torn in two—

"Cade? Cade, it's Quinn. Can you hear me?"

Cade heard the familiar voice as strong hands landed on his shoulder. He opened his eyes to see Quinn. His lover looked drawn and pale, his eyes bloodshot, like a man who'd gone to hell and back.

"Cade, you need to sit down." Quinn's firm voice cut through the haze in Cade's mind. Legs shaking, Cade allowed himself to be taken to the couch and sat down. Quinn sat next to him, running anxious fingers through his hair.

"I'm sorry that happened. Taliesin had no fucking right to do that to you. He knew just how it would affect you, the bastard." His voice was fierce, his eyes burning with golden fire.

Cade's face suffused with guilty colour and he closed his eyes in shame. "Christ, Quinn, I'm so sorry. I don't know what the hell happened. I couldn't control myself. He made me come in my pants, Quinn." His heart was squeezed tight in his chest as he wondered whether this whole thing constituted betrayal in Quinn's eyes and whether he would lose him. That made him feel worse and he started inhaling deeply, trying to catch a breath.

Quinn pulled him close, rubbing his back, his strong hands running down Cade's spine in soothing gestures. "Relax and breathe, Cade. Just think of somewhere still and quiet, a happy place, and take deep breaths. The urges will lessen, I promise. Breathe, honey."

Finally Cade was able to breathe properly as he stared at Quinn from haunted eyes. His nose wrinkled in distaste.

I need to change out of this soiled clothing. Hell, I can smell my own damn come.

"I'm glad you're back," he whispered shakily. "I'm so sorry, Quinn."

Quinn shook his head, his face tired. "I'd have been back sooner if it wasn't for Taliesin. That Withinner is getting ideas above his station. I'll have to deal with him later." Quinn's voice was harsh. "I know what he did."

Cade looked at him guiltily. "I'm sorry, it was overwhelming, the feeling. I couldn't help myself."

Quinn shook his head tiredly. "You wouldn't have been able to help yourself. The raw attraction between you two would have been even greater than what we had. You'd stand no chance if Taliesin wanted to make you his. It's why I haven't shown him to you before. I don't want to share you."

Quinn sounded vulnerable and Cade's heart melted at the thought that this Warlock king of his wanted Cade all to himself. He leaned in and kissed him fiercely, taking his mouth, all the pent-up desire he still had left over from the Withinner's touch igniting his blood and making him want Quinn even more. Quinn groaned and pulled Cade closer.

"I'm just glad you're home safe," Cade whispered. "I was worried about you. But right now I want to take a damn shower and get this spunk off me. I haven't come in my damn pants since I was a kid. Then you can tell me all about it after we make love. I really need to feel you right now."

"Is it me you want, Cade, or him?" Quinn pulled back and regarded Cade's face.

Cade flushed slightly, not sure himself. Seeing his expression, Quinn's face darkened. "I've had a tough day. I need to get home, take a shower and get to bed. I've got a lot to do tonight. I think it might be best if I left now and called you tomorrow. We can talk then." He turned to leave.

Cade pulled him back. "Wait. Please don't go."

Quinn regarded him thoughtfully. "Cade, no good can come of me staying tonight. It's really best if I leave now." He kissed the top of Cade's head swiftly and disappeared.

Cade watched him go with a sense of loss. He wanted to call out to Quinn that he was the one Cade loved, the one he wanted. But Quinn was gone too quickly and finally he closed the door and went to the bathroom alone to clean off the evidence of his betrayal.

Chapter 13

Quinn reached home tired, de-motivated and disheartened. He'd endured the pain of four Warlocks' deaths, travelled hundreds of miles to interrogate and kill a man, fought against his own Withinner and now he didn't even know whether Cade wanted him or his alter ego.

As he walked into the cold and dark entrance of his home, a sense of despondency shrouded him like never before. He knew he was tired and emotional, so he made allowances for himself. Quinn sighed as he poured himself a whisky and drank it down in one gulp, feeling better as he went upstairs to his bedroom to shower.

His bedroom was a long, wide room that spanned the length of his home. He'd installed huge floor-to-ceiling windows that looked out across the heath. His bed was a king-size four-poster that took up the centre of the room and was decked out in varying shades of grey and aubergine. In the corner there was a sitting area and a large plasma TV facing the bed.

In their two months together, Cade had never been in this house, let alone his bedroom. Quinn knew himself to be at risk in this house as most other Warlocks knew where he lived. He didn't want Cade exposed to the danger despite all the magyckal protection he had surrounding it. He'd tried hard to keep Jomo away for the same reason but the Kenyan was less easy to convince. Eventually he'd given into Jomo's constant badgering to have a home office at Quinn's house on the grounds of being frugal and saving money on big city rents.

Quinn undressed, dropping his clothes on the floor, and padded naked to the walk-in wet room in the corner of his bedroom. He turned on the water and stepped inside, enjoying the feel of the hot water on his skin, washing away the rigours of the day. He sensed the presence behind him and spun around, an incantation already forming on his lips to protect himself. A dark-haired man stood there, an astral figure, and hands reached out to him in entreaty. He closed his eyes, wishing him away but when he opened them, he was still there, arms still open in supplication, eyes watching him intently.

"Leave me alone, Adam," he muttered brokenly. "For God's sake, leave me the hell alone." His voice was despairing. He sank down in the wet room, his back against the wall, as he lifted his face to the water and let the rivulets roll down his cheeks like tears.

***

Andrew de Vere smiled in satisfaction as he stood on the deck of the yacht and looked out across the still waters of the Venetian San Marco Bay. The right side of his face stayed blank as usual, emotionless as there were slack muscles and deadened nerve endings. But the left side could faintly be seen to smile as he raised his brandy glass and toasted the night. It had been a long time coming but finally he felt he was in a position to begin his long claw back up the ladder into the position of power and respect that he expected as his right.

"Soon, Grand Master," he promised. "Soon you and I will meet again face to face and this time there *will* be only one of us left alive. Your time is coming, Fairmont. You have my word on that."

He turned as a young blonde woman in her early twenties came onto the deck, wearing nothing but a silky red teddy, her feet bare, her beautiful body doing justice to the flimsy garment she wore. He beckoned her over.

"Sophie, my love. Take a look out there—what do you see?" he gestured expansively with his brandy goblet across the bay.

Sophie Mercurio looked at him affectionately. "The world, Andrew. Yours for the taking, I imagine." She removed the brandy glass from his hand and set it on a small table then drew him closer, her hands stroking the damaged side of his face.

He watched her intently. "You believe that?"

She smiled slightly. "My love, you can do anything you put your mind to. You should be dead but you're still here. And you're stronger than ever before."

Her hands continued down and ran over his the broad, tight muscles of his chest, skimming up his powerful arms and neck, back up to his half-handsome face.

He reached out and pulled her to him roughly as he kissed her and slid his hands beneath the teddy, caressing her backside.

"I have a debt that is owed, one I've waited a long time to get payment for. And make no mistake, this time Quinn Fairmont is going to be paying the price for what he did to me and to Adam."

Sophie's face darkened at the sound of the man's name.

Andrew smiled cruelly. "I intend making Fairmont truly suffer this time. I'm going to take away everyone he holds dear, make him watch their suffering and then do to him what he did to me. Only this time he won't come back from it like I did."

He lifted Sophie against him, his arousal pressing against her stomach at the thought of what he was going to do to Quinn Fairmont. He drew back from her, pulling her roughly into the cabin, his hands already ripping at her lingerie as he pushed her back onto the long couch.

"Are you ready?" he whispered. "You know I can be very creative when I'm in one of my moods. I expect you to satisfy me accordingly."

He watched in pleasure as her pupils dilated and her lips parted as she readied herself for his onslaught.

***

Cade awoke late the next morning and for the first time since he'd started at the Institute, he called in and took a few personal days without arranging it beforehand. Professor Tickler-Brown was taken aback but understanding. Cade found himself an hour later standing on Quinn's doorstep, ringing an ornate bell, waiting for someone to answer.

Cade had seen Quinn's house from the street but up close it was even more awe inspiring and grand. Quinn had always been reluctant to bring him here, saying he'd be safer away from the house. He'd never quite been able to convince him that he didn't care about being safe but arguing with Quinn was like trying to convince a bull with a red flag in front of its face to stop charging.

He recognised Quinn's figure through the frosted glass of the door. Quinn opened it and Cade gasped at the sight of his pale face and haunted eyes. He didn't even allow Quinn the time to ask him what he was doing there when Cade reached forward and kissed him fiercely, hugging him so tightly they could both barely breathe.

"Quinn, don't ever leave me like that again," he muttered fiercely. "I had a crap night, I could hardly sleep and all I could think about was you. I know it's only been seven weeks, Quinn, but you'd better start getting used to having me around all the time."

Quinn buried his face in Cade's neck. "You're crazy, Cade. But I do want you around." He smiled as he hugged Cade back just as fiercely. "This day has just got infinitely better."

"Are we in a better mood now instead of being the partner from Hades?" Jomo's amused tones echoed down the hallway as he regarded the pair from the top of the staircase.

Quinn chuckled and turned to him, waving a hand in his direction. "Cade, I'd like you to meet Jomo Onyango, my business partner and, most of the time, my friend."

Cade looked up at the most debonair man that he'd ever seen descend the stairs. Immediately he was reminded of the model and actor Idris Elba. The man was tall, dark, and very handsome. Jomo, with an easy wide smile, came over to him, his hand held out. Cade shook it firmly.

"Cade, I am so glad to finally meet you face to face. I have heard every story imaginable about you from Quinn here who does not stop talking about you."

"Jomo, shut up," said Quinn uncomfortably. "Cade, take everything he says with a pinch of salt. The man's an inordinate embellisher of every story known to man."

Jomo winked at Cade. "He has been like the proverbial bear with a sore head today. I am so glad you came by to make his mood better."

Cade chuckled softly. "He does have his moods. But I'm glad I can make him feel better." He caressed Quinn's cheek, feeling the bristle of his beard beneath his fingers. "He's had a bit of a rough time lately." He looked around Quinn's home in wonder. "This is an amazing house, Quinn. Care to show me around? I'd love to see the bedroom. From what I can see, I need to spend more time in this place. It's pretty awesome." Cade grinned and took Quinn's hand.

"You're very nosy. And I happen to be working at the moment so the bedroom needs to be off limits or God knows what will happen."

Jomo waved a hand. "Don't mind me. I have no objections to the two of you making sweet passionate love if it makes Quinn stop being so grumpy. In fact, I'd insist on it."

Quinn grinned, his face more relaxed now. He squeezed Cade's hand and led him on a guided tour. He was obviously very proud of his home. It was a huge two-storey detached house, set back from the street and surrounded by trees, giving it an air of privacy he probably needed for his position. The house was contemporary and unique like the man himself. Jomo had tactfully disappeared as Quinn pulled Cade upstairs to the second floor.

"The library and my book collection are in the basement. I'll take you down there one day when we have some more time. The office is on the left-hand side of the wing through the double doors which Jomo has so kindly closed with him on the other side," he gestured toward the area. "And then this is my own private space. Cade, meet my bedroom."

Quinn grinned wickedly as he pulled Cade inside and closed the door behind him.

"I missed you," Quinn murmured as his hands slid under Cade's polo shirt and touched skin. Cade took a breath at the warmth of those hands on his body then slid out of their grasp, reaching down to unzip Quinn's trousers to drag them down his legs. His silk boxers followed and Cade licked his lips at the sight of Quinn's erection, swollen purple and strong and proud against his stomach. Quinn stood there, one eyebrow cocked in sardonic amusement as Cade's hands reached out to deftly unbutton his shirt, pushing it off his shoulders, his hands caressing Quinn's chest, tracing the hairline on his stomach down to his groin.

"Didn't I mention I was working today? Some of us have a living to make," Quinn murmured slyly.

Cade flapped a hand in disinterest. "Pfff. My needs take preference. And I am oh-so fucking needy…"

He pulled the now-naked Quinn impatiently over to the four-poster, his eyes widening at the ornate bed. "Now this is what I'd call a bed," he murmured as he pushed his lover down onto the bed. He gently flicked the tip of Quinn's cock and grinned when his lover's back arched at the sensation.

"My turn now," Cade whispered. He stood by the bed, watching Quinn's greedy eyes follow his every move as he undressed, slowly, teasingly, making sure every movement counted. He took his time pulling his shirt over his head, flexing his stomach and arms as he did so, seeing Quinn's tongue lick his lips and desire grow hot like flames in his tawny eyes. Cade tossed his shirt into the corner of the room, and then unzipped his jeans, making sure the zipper rasped slowly as he pulled it down. Cade was not wearing underwear and the look on Quinn's face as his eyes widened in appreciation made him hotter than hell.

He let his jeans fall to the floor and palmed his cock lazily, sliding his thumb over his tip, flinching at the sensation it caused. He smiled at the greedy look in Quinn's eyes.

"Is this what you wanted, Quinn?" he whispered as he crawled wantonly onto the bed on his knees. This man brought out his inner slut. "Me, bare skin and a needy cock and arse?"

Quinn growled loudly and reached out strong arms to pull Cade on top of him. His mouth covered Cade's as tongues duelled for supremacy. Cade licked his bottom lip, tugging it with his teeth then thrusting his tongue back into Quinn's mouth. For a while there was no sound in the room but the echo of their deep breaths, their murmurs of pleasure and small sighs. Cade moaned as Quinn's hand slid down the silk of his cock and he stroked him roughly, thrusting his tongue in Cade's ear as he did so, teasing the tip of him with his thumb until Cade gasped like a fish out of water. Quinn's teeth nipped at his piercing and pulled it none too gently, causing Cade to hiss in pain.

"Remember you are mine, not his," Quinn growled in his ear as his hands got stronger and Cade thought his dick might fall off with the force at which Quinn was jacking him off. He tried to nod and agree but he was so fraught with feeling in his groin that the gesture probably resembled more of a nodding dog on a car dashboard. His strangled "I'm yours" came out in barely discernible words as his climax built.

Quinn's hands were slick with Cade's essences and his hands on Cade's cock as his fingers stroked and pulled were instruments of pure torture. Cade's body tautened as he came with a groan, his body tossing against Quinn's sweaty skin, his hands clutching at Quinn's back, nails leaving scarlet welts on his shoulders. He'd been meaning to cut them as they were getting long but Cade felt a perverse pleasure that he could at least cause some injury to Quinn when he was in this mood. Thick spurts of creamy come jettisoned forth onto Quinn's hands, belly and chest and Cade collapsed on top of Quinn with a muffled moan and a feeling that the skin had been torn off his dick.

When Cade was finally still, Quinn motioned for him to lie on his stomach. Most of the time they made love face to face, as Cade liked being able to kiss Quinn, see his face scrunch up in concentration as he came, but today was obviously not going to be one of those times.

As Cade got on his elbows and knees, offering his arse to Quinn, he knew he was in for a rough ride. Quinn was in dominant and "I'm going to totally fuck you" mode. To his credit, it was a persona of Quinn's that Cade could really get used to.

What he wasn't prepared for was the lavish attention Quinn paid to his backside as his mouth sought that most intimate part of Cade and did its best to drive him totally crazy. Quinn's tongue lapped a long, hot lick up his crease, over his hole and then nipped his arse cheek—Christ, the man had actually fucking bit his arse—

before returning his attention to that very needy entrance between Cade's cheeks and mining him like a gold digger with a mission to find the deepest nugget of gold he could. Cade shuddered at the sensations of being probed with something that felt like a hot, wet, tentacle and whimpered as Quinn continued his assault down his tender passage.

"Fuck, Quinn, I'm going to come again," Cade managed to gasp in disbelief, hearing a satisfied chuckle behind him. Cade's cock had grown to alarming proportions again. He turned his head to see what was happening and Quinn grinned at him. Cade nearly came from that alone, the sultriness in his man's eyes turning his bones to jelly.

"Feel free to come as many time as you like, " Quinn returned to his feast and Cade closed his eyes as he laid his face into the bed sheets to try and hold back the noises he wanted to make. They weren't very manly, more like squeals a newborn pup would make trying to find his mother's teat. Cade was of two minds whether to be glad or sad when the rimming stopped and felt the heated tip of Quinn's cockhead as he pressed it against Cade's entrance.

"I'm thinking that was enough foreplay," Quinn murmured wickedly. "Now it's my turn." With one smooth slick move he pushed into Cade, who gritted his teeth and pressed his face deeper into the bed. If he was the Dartford Tunnel, Quinn was the damn three-storey semi truck bearing down on him, impossibly filling him and leaving no room for anything else.

Quinn groaned. "God, I love being inside you. You're my solace, do you know that? You're where I go in my head when I need to forget everything."

"I'm glad," Cade whispered. "I like being your distraction." His orgasm built as Quinn thrust in and out of him, and the constant pounding of his prostrate made his mouth dry and his brain swim. Cade cried out as he orgasmed for a second time, spewing thick ropes of come onto the bed underneath him. Quinn gripped his hips tightly as he shouted out loud, his roar of triumph echoing in the room as he came. Quinn's body finally stopped shaking and he lay across Cade's back, still inside him. Cade closed his eyes, feeling drowsy from the aftermath of two earth-moving climaxes. Quinn finally rolled off and lay beside him. There was a comfortable silence for a while as Cade traced the outline of Quinn's jaw. This was one of his favourite times—post-sex conversation. Other men fell asleep. Cade talked. He knew Quinn had long resigned himself to the fact that they wouldn't just fall asleep in other's arms, as appeared to be Quinn's preference.

"I hope Jomo isn't too traumatised by the noise we made," Cade murmured. "We were a bit loud."

Quinn laughed softly. "He's probably jealous as hell that he isn't getting any right now."

Cade ran his fingertips down the scar on Quinn's stomach. "I didn't have a chance to ask you how you were the other night when you got back from your trip. Did everything go okay?"

"I managed to find out a little about the person who caused all the deaths," Quinn said quietly. "I have some following up to do. Time is short and I don't want any more deaths on my conscience."

Cade frowned. "It wasn't your fault; you can't feel guilty. What happened to the Warlock who killed the others?"

Quinn was silent. "He died," he said shortly. "But he managed to tell me a few things before he did."

"Was he injured in the fight then and he died from his injuries?" Cade asked curiously.

Quinn sighed heavily. "I won't lie to you. I have enough secrets already. He died from my questioning."

Cade sat up and stared at him in horror. "You tortured him? Is that what you mean?"

Quinn sat up, his back rigid against the headboard. "I needed to find answers. The man wouldn't have told me otherwise. Yes, I tortured him. Then when he'd given me what I wanted, I killed him." His voice was flat and he looked into Cade's eyes. "This is a war and I'm one of those people who believe the ends justify the means. If I can save a few good lives whilst sacrificing one miserable one, I'll do it."

Cade wasn't sure how he felt. Quinn's face looked as if he expected a bad reaction from him. "Will the information he gave you help find who orchestrated the killings and perhaps stop him doing it again?" Cade asked quietly.

Quinn nodded. "I have a few leads to follow up tomorrow. I'm hoping it might lead to the Witchfinder. It might be the detail we need to try and stop him. I need to protect my people." He smiled twistedly. "You know the Spiderman saying. 'With great power comes great responsibility.'"

Cade leaned over and kissed him. "I can't judge what you did when you have the fate of the whole Warlock nation on your shoulders. I can't even begin to grasp what you have to do to protect it. All I want is for you to be safe while you do it. I couldn't bear it if anything happened to you."

Quinn drew a sigh of relief, pulling Cade closer, stroking his back as he snuggled into him. "I'll try my best to keep safe, I promise."

"I have some of my own questions to ask if you agree," Cade murmured. He'd been itching to find out more his Water Sprite abilities and after sex always seemed like a good time. What with everything going on in Quinn's life in the past two months, Cade hadn't liked to ask him too many questions about his own origins and his internet research on Fey beings could only take him so far.

"What kind of questions?" Quinn looked a little wary and Cade wondered in exasperation why this man of his hated answering questions and talking about himself.

"I want to find out more about what a Sprite is, what we're supposed to do, where we come from. That sort of ask. Nothing personal about you," he said drily. "God forbid you tell me something about your past, your childhood or anything too personal. But be warned, those questions are coming."

Quinn leaned back, a little more comfortable now he knew they weren't talking about him. "I wondered when you'd get around to asking me about yourself," he said softly, caressing Cade's palm with his thumb. "To be honest, I'm surprised you lasted this long." He grinned.

Cade noticed he'd completely skirted over the comment about the personal questions coming his way. He shrugged. "You had other things to think about. But now I really want to know."

Quinn sat back as he made himself comfortable. "Water Sprites are elementals. Some can shape shift, others can fly but one thing they can mostly all do is breathe in water and air. There are both male and female sprites, known by different names across the world: the Nix in Germany, the Nack in Scandinavia. They use music as a lure to draw people to them. You must have heard of Lorelei—she was a Sprite, luring men to their death. Sprites were also known to be great dancers." He grinned. "I can attest to that. There's nothing sexier than you than when you're on dance floor swinging those damn hips of yours."

Cade chuckled as Quinn spoke, seeing his passion for his topic and his eyes sparkling as he told him about his origins. "Sprites need water, moisture, to survive. In the stories, if a Sprite's source of water dried up, he would die with it. They can control the water but in the same way, it controls them, gives them life."

Cade ran a finger down his jawline. "That's good to know. Must be why I love the water so much. Even as a kid I was always around it, any time I could be. Tell me more of the good stuff. Are Sprites good lovers? Because you know I pride myself on that sort of thing." He winked at his lover.

Quinn glanced at him lazily, a wide grin on his face. "I read somewhere that Sprites are the sex addicts of the Fey world. This explains a lot. But I'm not complaining, I assure you. They were also reputed to be fairly jealous, and didn't take rejection lightly. They certainly wouldn't bear being cheated on and there are many tales of vengeful Sprites blinding and drowning unfaithful lovers. So I have been forewarned, I promise."

"As they should be," Cade muttered, his words belying his fascination at Quinn's story. This was literally something out of fairy tale and he was having a really difficult time believing in it all, despite everything he'd seen in his time with Quinn.

"They were also very handsome, which is easy to believe as I have one sitting right in front of me." Cade smiled at the adoring expression on Quinn's face as he leaned forward.

Cade shook his head in disbelief. "How do you know all this stuff? Have you got an encyclopaedia in your head?"

Quinn laughed. "I have Taliesin and a huge book collection and I read. Plus my father passed on a lot of his knowledge to me, as did my mother."

Cade didn't miss the shadow on Quinn's face as he thought of his parents and Cade knew sooner or later he'd want to hear more about them. But that could wait.

"So that's as much I know now," Quinn murmured. "We need to figure out exactly what your background is as we go and that will take time." He shrugged apologetically. "I don't have much to go on from where you're concerned." He frowned. "You told me you had an old trunk filled with stuff left from your father and your guardian—Sally, was it?"

Cade nodded, his face darkening as Quinn spoke. When he'd first told Quinn the story, his lover had been horrified that Cade had to face the death of so many people close to him, especially Sally's death being so close to home. Cade had said jokingly that he seemed to be a definite bad luck charm for anyone who loved him, and Quinn had better watch out. Quinn had pulled him close and said that there was no way a man like him could be bad luck. Life sometimes wasn't fair and he'd certainly had his share of unfairness but now he was there and Quinn wasn't planning on going anywhere soon.

Now, in the present, Quinn clasped his hands tightly. "Have you ever looked inside it to see what your past was all about? Perhaps there's a clue in there as to who your mother was, what happened to her and where she came from."

His voice was gentle as he gazed at Cade who shook his head. "I have looked into it. There were some papers that I worked through. I even had a genealogist try and find out more about my background with what we had but they never seemed able to find anything that made sense." He shrugged. "So I stopped eventually. Everywhere we went seemed to hit a dead end." He shifted in bed. "I suppose we should get cleaned up. I bags the bathroom first." He scooped up his clothes and disappeared into the palatial en suite.

Quinn watched Cade thoughtfully, thinking back to his words. It was a typical practice for Feys to shield their papers against human intervention, to try and hide the secret of their magyck and heritage. He suspected that this was what had happened with Cade and his genealogist. Cade's powers were so hidden deep inside, even he wouldn't have been able to trace back his true history. But Quinn knew he would be able to. The question was, did he want to? The answer was a definite no. He wasn't ready to hand Cade over to his magyckal heritage yet.

And therein lies the issue I have with you, Quinn, his Withinner retorted tartly. *You hide too much from him in your fear you will lose him. You are a coward, my friend.*

Quinn ignored Taliesin's taunt, although his chest surged with anger at being called a coward.

Fuck off, you poxy poet, Quinn muttered. *I'm trying to protect him, can't you see that?*

Taliesin's disbelieving snort made Quinn wish he could reach inside himself and throttle his Withinner, slowly and with malice. He turned his attention to his boyfriend who had come back into the room zipping up his trousers and shrugging into his shirt. "Cade, on the whole background thing—perhaps you didn't know what you were looking for. Now you do. So whenever you're ready I'll open it with you. Just tell me when."

Cade nodded. "I promise. When I'm ready we'll do it together." Taliesin scoffed again and Quinn scowled fiercely.

Cade looked at him. "Is your Withinner giving you bad news?" he asked in amusement.

Quinn glanced at him. "Nothing that you need to worry about. Did you have any more questions for me?"

Cade hesitated. "I know I've asked you this before but with everything else going on, I don't think I ever got a proper answer. I wondered whether there was any way I could perhaps ask your Withinner some questions that I really want answers to. You know I'm doing another dissertation on old British cultures and he'd really be able to give me a unique insight into what I'm researching."

Quinn breathed a deep sigh and leaned back as Cade watched him intently. "I think we might be able to come to some sort of arrangement," Quinn drawled finally. "If you let me have your questions, I'll dig down deep, try and get answers for you and what I can't answer, I'll ask him. Fair enough?"

Cade nodded, and Quinn smiled at the excitement on his lover's face. Knowing that he now had access to an ancient source of information that no one else in the world would ever have, Quinn guessed that the anthropologist in Cade felt a sense of extreme gloating satisfaction. "Right, I think it's 'clean me up' time," he murmured as he clambered out of bed. He turned to look at Cade. "Then I might be able to get back to work and earn that honest day's wage."

Chapter 14

The next morning, Quinn walked the Clapham Common Fairground. He observed everyone around him, his nose sensitive to anything Fey. He'd left Cade still firmly ensconced in his bedroom reading the morning papers and looking as if he really belonged there. His boyfriend had been fairly vocal about wanting to spend more time with Quinn at his home and eventually he'd worn him down to such a degree that he'd agreed they'd make it a regular thing, prudence be damned.

As Quinn wandered through the fairground, he'd already picked up the scent of another Fey, a young child, and a Warlock who'd nodded at him in respect as he passed by. He'd even found a very rare Calipoxor, a being that was able to shape shift into an animal, but still no Witchfinder scent. His skin prickled as he sensed someone behind him, no one threatening but a witch all the same. He turned slowly to see a young woman regarding him thoughtfully. She was very petite, barely five feet tall, with long blonde hair down to her waist and a fine, delicate face. She was beautiful. They regarded each other warily.

"Mary Hawthorne, I presume?" Quinn stepped toward her.

She nodded, her eyes watchful. "Grand Master. Percy told me where to find you. I got here as soon as I could." Her tone was deferential. Even witches respected the power of the ultimate Warlock leader.

He smiled. "Forget the titles, Mary. My name is Quinn." He held out his hand to her and she shook it. Quinn felt the static that flew between them as he observed her keenly.

"Have you found anything yet?" the witch asked quietly.

Quinn sighed, shaking his head. "Nothing. It's as if he wasn't ever here. This young man knows how to cover his tracks." He scowled. "I can't believe I'm hunting a fifteen-year-old boy."

"It's very clever, actually." Mary looked at him with soft eyes. "No one would suspect a teenager, and when it comes to actually killing him, surely even you would baulk at the thought of killing just a boy. That hesitation might just give him the advantage he needs to turn the tables."

Quinn frowned fiercely. "This *boy* killed four of my people. I can assure you I'll have no compunction about putting him down if it comes to that." Quinn motioned Mary over to a small cafe set up in the fairgrounds and they sat down at a table. "Have you any news for me on the cadmium situation and how we can fight it?"

Mary nodded. "We were very lucky to find the cadmium traces in Ross and the men who were killed in Scotland. Normally we wouldn't even have known about it. But because it was Litha, the bodies were more energised and it retained more of the poison longer. One of the other Warlocks is an Alchemist and he could smell it in their blood when the bodies were finally brought to the Lodge. He did a few tests and found the cadmium in the bloodstream and in the entry wounds."

Quinn listened in fascination. "So this stuff has the ability to pierce any protective shield we put around ourselves and once it's in our bloodstream, it poisons us?"

Mary sighed. "That's about the gist of it. We have no idea why it affects Warlocks the way it does. Cadmium is toxic to humans too, if they're overexposed. Your metabolism is so strong that it speeds things up so it seems to amplify things. It won't actually kill you but it does affect you badly and causes breathing and other functional difficulties. Then it weakens you enough for someone to place the final blow."

"How do we fight against it if it can get through our shields?" Quinn's voice was grim as he thought about the impact it could have.

Mary looked thoughtful. "There has been some research done about the properties of selenium to counteract cadmium damage. Your protection shields are composed of both organic and mineral elements, aren't they? I'd suggest you tell everyone to re-design their shields." The witch stopped and looked at Quinn doubtfully. "You can do that, right? Change the composition of the shields?"

When Quinn nodded, she continued. "Tell them to put increased dosages of selenium into their shield. Perhaps if you did some experiments, you might find the right level that you need to stop the weapons piercing the shields." Mary shrugged. "It's worth a shot."

Quinn nodded. "I agree. I'll get someone on it, thanks. Next question. What do we do if we get it in our bloodstream? Is there an antidote?"

Mary's face clouded. "There isn't one. Especially in this concentration. The best you can hope for is to strengthen your shields. I *can* put something together, a capsule perhaps that may slow the effects down—selenium, Vitamin D and other minerals that you can ingest. It may slow it down but I don't think it will stop it. It could help until we can figure out the right magyck to fight it properly. I'm working on it. If it's out there, I'll find it." The witch sounded confident.

"Then that will have to do. Thank you, you've been a real help. At least we know what we're fighting."

He reached out and touched her hand again, feeling the same tug in his loins he'd felt before. Mary must have noticed it too. She withdrew her hand quickly.

"Perhaps we should keep looking for the Witchfinder. I can sense him too. Between the two of us we might be able to canvass the area a little quicker."

Quinn looked grateful. "I'd appreciate the help. Keep your eye out for a teenager called Kyle, probably about fifteen years old with dirty brown hair. That's all I know. He's apparently a friend of this Witchfinder and we may be able to trace him back through him."

He stood up. "Let's meet back here in an hour with our updates."

The two parted company and Quinn continued his search. He was glad he had Mary on his side. She seemed very capable. He was intrigued by the spark between them though, and a little surprised at the slight sexual pull he'd felt. Witches and Warlocks may be part of the Fey family, but they didn't share the same Fey blood attraction between them. It was something he'd never pondered enough on to explain, accepting it as the natural order of things.

Quinn's father has been a Warlock but his mother had been a witch. His father had once laughingly told him that if they did share the attraction, there would be far more versions of Quinn running around. Quinn had never felt comfortable with his own dad sharing that rather intimate thought.

Quinn had been walking for about twenty minutes when he heard a loud shout. He turned to see a young boy weaving his way through the crowd at breakneck speed, a large, florid-faced man hot on his heels. Quinn watched in amusement as the man huffed and puffed behind the youngster. When the young boy was nearer to him, Quinn thrust out a leg lazily. The youngster tripped over it and went sprawling. The red-faced man was on him like a shot.

"You thieving little bastard! I'll teach you to take my wallet." His fist connected with the boy's chin, causing him to yowl in pain.

Quinn stepped forward, deftly taking the wallet from the boy's outstretched hand and giving it back to the man. "This belongs to you, I imagine."

The man nodded, as he pulled the youngster to his feet by the scruff of his shirt. "Thanks for the help. I'll get this little tosser over to the security office. They can call the police."

The boy looked sullen. "I found the wallet lying on the ground. I didn't fucking steal it, you wanker."

The man's face grew even redder at the boy's comments and Quinn grinned at the sight. He was finding this whole thing quite entertaining.

"What's your name, you little bastard?" Red Face snarled.

The boy gazed at him blankly. "I'm not telling you my name, you dimwit. If I don't tell you my name, you can't tell the Old Bill who I am and they can't do anything about it."

Quinn smiled at his naivety. "I think you'll find they'll get your name out of you one way or another," he drawled. "They may have to use the truncheons and a little bit of brute force, but I think you'll find giving us your name may be the path of least resistance."

The boy looked at him in confusion. "What? What the hell are you talking about? The police can't touch me. I'll sue them."

"I think you'll find fairground rules are a little different to the normal ones." Quinn was making it up as he went along. This boy didn't seem particularly intelligent. "I remember reading somewhere that in these grounds, at funfair time, the usual rules don't apply and the police have a certain carte blanche to question suspects."

The boy peered at him suspiciously. "I didn't steal no cart. I just took the wallet." He stopped as he realised what he'd just said.

Quinn smiled innocently. "Admission of guilt, heard by both of us."

He gestured to himself and Red Face who was looking a little puzzled himself at the drivel Quinn was telling the boy. "I think that makes things worse. You'd be better off giving this man your name. It'll go easier for you."

The boy looked at Quinn sulkily. He decided to concede. "Kyle Bannister. And you can't touch me anyway. I'm only fifteen."

Quinn's blood raced at the name and he regarded the boy intently. There was no such thing as coincidence in Quinn's book.

"Where's your friend, Kyle?" the Warlock asked quietly. "Don't you and he normally work together?"

Kyle flushed. "Jer isn't here. He had nothing to do with this. Leave him out of it."

"Jer?" Quinn questioned, his nostrils flaring and his hands clenching at his sides in anticipation. "What kind of a name is that?"

"It's short for Jeremy, you arsehole," the boy muttered. "And he'll make short work of the likes of you. He's a mean little bugger." His voice was proud.

Red-faced man took the boy by the collar again. "Right, Kyle," he spat. "Time to get you to the police."

Quinn reached out a hand and softly touched the man's shoulder. "You don't want to do that," he said softly. "I can take care of this. You have your wallet back. Best get back to the fun."

The enchantment in his hand passed into the man's shoulder and the man frowned, looking confused. "Right. I don't want to do that. I'll leave him to you, then." He turned and trundled off into the crowds.

Quinn breathed a sigh of relief as he turned back to Kyle who watched him warily. "Right, Kyle. It's just you and me now. I want to hear about Jeremy."

"I'm not telling you anything about Jeremy. He'll kill me if I say anything. Like I say, he's a mean little tosser." The boy was defiant but Quinn saw fear in his eyes at the thought of betraying his friend.

"You don't have a choice, I'm afraid, and I don't have time to argue." Quinn said softly. He laid his hand on the boy's shoulder and chanted a few words. The boy's eyes glazed over and Quinn led him unresistingly to a quiet corner of the fairground, behind one of the tents that dotted around the grounds. He needed to be careful not to be seen. He didn't want to be arrested as some sort of paedophile, trying to diddle a fifteen-year-old boy.

Kyle stood slack-jawed, his eyes blank as Quinn laid a hand on the top of his greasy hair. The energy journeyed downward as Quinn tried to draw the information he needed out of the boy's mind. It was a delicate enchantment, one that could cause damage to the subject if not done properly. Quinn was a master at it though, and he closed his eyes as he searched the boy's brain for the elusive Jeremy. He drew deep breaths at what he found in there, an unsavoury and tragic ream of memories that made him feel disgust and sympathy for the boy at the same time. Finally he found what he was looking for. He now had a name and a picture of the youth in his head, together with some of the places the two boys had been. It wasn't much but then there wasn't much more than this that Kyle seemed to know about him. Jeremy obviously kept his life private.

"Jeremy Payton. Thank you, Kyle."

Quinn took his hand off the youth's head. Kyle stood there, a faint strand of dribble in the corner of his mouth. Quinn placed his hands on either side of the boy's head and murmured a few words.

The boy's eyes slowly grew more aware and when he saw Quinn, he scurried back.

"Leave me the fuck alone, you fag!" Kyle hissed as his eyes searched around for something to hit Quinn with. Taliesin chuckled and he grinned at his Withinner's amusement.

"I can assure you that fag or not, I wouldn't be doing anything with the likes of you. You're not my type and you smell too badly. Now you need to forget this little tête à tête with me. You can do that, can't you?"

The soft tones of his voice and his intent stare into the youth's eyes were hypnotic. The boy's eyes glazed over once again and he shook his head as if wanting to get rid of something inside. Quinn repeated the words and Kyle closed his eyes, standing there quietly, looking for all the world as if he were asleep on his feet.

Quinn moved away quickly. The boy would be fully awake in a few seconds and would remember nothing. He wanted no warning to the infamous "Jer" that he was coming and the simple memory-wipe spell had done the trick admirably. Both he and Taliesin were grimly satisfied that he'd managed to get some information on this youth. He felt it in his bones. This was the one who'd ordered the attack on the Festival and killed Ross. Now all that remained was to meet back with Mary and perhaps discuss the next strategy to try and get Jeremy Payton in his sights.

Chapter 15

Cade was just about to leave Quinn's house to make his way back to the houseboat when he saw him arrive with a woman. He peered out of the kitchen window, standing behind the blinds so Quinn didn't see her. The woman was stunningly beautiful. Cade felt a surge of jealousy at the ease and familiarity the two seemed to have.

What the hell is he doing with her? The way she's looking at him, she must know him very well.

Cade knew Quinn said he preferred men but this woman could tempt anyone into regressing to heterosexual sex.

Quinn let himself in the front door as he chatted to the woman. He stopped, smiling at Cade widely as he saw him. "I thought you'd have gone back home by now. I'm glad you're still here. I've someone I'd like you to meet." He waved a hand in the woman's direction.

"Mary Hawthorne, I'd like you to meet my boyfriend, Cade Mairston."

He came over and kissed Cade, who felt a little better at both Quinn's action and his introduction. He hated the word "partner." In his book, that applied to business relationships. Cade stepped forward and shook the woman's hand, feeling a slight tingle on his hand as he did so.

Mary smiled gently, her eyes regarding Cade warmly. "Quinn's told me a lot about you, Cade. I'm pleased to meet you."

Quinn shrugged off his jacket and smiled at them both. "Mary's the witch who's been helping me with the situation we had in Scotland. We were at the fairground looking for the Witchfinder. I think we've found out who he is." He grinned widely, obviously pleased with the progress.

"That's good news," Cade said quietly. "What are you going to do about him now then? I hope you're not going to try and find him on your own. Even with your magyck surely it will be too dangerous?"

Quinn shook his head. "I won't be doing it alone. We need everyone looking out for this boy. We know his name now, what he looks like and where he likes to hang out. It's more than we had before. We'll just have to keep our eyes open for him. This is someone we don't want to underestimate."

He looked at Mary. "Sorry, I'm being rude. Can I get you something to drink? Cade?" Both Cade and Mary shook their heads. Quinn disappeared to make himself coffee.

Mary looked at Cade curiously. "Quinn tells me you're a Water Sprite? I've never met one before."

Cade smiled ruefully. "Neither had I until I met Quinn. I might be Sprite deep down but I don't feel much different to the old plain Cade. I love the water and if I don't swim every day I get very ratty but other than that I can't really say I know what a Sprite does. Or looks like. I think I must be a bit of a throwback."

Mary chuckled. "I'm sure that once you spend more time with Quinn, you'll find the inner Sprite in you. I'm sure he can teach you a lot about yourself. He's an incredible man. I can't say I've ever met one with as much energy and power as him before. He's truly incredible."

Her admiring tone made Cade's eyes narrow.

His man walked back into the room, sipping his coffee. "The alert is out. Everyone has his details now so they can be prepared if they see or sense him. We just have to be patient and see what comes up. He's got strong magyck himself masking him. He won't be easy to find but Kyle may lead us to him. Magnus is watching him." He smiled in satisfaction.

Mary chuckled. "He's not exactly inconspicuous. Are you sure that's a good idea?"

Cade had no idea who Magnus was and he felt a little left out at seeing the obvious camaraderie between Quinn and the witch.

Quinn grinned at his lover's puzzled frown. "Magnus is a seven-foot Warlock with a really bad temper. He may not be able to duck behind trees easily, but despite his size, he's a master at surveillance. How he does it we don't know. He'll do all right."

Mary smiled back at him warmly.

Cade had to ask. "Have you two known each other long—you and Mary?"

Quinn looked at him and laughed. "No. Believe it or not today is the first time we've ever met. Mary tracked me down at the fairgrounds. She's hopefully helping me with my cadmium problem."

Cade was perplexed. "Your cadmium problem? What's that?" he asked worriedly. "Is it something I should know about?"

"It's not an STD, I promise." Quinn grinned wickedly as Cade's face flushed. Quinn explained the situation, obviously trying hard to keep his amusement under control.

Cade's face cleared. "Oh, I see."

Another thing I can't really relate to. I'm not sure I like this witch, with her long blonde hair, sexy little body and obvious witchy connection to my Warlock. Female or not, she feels like a threat. I have no idea why I feel this way.

Cade became aware that he was scowling fiercely.

Quinn was looking at him quizzically. "Do you want me to explain it again? You look a little confused."

Cade glared at him. "I'm not an idiot, I understood the first time."

Quinn appeared taken aback by his vehemence and Cade sighed, aware Mary had a slight smile on her face at his words.

Bitch.

"Sorry. I've only had one cup of coffee this morning and no swim yet so I'm a little short-tempered."

Quinn's eyebrows rose ever so slightly and he moved over to kiss Cade's cheek. "Then perhaps you should have another cup of coffee or take a swim. Mary and I have some work to do on finding Jeremy so I'm going to take her up to the office. Combine our powers, see what we can find. I'll see you later at your place then?"

Huh, that was a brush-off if ever I've heard one. I'll just go home then, shall I?

Quinn missed Cade's dagger glare at him as he was too busy turning and beckoning for Mary to follow him.

Humph. I'm sure she'd like that, combining her powers with yours. As long as it's just her powers and she doesn't fancy combining anything else.

Cade knew his inner bitch was coming out but he really didn't like this woman. She felt *wrong* somehow.

Mary smiled back at Cade as she followed Quinn up the stairs. "It was lovely meeting you, Cade. I'm sure I'll be seeing you soon."

Cade watched as her pert backside ascended the stairs. He knew he was being unreasonable but he was feeling left out and a little useless at not being able to help. He gathered up his jacket and let himself out of Quinn's house. He couldn't help a backward glance up at the study window as he walked toward the tube station.

***

It was around eight in the evening when Quinn finally got to the houseboat and saw Cade sitting outside on the deck, Marco Polo on his lap. The dim lights from the bridle path alongside the canal shone faintly. The cat lifted his head and purred as Quinn approached. He scratched its head fondly.

"Hello, Marco. Have you been keeping this man of mine company?" He leaned down and kissed Cade.

"You taste of whisky," Cade murmured softly, winding his arms around Quinn's neck and pulling him down for a deeper kiss.

Quinn laughed. "I had a quick drink with Mary before she left." He sat down and pulled a chair up beside Cade. He'd not missed the sudden stiffening of Cade's body and he sighed inwardly.

What had he done now? Would he ever understand this man?

"Where do witches go when they leave then?" Cade asked curiously as his hands stroked Quinn's arm idly.

Quinn was bemused at the question. "I imagine her place in Chelsea, that's where she lives. There isn't a magyckal departure lounge, Cade. She doesn't just go poof in a puff of smoke and disappear." He grinned. "You've been watching too much TV."

Cade stood, up, brushed the cat off his lap and stormed inside. Quinn gazed after him in exasperation, surprised at the violence of Cade's reaction to his words.

What the hell have I said now? Jesus, it's like being with a ticking time bomb.

He got to his feet and wandered inside, seeing Cade at the far window, gazing out into the dark water. "What the hell did I say? Why are you so angry with me?"

Cade turned and Quinn saw the look on his face, a look of vulnerability he'd wasn't used to seeing. He moved closer to his boyfriend, drawing him into his arms, feeling his resistance then his surrender as he folded into him like a softly spread bedsheet.

"Please tell me what's wrong," Quinn said gently.

Cade's voice was muffled when he replied. "I just feel so useless because I don't know how it all works. I know nothing about who I am and how I got that way. I don't know what I can do or what being a Sprite is all about. It's very confusing and I really don't know what to make it of it all. I don't want to ask you all my questions yet because you have enough on your mind but I have so many." He turned his head and gazed out over the water. "And here you are facing all these dangers and I can't do anything to help you. And then you have perky little Mary being privy to stuff I don't even know about. It just gets my goat, that's all."

Quinn smiled softly as he nuzzled Cade's coconut-fragranced hair. "I want to keep you out of danger, not put you in it. And I know you have a lot of questions and I'll answer what I can whenever you ask. And besides, you are helping me. You're my reason, the one I want to be with when it all gets too much and the ghosts from the past come calling." His face shadowed. "You don't know what it means to me to be able to do that. You're my soulmate, Cade." He kissed the top of Cade's head softly, holding him tighter.

Cade looked up at him, his eyes uncertain. "I am?"

Quinn nodded. "You are. And more. I knew it from the moment I met you in the woods." He kissed him ardently, feeling Cade's mouth give way beneath his, hearing his soft sigh of satisfaction as he kissed him back.

When finally he released him, Quinn murmured in Cade's ear. "Perky little Mary? Do I sense a tinge of jealousy there?" He enjoyed a great sense of satisfaction in being able to provoke such a reaction in this man, to know that he felt this strongly about him to be this way. "I told you: I'm not interested in women anymore. Especially now I have you."

"She's very perky, in many ways," was Cade's muttered response. "And very beautiful. And a witch to boot. That's a lot to compete with if you ever decided to bat for both teams again. And I don't trust her. I don't know why."

Quinn lifted his face to his fiercely. "There *is* no competition; you're the one I want. I could never feel this way about anyone else."

Cade lifted his head and Quinn saw his eyes studying his face with an intensity that made him shiver in pleasurable anticipation.

"Then I guess you'd better prove that to me, hadn't you?" Cade whispered as he pulled Quinn into the cabin. "And I can be a very hard person to convince, so you'll have your work cut out for you."

Quinn chuckled as Cade pulled his tee shirt over his head and began to unzip his trousers. "I'm sure I can manage that." He slid his hands inside Cade's shirt, touching warm skin and hearing him gasp. "And Mary's not the only thing that's perky tonight, I can promise you."

Chapter 16

Quinn walked into his darkened house around midnight, threw his keys down on the small side table on the entrance and breathed a sigh of relief at being home. It had been a long and exhausting day. He rubbed a hand over his tired eyes as he walked into the lounge and took a bottle of whisky out from the large seven-foot tall wooden display unit against the far wall. He opened the cap, pouring a large measure into a glass then walked over with it to the picture windows, staring out into the darkness beyond as he sipped his drink.

They'd been tracking the elusive Jeremy Payton for the last four weeks. Once Quinn had his scent, there was no losing it. The boy was a creature of habit and the places Quinn had seen in Kyle's head were places he apparently came to frequently.

Quinn had teams in several places watching for the boy, making contact with people Jeremy came into contact with and so far it had worked in their favour as they built up a trail of the Witchfinder's activities. Several times they'd come close to finding him but he always seemed to avoid them at the last minute. It was as if he knew they were coming. Percy had even gone so far as to voice his concern that they had a traitor in their midst. On two occasions Quinn had felt the boy, known he was near but then exasperatingly, he just disappeared.

Quinn didn't want to believe that in the band of people he'd chosen to call friends, one of them might be betraying him. But he'd acknowledged that it had to be investigated. Percy had taken it upon himself to personally do it and report back to Quinn if he found anything suspicious. Percy had insisted on Quinn performing a fairly painful and lengthy memory search on him personally to satisfy himself that Percy wasn't the traitor. Quinn had done it but with a heavy heart at causing his friend such distress.

At least there had been no further Warlock deaths. That in itself was a blessing. Quinn imagined Jeremy was lying low to make sure he didn't give the Warlock team any ammunition to find him. It was a small mercy. He reached inside his jeans pocket and took out the small capsule that Mary had given him. The witch had been working hard to try and find something that the Warlocks could take to lessen any effect the cadmium might have on them. She'd come up with this pill and told him she needed someone to test it on. He'd immediately offered himself despite her violent protestations.

"I'm not giving anything to one of my people I haven't tried for myself." Quinn had said quietly but firmly. "Meet me at my place when we finish and we can test it then."

He had told Percy about his intended actions tonight and while Percy hadn't been particularly pleased, he'd accepted Quinn's decision. If anything went wrong at least Percy would know what had happened. The two men had a sixth sense between them and if Percy sensed any real danger, he'd promised he'd summon Nicholas and be with Quinn in a heartbeat.

Now Quinn stood waiting for Mary to make an appearance. He hadn't long to wait. Within a few minutes of him being home, he was letting her in his front door.

"Quinn, I still don't like this," Mary said softly. "I don't think you should be the one to test this theory I have. That's all I have you know, a theory."

"And a degree in chemistry as well as being one of the brightest Alchemists in the Magyck Circle and recommended by people I trust." Quinn smiled at her, trying to put her at ease. "Look at this way. If it goes wrong, at least I have the best person available to fix it."

She smiled faintly at his praise of her abilities but she still looked ill at ease as she stood before him.

"You have the knife with the cadmium extract?" Quinn asked.

She nodded. "I have it."

He took a deep breath. "Right. So I take this little devil that you've concocted, wait a few minutes, then you cut me with the knife, sending the cadmium into my bloodstream and then we see what happens from there. The expectation is that my body fights the effects of the cadmium, lessening any adverse effects. Is that about right?"

His words might sound laissez-faire but he had to admit he was nervous. Mary nodded, her blue eyes wide. Quinn popped the capsule into his mouth and washed it down with whisky. Mary watched him carefully, watching him, he imagined, for any negative reactions. They stood by the window in silence for a few minutes.

Finally Quinn turned to Mary. "Will that do it?"

He saw her back away. "I really don't think this is wise. Perhaps—"

He reached out and grabbed her wrist tightly, causing her to stop talking and wince.

His voice was steely. "You need to do this. Don't get cold feet on me now that I'm psyched up for it. Cut me," he commanded.

He held out his arm and saw her mesmerised gaze at the tanned skin of his forearm. She took out what looked like a thick handkerchief and spread it on the floor. Slowly she took the small athame, her witch knife, from her jacket pocket and took out a vial of a blue liquid. She opened the vial and poured a few drops onto the tip of her athame.

"This not what an athame is usually used for and it's certainly not usually so sharp. But I didn't want to use just any knife."

She took a deep breath and cut into his forearm, a long, two-inch cut that bled freely. He hissed with the pain as the blood welled up and drops fell onto the covering Mary had lay down on the floor.

She moved back, observing him, her eyes strangely bright. "How do you feel?"

He heard her voice from far away, as his vision blurred and the cadmium rushed into his blood stream. A metallic taste flooded his mouth, making him gag, wanting to throw up. His chest closed and his breathing became laboured. He reached out a hand against the window to steady himself. Taliesin roared in pain inside as well, his Withinner loudly protesting this turn of events. The cussing was extreme to say the least. He vaguely heard Mary's soft voice.

"Can you hear me? Give it a while. It will only be this bad the first time you take it. After that it will stay in your bloodstream and hopefully be able to keep fighting the cadmium, a lot less violently that you feel now. It will get worse before it gets better. Stay strong."

A wave of darkness clouded his mind and he staggered slightly on his feet, and then fell to the floor, his chest heaving for breath. He dimly saw the figure of Mary before him, her sandal-clad feet in front of his face. An incredible pressure echoed in his ears, and he wanted to scream with pain but the dryness in his mouth had rendered him incapable of making a sound. Just as he thought he was going to pass out, his vision started clearing and his breathing got easier. Quinn gasped, sucking in air. He sat up, the pressure in his ears lessening and becoming more bearable. Mary stood before him with an anxious smile.

"You're all right. It was only a few seconds, actually, and the effects are passing. Just take a few deep breaths."

He did as he was told and finally his body returned to normal. He could speak now, the dryness having disappeared and the metallic tang in his mouth fading. Taliesin growled fiercely.

By the Gods, Quinn, that was really painful. Are you sure this witch knows what she's doing?

Mary reached out a hand to help him up and he took it as he got to his feet. His voice was husky with pain when he spoke. "Jesus! That was awful. We can't have everyone going through that. The shock might kill some of the younger ones."

Any longer and Percy would probably have appeared on his doorstep.

Mary nodded. "It was a little extreme. I'm sure I can find something that will make it more bearable, it might just need a little less hemlock. Sorry, but you did insist on being the guinea pig."

Quinn looked up at her quickly, hearing something in her voice he hadn't expected to hear—a gloating satisfaction. But when he looked at her face all he could see was concern.

"Are you ready for the second part of the test? I need to cut you again, make sure its effects are going to last. By my calculations, this one pill should last at least a few weeks."

He gritted his teeth. "Ready. Go for it."

She cut him swiftly again, in the same place, parallel to the first cut. The original cut was already beginning to heal, the wound knitting together. Again, Quinn grimaced in pain as he waited for the reaction to the cadmium to set in. There was a slight tingle in his bloodstream and the dreadful metallic taste came back but he didn't feel as badly he had last time.

Mary watched his face, studying him and he in turn watched her back.

A smile of triumph crossed her face. "It looks like it works. By now you'd be on the floor, struggling for breath. I think we've found an antidote to the cadmium."

He heaved a long breath and looked at his forearm. The first cut was half closed, and there was a red, livid scab, which he knew would disappear in time. The second cut was also pulling together. It wouldn't look very nice for the next couple of days and both would be tender but at least it had been worth it.

He smiled at Mary. "*You* did it, you mean, you little gem. God, this is wonderful. When you fine-tune the formula we can distribute the pills out to everyone and at least put a programme in place that will protect them. We already know your advice about the selenium in the shields worked, so this is another bit of good news. You're incredible."

She smiled, her face rosy with his words. She leaned forward impulsively and kissed his cheek. Quinn's cock stirred in his jeans. He stepped back. It could only be some sort of rogue Fey affect. He hadn't found a woman sexually attractive since his last abortive relationship. It made him wonder what the hell was happening to him.

He pulled away further and Mary coloured slightly at his reaction. "I'm glad it worked," she said softly. "I'll get to work getting an improved formula ready, hopefully making the first reaction less intense. Then we can make a plan to distribute them."

She turned and picked up her bag. "It was very brave of you to test the first one. I'm glad I was able to help."

She walked out of the lounge and a few seconds later Quinn heard the front door close. He watched the figure of Mary Hawthorne walk swiftly down the tree-lined road until she was out of sight. He went upstairs to his bathroom to brush his teeth and get ready for bed.

He didn't notice that the blood-soaked cloth onto which he'd bled was no longer there.

***

Cade dove into the depths of the water in the pool, and with his usual strong and limber movements, he began swimming the length of the Olympic-sized pool at the Waterside Complex near Golders Green. He normally managed close to thirty lengths when he swam and he basked in the knowledge that had he wanted to enter the Olympics, he'd probably have won hands down. The water relaxed him, let his mind free and he could think of no better way to spend the evening after a hard day's work.

He'd be stopping off at Quinn's on the way home. He hadn't seen him since Friday night and he was feeling the effects. The last four weeks, Quinn had been so busy trying to track down this Jeremy character they'd had to sneak in any time they could to be together.

Cade completed his gruelling swim schedule and got out of the pool, walking over to the lounger to pick up his towel. There was a strange sensation, as if someone was watching him. He turned around and looked across the pool area. Other than a few other straggling swimmers and a couple of teenage boys larking around in the pool, there was no one there that looked particularly suspicious. He towelled his hair dry and walked over to change rooms to get into dry clothes.

In the pool, Jeremy Payton saw the tall, muscular form of the man he'd been asked to watch disappear into the change room. When the Witchhunters Alliance had asked him to follow this man, he'd been told he was a key factor to finding a very powerful Warlock, and one that he could help dispose of later. But in the meantime the Alliance had been very clear: he was to keep a low profile, stay away from any witches and Warlocks and no more killings for the short term, stirring up undue attention.

As the Witchfinder General, Jeremy worked alone and wasn't used to obeying the instructions of a secret band of witchhunters who seemed hell bent on destroying witches and Warlocks, but when they'd approached him with the promise of a lot of future activity, together with the lure of a lot of money if he helped them, he thought he might give it a little whirl. They'd been fairly helpful to him so far. If he got bored, he could always ignore them and do what he wanted anyway.

In the meantime the thought of what he would do to this man when they finally handed him over to him kept his murderous fantasies fuelled a little longer.

Chapter 17

Cade arrived at Quinn's house an hour later and let himself in with the key Quinn had given him. "Quinn? Are you here?"

A voice called out from upstairs. "Up here, in the office."

Cade walked up the curving staircase to the second floor and saw Quinn sitting behind his desk, frowning at his computer.

Cade smiled. "What's that face for? You look as if you've seen something you really don't like."

Quinn chuckled. "Just looking at the amount of email in my inbox. I've been a little dilatory in responding to anything for a while."

Cade walked around and stood behind him, pulling his head back so he could kiss him. Quinn swung around in his swivel chair and pulled Cade onto his lap. "I'd rather have you here in my arms so I can kiss you properly," he murmured as he proceeded to do just that.

There was no sound for a while other then the sound of various sighs and groans as the kiss grew in intensity. Finally they pulled apart.

"I love the taste of your mouth," Quinn whispered as his mouth found his ear and he trailed his tongue down it languorously. "In fact, I think we really should go to the bedroom where I can taste it properly and perhaps taste somewhere else as well. Jomo isn't in today so we have the house to ourselves."

Cade laughed softly. "I'd like that, Mr. Fairmont." He ran a hand down Quinn's inner arm and frowned, hearing his lover's soft hiss of pain. He sat up, his face concerned. "What's wrong?"

Quinn shook his head, his face a little pale. "Nothing to worry about. I cut myself on the forearm but it's healing. It's just a little tender."

"Let me see it. Take your shirt off." Quinn's face set and Cade shook his head. "You know I won't let this go and you'll be naked soon with me anyway. I'll see it then. What's the big secret?"

They both stood up and Cade unbuttoned Quinn's shirt. Once it was off, he exclaimed in horror at the two deep parallel cuts on Quinn's forearm. "Jesus, who did this to you? You didn't do this to yourself surely?"

Quinn sighed. "I needed to test the new antidote Mary had made and that meant cutting me and getting cadmium into my bloodstream. What you see there are the end results of the experiment we did Saturday night. They've healed quite a bit. In a couple of day's time there won't even be a scar."

Cade looked at him, horrified. "You used yourself as a guinea pig? Hell, what if something had gone wrong?"

Quinn shrugged. "I had Mary there with me. I'm sure she'd have fixed it. I did tell Percy about it just in case he needed to intervene."

Cade frowned. "I can't believe you didn't tell *me* what you were doing. You still should have had someone else physically with you. Mary's fine, I suppose, but I would have preferred to be there."

Quinn shook his head in bemusement. "You're not very fond of Mary, are you? Care to tell me why?"

Cade shrugged. "I'm not sure. I just don't trust her as much as you do. There's something a little off about her."

"Must be a Fey thing. I've had her thoroughly researched and she passes muster." He smiled at Cade. "Anyway, it was late, almost midnight. I didn't want to worry you."

Cade sighed. "Please don't treat me like I need protecting. That won't bode well for our relationship. I can look after myself and decide what worries me. And you alone, being cut by a witch and having a Warlock poison poured into you is something I want to know about. Before it happens, please."

Quinn nodded, seemingly amused at his stern tone. "Fair enough. Consider me chastened." He grinned. "Can we go to the bedroom now? I don't mind if you tell me off there, either. In fact, if you play the bossy schoolmaster I think that would bode well for our relationship."

Cade stood up and ran his hands over his bare chest. "I think I can manage that," he murmured. "Have you got a cane anywhere I can use?"

Cade smiled at Quinn's look of apprehension. "No cane? I suppose I can always slap your arse then. You might like that." From the look in Quinn's eyes, Cade thought he might well be amenable to that suggestion and he smiled inwardly.

Who would have thought that the mighty Quinn Fairmont might be down for a bit of slap and tickle? He'd have to see how that one went.

Cade regarded him in mock anxiety. "I'll slap your arse as long as you promise not to turn me into a frog or anything."

Quinn laughed as he took his hand and led him into the bedroom. "I've no use for you as a frog, Cade. I like you just as you are. Willing, sexy and human."

He swung the door shut behind them.

***

Andrew de Vere stood on his yacht contemplating the blinking lights of the harbour. By now, his tame witch would have done her job with the cadmium testing and Quinn Fairmont. She hadn't been happy with the plan at first, but with the use of his riding crop, he'd managed to convince her it was *his* plan and not hers to question.

Andrew sighed. Why was it that his minions never understood that it was the thrill of the hunt, of the chase, that made things so worthwhile?

He might have been able to have his witch subdue the Warlock while he was weak, bring him out of his home where he was magyckally protected against the likes of de Vere, bring him here and let de Vere to do with him as he saw fit. But de Vere didn't want it to be too easy anyway.

He wanted to destroy Quinn Fairmont first, emotionally, as Quinn had done to him when Adam had died. And the way to do that was by attacking his friends and then his lover. De Vere had started the ball rolling with the Warlock attacks to weaken Quinn. Next was the business partner Quinn was so fond of, then that rather sexy and nubile man that spent so much time with him.

Only then would de Vere be satisfied in taking Quinn's Withinner and destroying the human that remained. It would take a huge amount of magyck and planning. Quinn's Withinner would not allow his Warlock to be taken without a fight.

He sipped his drink, relishing in the smoky taste of the expensive whisky. "It's all part of the great plan, Fairmont," he murmured as he stood against the deck rail, enjoying the breeze on the part of his face where he still had nerve endings. "I'll make you suffer then bring you to me to finally destroy you. I want the classic movie showdown, you bastard. I deserve that. And as I'm having fun, why would I want it to be over too soon?"

He wanted to find out who the mole is in that ridiculous Witchhunters Alliance and destroy him or her too. Using that awful little child of a Witchhunter to help him get inside the organisation was a stroke of fucking genius in his book. He snorted in amusement. "Little bastard has no idea he's actually working for one of those he's sworn to kill."

He took another sip of his drink. "And best of all, I have my secret weapon." De Vere smiled in glee at the secret he harboured. "There's no fucking way when it comes to the crunch that Quinn and that arrogant Withinner will be able to defeat me. And then my poor Adam will have his revenge." His mood changed at the thought of his beautiful boy no longer being part of his life.

I miss you so much, my pet. So damned much.

"But I'll make sure Quinn gets his punishment, sweet boy," he whispered as he finished his whisky in one gulp. "Perhaps then you can rest."

A faint dark shadow swirled around his body, like mist rising off the sea.

Andrew smiled. "I feel you, angel," he murmured. "And it will be soon, I promise you."

Chapter 18

Jomo Onyango sat alone in the office at Quinn's house, his dark face frowning at something he was reading. His hand toyed absently with a letter opener, as he perused the contents of the document before him. The doorbell pealed and Jomo smiled.

Good. He needed a distraction from looking at all these financials. A visitor would be very welcome indeed.

He made his way down the spiralling staircase and opened the door. As he did so, a waft of smell assailed his nostrils, so fetid his eyes stung and watered. He had barely time to wonder what was happening when the blow struck him off his feet, hurling across the entrance hall to the other side. He hit his head as he landed and lay dazed and confused at the foot of the staircase.

He dimly heard a slight chuckle as he lay there and heard the sound of footsteps coming toward him. Jomo tried to open his eyes but it was too painful. He retched at the smell still pervading the hallway.

"Sorry about that," a low voice said in amusement from far away. "I think I overdid the sulphur." Jomo couldn't quite make out whether it was a male or a female voice. It sounded distorted, as if he was hearing it through water. "I'm sorry you had to get in the middle of this but I need to send Mr. Fairmont a message and I'm afraid you're it. Pull him closer to the door, you idiot. You know I can't go in there. It's protected."

The blurry figure moved toward the dazed Jomo, who was struggling to get up despite the voice's threat. As he was pulled unceremoniously toward the front door step he managed to speak. "Who the hell are you?"

The voice laughed. "You wouldn't believe me if I told you. It's a little beyond your understanding, my friend. All you need to know is that you're going to perform the ultimate sacrifice of being someone Quinn cares for and whom I'm going to take away from him. Permanently. Just lie back and relax. This won't take long. Then you can put him back where you found him, my dear."

A vice gripped Jomo's chest and he gasped, holding a hand to it as he struggled to breathe. The world grew darker and darker, the pain growing stronger, and then he remembered no more.

***

Quinn whistled softly as he approached the front door. He'd had a fairly good morning with the Consortium this morning, getting updates on the distribution of the pills Mary had made and the news had cheered him up. Finally something seemed to be going right. He looked up the garden path as he walked toward the front door. He was glad he'd managed to cancel the meeting he'd had. He was looking forward to perhaps getting Cade over for an early afternoon lovemaking session. He saw the figure of someone moving behind the frosted doors, someone that didn't look like Jomo. Jomo tended to take up this whole view. This person was decidedly smaller. Quinn's arm hairs stood up and he felt a distinct prickling on his skin.

Something wasn't right.

His strides grew more urgent up the path until he was almost running and he opened the front door, grabbing at the handle and hurtling into the hallway. Jomo was huddled at the bottom of the stairs, his eyes closed, blood running from a deep wound on his head. Quinn knelt down beside him anxiously.

Jesus, had he fallen down the stairs?

"Jomo?" he said urgently. "Jomo, can you hear me?" He faintly saw the rise and fall of his friend's chest and he reached into his pocket and pulled out his mobile to dial 999. Behind him there was a noise and he turned swiftly. It seemed to be coming from the hall closet at the far end of the entranceway. He made his way slowly toward it as the operator finally answered the 999 call.

Quinn spoke in staccato sentences. "I have an emergency. 77 Heathcoat Avenue, Hampstead Heath. I have a man who looks as if he's fallen down the stairs. He seems to be in bad way. Can you get an ambulance out immediately?"

"I have the location, sir." The operator's calm voice reassured him. "An ambulance is on its way. It should be there shortly. May I take your name?"

"Quinn Fairmont. This is my house. It's my business partner who's injured." Quinn had reached the closet now and he could hear a soft banging from inside.

"Right, sir. The ambulance is about five minutes away."

"Thanks." Quinn disconnected the call and looked back anxiously at Jomo. He wanted to be there with his friend but he needed to see what the noise in the cupboard was. He reached out and suddenly pulled the door open. Mary Hawthorne was huddled inside, her face bloody, her eyes dazed.

"Jesus, Mary. Come on. Let me help you out of there." Quinn reached in and pulled the witch to her feet. She leant into him, pressing himself against his chest. Despite the circumstances, a wave of desire for her washed over him. He pushed her away in confusion, holding her at arm's length.

"What the hell happened? What happened to Jomo?"

Mary shook her head, her face pale. "I came by to drop something off for you. The door was ajar and I pushed it open. Someone was standing over Jomo and I shouted at them. Then there was this almighty crash and I was hurtled backwards. I hit my head on the wall and the next thing I knew I was being shoved into that cupboard. Then I heard you on the phone out here."

"Did you see who it was?" Quinn's voice was grim as he left Mary to go kneel by the side of his friend.

Mary nodded. "Just a man. I have no idea who he was or what he wanted. Oh my God, Quinn, is he dead?"

Quinn shook his head. "No. Not far off though."

He tried to wake Jomo, his insides tightening when the man wouldn't respond. He had a nasty wound to his head and a faint scorch mark on the front of his shirt. The same scorch mark appeared to be repeated on his face, a nasty burn that ran along the length of his forehead. Quinn's blood ran cold. The mark on Jomo's chest looked like an energy burn, the same thing he'd used to kill Jimmy Christie. It was also used for memory wipes, a Warlock trick to ensure something couldn't be remembered. He'd used something very similar on Kyle but not to this extent. But a Warlock wouldn't have been able to get inside the house unless he'd had permission. Quinn's magyck protected him from that threat. He heard the sirens in the distance and motioned to Mary.

"Can you go stand outside and wave them in? The last thing I want to happen is they can't find the place or they go straight by." He looked at her warily. "I assume you're okay? I'd rather you didn't tell them about your being bundled in the cupboard. I don't want the police involved."

She nodded and disappeared out the hallway. Quinn reached down and laid a tender hand on his friend's forehead. It was cold and clammy.

"It'll be fine, Jomo. We'll get you to the hospital and you'll be fine in no time. I promise, old friend. I'm so sorry you got caught in the middle of this." Quinn heard the guilt in his voice and he closed his eyes, feeling sick.

There was a flurry of activity at the front door and two paramedics came in, all business, carrying their equipment.

"Mr. Fairmont, I assume this is our patient?" The older man knelt down beside Jomo, his younger colleague at his side. They fiddled and checked for a while then the older one looked up. "It looks like a heart attack to me. His heartbeat is very erratic. Did he have any history of heart trouble?"

Quinn shook his head tiredly. "No. He's as healthy as the proverbial horse."

The paramedic frowned. "He could have fallen hitting his head and then had a heart attack. We'll get him to the hospital and they can figure it out. In the meantime I'm treating this as a heart attack. His pulse is shallow, but it could have been worse." He frowned. "I don't know what this burn on his forehead is from though. It looks almost electrical."

Five minutes later Jomo was in the ambulance, Quinn at his side, on his way to the Royal Free Hospital whilst Mary stayed behind at the house. Once at the hospital, Jomo was wheeled into a glassed area for treatment, leaving Quinn pacing the hallway outside. He felt a sense of dread that someone had tried to hurt Jomo.

It was the one thing he'd always tried to avoid. He'd got too complacent and now his best friend was in the hospital with what looked like Warlock-induced energy burns and a nasty head wound. God knows what that memory burn would do to him. Quinn had a sense of helplessness and an immense sense of guilt at having Jomo pulled into his magyckal affairs.

Quinn stopped pacing and sat down on a hard hospital chair, his head in his hands as he wondered what to do next. Could it have been Jeremy that did this? Had he found out Quinn was looking for him and decided to teach him a lesson? Quinn knew the Witchfinder General has powers of his own but this seemed more Warlock than Witchhunter.

Quinn would invoke Taliesin later. Taliesin would be able to travel back and see what had happened, unless it was a Warlock, in which case they'd have protected themselves and Taliesin would be able to see nothing. There had been a distinct smell of sulphur at the front door, something Warlocks used to mask themselves. But at least then he'd know for sure whether it was one of his own doing this and be able to deal with it.

Quinn looked up as a doctor came out and looked around the room. He stood up.

"Mr. Fairmont?" The doctor waved him over and Quinn walked over.

The doctor smiled tiredly. "Your friend is doing okay. He'd had some sort of a heart attack; we're not quite sure exactly what caused it. He's stable and on medication and he'll need some rest." He frowned. "I have no idea what that burn is on his forehead. It's a definite scorch mark but I don't know how he got it. Do you have any idea?" He looked at Quinn curiously.

Quinn shook his head. "I wasn't there. I got home and found him lying on the floor. I'm afraid I've no idea what went on. Let's hope when he's awake he can tell us."

The doctor nodded thoughtfully. "Let's hope so. If you wait around a few minutes, a nurse will come out and take you to him." He nodded and disappeared. Quinn waited wearily for five minutes and saw a nurse approaching him with a smile.

"Mr. Fairmont? If you follow me, I'll take you to your partner." Her smile left him in no doubt that she thought they were together.

Quinn regarded her drily. "He's my business partner, not my *partner* partner. We're not a couple."

The nurse chuckled. "Sorry. We see all sorts here and it's difficult to be politically correct sometimes."

Quinn smiled slightly at her observation as he followed her down the corridor to a room at the end. She waved him in and left him standing over Jomo's bed. The Kenyan was pale, even by his standards, but he looked fairly comfortable and his breathing was easier.

Quinn sat down and watched him sleep. If whoever had tried to hurt Jomo was still around, Jomo wasn't safe even in the hospital. Whoever it was might try again. Quinn needed to get Jomo somewhere safe. He needed to make a few calls, get Jomo transferred elsewhere so he could send him to one of the Lodges where he could recover in peace.

He pulled out his phone and sent a few texts, waiting for the replies as he sat watching his friend sleep. Half an hour later he got the text he needed and sighed in relief. Percy was a master at organising this sort of thing. He'd got Jomo a transfer out of Royal Free to the Power retreat in Dorset. There he would be safe, under Warlock protection, at least for the time being. All Quinn needed to do was stay with him until the ambulance arrived to move him in a few hours' time. Then at least Quinn would have one fewer distraction to worry about. His next problem was protecting Cade. If they went after Jomo, they'd go after him. One of his other texts had been a request to have Magnus Onnarsson watch over him. He'd feel better having the seven-foot Warlock being Cade's bodyguard. He smiled wryly. The challenge would be getting Cade to agree to it.

***

Cade stormed around his houseboat, his hands gesticulating wildly as he faced down Quinn. He was not happy with the suggestion of a bodyguard.

"I don't need a seven-foot Lurch looking after me!" He turned and glared at Quinn, who was regarding him wearily. "I'm sure I'll be fine. No one's going to come looking for me here, are they?"

"I don't know," Quinn said as he watched Cade's angry pacing. "That's the whole idea of having someone look out for you. Because I don't know and I don't want to take that risk."

He leaned back on the couch, his face tired, his whole demeanour defeated. Cade's heart went out to him. Quinn had been through so much and here he was acting like the bitch from hell. Cade moved over to him, sitting beside him and placing his hands on his. Quinn's hands were colder than usual.

"I'm sorry I'm being such a prima donna. I just really value my privacy and the thought of having someone following me everywhere I go just doesn't sit well. Plus I've done martial arts. I can look after myself."

Quinn reached over and touched his cheek tenderly. "The one thing I don't need is to be worrying about you all the time. It's bad enough having Jomo hurt. I couldn't bear it if something happened to you. And whoever's doing this knows that's the one thing that would really make me lose focus."

Cade regarded him resignedly. "When you put it like that, and look at me with those beautiful brown puppy dog eyes, how can I refuse? But I don't want the man on top of me everywhere I go."

Quinn chuckled. "Believe me, the only man that's ever going to be on top of you—or behind you for that matter—is me."

Cade laughed at his words. "I asked for that, didn't I?" He caressed Quinn's face gently, a glint in his eye. "Seeing as how I'm so agreeable to having someone follow me around, I think I deserve a little reward, don't you?

Quinn grinned. "You want my body again?"

Cade shook his head. "No you arrogant sod, I want to ask you if you'd use Taliesin and those memory banks of yours to help me with my research for my latest dissertation. I have some questions I need answered and that Withinner of yours could do that."

Quinn's face darkened. "You know that means I may have to invoke him and that means drawing attention to us. And after the last time he was here, I'm not too keen on letting him be alone with you either."

"I realise that. But I'd really like to have the upper hand in my research and you could help me with it. I'm sure a big, strong man like you can keep me safe from the evil, randy sorcerer." Cade trailed his hands slowly down Quinn's hips, over the curve of his jeans, as he watched his face. He knew Quinn knew exactly what he was doing as a slight smile appeared at his obvious manipulation of Quinn's body.

"I'll think about it," Quinn said quietly.

"Thank you. Now I'll have that other reward you promised me earlier," he whispered as he leaned in to kiss Quinn, his hands stroking his bare arms in his sleeveless tee shirt. Cade slipped his hands around Quinn's waist, feeling the warm skin of his taut stomach beneath. Quinn groaned and pulled him closer, his mouth warm and hungry, his hands pulling Cade into his embrace. Cade shivered at the coolness of his hands then sighed in pleasure as Quinn's tongue found his and for a while there was nothing on their minds but the touch and feel of each other in the dimming twilight of an August sunset.

Chapter 19

Quinn readied himself to invoke his Withinner as he stood in the hallway of his home. He needed Taliesin to travel back to the day Jomo was attacked and perhaps get a sense of what had happened. It was a fairly tricky business doing the time-travel bit. Taliesin was adept at it but it made Quinn feel sick. He always came out of it feeling like he'd been sliced, diced and then put back together, which, he supposed in retrospect, was probably how it all worked. Quinn had no idea how his Withinner did it, and he doubted Taliesin knew the physics of it either. It was just something both of them took for granted.

Quinn was concerned about his Withinner. He'd become more and more difficult to manage as the relationship with Cade intensified, and he knew his other half was raring to have his fill of him. He didn't trust Taliesin anymore to do what he was told and that, for him, was a major problem. The one person he'd always been able to rely on was Taliesin. Meeting Cade had complicated matters for them both, and for the first time in both their lives, they had conflict between them of a nature not previously experienced. He sighed now as he willed Taliesin to come forward and hoped like hell that when the time came, he'd be able to revoke him without the usual battle of wills.

"*Taliesin, yn dod allan.*"

He repeated the phrase and finally Quinn felt himself being sucked back and the dark figure of the Withinner stood in the centre of Quinn's hallway, grasping his staff. His familiar was with him, the little golden dragonfly buzzing around in a frenzy, pleased to be let out.

"Still, Draigh." Taliesin growled and tapped his staff impatiently on the floor. "I need to concentrate on getting back to the other time and I can't do that with your infernal noise in my ears."

The dragonfly buzzed louder in protest.

The Withinner scowled. "I care not if you don't like the travelling in time. You have to come with me so stop your complaining."

Taliesin stood and looked around the hallway in quiet contemplation. He sensed something even now but he wasn't sure that Quinn was going to like the result of his travel. The smell of sulphur in the air was still strong and the chances were that Jomo's attacker was indeed a Warlock who would have masked him or herself.

Taliesin sighed and grasped his staff more firmly. Slowly, he made small circles with it, visualising the time he wanted to be, seeing Quinn's memories in his mind and making them travel back just that little bit to a slightly earlier time.

He saw the images in his mind, from the time Jomo was walking down the spiral staircase and opening the door but try as he could, from that time on there was nothing to see. It was as if, with the door opening, all visuals had been erased up until the time Quinn had found Jomo at the foot of the stairs. The smell of sulphur grew stronger and stronger, overpowering, and Taliesin heard the frantic buzzing of Draigh as the little dragonfly became more and more affected by the smell.

Finally, Taliesin opened his eyes and sighed heavily. "It's no use. There's nothing to see. Someone very powerful was masking themselves. At least we know it had to be a Warlock. But they did not actually enter the house. This I can tell. "He grimaced fiercely, his teeth glinting white in the darkness of the hallway. "Another Warlock traitor? This is becoming too much, Quinn. You need to stop this madness before it gets worse. Someone is working against us, someone very powerful and I don't like it at all. It smells putrid."

Draigh was perched on his shoulder, quiet now.

Taliesin felt Quinn trying to revoke him and he sighed then murmured, "Quinn, please let me be a little while longer. I need some growths off the heath for home. There is a sick child at stake. Enjoy my home that little bit longer. I lit the fire especially to keep you warm so you could stop your confounded whining about the cold. Leave me be just that little bit more and then I promise I will be a good boy and go back where you want me. You have my word I will behave myself."

Taliesin felt the pull from Quinn lessen and grinned wolfishly. His eyes narrowed in anticipation of what he was about to do. Whilst he'd been quietly doing his business on the other side, he'd come across an ancient chant which, together with some special moss from the heath from this time, would allow him to remain just that little bit longer and fight his revocation.

He'd only be able to do it once, as Quinn would become wise to it again and find a way to prevent him doing it a second time, but he thought it would be worth it this time just to see the man Cade again and perhaps get a bit further than he had last time.

He smiled as Quinn finally fully acquiesced to his request with fairly good grace. Taliesin's eyes narrowed. He'd known the mention of a sick child might sway Quinn's resolution to revoke him immediately. Humans were so emotional about their offspring. He'd have hell to pay after this night, he knew, for touching Quinn's new plaything. So he'd better make the most of it whilst he was here. He'd just have to avoid that giant of a Warlock Quinn had guarding the man, but he knew exactly how to do that. He was part Quinn after all.

***

Cade stood in the middle of his bedroom on the houseboat, packing away laundry. He turned to leave the room and started when he saw Quinn standing there.

"Quinn! I thought you were away tonight. I didn't hear you come on board."

Cade moved toward him with a smile, and then frowned as he noticed his stillness. He also had the unmistakeable prickle of longing as he got closer to him, the same feeling he'd had when they'd first met, only much stronger. As Cade reached out a hand to touch him Quinn's form shimmered. Cade retracted his hand with a startled gasp. The air went hazy and slowly a darker form took shape, one that he had seen and met before.

"Taliesin! What the hell are you doing here?"

The Withinner grinned at him. "I wanted to see you. Quinn has done such a great job keeping you from me that I needed to get creative."

He moved toward Cade, dropping his cloak to the floor and standing his staff against the wall. He wore a pair of tight leather breeches, a loose shirt of rough spun cotton and some sort of hide waistcoat with golden buttons over the shirt. Taliesin's chest rose and fell beneath the thin material and dark eyes regarded him with lust. The large bulge in his trousers made Cade swallow.

Christ. And I thought Quinn was big.

"How did you manage to look like Quinn just now?" he asked. *Quinn,* he thought desperately. *Where the hell are you? The damn bogeyman's just arrived.*

Taliesin shrugged his broad shoulders. "An incantation I found together with some special moss that enabled me to trick that giant of a fellow you have stationed outside. It allows me to resist Quinn revoking me for at least the next half an hour. I am part Quinn after all. It wasn't too difficult to do." He grinned wickedly. "Half an hour is all we need, I promise."

A small flying thing fluttered around the room, agitated and noisy and Cade ducked as it flew past his head. "What the hell is that?" he gasped.

Taliesin grinned. "My familiar. Her name is Draigh. She's a dragonfly. We've been together forever. Ignore her. She'll settle down. She doesn't like what I'm doing either."

He reached out a hand for him and Cade felt an irresistible pull. He'd never felt like this before, not even the first time with Quinn, and the emotions and sensations Taliesin was provoking were unbearable. Cade's heart beat furiously, his groin was hot, his prick erect and aching.

The Withinner's smile told Cade that he knew the turmoil he was creating. His breathing was deep, his lips wet from his constant licking as he moved toward him, his bulge noticeable and very large. The scent of musky arousal permeated the room if two mating and primal animals were about to fulfil their desires.

"Quinn won't like this, Taliesin," Cade stammered, trying to get away from the other man's allure by moving backward. Unfortunately Taliesin was moving closer to the bed. He smiled as he shrugged his magnificent shoulders. Cade had an overwhelming urge to bite into that muscled flesh.

"Quinn is not here," he said simply. "He has no power over me for the next half hour. Which means you and I can complete what we started with a kiss."

He started to unbutton his shirt, and Cade swallowed at the sight of his hairy chest, dark skin and the muscles that rippled across his stomach. The shirt was thrown onto the floor and

Taliesin reached out his hand, pulling Cade toward him roughly, his mouth grinding into his.

Cade's head swam with all thoughts carnal. "Taliesin. This isn't right. I'm with Quinn," he gasped, trying to pull his mouth away from his but failing miserably with the iron grip on his arm.

Christ, are the man's lips magnetic? Cade felt the pull of those full, fleshy lips and wanted nothing more than to bite them savagely.

The sorcerer grinned. "So am I." His hands reached out and deftly ripped the cotton shirt Cade wore apart. It dropped to the floor in two pieces.

Cade seemed rooted to the floor, unable to move. The animalism of the other man and his scent of sweat and bergamot turned his insides to mush and his mind to fluffy balls of cotton wool.

Taliesin's eyes gleamed at seeing Cade's bare, smooth chest. "You are magnificent, *cariad*," he whispered huskily. "You make me horny like the mountain *gafr*." He reached down and unzipped Cade's jeans, sliding them over his hips with his underwear and smiling in satisfaction at Cade's obvious tumescence.

Cade was on fire, his traitorous groin and cock burning with want. He knew a smidgeon of Welsh words. A *gafr* was a goat and by the look in Taliesin's greedy eyes, Cade was about to be rammed by one.

Taliesin pushed Cade back onto the bed. He licked his lips at the sight of Cade's rampant cock, swollen, red and already leaking copious amounts of pre-come.

Somewhere in Cade's mind he knew this was all wrong, but it was as if a haze had descended on his mind and he could no longer think independently of his cock and his arse, the ache in his channel intensifying as he watched Taliesin stand back and remove the rest of his clothing. His seducer climbed onto the bed and covered Cade with a body that was hot, iron-muscled and needy. His cock pulsed against Cade's and Cade was weak with desire, all rational thought now gone.

"I want to make you scream, make you mine. You are in agreement with this?" Taliesin's chest heaved with passion and he pulled away as he regarded Cade with heavy lidded eyes that were as dark as coal. "I wish to pleasure you, *cariad*, face to face, so I can watch your eyes, see your face when I come inside you," he whispered.

Cade had no words, his rational mind closing down at the effect the other man had on him. The feelings of guilt crept back into the dark recesses of his mind as he nodded. Taliesin's triumphant expression left Cade in no doubt that he knew Cade could no longer resist anything this man wanted to do to him. Taliesin growled loudly as he covered Cade again, his hands sliding over Cade's hips, fingers digging cruelly into his flesh. Cade cried out as teeth bit into the taut flesh of his shoulder, drawing blood.

Taliesin took his mouth once more in a kiss that seemed to suck out the very life from him. Cade tasted blood in his mouth at the violence of it.

"This is worth everything Quinn may say to me when he gets back," Taliesin's fingers reached down, coating them with their slick, combined essence and then his fingers slid inside Cade, making him cry out loudly as he pushed in, opening him up for entrance. Cade bit his lip with the pleasure and the pain of feeling those strong fingers probing and stretching. His head tossed from side to side as he moaned at the incredible feeling in every nerve ending he had in his body.

"Enough," Cade moaned, "I need to feel you inside me. No more foreplay."

Taliesin needed no urging. A thick, hot rod of pure hurt slid into Cade, and he cried out at feeling the other man's cock invade him, pound him as if there was no barriers. His rhythm matched the movement of his hips as they strove to meet each other. Cade's hands clutched his shoulders, nails digging deep into Taliesin's flesh, drawing blood and skin beneath his fingernails.

"Gods, you feel good, so tight. You can feel the connection too, can't you?" the sorcerer whispered as his one hand wrapped into Cade's hair, pulling it back and exposing his throat. He sucked on it greedily, causing small purple blemishes to appear.

Heat rose inside Cade and he knew he wasn't far from coming, the intense throbbing of his stomach and groin making him moan in pleasure. Sensation travelled from his feet up to his hips and finally to his cock. He hammered his fists against Taliesin's back as he came, biting into his shoulder, scraping his nails down his back. Taliesin hissed in pleasure as Cade's come sprayed over his chest and stomach.

He smiled at him, his dark eyes boring into Cade's. "I love seeing a man enjoy himself," he whispered into his ear, his tongue tickling inside. He clasped Cade's still-shuddering body closer to him, gasping for air as his climax took him to its peak. He cried out, some strange word Cade had never heard, his grunts and gasps in cadence with the jerking of his body.

Taliesin's nails scratched Cade's arm and he winced as he drew blood. The Withinner gave another loud, grunting howl as he came and Cade felt warmth in his channel from his semen. The fact there were no condoms, no safe sex, escaped him. The whole coupling—because that what was it had been—had been short lived but intense. There'd been room for no other outcome than fast and furious.

Taliesin's body slowly stopped its movement and relaxed on top of Cade's. He was heavy and sweaty, his breath in Cade's ears still warm. There was only the sound of deep and heavy breathing in the room as both of them waited for their heartbeats to get back to normal. A shudder of deep shame and fear wracked Cade's being and he finally reached up and shoved Taliesin violently to one side. "Get off me, you bastard," he snarled.

Taliesin looked at him in surprise. He moved, looking confused as Cade sat up and pulled the bed cover around his naked body.

"*Cariad.* Are you all right? Did I hurt you?" Taliesin seemed truly bewildered at his reaction.

Cade shook his head, trying not to let the hot tears welling in his eyes take flight. "Don't flatter yourself." He stood up, the duvet cover wrapped around his aching body. His arse burned like fire. "You need to fuck off back where you came from. I want you to leave. Now. You promised you'd let Quinn back when you'd had me. Well, you've done that. Now I just want you to go."

Taliesin sat up and gazed at him, perplexed. "What did I do to upset you so? I thought you enjoyed yourself."

Cade gazed at him, his eyes stone cold. "You made me betray Quinn. You made me betray the man I love. He'll never forgive me for this, no matter what you say about your Fey affect. I should have been stronger. I should have resisted you. And you should never have come here in the first place."

Taliesin shook his head. "You could no more resist me than I could you. You and Quinn did the same thing when you first met. Why is it different with me?"

"Because I love Quinn," Cade said quietly. "And I think he loves me. Well, loved me. You—all you wanted was pure sex. You wanted to get your itch scratched. And I helped you. I'll never forgive myself." Not only that but he'd had unprotected sex with a man that by Quinn's own account was a little bit of a philanderer on his home turf. God only knew what might happen now. His voice caught and he clutched the duvet. "Get dressed and go. Bring

Quinn back. He must be beside himself on the other side. But not here. I can't face him now. You need to do it somewhere else."

Taliesin stood up, his body rigid. He picked up his trousers and his shirt and silently dressed. When he was finished, he turned to Cade with a much softer expression on his face.

"I am sorry I upset you. That was not my intention. I never meant to hurt you. I was not aware you felt so strongly for Quinn. Human love is something I don't really understand. It is far too emotional for me."

He made a motion with his hand and the little familiar settled on his shoulder. He wrapped his cloak tightly around his body and picked up his staff. Cade thought he was going to speak but he changed his mind and disappeared into the dark of the night.

Cade sank to the floor, his body wracked with sobs. He could never face Quinn again after this. Quinn would never want to see him again, he knew. And he wouldn't blame him. He'd wrecked the best relationship he'd ever had and his world had just collapsed.

Chapter 20

Quinn was in the darkness of his living room, sitting still like a gorgon on a battlement of a castle. His face was pale, his eyes bloodshot. He'd half a bottle of whisky beside him that he'd been working his way through. But no matter how much he drank, the pain in his heart was still there.

The last time he'd been in this much pain was when he'd killed a man he cared for. He'd been back a few hours, after many vitriolic curses and muttered death threats against Taliesin. Taliesin had seemed fairly subdued when he'd been revoked, unusual for him, but it hadn't mattered to Quinn. He was full of fury for his Withinner, wanting nothing more to do with him. He felt betrayed, and for a Warlock, that was probably a death sentence for the Withinner relationship. He'd experienced every feeling, every emotion of Taliesin whilst Taliesin had been with Cade. There'd been no love involved, simply raw animal passion.

Quinn still felt his Withinner's orgasm and tasted Cade's desire for Taliesin in his mouth. His eyes stung with angry tears when he thought about it and he blinked them away furiously.

No matter how much he knew that the sex session had been fated to happen if the two met and that neither Taliesin nor Cade could have resisted the Fey pull, it still hurt. He was furious with Taliesin for his slyness in promoting it in the first place. His Withinner had been disloyal to him and that was something he couldn't countenance.

The jealousy he felt inside for what the two had experienced bit him to the core.

Without any protection too! God knows how Cade must be feeling in the aftermath. He is probably worried sick. Quinn knew there was nothing to worry about; Taliesin was a bit of a hound but he was a powerful Fey and not privy to the usual human sicknesses. What mattered now was getting to Cade to reassure him that Quinn didn't blame him for the forced seduction of his mind and body. He had to tell Cade that. Soon. Even if his insides burned with jealousy and rage at the fact someone else had experienced the delights of the body of the man he loved more than anyone else.

Perhaps one more drink would make his Withinner's betrayal more bearable and give him the courage to console Cade without spitting out words at him he'd no right to utter. He was taking another slug from the bottle when he heard Taliesin speak quietly.

Quinn. We need to talk.

"Fuck off." Quinn waved the whisky bottle in the air as he spoke out loud. "Leave me alone, you bastard. I never want to speak to you again."

You know that cannot happen. We are one. We cannot be apart.

"That's what you think, you Welsh git!" Quinn roared drunkenly. "If I never speak to you again it'll be too soon. You can forget ever seeing this side of the universe ever again. I'll get along on my own now. You, my friend, are history."

You know you will need me soon to fight what is coming. Do not be so stupid. I wish to apologise for what I did. It seems I made an error of judgement.

Quinn laughed loudly. "An error of judgement? I'll say you made a fucking error of judgement. You betrayed my trust with your fucking lies and screwed my boyfriend, you bastard. You hunted down the man I love. You gave him something that wasn't yours to give and took something that wasn't yours to take. We call that rape in my world. Now shut the fuck up and go away. Leave me alone. I mean it. Leave me alone."

Quinn threw the bottle across the room to smash and splinter against the wall, the whisky flying in the air and splashing amber-coloured rivulets against the wall.

He staggered up the stairs to his bedroom and fell onto his bed fully clothed. Taliesin was thankfully quiet. The room was spinning. To be honest, Quinn was surprised he wasn't puking his guts out already. He lay back on his pillow, closing his eyes, feeling sick in his stomach as the alcohol settled.

Jesus, I'm going to have one helluva hangover in the morning. Perhaps I'll wake up and just start again then I won't have to have a hangover.

He giggled slightly at the wisdom of his own words and let sleep claim him, falling thankfully into a deep dark cavern where he didn't have to feel anything at all.

The following morning Quinn awoke with a head that felt as if a dozen elephants were break dancing inside. He sat up, groaning as the light hit his eyes. As he did so, his stomach heaved and he just made it to the toilet before he hurled into the porcelain bowl. He vomited until his stomach was empty and he had the dry heaves. Finally he sat, pale and trembling, by the side of the toilet, not wanting to move from the spot.

Fifteen minutes later he finally stood up and made his way unsteadily to the shower. The hot water made him feel a little more human but still sick, his head pounding. He got out the shower, wrapping a towel around his waist, and rummaged in the medicine cabinet for three paracetamol, which he downed with water from the tap.

Quinn looked at his face in the steamed-up mirror and groaned at the sight. His eyes were bloodshot and sunken, his face deathly pale as a corpse left out in the elements for a week. He looked dreadful. He was supposed to go and see Jomo today to check on his progress but the way he looked, he'd be lucky to get anywhere without being arrested for being one of the walking dead. Perhaps he'd leave it until tomorrow. Quinn picked up his phone and felt his heart sink as he saw a missed call from Cade.

It was time to speak to him. He shouldn't have left it this long. Cade would be beside himself.

He got dressed and went down to the garage. His Jaguar XJ in racing green was his pride and joy and whilst he loved driving it, he hated the London traffic. But he needed to get to Little Venice and take Cade in his arms, explain that this was not his fault. He knew his man and Cade would be remorseful as all hell.

An hour later he stood on the deck of the houseboat. It was still and quiet, the curtains closed and looking abandoned. He knocked but there was no reply. Quinn tried the door. It was locked, but not for long.

With one short word from him, the door opened and Quinn stepped inside into the gloom of Cade's lounge. A shape lay huddled on the couch, covered by a large plaid blanket. Marco Polo looked up from his spot at Cade's feet as Quinn entered then slowly stretched and slid off the bed, padding toward the door. Quinn stroked the cat's upright tail as it slunk past him.

He sat down on the couch next to the sleeping man, and tried not to think of what had happened yesterday just a few feet away in the bedroom. He reached out a hand, moving the blanket away, smiling softly at the features revealed. Cade looked like a boy when he slept, long eyelashes curled against his fair skin, his beautiful lips relaxed and ready for kissing. He looked much younger.

Once again Quinn marvelled at the depth of his feeling for this man.

He'd heard what Cade had said to Taliesin yesterday, about loving Quinn and thinking Quinn loved him. Despite how furious he'd been with his Withinner, Quinn's heart had warmed at those words.

Perhaps this was the right time to put those same words into each other's hearts, cement them there like handprints in front of the theatre on the Hollywood Walk of Fame.

Cade snorted softly and Quinn reached out and brushed a wayward strand of hair tenderly from his cheek. Cade's eyes opened and as they focused and recognised Quinn, they darkened, their silver depths growing shadowed and wary.

"Quinn. I'm surprised you're here." His voice was husky with sleep and resignation.

Quinn quirked an eyebrow. "Why would you say that?"

Cade's eyes narrowed as he sat up, wincing as he did so. Quinn saw he was still fully clothed. "Because of what happened yesterday." His voice was flat. "You look like crap. Did I do that to you?" Cade's voice was sad and his hands clutched the blanket like an anxious child's. Quinn's heart stuttered and he reached out and cupped Cade's cheek.

Time to put his man's mind to rest.

Quinn leaned forward and pulled Cade's mouth to his, kissing him tenderly. Cade groaned into his mouth, a sound that made him hard as a rock. He wanted to take him right then and there, but he had to be patient.

Tongues mashed together as both men held onto each other's mouths with desperation. Finally they broke for air and Cade looked at Quinn with wide, surprised eyes.

"What was that for? Christ, Quinn, I let another man fuck me, how can you still want to kiss me like that?" He stood up in agitation, barefoot, hands waving as he spoke. "I'm so sorry it happened, I feel like a dirtbag but I couldn't help myself. That bloody Withinner of yours is too powerful; he's not even fucking human. I didn't know what to do. I—"

Quinn stood up and pulled Cade to him, locking him in the warmth of his arms, against his chest. "Cade, it's okay, baby. I know you couldn't help it." Cade's body relaxed against him and Quinn nuzzled the skin beneath his lover's ear. "You forget, I've lived with him since I was seven years old. I know how he can be. I don't blame you; I blame *him*, for everything." Cade's heart was beating wildly against Quinn's chest. "I should have come over last night, but I drank too much. I was upset at him, not you. Yes, I don't like what happened, but I don't blame you, Cade. You need to believe me when I tell you that."

Cade shifted and looked up at Quinn, eyes shimmering with tears. "I was so damned worried, Quinn. I thought I was going to lose you. I thought I'd stuffed everything up—"

Quinn kissed him again, more violently than before, and Cade moaned and surrendered to him. Quinn's heart swelled with love for his boyfriend. There was no way he was ever letting him go, not for anyone. He'd die before that happened.

Finally Quinn pulled away, leaving Cade looking dazed, his lips swollen and pink. Quinn wanted to start all over again, but it was time to talk.

He sat Cade down and took the seat beside him. "Taliesin and I have had words. We're not on speaking terms at the moment," Quinn said grimly. "He had no right to do that to you. He knew exactly what he was doing. He might call it seduction but I call it rape."

Cade opened his mouth to interject and Quinn laid a firm finger on it. "Hear me out. The attraction would have been useless for you to resist. He knew that and he still took advantage of you. I hate the fact that he did something so intimate with you. I have this rage deep inside at what you shared. I am so fucking mad with him at the moment that if I could rip him out of my heart and soul and throw him to the damn wolves, I would. But I can't. So I have to live with it. And so do you."

Cade nodded uncertainly. "Are you sure, Quinn? What if he does it again?" his face darkened. "Also, we had unprotected sex, Quinn."

Quinn snorted explosively. "Firstly, he won't ever fucking do that again. I'm his Warlock for God's sake and I'd find a way to rip his cheating heart out of his chest and make him eat the damn thing."

Cade giggled softly and Quinn smiled at that sound and the fact his lover's face was looking less like an animal caught in a trap about to die. "And you need have no worries about anything on the unsafe sex side. Taliesin doesn't suffer from the normal afflictions that humans suffer from." The relief is Cade's eyes spoke volumes. "And besides, he knows something now that perhaps he didn't realise before because I've never really it said out loud to anyone."

Cade face creased in a frown. "What's that?"

Quinn leaned forward and framed Cade's face with his hands. "That I love you," he murmured. "That I need you and without you, things just wouldn't be worth shit."

The flame in Cade's eyes grew larger, flickering light that turned the pupils of his eyes to black chips of pure crystalline fire.

"Wow, that's sort of romantic," he whispered teasingly, as he pulled Quinn's shirt from his chinos, and then slipped his hands underneath to touch Quinn's heated skin. "I get the sentiment at least."

Cade's hands were playing havoc with Quinn's breathing and he took a shuddering deep one as his lover nibbled his ear.

Cade whispered, "Perhaps you should show me just how much you love me? In a very intimate sort of gesture, like being inside me within the next few minutes? I'm still a little sore"—he flushed—"but I need this."

Quinn heard the hesitation in Cade's voice and knew instinctively he needed reassurance that Quinn didn't see him as sloppy seconds. Cade needed to know that despite Taliesin's taking of him, Quinn still wanted him in the same way he always had.

"I think we can manage that," Quinn murmured as Cade stood up and crooked his finger, beckoning him toward his bedroom. "But there's still one thing left to do."

Cade stopped and looked at him, those flames still flickering in his eyes. He looked uncertain. "I changed the sheets and stuff on the bed if that's what you mean—"

Quinn moved toward Cade and pushed him fiercely against the bulwark of the boat. "That's not what I meant," he growled. "I told you something. I want you to tell me something too."

Cade's body arched toward his in desire, his lips curved into a sly smile.

"I wonder what that could possibly be," he murmured, as he sucked Quinn's lower lip into his mouth. Quinn shuddered.

God, this man would be the death of him.

Cade took pity on him. "You want me to tell you I love you, my big, scary Warlock king? That I think about you all the time and I don't know what the hell I would do if I ever lost you? That I'm only ever yours?"

"Yes," Quinn breathed into Cade's mouth as he crushed them together. "That's exactly what I want to hear." His voice shook as Cade reached up and licked his ear.

"I love you, Quinn. Always. And I'm yours."

Quinn's heart pounded in his chest and he manhandled Cade into the small bedroom, pushing him down onto the bed, realising this was a replay of yesterday but not caring. He needed to mark

Cade as his, take him back and show his Withinner exactly who Cade belonged to.

"You're damn right you're mine," he growled.

Cade unzipped his pants and lifted his lean his lean hips to reveal strong, muscled legs and a cock that peeped over the top of his boxers. "So get down here and show that damned dark force of yours exactly how much it's just you and me."

Quinn needed no further urging.

Later that night as they lay together in sleepy contentment, Quinn knew there was something else he had to tell Cade about himself. He leaned up on an elbow and regarded Cade's drowsy face. "Cade? Are you awake?"

Sleepy grey eyes opened and regarded him. "I am now."

Quinn watched Cade's face carefully, seeing faint apprehension cross his face at Quinn's stare.

"What is it?" Cade asked quietly, more alert now. "You have a strange look on your face. I'm not sure I like it."

"Do you remember our first meeting at that charity dinner?" Quinn asked quietly. Cade snorted. "Of course I do. The one where you literally seduced me and fucked me senseless. Your Sir Galahad complex, I believe you called it?"

Quinn's face flushed guiltily at the memory of his relentless pursuit of Cade. His boyfriend took pity on him and ran his tongue over his lips before pulling him and taking his mouth in a kiss that left Quinn very aroused and breathless.

"I forgive you." Cade murmured. "How could I not when I lie here with you like this?"

Quinn laughed softly as he got his bearings again. "I wasn't totally to blame for that," he murmured. "I'd taken some Mirrabar blood on very good authority but although it quelled the urges for a while, it had nowhere near the 'quelling' effect it should have. When I was with Taliesin this last time, he explained why. He'd made some cryptic comment about it to me before but I'd forgotten." He looked at Cade, his eyes watchful. "You're not only Sprite; you have the blood of a healer too. You must be descended from a very powerful Sprite family. I stood no choice against your charms. The Fey blood attraction would have been incredibly heightened."

He smiled at the expression on Cade's face as he reached out and closed his mouth gently. "Taliesin said he sensed it when"—he stopped, a faint expression of distaste on his face—"when he was inside you last night. He said it was deeply buried but that it's there. It's also the reason he wanted you so much too."

Cade grinned then his face grew serious. "So what does it mean, being a Sprite with healing powers? How much can I heal, what does it involve?"

Quinn sighed and shook his head. "I'm not altogether sure. We'll find out as we carry on. But it means that whatever is dormant inside you is powerful and something that a lot of other Feys covet. So we'll take it slowly and try and find it all out among the three of us. I have no doubt something will come up soon."

Cade nodded, his eyes mischievous. "There isn't a double-entendre in that statement, is there? Because that would be a really corny thing to do."

Quinn reached down under the covers, grasping his lover's semi-hard cock in his hands.

"Well, now that you mention it," he murmured silkily. Cade's amused chuckle cut off sharply in a gasp as Quinn made his way down under the covers and took his lover in his mouth.

Chapter 21

The following morning, still aching and sore from the night's activities, and after a long and intense kiss from Cade to wish him on his way, Quinn drove down to the Warlock retreat in Dorset where Jomo was recovering. He knew he could get there instantly by invoking Taliesin but in his current state of mind, he wanted no contact with his Withinner. He'd do this next step the human way and Taliesin be damned.

The last status report he'd got from his team had advised that Jomo had woken up, very confused and with a fair amount of memory loss. Quinn needed to see exactly how much Jomo remembered. He'd spend some time down at the coast with him. Hopefully it would help him get his mind in gear for whatever needed doing next.

Magnus promised to keep watch on Cade despite his lover's sulky mutters that he could look after himself. Quinn had been ready to lock the man up in handcuffs and chain him to his bed to make him understand he was at risk.

Cade had declined his kind offer but the glint in his eye promised that it might become a distinct possibility in the future. They'd left things as an uneasy truce that Magnus would not crowd Cade and Cade would make sure he didn't go off alone.

The trip was uneventful as the car ate up the two hundred miles to the retreat. Quinn's thoughts were still filled with thoughts of Taliesin and Cade together and he stopped at the services area a few times to avail himself of strong coffee and pastries in an effort to cast the thoughts of them together out of his mind before he went crazy. He might have assured his lover that it hadn't been his fault but the thought of Taliesin taking Cade as he had still made his heart pound faster and the green fangs jealousy nip at his heart.

Quinn arrived around three o'clock in the afternoon. He parked the car and went inside. This was no ordinary clinic. The whole building was protected by magyck, not able to be seen by just anyone. Quinn walked in and was immediately greeted by a rather busty nurse who approached him with a smile.

"Good afternoon, Mr. Fairmont. We've been expecting you." She looked at him worriedly. "You don't look too well, sir. Is anything wrong?"

Quinn shook his head. "Something I ate, I think. I'll be fine. Where's my friend?"

"If you follow me, I'll take you to Mr. Onyango. He's feeling much better. It's just the memory loss really. The poor man is still a little confused about things. Perhaps you can help him remember."

"That's the idea," Quinn said as they walked. "I need to see if there's anything I can do to bring it all back for him. It depends how much he lost in the first place."

They'd reached a room in the left wing of the building and the nurse opened a door. "Mr Onyango is in here, Mr. Fairmont. Let me know if you need anything."

Quinn nodded. "Thanks. I will." He entered the room and saw his friend sitting in a large armchair gazing out at the coastline beyond the shoreline. Jomo turned as he came in.

He looked at Quinn quizzically. "Afternoon. Can I help you?"

Quinn's heart sank. "Jomo, it's me. It's Quinn. Don't you remember me?"

Jomo looked at him without any sign of recognition. "I'm afraid I don't. Since the heart attack my brain has been a little fuzzy." He smiled and Quinn saw a shade of the old Jomo in there.

"Do you mind if I sit down?" Quinn gestured to the other armchair.

Jomo chuckled. "Please do. I don't have many visitors so it's nice to have some company."

Quinn sat down, his heart heavy. Luckily Jomo was currently unattached and had no family close by. His parents and brother were in Kenya. Quinn had already told them he was fine, just recovering from a slight heart attack. He'd promised to keep them informed and had even offered to fly them over if they wanted to visit. He was still waiting to hear from them.

"My name is Quinn Fairmont," Quinn said quietly. "You and I are business partners in London and we're also best friends. We've known each other for the past fifteen years."

Jomo frowned. "You do seem familiar but I can't remember."

"How much do you remember, Jomo? Do you know who you are, who your family is?"

Jomo laughed. "Of course I remember my childhood, my family. I know who I am, thank God. It just seems to be certain people I can't remember yet. I'm told I know people, like you, but I just can't remember them. I know I'm a financial accountant, I know I'm a Virgo birth sign but some faces elude me. I know where I work, in a large house in Hampstead Heath."

"That's my house; we work from there running our business together. QuinnCo?"

Jomo nodded. "I remember all that. It's just you, I'm afraid. It's a strange one but anyone I know here in the UK I seem to have forgotten."

Quinn knew exactly what he was facing. It was a fairly complex Warlock memory block, able to be targeted at certain memories and areas of the brain. It appeared that whoever had performed this deliberate affliction on Jomo had hoped to erase anything at all about who they might be and look like. They'd gone far enough to erase anything that may lead back to them, taking no chances. They could have killed his friend but had chosen not to, instead leaving him a shell of what he'd been before. Quinn had no doubt that this cruelty had been the intention.

There were only a few people Quinn knew who could do such a memory erase; he was one of them and the other two were Percy and another Marshall called Justin Leichner, a very good friend of his.

The only other person capable of doing it he'd killed a long time ago.

Quinn trusted both Percy and Justin with his life and he knew *he* hadn't done it. That didn't leave him many other options. It wouldn't be easy to retrieve those memories given the complexity of the memory loss but when Jomo was strong enough he'd try.

Jomo was looking at him curiously. "They tell me you arranged for me to recuperate here. I have to thank you for that. It's a lovely place and I feel very at peace here. The care is first rate. I hope to be back on my feet soon." He smiled, his teeth white in his face, his eyes grateful.

Quinn grinned back, feeling a keen sense of loss that this man didn't remember him. "You just need to rest and get better. Then we can tackle that memory loss. The doctors tell me there are certain things they can do to try and bring it back. But you need to be a little stronger."

The two men sat chatting until finally Quinn stood up. "I need to speak to the doctors again. I'm glad we've had the chance to catch up. I'll be staying overnight anyway so I'll come over and see you later. Perhaps we can have a drink outside on the patio. I hope you remember you like whisky?"

The thought of another drink made him feel sick still but he'd do it if it meant it helped Jomo.

Jomo chuckled. "I do indeed. I'm not sure the doctors will approve of me having a drink even though I would love one." His voice was filled with longing.

Quinn grinned. "Don't worry. I'll convince them to let you have one. They owe me one. I'll see you later, my friend."

Jomo's eyes crinkled at the familiar address. "Now that I do remember." He said softly. "I like it."

Quinn put a hand on his shoulder and squeezed it. "Perhaps there's hope for you yet. "

He left the room to discuss Jomo's case with the resident doctor, who specialised in the arts of magyckal enchantment and Warlock wizardry. And it was as he'd thought: the memory loss was deep.

He sat outside in the late-afternoon August sunshine, watching the seagulls over the ocean, enjoying the light sea breeze on his face. Finally he rose and stretched, yawning. He needed to get some sleep before tonight. His head throbbed and his eyes were gritty and sore.

Quinn made his way to one of the large empty dormitory rooms set aside for visitors and saw with thankfulness that a bed had already been made up for him. He took off his shoes and lay down on the single bed, closing his eyes in relief. Some shut eye, perhaps a forbidden drink later with Jomo then some more sleep. Tomorrow he'd see what else could be done to help Jomo recover and then he could go home. Home to Cade.

***

Cade sat in his favourite spot on the deck of his houseboat, Marco Polo purring softly on his lap. He looked out over the water, up the canal at the other boats bobbing on the water. He'd been swimming all morning, sweeping through the water with long, aggressive strokes. The memories of last night's sex with Quinn remained with him and he'd smiled as he swum, remembering the intensity and passion.

Quinn had been pretty possessive and Cade had enjoyed the cool water of the lake easing his aching, pummelled arse. He was looking forward to more of the same, only this time, perhaps at a slower pace. He turned as a voice hailed him from the bank.

"Hey, sir! Is this yours?" A young boy stood there, waving a red tee shirt that seemed vaguely familiar.

Cade frowned. "Yes, that's mine. Where did you find it?"

He stood up to go fetch it, pushing Marco off his lap. The large form of Magnus regarded the young man intently as the large Warlock sat up from the bench on the sidewalk where he'd been reading his paper.

The boy moved forward with a grin. "It was wrapped around a bush over there. I thought it might have flown off your wash line." He gestured towards the makeshift clothesline Cade had set up at the back of his boat for various swimming towels and bathing costumes that he laid out there to dry.

Cade smiled as he stepped off the boat onto the bank to meet the youngster who was about twelve, round faced and cherubic, his blue eyes wide, with a fairly nice and polite grin.

He held out the shirt. "Here you go. I'm glad you didn't lose it. It's neat. It has the FCUK logo on it."

Cade smiled at him as he took it. "Thanks. It's one of my favourites. What's your name? Do you live around here?"

The boy shook his head. "I'm just down here visiting family. My name's Steve."

Cade held out his hand. "Nice to meet you, Steve."

The boy smiled. "I need to get on. My aunt's expecting me for dinner. Nice to meet you too." Steve turned around and continued whistling down the bank. Magnus stepped back, seemingly happier and Cade sighed.

Honestly, he knew there was some danger out there but a boy? Please.

He was still fed up that Quinn thought he needed protection like some swooning heroine from a romantic novel. Cade knew he could look after himself. Years of school fighting off bullies, being on archaeological digs while he did his studies and meeting some rather crazy characters and having an ex that was a martial arts expert had given him a few skills in self-preservation. He took the tee shirt inside, intending to pack it away. As he walked onto the deck he felt a slight dizziness.

Wow. Too much sun I think. I need to drink more water.

Cade draped the shirt on the bed and went to the kitchen to get a glass of water, his head growing lighter with each step. He held onto the sink with one hand as he splashed water on his face. There was a strange buzzing in his ears and his vision grew blurry. He looked out of the window at Magnus who was still reading his newspaper on the bench. Cade banged on the window glass, trying to attract his attention. Through eyes misting with darkness, he vaguely saw him look up, his face darkening as he saw Cade. He uncoiled his large frame from the bench and moved toward the boat. Cade was now hanging onto the sink with both hands, feeling as if he needed to be sick, his head spinning, his body trembling violently.

Magnus rushed inside with a look of concern. "Cade. You are very pale. Are you not feeling well?"

Cade shook his head then wished he hadn't as the boat spun again and everything went dim. "I'm not feeling well at all, Magnus. I think I'm going to pass out."

The room went black.

***

Magnus's heart stopped as he caught Cade before he hit the deck. "Fuck, what's wrong with you?" He laid the other man down on the floor, patting his cheek none too gently. "Cade? Can you hear me?" There was no response. Magnus cursed violently and pulled out his mobile to dial a number.

"Operator. May I help you?"

"I have a man here who has passed out and I can't get him to wake up. He said he was feeling ill and then just collapsed. Can you send an ambulance to this location? It's a houseboat called Lucky Devil on the Little Venice canal. Near the tow path."

"On its way to you now, sir. There is one nearby. Should be there in about two minutes."

"Thank you." Magnus put his phone down on the table and tried to rouse Cade again. His breathing was shallow, his face pale. Magnus waited in agonised impatience for the ambulance to arrive, hearing the siren long before it arrived. He went onto the bank, waving at the vehicle as it parked above on the road. Two paramedics got out and hurried down the embankment toward the boat.

Magnus waved them inside. "He's in there. He fainted and I can't get him to wake up."

The female paramedic looked at him with some trepidation. "Fine, sir, we'll manage this. It's a small area to work in so I'd appreciate it if you stay out here." She smiled at him. "You're not exactly a small man and we need the space."

Magnus nodded and paced the deck impatiently as they worked on Cade inside.

After five minutes the female paramedic came out, her face grave. "I can't be sure but it looks like he's had a minor stroke. We need to get him to the hospital straight away. My colleague and I will go with him. Would you like to follow? Do you have a car?"

Magnus nodded. "I have a motorbike up there. Which hospital are you taking him to?"

"A and E at St. Mary's. You can meet us there. We'll get the young man on the stretcher then see you there."

Magnus nodded. He waited until the two paramedics had Cade on the gurney and wheeled up the ramp to their ambulance. He closed and locked the door to the houseboat and disappeared to the roadside to fetch his bike.

Fifteen minutes later he was at the A and E Department at St. Mary's looking for the two paramedics and Cade. He'd already asked at the desk and the young lady had said no ambulance had arrived yet with a patient of that name. The man paced the waiting area impatiently, attracting worried glances from hospital staff and patients alike, as he muttered to himself fiercely. Finally he lost all patience and went over to the receptionist again who looked at him warily.

"Still nothing? Can you at least get hold of them and find out where they are?"

The receptionist sighed. "Tell me the pick-up point and I'll check the computer and see if I can get hold of anyone for you."

Magnus gave the address and approximate time of the paramedic arrival.

The receptionist looked at her screen and frowned. "I'm afraid the notes say that the ambulance was despatched as requested but when they got the address there was no one there. They put it down to a prank call and went on another call."

Magnus's blood ran cold. "An ambulance arrived there with two paramedics. I was there. I saw them."

The woman sighed. "I'm sorry, sir. I don't know what to say. The ambulance that was despatched when the 999 call came in was not the one that picked your friend up. There's no record of that anywhere, not even from another district. Perhaps it was a private one?"

She looked at Magnus enquiringly and he closed his eyes in despair. He'd been played. Someone had taken Cade from right under his nose. It was the only explanation.

He reached into his pocket with trembling fingers and pulled out his mobile, ignoring the receptionist's frown as he did so. Slowly he moved toward the entrance of the hospital to make his call and tell Quinn that the man Magnus had been guarding with his life had disappeared.

Chapter 22

Quinn was sitting on the patio with Jomo when the call from Magnus came in. He listened to the other Warlock's words, his face growing paler until he clicked off his mobile and covered his face with his hands.

Jomo watched him in concern. "What is it, what has happened?"

"Just some bad news from home, old friend. I need to get back there straight away. Someone I know is in trouble and I need to find him." Quinn stood up, his legs unsupportive. A dread coursed through his body he'd only ever felt once before.

Taliesin stirred inside him, sensing his distress.

Quinn? Something is wrong. Tell me.

Quinn ignored the Withinner and laid a hand on Jomo's shoulder. "I'm glad to see you're recovering. I'll come back and see you soon. Stay well."

He disappeared up the coastal path, heading for the top of the hill, out of sight of Jomo. Quinn needed to invoke Taliesin so he could get back home. He'd fetch his car later.

Quinn. What is the bad news?

"Someone's taken Cade; he's gone." Quinn heard the despair in his own voice.

He reached the top of the hill and stood in a copse of trees on the hill line, his face drawn but his voice fierce. "Taliesin, this time you'd better do exactly what I say. I need to find Cade. I need you to get me back and then I need you to disappear when I ask you so

I can form a plan to find him. Whatever our differences, this is more important. He's in real danger. Are we clear on this?"

His Withinner acquiesced and Quinn used his phrase to bring his Withinner forth. Within seconds Taliesin was standing in Quinn's place and within a further few seconds he too had disappeared. A minute later Quinn opened his eyes, finding himself back in the hallway at his home. He felt ill, never having gotten used to the time travel, and on top of the hangover he wanted to hurl. But he had no time for that now. The tall form of Magnus stood outside his front door. He unlocked it, letting the man in, watching as Magnus turned to him with haunted eyes and pale face.

"Mr. Quinn, I failed you. I let them take him. I am so sorry,"

Quinn laid a firm hand on his shoulder. "Magnus, it's okay. They were just cleverer than us. It happens. You saw a human twelve-year-old boy with a shirt in his hand. Nothing sinister about that. Did you bring it?"

Magnus nodded and drew the shirt from his pocket.

Quinn held it to his nose, grimacing at the smell. "It's soaked with natron. It's a salt that was used in the Egyptian time to dehydrate the bodies for mummification. With Cade being Sprite, it would have worked against him and dehydrated his body so rapidly he would have passed out like he did." He looked at Magnus. "There was no way anyone could have seen this coming. It's a natural mineral, not magyckal, so you wouldn't have been able to sense anything. It's Cade's reaction to it that was important. Although someone knew what it would do. Someone with a fairly advanced knowledge of alchemy."

Mary Hawthorne sprang to mind, but he dismissed that idea.
She'd helped them so far; surely she couldn't be involved.

"The question is now how do I find him. If he's been taken by anyone magyckal, they'll have made sure they cover their tracks.

Do you remember anything about the two paramedics that will be useful?"

Magnus shook his head. "They were both human. I only saw the woman. Dark hair, green eyes, quite plump, short." He shrugged helplessly. "There was nothing special about her that I can recall."

Quinn paced up and down frantically. "I haven't even been able to sense Cade. I've tried everything to try and get a bead on where he is. It's useless. Someone very powerful is protecting themselves and I'm damned if I know who it is. Even using Taliesin or any other Withinner to go back to that time, all we'll see is what you saw anyway. We won't be able to see anything else. We have no idea where they went."

He sounded desperate and Magnus hung his head in shame.

Quinn. You need to listen to me.

Quinn scowled. "Shut up, Taliesin. I'm not ready to listen to you yet, you bastard."

Magnus gazed at him in curiosity.

Quinn flushed. "We're having a bit of an altercation. He's persona non grata at the moment."

Magnus looked even more confused. He'd obviously never heard of a human Warlock rejecting his Withinner before.

Quinn, I can help. You need to let me do so. We can find Cade together.

Taliesin's voice was urgent. Quinn was unprepared for his pleading tone.

"Jesus, fine then. What do you have in mind?"

There was a slight silence then Taliesin spoke, fairly guiltily, Quinn thought.

I still have Cade's blood in my nails and his scent on me. My magyck is more powerful than yours. You know this. But if we combine both of our powers and emotions together using his blood as a lure we might be able to find him. We need to perform Unity.

Quinn's fury at his Withinner's first words about Cade's blood, drawn during their fuck session, rose to the fore. The Withinner obviously hadn't cleaned himself up yet, probably still revelling in the smell and the feel of Cade on him. Whilst Quinn found this distasteful, he acknowledged that it might help. *But Unity?*

"A Warlock hasn't performed Unity since that poor man Ethelred combined with his Withinner and both died screaming in agony," Quinn muttered. "You know that process is fairly unknown and very dangerous."

Quinn saw the apprehension on Magnus's face at his words as the other man shook his head violently.

"Mr. Quinn, that could be suicide. As powerful as you and Taliesin are together. That act hasn't been performed in decades to my knowledge."

"I know that," Quinn said testily. "I'm trying to convince Taliesin of that too."

It's the only way we will find him. You may track him down eventually but by then it will be too late. They mean to hurt you. Imagine what they are doing to him right now.

Quinn closed his eyes in dread at the thought. He knew Taliesin was right.

We are Quinn and Taliesin. You are a Fairmont, descended from one of the most powerful Warlock families in history and I am one of the most powerful sorcerers that ever lived. We can do this, Quinn. We have to. For Cade's sake.

Quinn's pulse quickened and his blood rushed faster through his veins. He didn't seem to have a choice.

"How do we do it?" he asked his Withinner, ignoring Magnus's gasp of horror.

Leave it to me. You need to use all your power to focus on me inside. Concentrate on me, my voice, and my feelings. Anything to bring you closer to me. Hate me if you must. Think of me with Cade yesterday. Think of me enjoying your man, feeling me inside him, his mouth on mine, his fingernails raking my back as he moans in pleasure beneath me. Yes, that's it, Quinn.

Taliesin chuckled in satisfaction as Quinn's powerful and angry emotions surged through his body. *It will be very painful, make no doubt. You may scream in agony before this is finished. Then we will be as one in my guise for we physically need what I have. Then we can combine our strengths as one. Cade's blood and his fluids will be our guide to finding him. They didn't anticipate this.*

Pressure built in Quinn's body, as if something inside was growing then trying to come out. He wondered vaguely through the pain if this was what the guy in *Alien* had felt like when the alien body had finally burst out of his body in a spew of blood and guts. Not only was the physical pain almost too much to bear, the psychic energy was excruciating. Taliesin's memories and feelings, tastes and sights all flooded his body like a tidal wave onto the shore, picking up anything in its path and sweeping it towards his mind in an inexorable passage towards his consciousness. He was not aware he was screaming, his body writhing on the floor as Magnus watched in both helplessness and fear. The pressure reached a crescendo and he fell into a pit of blackness.

He vaguely heard Magnus's worried voice in his ear as he slowly came to, his mouth filled with the metallic taste of blood where he'd bitten his tongue.

"Mr. Quinn? Are you able to wake up? "

Magnus's voice seemed to echo through his mind, almost too loud to bear. Quinn slowly opened his eyes, as the room spun around him.

Magnus helped him to his feet. "Christ, I hope that wasn't as horrible to bear as it was to watch. But from the sounds you made, I'd guess it was." He peered at Quinn carefully. "Are you still in there, Mr. Quinn?"

Quinn shook his head to clear the cobwebs. He felt Taliesin more than ever before and his Withinner's thoughts and feelings swirled around his head invasively. He swallowed.

"Yes. I'm here."

Even his voice sounded deeper and he saw Magnus's look of awe as he stood up. Quinn looked down at his hands, now covered in dark hair with the tinge of red blood beneath his fingernails. He looked in the hall mirror, seeing Taliesin in his usual garb looking back at him, his eyes dark and his face set.

Use the blood beneath my nails and the essence of your man. Concentrate on them, as we do this together. Smell him, feel him and taste him. Take his blood in your mouth, Quinn. Suck it. Concentrate.

Quinn took a deep breath and put his fingers in his mouth. He tasted Cade's blood in his mouth, smelled him and tasted his semen on Taliesin's fingers. He felt dizzy at the sensations it was causing.

The Warlock and the Withinner concentrated their powers on trying to sense the man they sought, seeing vivid pictures in their mind's eye as they went on a veritable Google Street View journey of sights, trying to hone in on where to find him. Quinn's head was pounding, his heart beating faster that he'd ever heard it do before.

I feel him. Taliesin's voice was triumphant. *He's not far from where we are now in our minds. See if you recognise it. Find a sign, anything that will tell us where he is.*

In his mind, Quinn saw a huge mansion set back from a country road, surrounded by trees with a small, winding country lane in its front. The driveway was curved around a large, ornate fountain, gushing water from what looked like a fish's mouth, and there was a grey Jeep pickup parked on the gravel of the driveway, together with a longer, sportier car, possibly a Maserati.

Quinn honed in on the number plate of the sports car. GB77ADV.

He filed it away for future reference, thinking something seemed familiar about it. There was a sign on the giant wooden door of the house, under the portcullis.

YEW TREE HOUSE 7 Glengorne Road

He's here, his Withinner gloated. *I feel him.*

Cade was nearby—Quinn felt it too. His lover was in a lot of pain and Quinn's blood grew hot with fury at whoever was causing it. The vision slowly cleared and Quinn stood, gasping with the effort it had taken. Magnus laid a hand on his arm.

"Mr. Quinn? Did you find him?"

He smiled tiredly. "Yes, I think we did." He walked over to the corner table in the entrance and took out a notepad, scribbling something on it and handing it to Magnus.

"Give this to Percy. Ask him to find out who the car belongs to and where this address is, immediately. Then I need to get down there, with some of you to bring him back. Tell Percy to make it quick."

He sank down onto the floor, his back against the stairs as he sat there, eyes closed.

We did it, we found your man. Does this make amends for what I did?

Quinn's Withinner sounded almost vulnerable as he asked the question. Quinn shook his head.

"I'm not ready to forgive you yet," he muttered quietly. "But I am man enough to say thank you for what you just did for Cade. I know it can't have been easy for you either."

He grimaced, feeling a sharp pain in his temple. He watched absently as a drop of blood plopped from his nose and landed on his shirtfront. He raised a hand to his face where it came away wet with blood. Taliesin's worried voice echoed in his head.

We need to separate. My form is proving too much for your human one to handle. The Unity was never meant to last this long or be this intense.

Quinn shook his head, wiping the blood away from his nose as it continued to drip.

"No, I need to stay this way a little longer. If we're going to defeat the bastard who has Cade, together in this form is the most powerful way to do it. I'll be fine."

He drew a sharp breath as the pain in his head grew in intensity. He tasted the metallic tang of blood in his mouth as it slithered down his throat, almost choking him.

You could die. We need to separate. Now. Before it's too late.

Quinn grinned savagely. "Your concern is touching, or is it your own neck you're trying to save? You don't want to change Warlocks because you think you have this one all figured out? I'm telling you I can manage. I need to get Cade back first."

He stood up unsteadily and made his way to the bathroom, where he held a wad of tissue to his nose. The blood soaked the tissue and he was already feeling weak. He put a wet washcloth against the bridge of his nose, holding his head back and waiting for the flow to stop.

Magnus appeared suddenly at the door. "Percy has the location. It's a house in Lambourn in Berkshire. The car is registered to an Evan Makepeace. He's still trying to find out a little about him but it's proving difficult. He seems to have covered his tracks. Percy has a team ready to meet us there to fetch Cade."

His eyes were full of worry as he looked at his Grand Master, noting his pale complexion and the bright red blood still running freely down his chin.

Quinn nodded. "Tell him to get down there and I'll meet him. We can form a plan of attack once we know exactly what we're up against. The advantage we have is that they don't know we're coming. Tell everyone to mask themselves and be as unobtrusive as possible. No one does anything until I get there."

Magnus nodded and vanished once again. Quinn put down the blood-sodden washcloth and regarded his face in the mirror. Taliesin's visage stared out at him, paler, with dried blood dotted across the bottom of his face and dark, sunken eyes. He smiled at his reflection, thinking it looked more like a snarl from a rabid dog, with his teeth stained with blood.

"Time to go, old son. I'm not sure how this all works now with us being united, but do your stuff and get me down there. We have a few arses to kick and at least this way, you get your wish and you can help."

Fine, Quinn. But you can't last much longer in this form. We need to make this quick.

"Just get me there. As you said earlier, I'm a Fairmont. I should be able to do this standing on my head."

He coughed as the blood still trickled down his throat.

"Ready when you are, Taliesin."

Chapter 23

Cade awoke to someone slapping his face none too lightly. He gasped as cold liquid doused his supine form, once then twice. Ice-cold water trickled over his face, into his mouth and drenched his body, leaving him shivering in the cold of the room he was in. He raised his head, unable to focus, from both waking up and the water in his eyes.

"Mr. Mairston. So good of you to join us." The words were jovial, the tone less so and Cade blinked his eyes towards the sound, trying to see who it was.

"I'm sorry I couldn't have made the water warmer before we rehydrated you, but unfortunately that would take too much effort and I'm really not inclined to bother. You Sprites are used to cold water anyway so it shouldn't be too much of a hardship." The voice was male and not particularly caring or friendly.

"Who are you and where the hell am I?" Cade tried to sit up but found himself bound to a long, high-backed chair, his ankles tied to the legs and his wrists secured to the armrests with what looked cable ties.

The voice chuckled. "Who I am doesn't matter yet to you and probably never will. That'll come later when I tell Quinn. Where are you? At one of my homes. Private, secluded, near the Downs and most importantly, no one knows about it. It's taken me a while to cover my tracks but I think I did it admirably."

The voice hardened. "You made the wrong connections, I'm afraid. Lucky for me, because now I have the means to send Quinn

Fairmont a message. One that he won't like, alas, but one can't always deliver promising news, can one?"

Cade could focus now. Through slightly blurry vision he saw a man standing in front of the chair he was bound to. He looked to be in his fifties, tall, about the same height as Quinn, with a powerful upper body, broad shoulders like an American linebacker in full uniform and pitch-black hair. His face looked strangely lopsided. He was very handsome despite the strange condition of his face. Cade swallowed, his throat dry and scratchy. "Why am I tied up? What do you want with me? If Quinn finds you, there'll be hell to pay—"

The man moved toward him swiftly, his arm striking out quickly, hitting Cade solidly on the left side of his mouth, causing his head to rock and his consciousness to buzz with the force of the blow. Cade's lip was already starting to swell and he tasted blood in his mouth.

"Sorry about that," the voice said softly. "I get a little enraged when I hear that man's name, especially coming out of a mouth as inviting as yours. I can appreciate an asset when I see it."

Cade saw his face coming toward him and his captor licked Cade's swollen lip lingeringly, clearing the blood from his mouth and then running his tongue over his own lips.

"You taste very good." His voice was soft and seductive, and Cade's blood chilled.

"Why am I here?" he muttered, a sense of dread permeating his body.

"You're my message, Cade. The one I want to send to that man you've been fucking. The one who thinks he's God's gift to the Warlock world simply because of whom he is and who his Withinner is. The man who tried to kill me and failed. The man who killed the one I loved above anything else. It's taken me a long time to claw myself back up out of the abyss and now it's my turn to cause him some grief and anguish." The voice turned amused.

"Unfortunately though, it ultimately becomes more your anguish. I can't deny your passing will be painful, as I really need him to know what fun I had with you before you finally die, but then, getting involved with a Warlock was always going to be a relationship risk, wasn't it?"

Cade swallowed at these words, fear creeping through his body like a cat slinking into the shadows. "You can kill me, but Quinn will come after you. He won't let it rest."

The voice laughed. "That's what I'm hoping for, my dear. I want him to come to me eventually, at a place I choose and when I choose. I love the hunt. It's about time we had another showdown, this time one that I will win."

He sighed as he moved behind Cade. "This is all getting rather boring. As much as I like conversation, discussions with the proverbial lamb to the slaughter aren't going to bring me any real satisfaction. But this will."

He laid his hand on the back of Cade's head. Agony built inside Cade's brain as if he had a hot iron impaling his skull. He smelt scorched hair and cried out in pain. The man stopped what he was doing, leaving Cade retching.

His torturer tut-tutted in amusement. "I find I have quite a talent for this type of thing. Not only that, I kind of enjoy it. That young boy you spoke to at your boat had no idea he was helping me get you here when I asked him to pretend he'd found your shirt. He was a pretty good actor, I have to say. He certainly earned his twenty-pound fee."

The man behind Cade savagely ripped his shirt open at the back, exposing his neck and shoulders. Something cold touched his skin as the stranger slowly and tenderly dragged the point of the steel blade down Cade's shoulder and spine. Goose bumps formed on his skin. The man leaned in and kissed them. "I've never tasted Sprite before," he murmured. "You have a very specific taste, like citrus fruit. It's quite pleasant." His voice grew savage. "I suppose Quinn has tasted more of you than he knows what to do with. The one I loved also had a wonderful taste. Like smoke and vanilla. I imagine Quinn missed that when *he* tasted him. He wouldn't have had the appreciation I did. This might hurt a bit. Sorry."

Cade screamed as the knife cut deeply into his skin, a long incision from the base of his neck, down the left side of his spine, almost to his waist. He retched again at the agony, coughing up bile in his mouth, gasping at the pain. He smelt blood, the coppery scent of it assaulting his nostrils. His head swam and he wondered dimly if he should pass out and leave the man to it. But his innate stubbornness wanted to try and fight this torture.

His captor walked around in front of him, the knife still dripping with his blood. He raised it slowly to Cade's mouth, wiping it across his lips. Cade gagged at the strong taste of his own fluids.

He watched from pain and hate-filled eyes as the handsome man slowly licked the blood off the blade, seeming to savour the taste.

"You bastard!" Cade whispered huskily, the pain in his back incredibly fierce. "You really are very brave, aren't you, hurting a man bound to a chair with no way to defend himself. That must make your mother very fucking proud." Cade knew it was foolish taunting someone who was obviously a psychopath but he was resigned to the fact that he was probably going to die here anyway. From the looks of it, slowly and painfully. He might as well get a word in while he still could.

The other man chuckled as he moved around in front of him. "Well, you do have courage; I'll say that for you. Quinn certainly knows how to pick them. For all the good it will do you."

The knife came toward Cade once again and he flinched, but the man only cut the remains of his torn shirt. The fabric was plucked from his body and thrown carelessly to one side.

He whistled quietly. "Will you look at that? You have a magnificent chest." His voice grew hard and vicious. "It's a pity I have to ruin it."

Cade closed his eyes as once again the knife did its work, this time cutting from his left shoulder down across his chest to the right, ending just above the right nipple. Again the pain was excruciating and he couldn't help letting out a sharp, piercing cry, his mind growing faint. The warm scent of blood permeated his nostrils, making him feel sicker. His head fell onto his ruined chest, eyes closing in despair as he saw what had been done to him, the deep, gaping wound leaking his life essence. Suddenly the other man spoke sharply, a tone of disbelief in his voice.

"He can't be here. How can he have found me? I was so careful. He shouldn't be able to breach my defences. That bastard and his Withinner are more powerful than I thought."

The voice sounded confused and Cade wanted to laugh, tell him that Quinn had come for him, that he was never going to get to kill him now. But he had no strength to form words. Cade heard a lot of noise from somewhere above him and heard the man swearing violently.

"That bastard has tracked me down. Someone must have told him. Have I been betrayed? Was it that witch or that stupid Witchhunter boy? I need to leave. I must get back to *Sept Rois*."

Through a pain-filled haze Cade's head was pulled back savagely. The man sounded panicked but the tone of malevolence was hard to miss.

"Sorry, son, it looks like I'll simply have to kill you quickly instead. This will only take a moment unfortunately. "

Cade saw the sharp dagger bearing down toward his throat. He closed his eyes tightly, not wanting to see his captor cut it as Cade waited for the inevitable. A sense of regret and loss flooded his body.

Sorry, Quinn. I'm so sorry I let myself be taken. I love you.

There was a sudden bright flash and a slamming sound. The figure in front of him was wrenched away from him violently as a familiar voice cursed with fury and grief.

Cade closed his eyes again, thankful that the knife had not done its dirty work even as he wondered what the hell Taliesin was doing here and why the Withinner was holding him, calling him endearments he would have never have expected to hear from him. Then his world went dark.

Quinn stood at Cade's side, his face soaked in blood, both from his nosebleeds and from the deep gash on his cheek where the knife of the man tormenting Cade had lashed out. The Warlock himself had vanished as Quinn had wrenched him away from Cade, his knife making one more bloody sacrifice on Quinn's cheek. Quinn hadn't managed to see the man too clearly. His vision was distorted from the constant migraine-like pain in his head. The other Warlock had invoked his own Withinner, a small, dark and compact man who'd vanished within seconds. He seemed familiar to Quinn but he'd no time to think about that now. The sight of Cade sitting slumped in the chair, his chest running crimson with blood and his face as pale as dry clay, made his heart stop.

Quinn growled in anger and moved swiftly to his lover's side, standing over him, murmuring his name and stroking his cheek, hoping he could hear him.

"Cade? Hold on, my love, I'm going to get you free and then we'll sort out those wounds. Just hold on. It'll be okay." His voice choked and hot tears threatened to spill from gritty eyes.

Quinn touched the bonds holding Cade's wrists and the clips fell to the ground as if they were dust. He did the same to his ankles, then, despite his own weakening body, he picked Cade tenderly up in his arms, taking him over to a large table in the corner. Quinn laid his boyfriend's still body gently down on the table, murmuring to him, his chest heavy with dread as he saw both cuts still freely welling blood. "We have to heal him, Taliesin. Help me."

Cade's breathing was shallow, his face white. His eyelids were almost translucent and Quinn knew he had to work fast. He spoke though gritted teeth as the pain in his head grew fiercer. He'd been fighting it since the battle had started above ground in the house. The other Warlock's magyckal defences had been easily breached with him and Taliesin being unified and they'd managed to overcome the few people up there. They hadn't been expecting a full-on Warlock assault. When they'd made their way down to this basement, the pressure in Quinn's head had grown stronger. His vision was blurred, his jaw clenched against the pain he felt.

Quinn, we have to separate. We can heal him that way too. You need to come out of me. You're no use to anyone dead, least of all Cade.

"But we can heal him better this way, can't we? Together like this it will be much quicker and cleaner for Cade. Help me, please. I can hold out a little longer." Quinn could hear the exasperated sigh of his Withinner.

You are the most stubborn human of all humans I have ever met. Soon to be a dead human if we don't act soon. Quickly. Say what you have to say and I will help. Make haste. I can only protect you so far. My power to keep you safe is weakening too.

Quinn ignored the constant stream of blood running freely from his nose and closed his eyes as he muttered an incantation over Cade's wounds, holding his hands above them. It took a lot of energy to heal and he had very little left. But what he had he would give to Cade.

Slowly, joined with his Withinner's power, Quinn watched Cade's wounds start to knit together as the blood flow stopped and the skin pulled together. The agony in Quinn's head was intensifying, the jagged spurts of pain in his temple too much to bear. He wanted to be sick but held off as he chanted quietly. Finally he could do it no longer. His hands fell to his sides in exhaustion. His head was so filled with pain that he could no longer remember the words to anything. Taliesin exclaimed loudly.

Quinn! I am going to separate us. I have to do it now or you will die. This will hurt again, so be warned.

Quinn was beyond caring. His body was already so racked with pain that when he Taliesin began the action of separating them, the agony he felt was something he embraced with open arms, as it caused the darkness to claim him into its blackness as it whispered insidiously into his ear.

Chapter 24

Cade awoke to the sounds of Ravel's "Bolero" filtering softly through the air. The haunting strains of the music soothed him. For a moment he lay there in the bed, not remembering the events of the past day, until he moved and felt a twinge of discomfort in his back that made him hiss in pain and all the memories come flooding back.

He tried to sit up, but it hurt too much and he settled back against the pillow. As he did a woman walked in and smiled as she saw Cade awake.

"Mr. Mairston. You're looking a lot better. How are you feeling?"

Cade looked at her woozily. "Where am I?"

"You're in one of the magyck clinical Lodges we run. This one is in Dorset, one of the more advanced ones. We have great facilities here, and it's top of the range in healing magyck. I understand a friend of yours is here too—Jomo Onyango. Perhaps when you're up you can share a moment with him. Of course, he simply believes this is a normal hospital, so please don't say anything to him about the magyck part of it. That's our little secret." She grinned.

"Who are you? Is Quinn here too?"

The woman's smile faltered a little. "My name is Ursula. I'm a nurse. One of the doctors will be in to see you soon and explain everything to you. Until then, just stay quiet and try not to overdo anything. Your back is still a little bit of a mess, I'm afraid."

She bustled out and Cade realised his question about Quinn hadn't been answered. He struggled to sit up, wincing at the tight feeling in his back. Finally he was upright, his legs out of the bed as he sat on the side, frowning at the hospital garb he wore.

"God, how stereotypical is this thing," he muttered. "Shapeless, dull, and my backside hanging out for all to see."

"I see you're feeling better, Cade." The soft voice behind him made him turn and stare at the man. He was a short, stocky and round with a bald head and a gentle voice.

"Do I know you?" Cade's eyes narrowed suspiciously.

"My name is Percy Ballantyne. I'm Quinn's Marshall. He may have spoken of me. I certainly know all about you from him." He smiled.

Cade nodded. "You were the one who called him about the Warlock killings. I'm glad to meet you at last, Mr. Ballantyne. Perhaps you can tell me where Quinn is? The nurse that was here seemed to avoid answering the question."

Percy moved over to Cade, sitting down beside him on the bed, his face grave.

"Firstly call me Percy, please. And Quinn is here in the clinic. He's not in very good shape, I'm afraid. We're trying to heal him but it's taking some time."

Cade's heart lurched inside. "What's wrong with him? I saw Taliesin at the place they took me to, but I didn't see Quinn. Can I see him?"

Percy leaned over and patted his shoulder uncomfortably. "It's a little complicated. Quinn is in a coma."

Cade drew a horrified breath and clasped Percy's hand tightly. "A coma? How did that happen?"

"In order to find you, Quinn and Taliesin had to perform some rather unusual magyck called a Unity. It basically involves combining the two of them to make them stronger. It's a very rare incantation and one that normally isn't performed because of the danger to the human Warlock. You did see Taliesin's body but it was Quinn controlling him inside. It's a long story and one I'm sure Quinn will tell you when he's awake."

Percy's voice was wary. "But the Unity lasted many hours longer than it was ever meant to do. It meant Quinn's mind and body sustained some damage in the process. Taliesin managed to keep him alive long enough to get him back here but he was extremely damaged when he arrived. It's taking all our combined powers to heal him."

Cade stared at Percy. "I want to see him, Percy. Please."

Percy nodded. "Let me get you a wheelchair." He raised an admonishing finger at Cade's protestation. "Cade, you were badly injured yourself. Quinn managed to heal most of your injuries, specifically the one to your chest, but he ran out of energy and your back is still fairly raw. We've done what we can, given the damage, and it will heal. It'll just take a little while. The knife the Warlock used was enchanted and was specially engineered to leave lasting damage. So we want to try and keep you as comfortable as possible while it heals. That means not putting too much strain on it. So—the wheelchair, yes?"

Cade nodded. Percy raised a hand and a young nurse pushed in a wheelchair. Percy helped Cade into it and then took the handles and manoeuvred it out of the room. Cade saw the ocean out of the windows, steel blue yet inviting. He had an urge to swim and never stop.

"There's a large freshwater pool at the back," Percy said, as if reading his thoughts. "In a day's time or so you can swim to your heart's content. It will probably do you a lot of good."

"Tell me exactly how bad Quinn is," Cade asked Percy softly. "No lies, please. I want to know the truth."

Percy's face darkened and he took a deep breath. "The only thing keeping Quinn alive when he reached here was Taliesin. Quinn himself was virtually dead."

Cade closed his eyes and swallowed, his entire body cold and shivery. The ache in his chest was indescribable.

"Taliesin performed the separation but the shock stopped Quinn's heart," Percy said quietly. "Quinn had already done more than humanly possible anyway; I have no idea how he managed to hold out as long as he did. Taliesin got him back here with a faint spark of life and we immediately started the process of trying to get him back." Percy sighed heavily. "We managed to get his heart restarted and heal some of his internal injuries but it's the brain we're worried about. He sustained massive bleeding in there due to the psychic pressures, plus he lost a lot of blood. We won't know what will happen until he wakes up." He smiled sadly.

Cade heard the unspoken concern. *If he wakes up.*

Percy laid a hand on his undamaged shoulder. "Obviously Taliesin and all the other Warlocks and Withinners are doing what they can. He's on a sort of a magyckal life support system."

They'd reached a room now and Percy opened the door and pushed Cade inside. Quinn lay there, his face white and his closed eyes sunken in his gaunt face. The golden shine that normally radiated from his man was gone, in its place a listless paleness that coated Cade with pain and sadness.

Cade couldn't help himself. He stepped out of the chair, despite Percy's exclamations and moved swiftly over to the bed. Percy clucked in annoyance behind him but Cade didn't care. He needed Quinn. He sat down carefully on the side of the bed and leaned down to kiss Quinn's cold lips, whispering slowly as warm tears welled in his eyes.

"Quinn? Sweetheart, it's Cade. You saved me. So you come back from wherever you are, you stubborn bastard, so you can be with me. Don't make me come in there and get you, because you know I will."

Cade held Quinn's freezing hands and stroked his forehead as he whispered to him. Percy stood then turned, leaving the two of them alone.

***

It was early morning. Cade slept, hands stretched protectively over Quinn.

It had been almost four days since he'd first seen him unconscious and so colourless he'd been terrified. In that time he'd hardly left his side. Impatient for him to wake up, Cade had played music, read to him, threatened him and tried to kiss him awake but still he slept on. Cade took solace in the fact Quinn's breathing was steady, and his face, while still pale, seemed a better colour.

Cade yawned, sitting up and stretching, looking out of the window at the sea beyond. He turned to look down at Quinn and gasped at seeing his eyes open and staring up at him. They were blank, scarcely any light in them and Cade took a deep breath, fearing the worst. Then Quinn blinked and his eyes grew more focused. The deep brown eyes he loved so much looked into his as he said huskily, "Cade?"

Cade smiled in relief, bending down to press his lips to his, feeling his warm, stale breath on his cheek. "Quinn. It's about time, you arsehole."

Quinn reached out a hand and Cade took it, kissing it gently as he lay back down beside him, waiting for him to speak.

Quinn squeezed his hand and tried to smile, weakly but a Quinn smile all the same. "I would have been here sooner but I missed the bus."

Cade stared at Quinn's beloved face with a lump in his throat. "God, it's so good to see you awake. I was so worried about you, everyone was. How are you feeling?"

Quinn closed his eyes in fatigue then opened them. "Tired, and like said bus ran me over. I ache everywhere." He gripped his hand fiercely. "How are you? When I saw what that bastard had done to you"—his voice broke off with anguish—"I thought I'd lost you. I tried to heal you but it just took so long and I couldn't do it anymore. I'm so sorry."

Cade leaned down, stroking his cheek. "You saved me. You and Taliesin. But you took too much on. It nearly cost you your life trying to save mine. I can never repay that."

Quinn reached up and caressed his cheek gently. "No repayment needed. I love you. It was an easy decision to make, believe me."

Cade leaned down and kissed him deeply, feeling his mouth move beneath his. "I love you too. With everything I have."

Quinn reached up and put a finger on his lips. "Taliesin was the one who actually found the way to track you down. Then he kept me alive all the way through and is still healing me." His voice shook. "Was Percy able to heal what I couldn't?"

Cade looked at him gently. "The one in front doesn't look that bad. There is a scar but I'll still be sexy enough in my Speedo." He grinned. "The one on my back, that's still a bit tender. It didn't heal as well, but I'm alive. I can live with a scar. But I couldn't live without you."

Cade reached out a hand, gently stroking his lover's forehead and Quinn closed his eyes. Within a minute he was asleep again but it didn't seem as deep, one more born of exhaustion.

Cade gently pulled the covers over Quinn and went in search of a well-deserved cup of coffee. Quinn awoke later that afternoon, his eyes once again opening and focusing on Cade, who sat by his side reading a book. Quinn's eyes watched him and Cade leaned in to kiss his cheek softly. "Hey there, sleepy head. Feeling better now?"

Quinn nodded, reaching for his hand. "I feel stronger. Taliesin has really been working his magyck. Not to mention you. I knew you were here, I sensed you." He grinned slightly. "I was being kissed to death so I thought I'd better get back so you can do the real thing with me awake instead. That's an invitation, by the way, as long as you don't mind afternoon breath."

Cade reached over and kissed him thoroughly, running his hands through Quinn's unruly and spiky bed hair. "I'm so glad you're back. I was so worried I was going to lose you."

Quinn caressed Cade's cheek. "I was worried myself too, don't worry. That Unity thing is not something I want to try again anytime soon." He closed his eyes, his face weary. "I can't remember everything." He looked at Cade with darkened eyes. "There are things I have trouble with. I thought I recognised the other Warlock's Withinner; it's just there on the edge of my memory, but not quite there. I have this feeling there's something I should know but I don't." His voice was frustrated. "I might have got you back but I'm no closer to knowing who the hell this is doing this."

"I saw him." Cade sat back.

Quinn's face became more animated. "God, I hadn't realised you'd seen him. That sounds very careless of him. Not like a Warlock of his calibre at all." Quinn struggled to sit and Cade propped more pillows under him so he was upright.

Cade nodded dryly. "He didn't plan on me living to tell anyone about him. He was very confident, very cocksure and I felt pure evil when he was close." He shivered. "He was a psychopath, that's for sure. And he really hates you. All he wanted was to make me suffer and then let you know how much pain he'd caused me."

Quinn's face darkened and his lips twitched. "Tell me what he looked like."

Cade thought back to his ordeal. "He was about your height, black hair, quite handsome. Much older though. There was something wrong with the right side of his face. It was stiff, as if he couldn't move it—" he stopped suddenly and grimaced as Quinn's hand tightened on his, his longer nails from his days in the hospital bed digging into Cade's skin. "Christ, that hurt! What is it?"

"The right side of his face? Are you sure?" Quinn's voice was expressionless. His face looked frozen, but his eyes betrayed the turmoil he was feeling, staring at Cade with despair.

Cade nodded. "Yes. It was as if he had a mask there, smooth skin that didn't move. Why, do you know who it is?"

Quinn's face paled and he slumped back against the pillows. "It can't be him," he muttered, passing a shaking hand across his eyes. "I killed him, I'm sure I did. He surely couldn't have survived."

"You know who this might be?" Cade took Quinn's hand in his again as he looked at him.

Quinn was quiet, then finally nodded. "It sounds like someone I thought was dead." He turned and looked out of the window at the sea outside. "Tell me everything else he said to you."

"He said you'd killed the person he loved more than anyone else." Quinn's hand tightened on his again and he winced and looked at him curiously. "He also seemed to think you and he had this person in common." He flushed slightly. "He said something about you tasting him and not appreciating what he tasted like. It was a little obscure. I wasn't sure what he meant."

Quinn's face tightened and the look of desolation in his eyes was more than Cade could bear. "Quinn, tell me who you think this is. And who was the man he was talking about?"

Quinn stared at Cade as if he wasn't there. For a moment Cade thought he'd gone somewhere, somewhere where he didn't have to answer the question. Finally his eyes refocused on Cade and he closed them, leaning back against his pillow with a deep and juddering sigh.

"The man who attacked you is named Andrew de Vere. He's someone I knew many years ago, someone who isn't a friend, to put it mildly." He laughed bitterly. "Andrew has coveted Taliesin ever since I can remember. One day he decided to try and take him away from me." He turned his head and gazed out of the window. "It didn't go so well for either of us. But I thought I'd killed him. Only it seems he's risen from the proverbial dead and come back to haunt me like—" he cut himself short. "I don't know how he survived."

"What happened to his face?" Cade asked quietly.

"Me. It was an energy surge that slowed him down but destroyed that side of his face. It was what helped me finish him off. At least, I thought I had."

"And who was the man he referred to? What part did he play in all this?"

Quinn's face twisted with pain. "The man was Adam. The one you saw me in the papers with. He turned out to be de Vere's spy." His voice was choked with emotion.

Cade knew then that Adam had meant a lot to him. His heart ached inside at both Quinn's pain and the fact that he'd cared so much about this man.

Quinn stared at him, his eyes blank. "Andrew knew Adam long before I did. He'd known him since he was a child. Adam was like a son to Andrew. He used Adam to get to know me so he could get someone inside my home, into my life. Andrew was besotted with Adam, but still used him, pushed him into another man's arms and bed. Andrew hoped he'd gain my trust so Andrew could get closer to me, to steal Taliesin. De Vere loved the game of always being one up on everyone and he enjoyed seeing me with Adam knowing what was really going on. It got him off."

Quinn closed his eyes. "The first part of his plan worked. I fell in love with Adam. We were together a year and I was planning on asking him to marry me. Little did I know he was knowingly working for de Vere all along." He took a deep breath again. "He's the one who gave me the scar on my hip. The night de Vere decided the game was over because now I had so much to lose, he came to take Taliesin. Adam was with me and I went to protect him from de Vere and instead Adam turned on me and slashed me with a bloody great dagger." His face was bleak. "It was an advantage for them I wasn't expecting. They nearly killed me and succeeded in taking Taliesin. De Vere had told Adam to slow me down so he could finish me off himself. He always was an arrogant bastard."

Cade's heart broke at the fact that a man could try protect the man he loved and instead ended up betrayed and nearly mortally wounded by him. "God, I'm so sorry," he whispered. "I can't even imagine how you felt."

Quinn nodded absently. "It threw me. I wasn't expecting it. Adam was a really good actor. I truly believed he loved me." He gave a twisted smile.

"How did you manage to get out of the situation?" Cade stroked his arm gently, his lover's muscles rigid beneath his fingers.

Quinn looked at him. "I killed Adam." His voice was grim. "I had no choice. I was weak from where he'd stabbed me, and he was still trying to finish me off as I lay bleeding. Taliesin was doing his best to help, but in the end, the only thing I could do was destroy Adam to gain the advantage *I* needed over Andrew. To survive. But Adam was human. Enchanted but still human. De

Vere tended to forget that sometimes and thought Adam was inviolate under his protection. To some extent he was, but I was more powerful than Andrew. He forgot that too."

His face was grim. "I summonsed whatever energy I had and directed it at Adam. He stood no chance. He knew I loved him and he thought I wouldn't be able to hurt him. I proved him wrong." Quinn sighed. "Adam was de Vere's Achilles' heel. His death threw him long enough for me to do what I had to do. I saw de Vere die, I'm sure of it. I passed out. When I came to, I was in the Lodge, right here," He waved around him. "Percy told me de Vere's body had disappeared but that wasn't unusual. Sometimes as a Warlock dies, Withinners will transport them somewhere else. We've heard nothing more since that whole event until now. That was nine months ago."

He leaned back, exhausted at the telling of his story.

Cade reached forward and kissed his forehead softly. "You need to rest and get some sleep."

Quinn shook his head firmly. "No time for that. You need to call Percy in here. I need to speak to him urgently."

Cade looked at him in exasperation. "Surely this can wait?"

"I need Percy, now." Quinn's voice was pure steel. "I need to get out of this bed and we need to think about what you've just told me. It changes everything if this is Andrew."

Cade regarded him for a moment then shrugged. "I'll go find Percy for you. But don't overdo it. I know you're king of the Warlocks and all that but you still need to heal properly."

"As said king of the Warlocks, I have greater responsibilities beyond either you or me. De Vere means trouble for all of us. Now I know it's him, I imagine all the recent killings string together somehow. He's involved, I know it." Quinn smiled gently at Cade's expression. "This is bigger than both of us. But don't look so worried. I promise I'll be careful."

"Like last time?" Cade turned and looked at back at him as he left the room. "I know you were doing it for me but you nearly died. I couldn't face that again."

Cade left the room leaving Quinn staring into space. He found Percy standing looking out over the sea. He turned as Cade came up behind him.

"He's awake. He asked me to come and find you." Cade regarded him seriously. "Please try making him see he's not immortal. He thinks he is but he's not."

Percy chuckled softly. "You haven't known Quinn as long as I have. That man doesn't understand the meaning of 'you can't.' He's the most single minded and driven bastard I've ever met. Don't let that bookish exterior fool you. He didn't get to be Grand Master at the young age of twenty-one without having to prove himself to a lot of very powerful people. His father was the same, although he was twenty-four when he gained the title."

Cade scowled. "That may be. But he's still mine and I'm not averse to using a little emotional blackmail or physical force to get him to listen to me if I have to."

Percy grinned as he walked out of the room to see Quinn. "I have no doubt you're probably the one person who can get him to do something he may not want to do. That man worships you. I've never seen him this way before with any man, even Adam." He stopped, as if wondering if he'd said something he shouldn't.

Cade sighed. "I know about Adam. Quinn's just told me. That's actually part of why he wants to see you so urgently."

Percy frowned in puzzlement as he disappeared. Cade however was strangely elated at his last words. He'd never been worshipped before and he had to admit it gave him a strange sense of power. As long as he could use that to try and convince Quinn to be careful, it would all be worth it.

Chapter 25

Quinn frowned as he sat in the bed in his clinic room, looking out at the sea beyond. He was still weak, but growing stronger every day. The table beside him was scattered with documents, reports and various other magyckal paraphernalia Quinn was using to try to track down de Vere. But the man had once again hidden his tracks so well that finding him was proving difficult. Quinn threw the latest report he'd been reading across the room with a snarl. He'd the combined force of hundreds of thousands of Warlocks at his disposal and he was no closer to finding the bastard than he'd been before. He took off his reading glasses and rubbed his eyes tiredly.

"I'm not sure that's going to help," said Cade's amused voice from behind him.

He turned with a smile as Cade came over and ran fingers through his hair. "Whilst I love to see you all angry and sexy, it's stressing you out and in your condition, that's not a wise idea." He walked over to the scattered papers to pick them up and Quinn reached out a hand, pulling him onto the bed against him. Cade wriggled beside him, and Quinn felt the familiar stirrings in his groin when this man was close.

"Leave them there," he said quietly. "I'll pick them up." He pulled Cade close to him, hugging him, enjoying the scent of sandalwood and musk.

Cade ruffled his hair, knowing how much it irritated him. "I know you're anxious to find this bastard. So am I. I want to watch while you burn his eyes out and make him self-combust. But you need to relax. I don't want those nosebleeds starting again."

Quinn sighed. "I know and I'm trying. I just feel helpless not being able to find him. He could be out there plotting his next move even as we sit here. I have no leads, no bright ideas as to where he might be and the Consortium hasn't been able to find one scrap of magyckal activity that might indicate where he is. He's just disappeared like a puff of smoke."

Cade sat straight up, regarding him carefully. "Have you given any further thought to my suggestion? I told you I don't mind if it helps."

Quinn shook his head vehemently. "Don't even go there. I'm not getting inside your mind to see if you missed telling me anything. I appreciate the offer but I'm not going to do it to you. It will be painful with you in your current state; you're still healing too. I really don't want to put you through that after what you went through."

"As opposed to what *you* went through?" Cade stood up and walked over to the papers, ignoring Quinn's muttered request to leave them, as he bent down and picked them up. "He said a lot of things. There might be one snippet of information that I heard that might help you. Something I forgot. He had verbal diarrhoea."

Cade knelt down beside Quinn. "You told me this was bigger than both of us. You're letting your emotions for me stand in the way of doing what you know you should do, what you *would* do had I been anyone else. I don't think I can let them happen. I don't want the whole fate of the Warlock nation resting on my shoulders because I might know something that could help you that you won't let me share."

"Cade is right." The quiet voice of Percy Montgomery intruded in the still room. "I've been waiting for you to recover to tell you much the same thing." He walked into the room, regarding his Grand Master thoughtfully as he smiled at Cade.

Quinn frowned fiercely, his eyes flashing dangerously "Percy, don't deign to tell me what to do. I'll decide what's best for the Consortium. And probing Cade's memories is not something I'm doing. It could damage him, being Fey himself."

"Quinn, forgive me, but you aren't thinking with the right hat on. As your Marshall, it's my duty to tell you the truth and that truth is that you are too emotionally invested at the moment. We have no other leads. I have people out there putting themselves in danger to try and get you information. You owe it to them to follow up every unexplored avenue you can. That includes seeing if Cade holds any more information. If not, at least we'll know and we can tell the people out there that we did our best. At the moment, that's not something I can tell them."

Anger surged in Quinn's chest as he stood up from the bed, his head slightly dizzy from the change in altitude. He glowered at Percy with all the force of his rather leonine being. "Don't you tell me what to fucking do!" he snarled, his voice taut with fury. "You may be my Marshall but I'm Grand Master and I'll decide what happens!" He swayed and grabbed hold of the side of the bed.

Hell, those may be fighting words but I must look like an invalid...which sort of defeats the objective.

Cade moved forward with a deep sigh. "For God's sake, stop being such a fucking drama queen! You know deep inside Percy's right. You *should* be doing this."

Quinn turned slowly to face him, seeing Percy regarding Cade with an amused smile. Cade had an irritated expression on his face, raised eyebrows challenging him. Quinn shook his head in disbelief. "Christ, this just gets better and better! Now I'm a drama queen?"

Cade cocked his head to one side as he nodded slightly.

Quinn felt very out of sorts. No one had ever told him that before. "Well, I suppose that tells me, doesn't it?" he said dangerously. "We can't have that, can we?" He knew he was being childish but he couldn't seem to help himself. He also knew deep inside that both of them were right, which didn't help his mood. "Fine, if you both feel so strongly about it, then I suppose I have no option, do I?" He found his feet and took Cade's hand in his, pulling him toward him.

"Sit down; I think I can manage to do this with what little strength I have left." He held up a warning finger at Percy's interjection. "Don't say a word. If this is getting done, *I'm* the one doing it."

Percy was a wise man and Quinn knew he knew when to back off. His Marshall sat down on the corner chair, watching as Quinn seated Cade on the bed as he stood over him. Cade looked at him calmly and Quinn's bravado disappeared.

"Cade, this may hurt. I'll try not to go too deep—that could be dangerous for you. Are you ready for me to do this?"

Cade nodded, taking his hand in his. "I'll be fine. Do your voodoo magyck on me like you normally do." He smiled wickedly. "And don't hold back either. I can take it. If there's anything in there I want you to find it."

I will help you contain the power, Quinn, so you do not damage your man. Trust me on that.

Quinn took a deep breath and laid his hand on top of Cade's head. His boyfriend closed his eyes as Quinn started to chant softly, willing memories and visions out of Cade's memory. Cade's hand tightened in his and he drew a sharp drawn breath as Quinn dug deeper. Magyckal procedures like this were always risky and with Cade being Fey and having undergone the torture he had, Quinn had no idea what this might do to his psyche.

Quinn tasted Cade's memories like soft tones of lemon and vanilla, the essence flooding his mouth as the pictures, sights and sounds flooded his mind like snippets from a film. He tried hard not to absorb Cade's emotions of that time, fearing they'd distract him, but deep below he felt Cade's pain and fear as well as his anger and he drew a deep breath himself at the feelings being invoked within him. Taliesin was angry too at what had been done to Cade, but he was also proud.

He is brave and noble, this man of yours. You chose well, Quinn.

The room spun slightly when Quinn heard de Vere's voice, one he'd heard in his nightmares for a very long time.

He knew that one of the reasons he'd avoided what he could admit now was the inevitable action he had to take. He would have to hear the man's voice and see his face.

His thoughts raced as he heard de Vere's words, his mind absorbing them, the emotions they provoked too raw for him to manage. Finally, with a gasp of relief, he opened his eyes and lifted his hand from Cade's head. He looked down at him anxiously.

Cade sat, head bowed. He was shaking, his breath coming in short, sharp bursts.

"Cade? Are you all right?" Quinn saw the faint nod.

Cade replied with a slight quaver in his voice. "I'm fine. I wouldn't want to do that too often, it actually does hurt, but I'm fine, I think." Cade looked up at him, his face pale, and eyes questioning. "Did you find anything useful?"

Quinn nodded in relief. "You were right. The man was in a chatty mood. He didn't think you'd survive, that's for sure, or he wouldn't have lost control like that and blabbed so much. He was always fucking arrogant. Luckily for us, that is one of his failings."

He turned to Percy. "Andrew mentioned a witch and the Witchhunter. He thought he might have been betrayed by one of them. I'm not sure about the boy, as I don't know why he'd be working with the likes of Andrew. But it brings greater urgency to the fact that we need to find this Jeremy Payton and find out if there's any connection. We need to increase our efforts." Quinn sighed heavily. "As for the witch—I'm beginning to think your instinct about Mary was perhaps the right one, Cade. It could be her he's referring to. Percy, we need to follow up on that, make sure we know she's who she says she is. Dig out anything we can find, get anyone involved that might give us some more insight. We need to act on a suspicion no matter how nebulous it might seem. De Vere said something else very interesting. He mentioned going back to '*Sept Rois.*' My French is rusty but I think it means Seven Kings. I don't know if it's a place or what but we need to find out. Put someone on it immediately," he commanded Percy. "See if we can find any connection, no matter how tenuous. Tell them to look at links with the number seven, the names de Vere, Makepeace or Adam."

Percy nodded and left the room. Quinn's legs were shaking and he sat down next to Cade quickly before he collapsed. Blood trickled slowly from his nose. Cade picked up a tissue from the table and wiped it gently. Then he helped Quinn into the bed again and settled him under the covers.

"God, you should have let Percy do this. What the hell am I going to do with you, you stubborn bastard?"

"You're not being very complimentary toward me today," Quinn murmured as he lay back with closed eyes. "I'm not sure I can take any more insults without feeling the urge to turn you into that frog you mentioned the other day."

Cade chuckled softly and Quinn opened his eyes as his lover's mouth found his. He closed them again, enjoying the feel of lips against his and the smell of Cade's hair like oranges in his nostrils. Quinn opened them again as Cade stood up, going over and closing the door, locking it as he turned back. He felt a frisson of pleasurable anticipation at the sultry look in Cade's eyes. He knew it well.

"I think you deserve a little more TLC that you've been getting," he said huskily. "Despite your threats to turn me into an amphibian, I still feel the need to jump your bones and relieve a little tension. All you have to do is sit there. I'll try not to kill you, I promise."

Quinn laughed quietly as Cade sat next to him. "I don't mind dying this way. Do your best—" Quinn's voice was cut off as Cade covered his mouth, his tongue darting into Quinn's, causing him to groan in pleasure. In turn he slid his warm hands under Cade's loose tee shirt, finding warm skin. Cade pulled his shirt over his head, throwing it behind him.

Quinn took in a breath at the sight of the faint red scar on Cade's chest, tenderly tracing it with his fingers before kissing it softly. Cade's fingers lifted Quinn's loose sweatshirt off over his head and it joined the other clothing on the floor. His hands caressed Quinn's chest and the muscles of his stomach, and then he reached down and slid his hands into the waistband of his loose sweatpants, caressing the skin of his hip. Cade trailed his tongue down the side of Quinn's chin, across his scar then onto his throat, finally down to his shoulder, nipping the taut muscle, once then twice, causing him to hiss in both pain and bliss.

"Hell, watch what you're doing with those teeth of yours," Quinn muttered in between kisses. Cade smiled against his skin and reached down again into Quinn's sweats, grasping his very erect cock in his strong, warm hands, and started to stroke, pull and caress his prick with expertise. Quinn's eyes closed in pure bliss.

"I intend making you come in your pants," Cade whispered as Quinn's body responded to his lover's movements. "Like a teenager, not that bossy alpha animal that you are." He nipped Quinn's shoulder again. "Open your eyes and watch me jack you off."

Cade's words simply inflamed Quinn further than he thought was possible and he groaned loudly, his good intentions of doing what he wanted all gone as the heat in his loins built to an almost unbearable intensity.

He tried to keep his eyes open as instructed and watch his lover's hand move like a small animal in his pants but the feelings were too great and he leaned back, closing his eyes instinctively, as his body shuddered in a wave of tremors that would have registered on the Richter scale. He gasped in Cade's ear, thinking his heart would jump out of his chest like a salmon swimming upstream.

"Christ, I thought you said you *weren't* trying to kill me?"

Cade chuckled as he removed his semen-coated hands from Quinn's pants, then Quinn watched in awe as Cade proceeded to lick them clean with slow, languorous flicks of his tongue. When he started sucking on his own fingers, Quinn's cock stirred once more into launch mode.

"Christ, you are bad," he said huskily as Cade grinned and finished his feast.

Cade nodded solemnly. "Oh yes, I'm very bad," he murmured, palming Quinn's hardening crotch with a knowing smile. "And later you can discipline me. We can't do it now because I tend to be too loud when you're inside me. And we can't have the whole damn hospital knowing what we're doing, can we?" He grinned wickedly at Quinn's expression and leaned forward, semen-scented breath washing over Quinn's mouth as he kissed him. "So I'll take a rain check and store it all up just for you."

He stroked Quinn's hair gently in soft strokes that made Quinn want to purr. "I think you really needed that, Mr. Fairmont. It's been a while."

"I really did, Mr. Mairston," Quinn murmured. "And I lived to tell the tale. I had my doubts, I can tell you. I thought my heart was going to stop again." He grinned lazily. "I agree with you on the going-full-monty part. You do tend to be fairly vocal as well as foul mouthed and I can't have everyone here knowing that you're screwing the life out of me. That strikes me as being very bad Warlock king street cred. I do have a reputation to maintain."

"I can't help it you make me feel that way," Cade said laughingly and leaned over to caress his jaw line gently. "I suppose we should get out of this bed and take a shower. I'm sure you've got a lot of Warlocky stuff to do and I for one intend going for a very long swim in that pool before I get too grumpy."

Cade disentangled himself from Quinn. But Quinn reached out and pulled him in for another long, deep kiss, running his hands down Cade's back, touching the still-healing scar there gently, before clasping his arse and kneading his cheeks like a cat. For a while there was only each other and the slow beating of hearts under skin that pressed together as if it were melded together. When Quinn finally released Cade, his boyfriend drew back the covers and raised an eyebrow. "It seems such a shame to waste that. And I am pretty hungry…" He licked his lips lasciviously.

Quinn laughed softly, needing no urging.

Chapter 26

Andrew de Vere paced the deck of his boat, *Sept Rois*, where it lay moored in the Essex Marina. The expression on his face was black and thunderous. His hands clenched and unclenched by his side with each step as he paced in the dim evening twilight.

Sophie Mercurio watched him from the inner cabin where she sat with a glass of wine. Andrew could see she was scared of his mood and it gave him great satisfaction. He'd already punished her for something last night with his riding crop; what, he couldn't quite remember. The welts blossoming on her tender skin had given him great pleasure. The woman was so obsessed with him she'd do anything to please him. And she liked it rough too, something which made her the perfect partner—for now.

He got tired of pacing and stormed into the cabin regarding Sophie belligerently. "I'm glad to see you looking so relaxed when this whole fucking thing is falling apart around us. But please, you sit and enjoy yourself."

Sophie sighed. "Andrew, you know we can recover from this mishap."

Andrew glared at her dangerously and she flinched. "Mishap?" he said softly. "Really? That's the word you would use to describe our current situation?" Without warning he reached out and took hold of her hair, pulling her head back viciously until tears formed in her eyes. He reached down across the armchair and spat words into her ear.

"You stupid bitch. This is not something we can simply ignore. This is Quinn fucking Fairmont we're talking about and I want him dead so badly I can taste it like bile. But he's been forewarned and the protection he has now is like nothing you ever have seen before. The only thing I have in my favour, darling, is you."

He gave her hair one last furious twist and released it, leaving Sophie pale faced on the couch.

"I wanted to ruin this man emotionally before the end. It's just not enough to kill him. At least I finished the job with his friend. Damaged-goods always goes down so well. Then that cocky son of a bitch that he's fucking gets away. That wasn't supposed to happen, Sophie. There's no way now we'll even get close again like last time, he'll be too much on his guard. He probably knows it's me now and he knows how to keep himself hidden from me. I no longer have the advantage."

"You have me still. I can get close enough to him and his partner. He doesn't suspect a thing. They're focused on you."

Sophie Mercurio, aka Mary Hawthorne, stood up and walked over to her lover, wrapping her arms around his neck as she leaned into him.

He regarded her flatly. "You don't have the power to destroy him or the lover. Whatever you throw at them, he and that Withinner of his will fight. The Consortium has powerful magyck protecting them both and it won't be easy to get through it. I need to get him in a compromised position and he won't allow that to happen again easily. He'll trust no one including you. I need another plan." He removed Sophie's arms from his neck and walked over to the cocktail cabinet to pour himself a whisky.

Sophie watched him, her eyes like that of a puppy that had been kicked. As she spoke, her voice trembled. "You needed someone on the inside giving you information and I did that. I killed the witch and took her place. I managed to convince that horrible young Witchfinder that we were humans fighting witches so he'd kill those Warlocks so I could get close to Quinn with the antidote he needed. Again, he trusted me. How could he *not* trust the person who's helping him protect his people? I adapted when he came home unexpectedly and I wasn't quite finished staging the scene with his friend. Surely we can do something again that will bring him out in the open. I have an idea or two."

"Pray tell." said de Vere smoothly. "I'm all ears." He sat on the couch, sipping his whisky as he watched her, his eyes narrowed.

"He has a definite weakness. The man, Cade Mairston. He's the key to all this."

Andrew waved his hand impatiently. "Sophie, you're preaching to the choir. I know that's his fucking weak spot."

"My idea is to cause turmoil between them, drive them apart. That way we'll separate them, making them weaker. Quinn will be distracted. Perhaps enough that he'll let his guard down and I can get him somewhere you need him to be." She smiled. "The last time he got upset, he finished half a bottle of whisky and passed out. His emotions take over when it comes to his lover."

De Vere mused over her plan as he fingered his chin thoughtfully. "How do you propose driving this wedge between them? The man's gay, if you hadn't noticed. He's not into what you have between your legs."

Sophie smiled although he saw her face tighten at his deliberately cruel words. "I tried a slight experiment. I gave myself a small transfusion of Fey blood the first time I met him to see the result. It worked. His hormones went a little crazy and he felt an attraction. Quinn was bisexual and he only stopped being that way about six years ago. If I gave myself more Fey blood it would lead to him having the same sexual attraction he'd have for a Fey and then I could orchestrate it that Cade found out, or better still, walks in on us. I doubt he's the understanding kind. This is the human way to do it, Andrew. Good old fashioned lust and betrayal.

Nothing the Consortium can foresee or mitigate. But it will cause some real pain."

De Vere nodded. "Not bad. There may be some use to you after all."

Sophie flushed. "I thought that then, when he's out of the picture, Quinn's guard will be down. Then who knows, he may even turn to me as solace. I can keep up the transfusions to keep it interesting. It may be the only way we can weaken him. Between us we can create a hex too, something that will mess with his mind and perhaps slow him down, weaken him."

Andrew nodded. "History repeating itself. I like that idea. Without the destruction of your good self, of course," he qualified quickly as Sophie's face tightened at his words.

I need to keep the minions sweet, make them feel needed.

Sophie became more animated. "And if need be, you can still go after the lover. He'll be less protected on his own and that'll give him something else to think about once you've destroyed him. I think you'd call it collateral damage?"

She started as de Vere's arms reached out and grabbed her, pulling her down onto the couch.

"Not bad, my darling," he whispered. "I quite like the whole idea. You may have something there."

Sophie sighed as his hands begun to unzip the back of her dress. Andrew knew she was anticipating a delightfully rough night and he intended to see that she got it.

Chapter 27

Quinn was happy to finally be home. He sat in his study, his reading glasses perched on the end of his nose as he looked at the report that Percy had sent him. He sat back in his chair, taking his glasses off, pinching the bridge of his nose in tiredness. He looked up at a knock at the door, seeing Cade standing there.

"Quinn? Percy and Magnus are here to see you. They're downstairs." He frowned. "They wouldn't come up until you'd said it was okay."

Quinn stood up and stretched. "No problem, I'll come down. It's more comfortable downstairs anyway."

Cade shook his head in wonder. "They're really in awe of you, aren't they? What do they know that I don't that makes you such a force to be reckoned with? Is it just the whole Grand Master thingamajig?"

Quinn chuckled. "God, you're so irreverent of tradition. The whole Grand Master thingamajig as you so eloquently put it is a tradition over one thousand years old, and traditions are hard to break in my world. Percy and Magnus are old school." He grimaced as he stretched. "Hell, I'm only thirty-six and listen to my bones. I'm getting old."

"You're four days from your birthday, sweetheart. So I'm afraid you're closer to thirty-seven whether you like it or not," Cade said wickedly.

Quinn gazed at him suspiciously. "How do you know when my birthday is? Has Percy been blabbing? And you're only a year younger than me so you can't talk."

He disliked birthday celebrations, avoiding them like a hen in a fox lair.

"The eighteenth of August, Quinn. The tabloids love to print everything about you and since you wouldn't tell me when it was, I simply found out on the Internet."

Cade laughed at the disgusted expression on his face. "Now you'd better get down to your court below and just hope that I haven't ordered you one of those stripper-grams for your special day."

Quinn chuckled softly. "If there's one thing I do know it's that you wouldn't want another man or woman with their hands all over my body." Cade scowled at how true his words were and Quinn gloated in satisfaction. "But feel free to get me one if you can get over it—I like a little bit of variety every now and then. A blond of either gender would be nice and make a change."

His witty parting shot as he left his study was somewhat spoiled by a large pebble lobbed at him, causing him to exclaim loudly in surprise as it hit him squarely on the back of his head.

"That's not what that flower display is used for," he called out as he descended the stairs, rubbing the tender spot. Percy and Magnus looked up at him in surprise. He shrugged. "Cade threw something at me. It must have been something I said."

He grinned as he invited them through to the large drawing room with its view of the heath in the darkening twilight. Once they were settled, Quinn turned to them enquiringly. They both looked ill at ease and Percy's face was grim.

"What's wrong?" Quinn asked. "You two look very unhappy about something."

Percy looked down at the floor, his eyes unable to meet Quinn's for some reason. "We have some good news and some bad news, Grand Master."

"Tell me." Quinn observed them narrowly.

Percy looked up. "I fucked up. I planted a stranger in your midst without even realising it. Mary Hawthorne *isn't* who she said she was."

Quinn's eyes narrowed dangerously as he leaned forward in his armchair. "Then who the hell is she? And why didn't you know it wasn't her?" He looked at them bleakly. "Is that the good news or the bad news?" His heart was beating erratically and he had to struggle to control his rising anxiety.

Magnus shifted uncomfortably in his chair. "It's the bad news, Mr. Quinn. The good news is that we think we know who she is and we think we've found de Vere."

Quinn visibly relaxed at this news, and he sat back in his armchair again. "Right, then. Start at the beginning and don't leave anything out." His voice was mildly threatening.

Percy sighed. "We looked for anything that we could find that looked remotely like *Sept Rois*. We found places, restaurants, an S and M club in London"—he grinned slightly at Quinn's expression—"and hundreds of other weird and wonderful places. But there was only one that had de Vere Makepeace's name against it—along with other Latin aliases, which is how we found it. He's been inordinately careless and the man's arrogance defies belief. There is a yacht named *Sept Rois* currently moored out in the Essex Marina on Wallasea Island on the River Crouch. I have people watching it circumspectly. They've been taking video footage of the activity on board and streaming it back." He swallowed. "I think you should see it."

He motioned to Magnus who slipped a DVD out of his pocket and handed it silently to Quinn. He regarded it thoughtfully then slipped it into the DVD player, switching on the television.

"I need my glasses," he muttered, pausing the playback and disappearing up the stairway toward his office. He came down a few minutes later and slid them onto his nose as he sat down again.

Damned things. I'm a master Warlock and I can't see a thing without a pair of glasses on my nose.

The three men leaned forward expectantly as a picture of the yacht came into view, slightly blurry, and rather skewed. Quinn looked at Percy with a raised eyebrow.

"They're not cameramen, Quinn," Percy said quietly. "The youngster that was filming is only twenty years old and fairly new at the whole surveillance thing. Keep watching."

Quinn watched as a man came onto the deck. He stiffened at the sight of the figure, his skin prickling like a thousand bee stings delivered all at once. The video camera zoomed in, slightly out of focus and fairly erratically, but Quinn saw the face of de Vere. He hissed between his clenched teeth, his fingers curling into fists as he saw the face of the man he thought he'd killed. He watched as a young woman joined him on the deck. Quinn closed his eyes in despair as he saw the beautiful face of Mary Hawthorne lean in and kiss de Vere, her hands winding hungrily in his hair as he pulled her closer to him.

Quinn sensed both Percy and Magnus watching him in trepidation. He watched as de Vere and Mary clung together, the adoration for the man evident in her body language. When it got to the part where he was removing her clothing, Quinn paused the footage. He had no desire to watch them enjoy each other any further.

"That fucking bitch."

He turned at the sound of Cade's voice, a voice coated in hatred, sounding very unlike his usually laid-back lover. It caused the hair on Quinn's arms to stand up. Cade stood staring at the TV screen at the half-naked couple, his face rigid and grey eyes flashing. He looked at Quinn and then at Percy and Magnus.

"I knew I didn't like that woman. There was always something off about her." Cade seemed to realise suddenly he'd interrupted them and his face flushed. "I'm sorry about butting in, what with your high council meeting or whatever you call it, but I saw the footage." He turned to Percy. "How in hell's name does someone like her get to march in here and pretend to be someone else what with all the security and magyck-y stuff you guys do to protect yourselves? Did no one realise this woman was a fake?"

Quinn hastened to quell Cade's rising temper, seeing the guilty and woebegone looks on both Percy and Magnus' face. "Cade, you're quite right to ask those questions and I'll be doing the same thing, believe me. But the damage is done now—"

Cade interrupted him fiercely. "They nearly killed you! Not to mention slicing and dicing me. That bitch has probably been telling that psychopath everything that's been happening, giving him all the detail he needed to kidnap me and try to kill you. How can you be so calm about it?" His voice pitched higher as he strode round the room.

Quinn stood up swiftly, moving over to Cade whilst Percy and Magnus sat glumly watching. He pulled him close, feeling his lover's agitation. "It's all right. This is good news. We've found them both and they don't know we know about Mary. It gives us a huge advantage."

"Her real name is Sophie Mercurio," said Percy softly. "She's been with him for about six months. She *is* a witch; she didn't fake that. The real Mary Hawthorne was found dead in a cave in Norfolk. She'd been dead some time and it looked like there was a major memory drain with the burns on her forehead. I imagine that was de Vere passing on the information to Sophie so she could be more believable. He's the only one powerful enough to do that. He also helped her mask herself to us."

Percy looked down at his feet. "She passed all the screening we put her through before we directed her to you in that fairground that day. There was no reason to suspect she wasn't who she said she was, but I'm sorry for putting you and Cade in danger, Grand Master. It was unforgiveable and I'm quite ready to take the consequences."

Magnus spoke for the first time. "I stand with him on that, sir. I was the one who thought of Mary in the first place. I knew her well a very long time ago. They must have found someone who resembled the real one well enough to fool me. It had been twenty years since I last saw her as a young lass. I am so sorry, sir." His voice caught and Quinn wondered just how well the two had known each other.

He reached out a hand, placing it on Magnus's shoulder. "I'm sorry you lost an old friend, Magnus," he said softly. "And whilst I appreciate the sentiments, gentlemen, throwing yourselves on your swords isn't the answer. It was a very clever plot and one that wouldn't have easily been found out. De Vere made sure of that."

The two men visibly relaxed.

Quinn was quiet. "She would have needed a reason to get involved and the only reason we needed her to come on board in the first place was because of the cadmium issue." He regarded Percy thoughtfully. "It raises the question that perhaps that was engineered to enable her to get on board? We already know that de Vere mentioned the Witchfinder General. And that's a really scary thought—that de Vere could convince a Witchhunter to work with him to kill Warlocks to attract our attention. How in hell's name could he get that right?"

Percy looked uncomfortable and Quinn looked at him, his nostrils flaring. "You know something. Spill it." He released Cade and sat down again, patting the seat beside him for him to sit next to him. Percy continued with his story.

"We had news from Daniel."

Percy continued. "Recently the Witchhunters Alliance has had an influx of capital and man power into their ranks. Someone has been rejuvenating them and reorganising them to be much more streamlined. Daniel's been investigating and he told us that the person at the top that's been doing this is a man calling himself Andreas Facite." He smiled bitterly. "Given what we know now, it's no big surprise who that is."

"Christ, I don't believe it. The gall of the man." Quinn's face darkened.

Cade looked at him in confusion. "You know him?"

Quinn nodded. "Andreas Facite is just a bastard Latin translation of Andrew Makepeace. It's de Vere."

"Wow. You know Latin too." Cade's voice was reverent and despite the seriousness of the situation, Quinn grinned at his impressed expression.

Percy smiled. "He's been a master puppeteer, controlling them from afar using other humans to do his dirty work so they aren't tipped off. We think this is how he's convinced Payton to work for him. We believe the boy thinks he's working for a witch-hunting group, not a bunch of Warlocks and witches." He chuckled grimly. "When the Witchfinder General finds out he's been duped, he's not going to be happy. Bad news for us though. It may make him even more hell bent on our destruction for making a fool of him."

Quinn leaned back, his lips pursed, his long legs stretched out in front of him. He ran a hand through his hair.

"This is becoming very messy," he muttered. "If Cade hadn't been kidnapped and we hadn't managed to find him in time, this plan could have worked to destroy us in a way we could never have envisaged. It's pretty Machiavellian but exactly what I'd expect of de Vere. I'd imagine he was behind what happened to Jomo too." His voice was bitter.

Quinn. May I speak?

Taliesin's quiet voice echoed in his mind and he frowned. He raised a hand to stay the conversation in the room. His Withinner had been very silent lately, hardly communicating and when he did, he was deferential to the point of being over polite. Quinn wasn't sure he liked this new Taliesin, despite his own recent virulent expostulations telling his Withinner to keep a low profile and stay the hell away from him. Quinn still hadn't quite forgiven him for seducing Cade although recent events had overshadowed his original fury at the action. Taliesin *had* saved his life. Twice.

He sighed. "Speak, Taliesin. Have your say."

The group looked at him as they waited for Quinn to communicate with his Withinner.

We have known de Vere a long time. He is a diabolical and manipulative weasel that should have died all those months ago. How he survived what we did to him is something we have to find out. But more pressing is this Witchfinder General. We need to find this boy. He might be the key to defeating de Vere. If we can pit them against each other it will distract, even weaken de Vere long enough for us to make a plan and kill him once and for all. It will be very difficult to take him on again, especially in your weakened state.

Quinn scowled at the reminder of his current situation.

It may also mean that the boy will leave us alone for a while as he concentrates on de Vere.

Quinn nodded at Taliesin's words, seeing the exasperation on Cade's face that he couldn't hear what was being said. Percy and Magnus sat quietly, willing to wait it out until their leader passed on his Withinner's comments.

"Not a bad strategy," Quinn murmured. "We are trying to find the boy though."

He looked at Percy. "How is the hunt for Jeremy Payton coming along? What do we need to do to intensify the search?"

Percy shook his head. "The boy is well hidden. He's been very quiet and there are no fresh leads to follow. I have everyone I can out looking for him."

Quinn shook his head emphatically. "That's not enough. We need to force his hand. Taliesin is proposing when we find him, we sic him on de Vere; let them fight it out. It'll distract de Vere long enough for us to make a fresh plan to get rid of him. We need to attract this Witchfinder General somehow so we can get our message across. Any ideas?"

Cade leaned forward. "You told me that each time you seem to get close to Jeremy, he just eludes you." He looked at Percy. "You even made a comment about having a traitor in your midst. What if it was Mary—isn't that the logical assumption? Perhaps what you need to do is keep Mary on board, leak some information to her that hopefully she'll believe and then use that to track him down."

"But if it's Mary, and I think you're right, it is her, Mary's been warning him when we're coming," Quinn said quietly. "She's keeping him *away* from us every time we get a sniff as to where he might be. What information could we possibly give her that will put him *in* our sights?"

Cade looked at him, his eyes bright. "She obviously has links to where he is. So you tell her you've found Jeremy again. But you also tell her he's discovered he's been inadvertently working for a Warlock instead of a witch-hunting group. That he's furious and he's going after the top guy—this Latin person. She'll do anything to protect de Vere; we know that. She'll either try to destroy Jeremy herself and you can follow her or she'll send him to you to do it. I'd imagine the latter. It's a more sure way of destroying him. It will also give her an out with de Vere if he finds out what she's done. She can simply say she was too late to warn him. She's a woman in love, and she'll do anything to protect the man she loves regardless of the consequences. I would."

Quinn watched him with open awe, his fierce man with flashing silver eyes. Taliesin chuckled.

He gets better every day. He is a mighty warrior and a great strategist, your Cade. This could work in drawing him out using the traitorous witch. Once you know where he is, you can tell him the truth somehow, using humans, and point him in de Vere's direction. You'll be able to track him every step of the way, using him like a puppet. It's a good plan. We won't get to de Vere without him being distracted and the witch won't betray him. You know how good he is at enchanting people. She'll die first and that serves no purpose.

Quinn nodded. "Cade, I think you might be a genius. It's a good way to draw him out. It's the only plan we have so we need to make it work." His face darkened. "It will be difficult, though, pretending we don't know who this witch really is. I can't afford any slipups. We need to keep it between us and tell no one else. Our only advantage is they don't know we know what we do."

He turned to Percy. "You don't let that yacht and de Vere out of your sights." he commanded. "I want nothing to be done that will make him suspicious, but I want to know where he is at all times. I want to be informed the minute *anything* changes. And I mean the *minute* it changes, not a minute after. I'll deal with Mary Hawthorne and start setting the stage for the new act."

He turned to Cade. "I know you. You're going to find it difficult to pretend you don't know who she really is. You need to stay away from her altogether," he said firmly.

Quinn fully expected an argumentative Cade to raise his objections at this autocratic decree of his and was surprised when he simply nodded.

Cade spotted his disbelief and smiled slightly. "Quinn, I'm not an idiot. I know I'd want to scratch her eyes out and beat her senseless. I can't argue with you on that one."

Quinn was nonplussed. "Well, that settles it. Everyone knows their part." He laughed cynically. "Perhaps we'll get lucky when we tell Jeremy about de Vere and he'll actually do the job for us. Although I doubt he's powerful enough to do it easily." His voice hardened. "Besides, I want to do it myself. I failed once. I don't intend doing it again."

Both Percy and Magnus nodded and departed. Once they'd gone, Quinn leaned wearily back in his seat, Cade gently stroking his forehead and running his hands through his hair. "Quinn, there's something we still have to get out in the open. We need to talk a bit more about what happened between Taliesin and me."

Quinn opened his eyes, shaking his head vehemently. "No way, it's late, I'm tired and I just want to go to bed. That is a conversation for another day."

Like never, he thought. *If I ignore it long enough, it'll go away.*

"No, I need to talk about this now. This isn't just about you."

Quinn scowled ferociously and made as if to get up out of his chair but Cade pulled him back down with force.

He glared at him in exasperation. "Let me go. We spoke about that and I thought it was all over." He stood up and started walking out of the room. Cade's quiet voice stopped him in his tracks.

"Quinn Fairmont, if you walk away from me now I shall leave and not come back until you *are* ready to talk about it."

Quinn heard the tremble and the finality in his lover's voice and he clenched his hands into fists as Cade spoke his next words.

"You're going to be going up against a man who's trying to kill you, who tried to kill me and one with whom you have a lot of history. I need you to be the strongest you can be and with things between you and Taliesin at the moment, I don't believe you are."

Quinn closed his eyes, knowing Cade was right but still not wanting to open the door to that night for fear it would drive him crazy with jealousy.

"I know you forgave me but I still think something is eating you up inside. I can see it sometimes. You two need to make it up. You need each other. I know you've been skirting around the issue but it's true. And the only way you can do that is if we talk about what happened."

Cade stood up and walked over to him and Cade's strong arms encircled his waist as he laid his head on Quinn's shoulder. His body was rigid and he felt Cade's breath against his ear as he held him.

Finally Quinn sighed and turned to Cade's earnest face and saw an expression of desolation. Quinn's heart ached. He supposed this was as difficult for Cade as it was for him.

"Fine." He sighed as he sat down again, and waved a hand at Cade. "Have your say."

Cade swallowed and sat down beside him, taking his hands in his. "I know you told me that it was just this whole Fey attraction and I couldn't have resisted it any more than I could when I first met you. And with Taliesin it was so much more powerful."

Quinn drew a breath at those words, not looking at Cade, not wanting to imagine the heat of the feelings that would have been burning within both Cade and his Withinner, even as he felt envious of them. He sensed Taliesin listening but the Withinner made no comment.

"But even though it was so…intense"—Cade cleared his throat—"it was just sex. I didn't feel anything emotionally other than the physical feelings at the time, the sexual attraction. What we have is emotional. It's more than sex, more than just bodies mating, which is all it was with Taliesin." Quinn flinched at the pictures his mind conjured up even though he'd been there at the time.

Cade squeezed his hands. "I love you, Quinn. I feel empty when you're not around; I miss your smile when it's not there, which is a lot lately, and I miss you, every bit of you. I've never felt this way about any man before and I don't believe it's just the genetics of Warlock and Fey. What I feel for you I will never feel for another man. Ever."

Quinn gazed into Cade's pale face, feeling a sense of sudden peace at his words. "Believe me I know how persuasive Taliesin can be. You didn't stand a chance against him. He's a Fey and I couldn't have expected anything different of you. Of him, yes, but of you, never." His Withinner squirmed in guilt at his words and Quinn felt content. "I never wanted to blame you but I have to confess it rankled knowing what he did to you. I'm the only one that should ever be inside you or touch you that way. I know I need to let it go too, with Taliesin. You are the best thing that ever happened to me and I feel like I can finally put everything in my past to rest and move on."

He raised Cade's face to his, taking his lips in a kiss that in his imagination seared Cade's soul, tattooing Quinn's name upon it, claiming him forever as his own. Cade kissed him back and Quinn felt his desire and love for him in every movement of his mouth on his. Finally they pulled apart, breathing heavily.

"I need to make love to you right now," Quinn whispered urgently, pulling Cade up the wide staircase toward the bedroom. "I need to show you just how mine you are and I have a lot of ideas on just how to do that."

Quinn pushed the bedroom door open with his foot as he pulled Cade back into his arms.

Taliesin, old son, eat your heart out. This man is mine, Withinner. You may have had his body but you'll never have his heart.

***

Later that night they lay together, spent and satiated, the only sound in the bedroom the ticking of the clock on the bedroom wall.

Cade murmured sleepily against Quinn's chest as his hands stroked his stomach gently. "I have to say you can be very inventive. I had no idea it was humanly possible for arms and legs to do all those things let alone get into positions like the way you did tonight."

Quinn chuckled. "You bring out the beast in me. I have to confess I've read a lot of the *Kama Sutra* over the years but putting it into practice becomes a whole new ballgame." He hastened to qualify his statement. "In scholarly pursuit, of course. I have a copy in my library that I like to refer to every now and then."

Cade thumped him lightly on the shoulder. "I'll bet. Just don't try those moves with anyone else, or I'll break your legs."

Quinn rolled over, lying on one elbow to regard him more seriously. "I meant what I said earlier, you know. It's really all right. I think I've come to terms with it and I suppose that means I've sort of forgiven Taliesin. I have a feeling he won't do anything like that again."

His Withinner stirred inside, slightly mutinous but grudgingly acquiescent to his statement.

You have my word. I cannot bear such a sulk again as the one you went through. It was painful in its extreme to witness.

Quinn grinned in the darkness. "Even Taliesin's happy times have been very infrequent recently. I think he's going through a very dry spell. The only action he's been getting is mine."

Cade snorted in laughter. Taliesin snarled.

Do not mock me in my time of crisis. This place is like a cursed desert with no rain in sight. My mood has driven away even the most willing. Perhaps now you have forgiven me, I can begin my pursuits again.

"He's really pissed off," Quinn chuckled loudly.

"It's very disconcerting hearing you talk to your own brain," Cade murmured. "Someone going's to lock you up one day." He sat up, the bedcover dropping to his waist as Quinn watched him lazily with predatory eyes. "So the two of you are friends again? You have each other's backs?"

"Yes, we're fine so stop worrying. Our next priority is spinning Mary a yarn that she'll believe and see whether she falls for it. I'll arrange to see her tomorrow. I'll have her come over here to discuss the search for Jeremy and ask about the refinements to the cadmium capsule she designed. Although knowing what I do now I don't intend being her guinea pig. God knows what her plan is." He sighed sadly. "I can't believe four Warlocks died just so she could get her hooks into me and feed information back to de Vere. They don't seem to care who they destroy. I always knew de Vere was a sociopath but this seems extreme even for him."

His words appeared to give Cade an opening into something he'd been waiting for because he sat up, brows furrowing. "Where do you think de Vere's been all this time and how do you think he survived what you did to him?"

"The million-dollar question. I have no idea. The last time I saw him he was lying bloodied and virtually dead with a face that was on fire and a great big dagger sticking out of his chest. The same one Adam used on me. I wasn't much better off except without the burning face but Taliesin was able to keep me alive long enough to get to Percy."

Cade stared at him in disbelief at his matter-of-fact words about how close he'd been to death yet again.

Quinn grinned at the look on his face. "It's an occupational hazard in my line of work. But I promise to try and keep it to a minimum." His tone grew serious. "I don't know where he's been since. Lying low obviously, healing, getting back to his usual nasty self and charming more susceptible people into doing his bidding." Quinn heard the bitterness in his voice even as he spoke.

"Quinn, about that night. The night you killed Adam." Cade reached up, cupping his face in warm hands.

Quinn flinched, looking over at him. Cade continued. "It was a terrible thing to have to do. I get the feeling you still feel very guilty about it. But you didn't have a choice. You need to forgive yourself. You said with me here you could put your past behind you and move on. Is that one of the things you've left behind?"

Quinn sat up, the bedclothes falling around his waist and stared into the darkness at the foot of the bed. "I'm trying. You've made it easier but I still remember I killed a man I loved in a terrible way." The nightmare of that night revisited him. He still saw Adam's wiry frame in flames, heard his agonised, dying screams echoing through his head. He shuddered. "I was in pain, I used too much magyck and he just…burnt up…in front of me, in absolute agony. I didn't mean it to happen like that but I was confused and Taliesin was helping me and between us the power was too much."

He was aware he was rambling and Cade's strong arms encircled his waist as he laid his head against his stomach.

"I still see him, in the dark, and sometimes when I'm in the shower, I feel him and he reaches out to me, blaming me…" His voice caught and he bowed his head as his eyes stung with tears he hadn't yet been able to shed. He blinked them away fiercely. "I know I had to do it but it doesn't make it any easier."

Cade spoke, his voice slightly tremulous. "It sounds like you still love him a little bit."

Quinn shook his head fiercely. "No, not love. That died when he slit my stomach open and looked at me, gloating, telling me he'd never loved me and that I was a fool." His voice was harsh. "But Adam was human, not a Fey. He was enchanted by de Vere and didn't know any better. A little like you and Taliesin that one night. I killed a human; I burned him to death and that—that's why it upsets me so much."

He swallowed as he leaned back against the pillow, hearing Taliesin speak almost affectionately.

You have had this burden too long, my friend. You need to let it go. We have much to do and this guilt you bear can only get in the way. You may have lost that man but you saved the one you now have in your arms. Feast on that and grow stronger.

Cade kissed him softly on his cheek. "I'm sorry I opened old wounds but I needed to know for myself. You can't heal unless you tell someone about what's bothering you."

Quinn lay down and Cade snuggled up to him, pulling the covers up and draping his arms protectively across his stomach. Quinn closed his eyes, feeling better for having shared his guilt. He pulled Cade into him, nuzzling soft, dark hair. "I love *you*, with everything I have. Remember that."

"Back at you. Now close your eyes and go to sleep, big boy. You've got a tough day ahead of you tomorrow." Cade snorted. "I wish I was with you so I could smack that woman around the head a few times. But I'll be a good boy and stay away, I promise."

"Cade, you could never be a good boy. But I'd never want you to be."

There was a low chuckle in the darkness. Quinn closed his eyes, feeling his lover's breath against his chest, smelling the scent of his hair and thought, for one fleeting moment, that everything would be all right.

Chapter 28

Quinn sat in his office, his chest tight with nerves as he waited for Mary Hawthorne to walk through his office door for their meeting. He'd gone over his story with both Cade and Percy, checking to see that it would make sense when he finally relayed it to Mary. Quinn hoped like hell he could pull this one off. He was no actor and this would require a fair bit of talent in that discipline. He sipped his coffee as he read through some of his business grant requests. With Jomo still being out of action, Quinn was singlehandedly running the business and it was taking a fair amount of his time to do it. He heard the doorbell and his heart lurched as he laid his glasses down on his desk and went downstairs to open the door for Mary Hawthorne.

She stood outside, looking as lovely as ever, in a short, deep red dress, her feet encased in high heels and looking like something out of a fashion magazine. He stared at her, a little surprised at her outfit. Normally he'd only ever seen her in jeans and tee shirts or flowing dresses before. This was a completely new Mary and knowing what he did now about her, he had a strange feeling it was intended.

"Mary, you look lovely. Come on in. I've just made coffee if you'd like a cup?" Quinn motioned her inside, shutting the door behind her, feeling a slight dizziness as she walked past him.

Mary laughed. "No thanks. I've been at a fashion show all morning and they've plied me with so much tea and coffee it's a wonder I'm not floating in here like the Queen Mary."

She smiled at him, laying a hand on his arm and again he had that strange sensation in his chinos that said his body was attracted to this woman.

Quinn moved away from her swiftly, wanting to keep his distance until he could figure out what was going on with his traitorous nether regions. He hadn't had the urge for a female body in a long time.

"Right, well, let's go upstairs then, to the study and you can fill me in on the latest news about the search for our Witchfinder General."

"Is Cade here?" Mary asked him enquiringly. "I wanted to say hello to him."

Quinn shook his head. "No, he's at work. He has a fairly hectic teaching schedule at the moment so it's keeping him busy." He didn't miss the faint trace of annoyance on Mary's face at his words and he wondered what that was all about. Quinn led the way up the staircase, his nostrils flaring at the scent of the woman following close behind him. He was feeling very confused. This wasn't quite how he'd envisaged this going, this definite sense of lust for the witch making his head swim slightly and his heart beat faster. Something wasn't quite right and he was very much on the back foot despite his carefully laid plan.

I sense Fey, Quinn.

His Withinner's harsh tones echoed in his slightly dizzy mind.

Something is wrong. Witches are not Fey. This woman is up to something. Be on your guard.

"I would if I could think straight," he muttered darkly.

Mary asked enquiringly, "Quinn? Did you say something?"

He shook his head as he reached the top of the stairs and beckoned her into his study.

"No, just talking to myself. Have a seat; I'll be with you in a second."

He smiled and disappeared into the bathroom, closing the door and leaning against it thankfully.

Christ, what the hell was wrong with him? He wanted to shag this woman so badly it was unbearable. His trousers were constricted, the sensitivity unbearable.

He took a deep breath, splashed some cold water on his face and tried to let the feelings inside him subside. His Withinner spoke urgently.

Quinn. I can sense the feeling in your loins. It feels like a Fey reaction. You need to stop it, quickly.

"Stay the hell away from my loins. How do I stop it anyway?" Quinn growled angrily. "Short of staying in here and finding an excuse to have a meeting from behind the bathroom door, I don't see what I can do!"

Have you no more Mirrabar blood? That should do the trick.

Quinn sorted. "And a fat lot of good that did me when I met Cade. That stuff hardly worked." He remembered he'd put a second vial in the cabinet and he opened the door and took it out, regarding it thoughtfully.

You know why it didn't work as expected with Cade. I have explained that. That attraction was more than simply Fey, Quinn.

Quinn frowned. "Oh. Right." It showed how disturbed his mind was when he forgot that sort of thing.

Drink the vial you hold in your hand and it will work. I promise you. What is your alternative, pray tell?

His Withinner's withering tone made Quinn scowl deeply.

"Christ, you can be a damn bossy sod."

Stop blabbering and drink the blood, you ass.

Quinn opened the vial and raised it to his mouth as he drained the vial, gagging at the disgusting taste and almost retching into the toilet bowl. Taliesin laughed.

I swear you have grown soft like the rosy buttock cheeks of a woman.

"Fuck you. At least I'm a person and not a horse's arse."

Quinn wiped his mouth and looked in the mirror as Taliesin chuckle at his words. The familiar ice coldness of the liquid entered his body. He started at a sudden knock on the door.

"Are you all right in there? You've been a while." Mary's voice sounded anxious and yet he sensed the tone of satisfaction.

"Fine. I'll be out in a minute." Quinn glowered at the mirror.

She probably thinks I've been in here relieving my tension. Christ, that's all I need, having her thinking I've been jerking off in the bathroom!

He took one last deep breath and opened the bathroom door. Mary stood outside, her face concerned but her eyes glinting with triumph.

"Are you sure you're okay? You look a little pale."

He nodded. "Honestly, I'm fine. I had a nosebleed and just had to clear my head for a moment. It happens sometimes after the Unity episode. Quite a few things have changed since doing that. My body seems to react differently to things now."

Quinn hoped by saying this, it might plant some seed of realisation that he was physically different which might explain his lack of reaction to whatever she had planned in terms of seducing him. After all, a Unity with one's Withinner was a fairly unknown quantity and anything was possible.

Whilst the urges to ravish this woman were still there, the desire was abating and he felt a distinct sense of relief. He sat down behind his desk, glad he could hide the tumescence at his groin, and smiled at her. "So, tell me your news then I'll tell you mine. I think you'll like what I have to say. It's an incredible break through."

She started slightly and her brows furrowed, and he imagined she was wondering how he was so calm in her presence. She leaned back, crossing her legs, giving him a deliberate view of her thigh and a well turned-out ankle.

She spoke softly. "The news on finding the Witchfinder isn't that good. He's really gone to ground and whilst there have been a few good leads and sightings, every time we get there we seem to be that little bit too late."

Quinn leaned forward. "Why do you think we keep missing him? Are we not keeping our plans secret enough? What can I do to help?"

He watched as she considered her words carefully. "I think we may have an informer in our midst. Someone who's tipping him off. I've mentioned this before."

Quinn leaned back in his chair, appraising her face with narrowed eyes. "Have you any opinion as to who this might be? I have to say that if I find out someone has been warning this boy, I'll be inclined to deal with them very severely. Like I did with Jimmy Christie." His voice hardened. "You need to tell me who you think it might be so I can deal with it."

"I don't want to make accusations when I don't have any proof—"

He interrupted her, standing up and hitting the desk with his fist, causing her to jump back, startled. "I trust your judgement. You've helped us this far and I value your opinion. Now tell me who you suspect. This is no time for protecting people. There's too much at stake."

The witch looked down at her hands as she toyed with the ring on her finger, and then looked up at him. "I think it might be Percy." Her voice was quiet and Quinn's fury rose unbidden in his chest at her duplicity in accusing one of the few people he had total faith in.

"Why do you believe that? Have you any evidence at all?" He turned and looked out of the picture window at the heath beyond, his face stony as he tried hard not to show his disgust at what she was doing.

Mary stood up and came up to him, and he sensed her perfume and the essence of her. He closed his eyes, fighting the last remaining feelings of attraction in his body. The Mirrabar blood was working but it would only do so much. He thought of Cade, his grey, loving eyes, his face and his low laugh and the taut, male lines of his body. The images helped dissipate the urges he was feeling for the woman.

Mary laid a hand on his arm, and he experienced a distinct tingle, like something worming itself into his arm. He pulled it away sharply and she moved back, watching him.

"He's been leading all the raids on where we think Jeremy is, he was in the thick of the fighting up in Scotland when the other Warlocks were killed and came out unscathed, almost as if he knew it was going to happen. It's nothing concrete, just a gut instinct. If I'm wrong, I will be happy to apologise, but if I'm right"—she shrugged—"we may just get the break we're looking for."

Bile rose in his throat at her deviousness but he managed to suppress it as he turned to face her. She stared at him, her lips parted, and she moved closer to him. There was confusion in her eyes that whatever plan she'd had to seduce him hadn't worked. He hoped his earlier comment about the possible after-effects of Unity would allay any suspicions she might have if she gave further though to it later. He hadn't been prepared to go with the alternative.

He nodded curtly. "Fine. I'll investigate your allegation and see what comes of it. Thank you for telling me."

He sat down again at his desk, leaning forward to look at a document, pretending to re-read it. She watched in silence. Finally he sighed and held it up.

"I have some very good news here anyway. I received some information from another source, which may just give us an edge. It looks like we have another avenue to follow to track Jeremy down."

Her face became watchful as Quinn continued.

"The arrogant Mr. de Vere has overstepped his mark somewhat." Quinn saw her nostrils flare at his disdainful tone about the man she loved. "Apparently he's been masquerading as a Witchhunter with the Witchhunters Alliance, convincing our Witchfinder General that he's on the side of the proverbial angels." Quinn laughed sardonically. "It seems de Vere has been using the Alliance for his own nefarious ends and our young man Jeremy has found about it. And may I say he's really not too happy about being duped by a Warlock and being played for a fool. The word is he's going after him and he knows where to find him."

Quinn shrugged. "It'll suit our purpose if he does find the traitorous bastard and kill de Vere for us. Save me doing it again." Quinn saw Mary's hands tighten in her lap.

Good, she's getting riled. Enjoy the feeling, bitch.

"If nothing else, it means we might be able to track the extra magyckal activity and get a bead on both of them. Best-case scenario is they kill each other but I can't afford to leave that to chance." He pushed his chair away from his desk, stretching his legs lazily in front of him. "I'm working on something at the moment with the Consortium which will hopefully amplify the Witchfinder's presence when he starts up again. It's a long shot but they seem to think it might work. He has to slip up some time. We need a break. As you know, he's been very quiet lately. If we can find him, we can perhaps find de Vere."

He looked at her enquiringly. "What do you think?"

Mary pasted a smile on her face that looked forced. "It sounds a little iffy. We're relying on a young Witchfinder to track down a very powerful Warlock in the hope of destroying him. Is that possible?"

Quinn pulled his chair in closer to his desk and leaned his elbows on it, steepling his fingers. "Hell yes. Don't underestimate the Witchfinder. He's been around since the sixteenth century and Taliesin has seen firsthand what this man is capable of. Don't be distracted by the fact that he's a fifteen-year-old boy. He knows exactly what he's doing and he's using all his inherited hunting knowledge as a Mannacrux to get him where he wants to be. If he knows where de Vere is, and if anyone can get to de Vere, it'll be him."

He laughed in satisfaction. "I'd like to be a fly on the wall when he does. I'd really enjoy seeing the other side of de Vere's face burst into flames."

Quinn felt the hate for him emanating from the witch and he was surprised that her emotions were running so high. Surely she knew he'd sense them? He couldn't let that pass; she'd get suspicious that he'd not mentioned it.

He rolled his chair back again and observed her. "Mary, you seem very emotional about all this. I can feel it. Are you all right?"

She started and there was sudden fear in her eyes that he'd picked up on her feelings but she recovered the situation very quickly. "I can't help it. I remember you being in a coma and the scars on Cade's body and I feel very angry that we can't track down de Vere down and deal with him rather than wait for some Witchfinder to do it for us. I'm sorry if you feel it; I'm not normally this transparent. But this really riles me."

He nodded in apparent sympathy even as her lying words made him ill. "I know what you mean. I have the same feelings myself. But don't worry; we'll get the bastard eventually."

Quinn smiled at her. "So, that's the plan for the short term. How is everything going with the new capsules for the cadmium exposure? Have you managed to make the reaction a little less painful yet?"

Mary appeared very distracted. "Yes, I've given the latest batch over to the Consortium to do some testing. I believe it will make the reaction much less intense but still offer the same protection."

"Well done, I'm really glad we have you on our side."

Quinn smiled at the woman even though he wanted nothing more than to place his hand on her chest and burn her through to her backbone. He was having trouble suppressing that urge.

She stood up. "I've nothing much more to report back on, so I should leave you to your work."

He nodded as he stood up. "Thanks for the visit. Keep me informed if you hear anything else that may be useful. I'll do the same on my side."

She waved a hand at him. "Don't worry about seeing me out. I know my way. I'll be in touch."

Mary Hawthorne smiled faintly as she picked up her bag and walked down the staircase to the front door. Quinn stood at the top, on the landing and watched her leave, waving a hand in goodbye as she turned back. When the front door finally swung shut behind her, he sighed in relief. The trap had been set. Now all he had to do was wait until the predator took the bait.

Chapter 29

Cade watched Quinn avidly as he lay back in bed with a sigh of contentment, his arms behind his head as he closed his eyes. He loved the sight of his lover's muscled chest and the flat plane of his stomach and he wanted nothing more than to run his tongue over it—again.

"This is bliss." Quinn sighed. "The best part of the day without a doubt."

"Did you have a tough day?" Cade ran a hand down Quinn's arm, making him shiver as he decided what to do to him next. "You still need to tell me how it went with Mary."

Quinn's face darkened at the woman's name. "It took every ounce of self-control I had not to hurt her," he muttered. "The bitch sat there, as innocent as you please, and told me bare-faced lies. She even had the gall to accuse Percy of being a traitor!" He grimaced guiltily. "I might have overdone it a bit, running down her current paramour, but I couldn't help myself."

"Do you think she believed your story, then?" Cade asked as he slowly kissed Quinn's chest, little butterfly kisses that made him sigh in pleasure. He'd just come out the shower and tasted like soap and sandalwood from the shower gel he used.

"How can I answer you when you're doing that?" Quinn said softly. "I thought we were having a serious conversation here."

Cade sat up with an exasperated sigh. "Fine. I'll leave you alone."

His boyfriend grinned. "Not for too long, I hope."

Cade sat back, the bedcovers drawn up around his waist, giving him full view of his bare chest and tenting erection. He grinned at Quinn and the look of greed on his face.

"Self-control, Quinn. Get some. You were saying?"

Quinn managed to move his eyes away from Cade's attributes and focus on his eyes.

"There was something going on." He shifted uncomfortably. "I don't know why but there seemed to be some sort of crazy Fey attraction between us. It was very distracting, which I think was the point of the whole thing."

Cade sat up at his words, his face fierce. "How is that possible? You told me witches didn't have Fey blood. And you're no longer interested in women. Did you and she—"

Quinn shook his head vehemently. "Of course I well didn't. I took some more Mirrabar blood and that quelled the attraction, mostly. It took a bit of self-control, but I managed." He sounded proud of himself.

Cade's eyes narrowed dangerously. "Like I said—how is that possible? And what if she tries it again? What if this time you have no Mirror-whatsit blood and you end up screwing like rabbits? I really don't like this—"

His jealous tirade was cut off as Quinn pulled him toward him, covering his mouth with his. Cade sank into him, his groin aching and swelling as their kiss grew deeper.

Quinn finally released him, his brown eyes almost black as he whispered in his ear. "I promise I will always have enough Mirrabar blood around to fight any urges. I don't know what she did. All I can think of is that she injected herself with Fey blood somehow, which is a very extreme thing to do, but one I think she's more than capable of. I don't know what her end game was, probably to distract me, put me off guard."

Cade wasn't convinced. "I really dislike Little Miss Perky, have I mentioned that?" he said darkly. "I'll be glad when she gets her comeuppance and is out of the picture."

Quinn chuckled. "As soon as she does what we hope, which is steer Jeremy our way, we'll deal with Little Miss Perky, I promise. I have a few ideas as to what to do with her myself. I need to make another example, I think."

His tone was grim and Cade pitied the woman being on the wrong side of his Warlock king, but only for a split second. Mary Hawthorne aka Sophie Mercurio deserved everything she was going to get.

As did Quinn. Cade's hands moved under the bedcovers, down to Cade's groin, caressing him as he slowly leaned in to nibble Quinn's bottom lip, meeting his eyes. His lover's one eyebrow raised in a gesture Cade always found terribly sexy.

"Are we finished talking the serious stuff then?" Quinn murmured sultrily. He sat upright, his hands circling Cade's waist as he pulled him over, half on top of him, his hands sliding down to Cade's backside and pulling him up, inviting him to straddle him. Cade manoeuvred himself on top of him, leaning forward to kiss him hungrily. Quinn's hips were already moving beneath him and Cade grinned in mock annoyance as he removed his mouth from his.

"Patience, Quinn. I had something in mind for you before we get to the real action stuff. Do you think you can bear with me a little bit longer?"

Quinn chuckled as his mouth found Cade's hardened nipples and he got a fairly muffled reply as he feasted on first one, then the other. "I suppose I can let you have your way with me that little bit longer. What exactly *did* you have in mind?"

Quinn's bed was a king size wooden four-poster with an ornate headboard. Cade leaned over slightly to his right and opened his side table drawer, drawing out two long swathes of red silk that he wrapped around his hands and then trailed over Quinn's chest.

"I want to tie you up," he whispered, watching Quinn's pupils dilate and his breath become even more uneven. "We haven't done that before and I thought we could take turns. You first."

"Christ." Quinn's voice was husky with desire. "You are such a bad man. You drive me crazy, do you know that? How long have you been hiding that in there?"

"Long enough." Cade smiled, his own breath deepening as Quinn's arousal stirred underneath his backside. "Now hold up your wrists and relax. I promise I'll be gentle."

Quinn groaned faintly as Cade took his one wrist and placed it where he wanted it against the wooden post, tying the red silk around it fairly tightly and knotting it. He did the same to the other one and then leaned back. He nodded. "That'll do. I like the idea of my big, tough Warlock king being at my mercy."

Quinn looked at him with darkened eyes. "I'm always at your mercy, have no doubt about that."

Cade laughed softly and kissed him, his tongue thrusting deeply into his mouth, his hands caressing Quinn's chest and stomach. He positioned himself on top of Quinn, whose eyes followed his every move. He eye-fucked Cade from the top of his head, down his chest to finally rest and focus on the cock that rose hard and ready from Cade's thatch of dark pubic hair.

Quinn himself was at full mast underneath Cade, who grinned as reached for the lube he'd hidden under his pillow. Slowly, teasingly, he opened the cap and squeezed some onto his fingers. Then as Quinn watched in hungry, breathless anticipation, Cade reached behind him and found his own entrance, fingering himself, hissing at the feel of his own fingers in his arse. His lover's breathing grew harsher, a low growl starting in his throat and turning into a loud groan as Cade finished what he was doing and lowered himself onto Quinn's eager cock. Cade's hands flattened themselves palm down on Quinn's tight stomach as he took Quinn inside him. He moved on top of Quinn, his slow, deliberate movements causing Quinn's body to move beneath him.

Cade lifted and lowered himself, loving the way Quinn watched, mesmerised, as his cock went in and out of Cade's body. He loved the fact that he was in charge of this amazingly sexy and complicated man, his for the taking. With his hands tied, Quinn's only weapons were his mouth and his cock, and he used both of them to best advantage as he sought Cade's mouth out greedily and met each movement of his hips with one of his own. Cade drank in the smell and the taste of him, his eyes watching the play of emotions across Quinn's face, and he thought he could never be in a better place than this one. Finally after what seemed an age, their motions together grew more urgent and Cade kissed him violently, as Quinn's moans grew louder and they matched each other in volume and intensity.

"God, this feels so good," Cade gasped. "I think I'm going to come just like this." He sensed Quinn was near as well.

"Don't stop what you're doing," Quinn groaned. "Whatever you do, just keep going."

"I couldn't stop if I tried," Cade groaned as his head went back and the shudders of his climax racked his body. Hot, wet streams of come covered them both, bellies and chests.

Cade held onto Quinn tightly as he climaxed soon after, his cries of pleasure muffled by Cade's lips as their mouths ground together in shared passion, their bodies pressing together, sweat to sweat, until finally both of them were still and gasping in the aftermath.

"Jesus!" Quinn gasped, his breath heaving. "I think that's the second time you've tried to kill me through sex. Third time might be the charm."

Cade still sat on top of him, satiated cock bobbing as he laughed and ran his hands through his damp, sweaty hair. "You make it so easy. You turn me on like never before."

"Perhaps you could untie me now, though?" Quinn tugged at his bindings as Cade watched him slyly.

"Actually, I think I might take a few photos first for my personal collection," Cade said wickedly as he moved off him and swung his legs out of bed.

Quinn looked at him in apprehension. "Don't you dare. I don't need those sorts of pictures floating around."

Cade chortled as he padded naked to the dresser and found his mobile phone.

"Cade, I'm serious. Don't you fucking take any photos of me like this. And you need to untie me. Now."

His Warlock king's imperious command went straight over Cade's head as he chuckled, taking a couple of pictures with his phone while Quinn looked on in frustration. "Sorry. My game, my rules. I promise you I'll keep them very safe. It's for me to look at when you're not around and I want to have my own happy time."

Quinn watched with narrowed eyes and flared nostrils as Cade put the phone back on the dresser. "And it's password protected, too, so you won't be able to go in and delete anything." Cade saw his mouth twitch and knew he'd been going to do just that. He'd probably have some witchy spell he'd use when Cade wasn't around to destroy it but he'd take that chance. He'd already uploaded the images to his Dropbox folder and Cade doubted slyly Quinn would think of getting to that one.

He walked back over to Quinn and straddled him again, sitting on his stomach as he reached over and undid the silk ties one by one. Quinn watched him carefully, the air with fraught with tension. Once he'd finished, Cade leaned back and regarded him with amusement as Quinn flexed his wrists, getting the kinks out of them.

"Was that everything you expected?" Cade asked sweetly, holding back a laugh at the look of speculation on Quinn's face. "Just remember you owe me one now, next time it's my turn to be tied up."

Quinn regarded him thoughtfully. "I can safely say I look forward to that one." He reached over and caressed Cade's cheek but with a glint in his eyes. "You do know I could have magycked those ties off at any time I wanted? I wanted to see how far you'd take this whole control thing. And you'd better be prepared for *my* photo shoot."

Cade sniffed. "I can live with that. I'm not as uptight as you about naked photos."

Quinn reached over and pushed him to one side of the bed, covering his body with his as he held Cade's hands tightly above his head. He leaned in and bit his neck gently, sucking at the skin.

Cade scowled. "Stop that. You know I don't like love bites. It's juvenile."

Quinn stopped what he was doing and looked at him lazily. "Really? Well, I never. Too bad I'm not going to listen to you then, isn't it?"

He continued his sucking of Cade's neck as he struggled beneath him trying to get free. But Cade knew there was no way he'd be able to fight Quinn off. The man was as strong as an ox and just as tough. When he was finished, Quinn rolled off him, regarding the purpling bruise with satisfaction.

"You bastard!" Cade hissed. "Now I'm going to have keep it covered up so people don't think I'm some sort of eighteen-year-old jock making out under the bleachers with the other college jock."

"Cade, baby, I don't think anyone will think you're eighteen," Quinn remarked as he got out of the bed with alacrity to avoid a fierce slap. He chuckled as he pulled on his jogging bottoms. "I'm going to get a glass of wine. I'm a little jazzed up from that session and I need something to help me sleep. Do you want anything?"

Cade shook his head mutinously as he lay back in bed. Quinn laughed at him as he left the room.

"You play with fire, you get burned," he called out as he descended the staircase.

"Yeah? Well, just you wait, clever clogs. I'll have my revenge." He chuckled at his bad thoughts and lay back in the bed, pulling the covers over, waiting for Quinn to come back to bed. He was half dozing when he heard the sound of a glass shatter as it hit the floor.

He bolted upright in bed. "Quinn? Are you all right?" There was no sound from downstairs. He got out of bed, pulling on his boxers then he moved across to the door and peered out into the hallway. "Is everything okay?"

There was still no reply from downstairs and he started down the stairs slowly, seeing the light on in the kitchen but hearing nothing. His heart beat faster as he reached the kitchen and slowly pushed the door open. Quinn was hunched in a corner, his eyes closed, blood trickling from his nose, his face white as chalk. Cade rushed over to him, trying to avoid the shattered pieces of glass on the floor from meeting his bare feet.

"God, what's wrong, what's happened?"

Quinn shook his head, as if trying to shake something out of it. His eyes were screwed shut as if in pain, his whole body trembling. He seemed to be muttering something over and over again but Cade couldn't hear what he was saying. It sounded like *"relinkwi me solus"* but he had no idea what the words meant. Quinn looked up at him and Cade drew back slightly. Quinn's eyes were slits of black ice regarding him with such malevolence that he felt a stab of fear. Cade reached out a hand tentatively to touch Quinn's shoulder and he snarled, knocking the hand away with such force that it smacked against the wall. Cade cried out in pain and his cry seemed to bring Quinn to his senses. His face cleared slowly, as he blinked at Cade dazedly. "I'm sorry. I didn't realise it was you. I thought it was him." He leaned back against the wall, his nosebleed dripping onto his chest in steady constant drops. He spoke softly to himself. "I won't hurt him, Taliesin. Stop worrying."

Cade frowned. "We need to stop this bleeding. Come on, let me help you up." He stood up, reaching out a hand and helping Quinn to his feet, where he stood, slightly unsteady.

"Come across to the bathroom. We need to get a cold washcloth to stop that." Cade pulled him over to the bathroom and made him sit down on the toilet seat whilst he soaked a cloth with cold water and laid it across the bridge of his nose. Quinn leaned back, his face still snow white. Cade waited silently for the washcloth to do its work. Quinn said nothing, simply sat there with his eyes closed.

Cade's whole body filled with fear for Quinn, fear that something was terribly wrong with him. Finally his lover raised his head and took the washcloth off, putting it into the basin. His nosebleed had stopped and he stood up, regarding himself in the mirror then picked the cloth up again and cleaned the blood off his nose and chest. Cade saw his eyes were pure black, no iris to be seen. It was a very disconcerting sight.

"What the hell happened?" Cade's voice was quiet. He'd never felt so scared, not even when he was being tortured by Andrew.

Quinn heaved a shuddering sigh. "I was downstairs getting the wine and I smelt something burning. I couldn't figure out where it was coming from. I looked around and then someone tapped me on the shoulder." He swallowed, his voice raw. "I thought it was you but it wasn't. It was Adam. He was on fire, and the smell of burning flesh was sickening. I heard him screaming and he kept pushing me in the chest with his hand—claw, more like it. I felt this pain and looked down and I was on fire too. I tried to put out the flames but it didn't seem to work and Adam kept coming closer and eventually"—his voice trembled—"I don't remember what happened then until you cried out."

"You were saying something, it sounded like 'relinkwi me solus.' What the hell does that mean?"

Quinn smiled faintly. "Bad pronunciation, but I imagine I was saying '*Relinquere me solus,*' which is Latin for 'leave me alone.'" I sometimes revert to Latin when I'm really stressed. It's a Warlock thing."

Cade saw he was trying to put his mind at ease but he wanted none of it. "Why did this happen?" He reached out and cupped Quinn's cheek. "Have you had it this bad before? Your eyes have gone all black."

Quinn shook his head. "I sometimes see him, but not like this. This was extreme. I don't know why. Taliesin feels it too. The eye thing…it happens sometimes."

He looked exhausted and Cade hugged him, kissing his neck and wrapping his arms around his waist. "You need to come back to bed and try and sleep. Let's go upstairs and perhaps we can make more sense of this in the morning when we've had a good night's sleep." Privately he thought neither of them would get a good night's sleep tonight but it sounded good just saying the words.

They walked silently up the stairs to the bedroom and got back into bed, each of them quiet, busy with their own thoughts. Cade snuggled into Quinn, stroking his stomach and running his hand through his hair, listening to his breathing slowly deepen as he fell asleep. He stayed awake for some time afterward, wondering what the hell had happened and how Quinn was going to protect himself from any demons he needed to face. It looked like there was nowhere really safe to go.

Chapter 30

Jeremy Payton scowled ferociously as he unlocked his letter drop box in the bus station for the latest information from the Witchhunters Alliance. They'd been leaving him messages less frequently recently, ever since they'd told him to lie low and stop killing witches and Warlocks. He had a severe case of withdrawal at the moment and seriously doubted that he'd been able to carry on this way. He really needed to kill something. He liked the money they were giving him, and they'd promised him a huge killing bonus when whatever it was that they were planning was over, but he was really feeling the pinch at the moment.

His face brightened when he saw the familiar piece of yellow notepaper in his letterbox. He drew it out, checking no one was watching and went over to the seating area to read it. The writing was large and flowing, written in a cursive scrawl he struggled to read.

Jeremy

Good news. Thank you for being so patient whilst we resolve our own affairs. It has come to our attention that a combined coven of witches and Warlocks is convening Friday night at the address on the back of this note. Feel free to fulfil your duty and visit them. We wish you every success in your endeavour and will be in touch again soon.

The Alliance

Jeremy grinned. That was more like it. He turned the note over and saw the address on the back. 311 Haven Avenue, Islington, London. The boy smiled as he stuffed the note in his grubby back pocket. A coven! That meant a lot of the buggers. He'd be able to get his frustrations out at a central sitting. Jeremy sniggered and swaggered out of the bus station, with a lighter step than before. He'd be there. You could count on that.

***

Cade was pottering on the deck of his houseboat one late evening when Quinn arrived to visit. Cade had been decidedly inconspicuous at his own home and although he'd been going home to feed Marco Polo and say hello, he felt very guilty that the cat had been left much to his own devices. If he was intending spending more time at Quinn's, he'd have to perhaps think about taking the cat with him when he did. He smiled at Quinn as he came on board, noting the dark shadows under his eyes and the pallor of his face.

Quinn smiled faintly as he kissed him. "You taste of strawberries," he said softly as he went inside and seated himself on the couch.

Cade motioned to a fruit basket on the centre table. "I bought some at the Friday market this morning outside work. Help yourself."

Quinn shook his head, leaning back wearily against the back of the couch, absently stroking Marco Polo as the cat jumped onto his lap. "Not hungry, thanks."

Cade sat down beside him. "Are you still having those day-mares?"

He nodded tiredly. "Quite a few since that last one Wednesday night. Percy thinks I've been hexed."

Cade stared at him. "Hexed? What the hell is that?"

"It's a very powerful spell witches and Warlocks use to make something bad happen to you. Normally I'd be immune to those sorts of things, but a Warlock with de Vere's power, he'd be able to do it. Percy thinks Mary passed it on to me the other day. They can be transmitted fairly easily. I did feel a slight sting on my arm when she touched me but I put it down to the Fey thing." He sighed. "I was so busy trying to suppress those urges, I guess I got distracted. I imagine that was the plan all along and de Vere wants me to suffer over and over again for killing Adam. It's certainly a distraction that's working."

Cade looked at him in horror. "What can you do to stop it?"

Quinn shook his head. "Not a lot. Taliesin's working on something but a hex is a powerful piece of magyck when it's given by someone like de Vere. It will take time to fight it. Percy's seeing what he can find out about stopping it too. Anyway, enough about me. How is work?"

Cade shrugged. "Paling into insignificance with what's been going on in my personal life. I'm really struggling to concentrate on my teaching classes. I'm sure Tickler-Brown is about to fire me."

Quinn laughed at his expression of gloom. "He can't do that. I contribute to the Institute's coffers and if he did that, I promise you he'd lose his funding." His voice was firm.

Cade grinned. "I'll have to remember that. But I've no excuse. He's right to be a little frustrated with me at the moment. I'm really not focusing."

Quinn reached over and took his hand. "Life has got a lot more complicated since meeting me, hasn't it? Any regrets?"

Cade shook his head. "Absolutely none. I can't imagine not having you around. You're worth all the trouble, I promise you." His face shadowed. "I'm just sorry we haven't really celebrated your birthday yet. You haven't been feeling well and you've been so busy, I haven't been able to plan anything."

Quinn wrapped his arms around him. "You're my birthday. All I need is right here in my arms." He was just pulling Cade in closer for a kiss when his mobile rang. He frowned and then his face darkened as he saw who the caller was.

"It's Mary." He answered the phone curtly. "Quinn Fairmont. Evening, Mary."

His face hardened as he listened to the witch's words. "I see. Well, that's a real breakthrough. That's really good news."

He clenched his fist against his side at the next words. "No, I won't tell Percy. I have an ongoing investigation on that one and I'll share the results with you really soon. Thanks for letting me know. Text the address to this phone and I'll get someone on it. Goodbye, Mary."

He clicked off his phone and put it back in his pocket, his face thunderous.

"That bitch!" he muttered darkly. "The sooner I can deal with her, the better. It's killing me having to be civil to the likes of her miserable skin."

Cade raised his eyebrows. "Are you going to share?"

Quinn nodded shortly. "It looks like your plan worked. She's just told me she has a new lead on Jeremy and as long as I don't tell poor old Percy about it, we might be able to get him this time." He scowled ferociously.

Cade laid a hand on his arm. "So the plan is now that someone meets Jeremy and spills the beans about de Vere conning him with the Witchhunters Alliance and we hope he gets angry enough to go after him? Hopefully they'll kill each other but if they don't, will they be weakened? Can they be gone after individually? Once you tell him to where to look of course, on his yacht." He looked at

Quinn anxiously. "De Vere hasn't disappeared, has he? He is still on his yacht?"

Quinn nodded. "He's still there. I've got permanent eyes on him and he hasn't moved. Mary's still visiting him."

"Who's going to talk to Jeremy? It can't be you or another Warlock because he'll sense it," Cade said worriedly.

Quinn nodded. "We have certain human alliances we can call on for this kind of thing, Cade. I have someone I trust with the skills to approach Jeremy and tell him he's been duped. Someone that can look after himself even against the Witchfinder General." He chuckled humourlessly. "Daniel will give Jeremy a run for his money, I promise you."

Cade sat back, a look of relief on his face. "So we wait now for Daniel to do his thing and see what happens."

Quinn leaned forward, his eyes shadowed. "I'm single-handedly starting a war here. Make no bones about that. The Consortium may all be in agreement with me but I am pitting Witchfinder General against Warlock. There could be casualties. I need you to realise that my hands are not clean on this."

Cade heard the pain in Quinn's voice. He shook his head vehemently. "You have no choice. They're both mortal enemies of yours and your people and you have to protect everyone. There have been too many deaths already." Cade knew the days ahead would be fairly dark and it would take everything he had to help Quinn get through it. As strong as Quinn was, he was going to face some difficult decisions.

***

Quinn sat in his darkened lounge, gazing out over the glimmering lights of the heath. The house was quiet save the ticking of the wall clock. He'd sent Cade home earlier, telling him he had a Consortium meeting he was holding in his home. It wasn't the truth. He'd simply wanted Cade away from the house when Percy came round later tonight. He had a feeling it was going to be very eventful. His lover was better off on his boat with Magnus watching over him. Quinn needed one less distraction at the moment. He was also exhausted from the unrelenting hex activity and the voices in his head. The effects had grown worse and although he could fight off some of it, it was a constant battle to stay sane. He knew without a doubt that this was all something designed to wear him down, lose focus and drive him crazy and he acknowledged tiredly to himself that it was working. Taliesin had also expressed a very fervent expletive at the constant interruptions and emotional drain running through Quinn. His Withinner was feeling the effects too.

He heard the faint knock at the door and got up wearily to answer it. Percy stood there, his face grave as he saw Quinn.

"Jesus, Quinn. You look dreadful." He came inside, taking off his coat and hanging it up on the coat stand in the entrance. "You'd better hope this stuff works, or God knows what you'll look like tomorrow."

The "stuff" he was referring to was clenched in his hand, a strange luminescent collection of various plants, waving fronds and what looked like long, sausage-like pods.

"Nicholas was adamant this would work to counteract the hex. Certainly enough to make it more manageable. He's been scouring every book and old text he's got trying to get this stuff together. It's taken a while, I can tell you. Some of this stuff is from the most obscure places imaginable."

Percy's Withinner was Nicholas Flamel, a powerful alchemist. From the stories Percy had told Quinn, his Withinner had been incensed at not being able to help when the original problem of the cadmium had been discovered. Because it was virtually a new mineral to a fourteenth-century alchemist, "Mary Hawthorne" had pipped him to the post. But in matters of ancient magyckal activity and antidotes, Nicholas was beyond compare.

Quinn closed the door and turned to Percy, who reached into his pocket and pulled out a handkerchief.

"You're bleeding again," he said quietly. "We need to get this counter-hex done soon or you're going to be in bad shape. And you're not in that good enough shape as it is after recent events."

"Thanks for that vote of confidence." Quinn said drily as he let Percy carefully wipe up the blood from under his nose. "But I agree. Whatever you need to do, just do it. We'll manage."

Percy motioned to Quinn to sit down on the couch. "Close your eyes and think of England," he said, chuckling. "It shouldn't hurt too much but there could be a bit of pain."

"Carry on," Quinn said in resignation. "I can't take much more of this current situation. A little bit more pain isn't going to matter."

"It needs to get into your bloodstream. That's where the hex is now and that's where we need to attack it from."

Quinn lay back, his eyes closed, listening to Percy's chants, the voice growing more French as Percy's Withinner materialised to perform the magyck. The cadence of the alchemist's voice was mesmerising and Quinn grew dizzy. His body started to tremble and his extremities grew cold. He opened his eyes to see Nicholas holding the plants and the other things he'd brought slowly transform into a golden puddle of light, a floating ball before his fingers, one that stayed suspended in the air as Nicholas slowly drew the ball together in his hands. He gently grasped both edges of the ball and stretched it, changing it into a liquid stream of what looked like pure fire. Quinn gazed, mesmerized, at the sight.

Nicholas caught his eye and smiled softly. "As I said, this will hurt a bit, Grand Master. But it should be very bearable after what you have already been through. Are you ready?"

The soft Gallic accent echoed in Quinn's brain, which now was feeling as if a thousand bees were buzzing in it. He nodded, bracing himself for whatever was to come.

He wasn't prepared for the agony he felt as Nicholas slowly laid his hand on his chest and fed the golden stream of light into Quinn's body. It was as if someone had taken a very sharp knife and was trying to prise his breastbone open whilst he was awake, gouging like an inexperienced butcher.

Nicholas's eyes grew wide at the unexpected reaction as Quinn's body jerked, his agonised cries and those of his own Withinner echoing through the house.

The fire stream burnt its way into Quinn's body, wrapping itself around his heart, his lungs and anywhere else it could find, searing them with liquid fire. He couldn't breathe and his mind grew dark with pain even as his body jerked like a marionette's, arms and legs spontaneously kicking and flailing. He was burning from the inside and the agony was such that he retched, vomiting up that night's dinner.

Nicholas's face was pale and anxious as he bent over him. Quinn vaguely heard a voice, sounding like Cade's, shouting at someone and then there was a final explosion of light in his head and blessedly he felt no more.

***

Cade stood in horror at the lounge door as he witnessed Quinn's agonised throes. As he watched, Nicholas disappeared and Percy stood in his place, on his knees by the still-spasmodically jerking Quinn. Blood rushed from Quinn's nose—not fresh blood, but huge, dark and clotted gouts of it. His mouth was stained with vomit.

Cade rushed into the room. "Jesus, Percy, what the hell is going on? What's happened to him? You have to stop it!"

He knelt down beside his lover, whose body twitched spasmodically. Quinn's eyes were closed, sunken back into his head and his face was so white Cade thought he was dead.

"I don't know what's happened." Percy's voice was desperate. "This shouldn't have happened. The reaction is far too extreme."

"Help him for God's sake. He's dying, damn it. I can hardly hear his heartbeat."

Cade had his head to Quinn's chest, his fingers desperately trying to find a pulse. Quinn's body was still now but the blood still gushed from his nose.

Percy watched his friend in distress. "Cade, I don't know how to fix this. Neither does Nicholas. I need to get him to the clinic again. We need Taliesin."

Even as he spoke, Cade gasped as Quinn's body materialised into Taliesin's, lying supine on the floor, his dark features racked with pain, the same blood falling from his nose. He tried to sit up, his features grimacing painfully. Cade reached out a hand to help him. The Withinner took his hand as he struggled to a sitting position, his voice filled with agony.

"Percy, I have to get Quinn back to the Power retreat urgently. You need to get Nicholas there. Quinn needs specialised magyckal attention and I can help from there. The hex went deeper than anyone knew. De Vere knew we might reverse it and he cunningly adapted it to make Quinn suffer should we try. If you don't do this, he will not survive. That is sure."

Cade stepped forward, his eyes filling with angry tears, his voice desperate. "Promise me, Taliesin. Promise me you'll heal him. Please."

The Withinner nodded, with no hesitation. "I will try save him. You have my word."

Seconds later Taliesin and Quinn had simply disappeared. Percy looked at Cade awkwardly. "I have to go. Taliesin will need

Nicholas and every other Withinner we can summon. The Power retreat is the best place for him now. I need to get us there."

Cade nodded dully. "Just save him for me, please."

Percy nodded. "I'll come back as soon as I'm done. You have my word." Percy patted his shoulder and was gone too.

Some hours later, having cleaned up the blood and sick from the floor, a pale-faced Cade sat in the lounge, a large glass of whisky in his hand. Cade gazed unseeingly out at the heath.

How many times was he expected to lose the man he loved? Was Fate conspiring against them to make things as fucking difficult as they could?

He took a sip of his whisky then sighed, put the glass down and stood up. There was nothing to be gained sitting here stewing in his own fear and loss and drinking himself into oblivion. He needed to get some sleep and wait for Percy's return. Quinn would need him strong and positive, not weak and hungover. Best to go to bed, to try and while away the waiting time with sweet dreams of him and Quinn rather than agonise over what might be. With a heavy heart, Cade made his way to his bed alone.

Chapter 31

Cade was awakened by a knocking at the front door and sat up, peering blearily at his watch. It was seven a.m. He pulled on a pair of sweats and ran down the stairs to open the door to see an ashen-faced Percy standing on the doorstep.

"How is Quinn?" were Cade's first words.

Percy nodded. "Stable. It was pretty touch and go but we managed to cleanse him of the hex and repair some of the damage. He's resting now with a lot of energy flowing his way as people take turns flooding the room, so I'm back to take a break then I'll take my turn again later. But he's rallying. I'm sorry you can't be there but you couldn't see him anyway. He's in isolation in one of the magyckal areas." His voice faltered and Cade felt a sense of shame that he hadn't invited the man in. He looked wrecked.

"Come in Percy, please. Sorry, I forgot my manners." He ushered Percy into the lounge, made him sit down and then sat down beside him. Percy leaned back tiredly, his eyes closed, and Cade simply waited. He had so many questions but Percy looked as if he needed a moment. Just as Percy's eyes opened, his mobile rang. He gave a tired sigh and answered it. Cade listened to some of the conversation, which seemed to be Consortium business and an update on the meeting with Jeremy Payton. Finally Percy finished and put his phone back in his pocket.

Cade looked up. "I forgot I had his reading glasses in my jacket last night." he said quietly. "I thought he might need them so I thought I'd bring them over quickly. I wasn't expecting what I found." He shivered at the memory of Quinn's broken body lying on the floor.

Percy nodded, sighing wearily. "If anyone can fight this, it's Quinn. He's a tough bastard and he has Taliesin. Christ, I'd never seen anything like that before in my life."

He sat, staring down at the floor. "That was Daniel on the phone. He said the meeting with Jeremy went all right, that's he's a nasty little bastard who deserves everything he's going to get but for now, he's so riled at de Vere tricking him that his focus has at least shifted from us. Daniel says he doesn't think he suspected anything. He managed to convince him he was from the real Witchhunters Alliance, not difficult to do considering who he is." He sighed. "I didn't tell him about Quinn. He's got enough on his plate and that will just upset him unduly."

"Who is this Daniel anyway?" Cade said tiredly. "I've been meaning to ask. Quinn seems to think a lot of him."

Percy sighed. "It all sounds so stereotypical, but Daniel is the leader of RAW—Resistance Against Witchhunters." He smiled slightly at Cade's look of disbelief. "I know. It sounds silly even to me and I know how powerful the organisation is. It's very deeply buried and we've managed to keep it fairly small and very secret. WA knows it exists but they haven't been able to find out much about it let alone who leads it. Daniel runs it with an iron fist. The difference with Daniel is that he's a human leading a bunch of magyckal beings. RAW is composed of humans, witches and Warlocks, who work together against the Witchhunters Alliance, because, make no mistake, we don't underestimate them. As Dan is human, he manages to attract a lot less suspicion than anyone else. He has one very big foot inside WA as a human, knows everything that goes on, and is very well thought of in there. The WA think Daniel's trying to infiltrate RAW and that's the beauty of it. He's the Consortium equivalent of a double agent, I suppose.

He feeds the WA information on the Consortium, the Praetorium, RAW, anything he feels he can give away that will make them feel he's contributing but nothing that would seriously damage any of these organisations. It was Quinn's idea."

"How can Daniel be with the WA and fight them at the same time? Surely that must cause him a real conflict of interest?" Despite his grief and worry for Quinn, Cade was curious as to how someone could be so dually represented on different sides. "And what's the Praetorium?"

Percy's face clouded. "The Praetorium is the witch's equivalent of the Consortium. It's run by a very powerful witch. And make no mistake, Daniel's first allegiance is to RAW. His late wife was a witch, hunted and killed by WA. He'll do anything to destroy them." Percy glanced at Cade. "You've heard Quinn talk about the end justifying the means, Cade?"

Cade nodded.

"Well, Quinn truly believes that. It's not just lip service and he can be a very ruthless bastard when he wants to be. I told you once he was single minded and driven and fully earned his title of Grand Master. Having Daniel in the WA serves a good purpose even if it destroys him every time he has to listen to another story about how they hunted one of us down and killed us. Sometimes Daniel's even had to sanction a killing."

Percy's face was grim. "And Quinn has to deal with that. He'll try and stop it, have no doubt, but sometimes I wonder if he'd let it happen if there was a risk of exposing Daniel."

His face darkened. "Quinn believes in the bigger picture, a burden he's had to shoulder since he took on the mantle he has." He took a deep breath. "Daniel is Quinn's family, Cade. He's Quinn's uncle by marriage. Daniel's wife Moira was Quinn's aunt on his mother's side. Quinn's mother was a witch, his father a Warlock."

Cade gasped at the news, his eyes widening. "I had no idea Quinn had any family left, never mind having two Fey beings for parents."

"Moira was murdered four years ago by the Alliance. Daniel and Moira virtually raised Quinn when his parents died. Daniel is more than an uncle to him. He's a father figure." He shifted in his chair. "It's actually an incredible story and all Quinn's idea. When Moira died, Daniel—that's not his real name by the way, just the one he has now, his real name was Sam—wanted to get revenge. Quinn convinced him he'd be better off working on a longer term basis to bring the Alliance down rather than go off half cocked and kill a few of them."

Cade heaved a sharp breath as Percy continued. "So Quinn 'arranged' the death of the original man, his true uncle Sam, so that there were no ties and resurrected the Daniel persona. Daniel even underwent psychical plastic surgery to alter his appearance. The witch killings were fairly high profile and everybody knew Sam's face. So he gave up his old life and created a new one as leader of RAW and a mole in the Alliance."

He stopped and passed a weary hand over his eyes. Cade was shell-shocked at the mysterious murky world his lover commanded.

"It also means that the familial ties between Sam and Quinn had to be severed completely. The two of them could never have a normal family relationship again; it would have given Daniel away. So the only time they meet now is in places where they are protected, like the Consortium. It's been rough on both of them—they are very close—and to have another father taken away from him was tough on Quinn. But he was prepared to do it for the good of the Consortium and the causes he believes in."

Cade leaned back, aghast at news Quinn had never told him. "I don't know anything about him, do I?" he said softly. "I love him, I share a bed with him but still he's a complete mystery to me."

Percy saw his expression and reached out and squeezed his shoulder.

"Cade, don't blame Quinn for not telling you anything. You've only known him about four months. That's nothing, a mere blip in time. You still have a lifetime together and you're going to need a lifetime to find out what makes Quinn tick, I can tell you."

He grinned wryly. "He'll probably have my nuts for telling you what I have so far. Quinn is a very private person. He's fiercely protective about those he loves, of which you are one, and he's also fiercely loyal to the Consortium. He's very aware of his birthright and responsibilities as a Fairmont and he'll do anything to live up to it."

"And yet he's not here with me," Cade whispered. "What do you think is happening? Do you think Taliesin can fix him? It's all very frustrating and it makes my head hurt."

Percy grinned slightly. "I'm a Warlock and my head is hurting too. There's just so much going on." He stood up and looked at his watch. "It's almost midnight. Would you mind if I used the spare room and I'll stay here tonight? I'll go home tomorrow, but I want to stay here with you, keep an eye on you. It's the least I can do for Quinn." He chuckled. "I have no doubt Magnus is lurking somewhere close by too, so you'll be well looked after with the two of us here."

Cade felt relieved that he wouldn't be left alone. "Of course. You know where the bedroom is. Make yourself comfortable."

He stood up to say goodnight and watched Percy mount the staircase to the guest room. Cade followed him up a few minutes later, switching off the lights. He got into bed, thinking about Quinn and what he might be going through. His fists tightened at his sides. He felt so impotent at being unable to help in any way. It took him a long time to get to sleep and when he finally dozed off, he hugged Quinn's pillow close, smelling his scent and feeling a little closer to him.

***

The next few days passed in a haze for Cade as he waited for Quinn's recovery and for him to come home.

Cade stood now at the edge of the heath pond, gazing out over the water, ready to swim his way out of his doldrums and for a short time, try and forget Quinn wasn't home.

Percy gave him regular reports and it appeared that Quinn was getting better, although still being held in a magyckal coma while he healed. Cade had called work and taken some personal time. There was no way he could drag himself into the office and pretend everything was normal. Life hadn't been normal since meeting Quinn and although he wouldn't have it any other way, the strain of this very unorthodox relationship and Quinn's regular habit of nearly dying was beginning to take its toll.

He launched himself into the water and headed out for the buoy in the middle of the pond. His arms wheeled through the water like pistons, and he treasured the feel of the cold water on his skin, the sensation of weightlessness and freedom that came from being suspended in the water. Cade reached the buoy and stretched out a hand to touch it for luck as he always did, and said a short prayer that Quinn would soon be home. Then, as Cade hung onto the buoy, getting his breath back for the swim back to shore, he noticed a strange luminescence on the water a few feet from him. He narrowed his eyes trying to see it better, and finally, unable to make out what it might be, he held his breath and disappeared under the surface. Cade was adept at holding his breath. He had scored a personal best time of nearly four minutes, something that had made the lifeguards at the pool he swam at very twitchy as they walked up and down the pool side, hoping that he would make it back up.

As he peered into the water, the light seemed to shift, drifting toward him inch by inch. Curious, he reached out and touched it as it got in front of him. He was surprised at the fact that he wasn't scared, that whatever it was seemed benign and wasn't looking to harm him. Cade had no idea why he knew this. As he made contact with the substance, warmth spread through him like a sudden drift of heat passing through his body.

He closed his eyes as he embraced it, hearing vague whispers echoing in his ears. Cade couldn't understand any of them but he knew it wasn't English. He let the feeling of completeness soak through his skin until finally he could hold his breath no longer. With a spurt of energy, he drove upward through the water to the surface, breaking through with a gasp, and he sucked in a deep breath of air.

When he looked across the pond again, the luminescence had gone and he was left with a sense of loss. Something deep inside him said that he'd just made first contact with his kind, another Sprite perhaps. Cade waited patiently in the water, hoping that it would come back but after ten minutes, the sensation of warmth has dissipated and his skin was cold and goose pimply. He knew he needed to get out the water and get warm. It was with a deep sense of reluctance that he made the long swim back to the shore, back to dry land and home, where he hoped perhaps Quinn would be waiting.

Chapter 32

Quinn sat on the edge of the bed in the darkness, still feeling as fragile as glass but relieved to be home and to find Cade sleeping in his bed, hugging Quinn's favourite sweatshirt. Quinn smiled tenderly at the sight as he reached out a hand and softly moved a tendril of hair from Cade's forehead then leaned forward and kissed his cheek.

"Wake up, sleepy," he murmured. "Open those beautiful eyes of yours."

Cade's eyes opened at the sound of his voice. Quinn saw unfocused sleepy eyes regard him hazily then a huge grin split Cade's face as he sat up, covers falling to his waist. He reached out for Quinn, pulling him into a warm embrace, as his cheek rubbed against Quinn's bristled one. That simple movement of affection had Quinn's heart swelling with emotion.

"You're back." Cade murmured softly. "How do you feel? Did Taliesin manage to heal you? What the fuck took you so long? It's been killing me waiting—"

Quinn kissed him softly, shutting off the flow of questions. He was shattered beyond belief but thankful he was still alive and back with his lover. "I've just got back. I'm better but still a little fragile so be gentle with me," he whispered against Cade's ear. "That means no death by sex, please. I don't think I could survive it, even though I'd love to."

Cade pulled him down to lie beside him, his hands drawing him possessively closer, lips close to his ear as he snuggled into him like a puppy burrowing into its mother's side. Quinn thought wryly it was as close as his boyfriend could get without crawling inside him.

"I don't care what he did," Cade whispered huskily. "He promised to bring you back to me and he did. That was five days ago. Five days, you miserable bastard. I've been insane with fucking worry. I had updates but I've been out of my mind. The powers that be wouldn't let me be with you; they said you were in isolation."

"I know," Quinn whispered. "I'm sorry. It was rough going and Taliesin wouldn't bring me back until he was sure I was strong enough. You know him—he's a bossy boots."

His Withinner stirred at his description. Taliesin had suffered greatly trying to heal them both and Quinn knew if his Withinner had been anyone else, he wouldn't be sitting here right now with the man he loved.

Cade smiled, his hands touching him constantly as if trying to make sure he was really there. Quinn closed his eyes, lying back on the bed, feeling the tiredness sweep through him. It seemed that this feeling was ever present, this constant exhaustion. He wondered wryly just how long he could sustain it.

"It was touch and go again," he murmured as he stroked Cade's smooth, warm shoulder. "Whatever de Vere had done took Taliesin a long time to get rid of. My poor Withinner certainly earned his medal this time. It took a lot to heal me—again." He shivered. "I never want to go through that again. De Vere really outdid himself with that hex."

"Tell Taliesin thank you," Cade said softly. "Please tell him I'm very grateful and I owe him one."

Taliesin huffed in disagreement. *He owes me nothing. We are even now. I've made up for my digression. Tell him that.*

Quinn grinned. "He says you're even. You don't owe him anything. He wanted to make up to you for what he did." He sat up and regarded Cade carefully. "Did Daniel manage to resolve things with Jeremy? What have I missed? Has a war started yet?"

Cade reached up and put his finger against his lips. "No work talk. But yes, Uncle Daniel did have the conversation with Jeremy and directed him toward de Vere. It's been quiet so far. Percy has been close to everything, managing things for you whilst you've been gone. I'm sure he'll fill you in tomorrow when you see him."

Quinn regarded him carefully. "*Uncle* Daniel? Has Percy been spilling the beans about me? What else did he tell you?" He kept his voice neutral but he didn't like too much of his private life being disclosed even to Cade. The less he knew, the safer he'd be. Experience had taught him that.

Cade shrugged, brushing a lock of hair out of Quinn's eyes. "I know he's the leader of the Resistance, which, by the way, makes me embarrassed to say it as it sounds so hackneyed. That he was married to your aunt, who was killed by the Alliance. That's all he told me. So take that scowl off your face and cut Percy some slack. He was as traumatised as I was at what happened to you and needed to share something about you."

Quinn was relieved that Percy hadn't told Cade much more. He'd a lot of secrets in his closet and if anyone was going to tell Cade about them, it would be him alone. And there were some he'd never share with him.

"I'm glad you're here. I missed you." Cade's voice caught.

Quinn cradled Cade's face in his hands and gave him a soft, sweet kiss. "I'm here so go back to sleep, and we'll talk later. It's two in the morning. I love you."

"I love you too. Welcome home, Quinn."

***

The following morning Quinn slept in and woke up around ten. The other side of his bed was empty and he stretched and yawned.

He padded naked to the shower, wondering with a frown how his clothes had been taken off as he was sure he'd been wearing them when he'd fallen asleep. He was getting dressed into jeans and a shirt when the doorbell rang. He heard Cade answer the door and at the voice he heard next, he was down the stairs in a shot, taking them two at a time.

Cade faced Mary Hawthorne and Quinn saw from his body posture that Cade wasn't happy. His back was rigid, hands clenched into fists at his sides. He was like a bull terrier poised to rip someone's throat out.

Christ. I need to get these two away from each other before Cade goes ballistic and blows our cover.

He walked swiftly over to them, nodding to Mary. He turned Cade around to face him and kissed him deeply, all the time holding his arms down by his sides and squeezing them in warning.

"Morning, honey. Where's that coffee you promised me? I've been waiting ages. Mary, it's good to see you. Shall we go through to the lounge? Would you like coffee too?"

He took Mary firmly by the arm, leading her through to the lounge, leaving Cade standing behind and glaring daggers at the witch.

Mary looked at him in confusion. "Quinn, I thought you were away? Cade told me you'd gone on a sudden business trip and they weren't sure when you'd get back."

Quinn shrugged as he sat down in an armchair and motioned for her to do the same. "I got back this morning. It was cut short. What can I help you with?" He looked at her enquiringly.

She gazed at him narrowly. "That information I gave you the other night. Did you act on it?"

He pretended to look puzzled. "The address you gave us for Jeremy Payton? Yes, I sent a team down there. They didn't find him."

Mary frowned. "He was there. Your team should have found him there. I don't understand. The information was very good. You didn't tell Percy about it, did you, so he could warn him?" She stared at him and Quinn wanted nothing more that to blast her with a ball of fire and watch her shrivel up.

"No, I didn't tell Percy. And please don't question my actions or those of my team." His voice was steely and she flushed. "I can assure you we didn't find Jeremy so your information couldn't have been as good as you thought it was."

Her voice was quiet when she spoke. "I'm sorry. I didn't mean to question you. It's just I really thought we'd got him this time. Perhaps next time."

She shifted uncomfortably. "You look tired. Are you feeling all right?"

He nodded. "I've had some nosebleeds and spells of dizziness recently but nothing I can't handle. Thank you for asking."

He watched Cade warily as he brought a tray in with two cups of coffee. His boyfriend caught his eye but ignored his warning glance. "Your coffee, guys. You don't mind if I sit here and listen, do you?" He sat down, his long legs curled up beneath him on the couch. Quinn glared at him. Cade smiled at him sweetly.

"Have you any other leads on Jeremy for us?" Quinn asked. "I know we need to step up the search for him, so anything else you can find out would be useful."

"I'll try and run through my sources. I think you're right. We need to increase our efforts and find this monster before he hurts anyone else. It's taking far too long and soon we're going to run out of time." Mary leaned forward and took a sip of coffee. Quinn didn't miss Cade's sly smile and he groaned inwardly.

Jesus, what the hell had he done to the woman's coffee? The man was a menace even if he worshipped the ground he walked on.

Mary drank her coffee as she glanced at Cade. "Is everything all right at work, Cade? And how are things with that lovely cat of yours? He must be a bit lonely on the boat seeing as how you're here so often."

Cade smiled but his eyes were flat. "Work is good, thanks. And Marco is fine. He's a cat; he's used to being by himself. But I did think if I was going to spend more time here, I might bring him here for a while so he has some company."

Quinn started at those words. He hadn't been aware of that plan.

Mary turned to Quinn. "How's Jomo? Is he getting any better?"

Quinn's anger surged at the nerve of the woman mentioning his friend, the one she'd probably had a part in attacking.

"He's very well. Physically he's fine. But Percy and the others are still trying to restore some of his memories. It's a long process. He wants to come back to work next week, but I'm trying to convince him to stay where he is for the time being. It's safer at the moment until all this madness is over and we have the Witchfinder General and de Vere all wrapped up."

Quinn's mobile rang and he excused himself to answer it. "Quinn Fairmont."

"Quinn? It's Daniel. How are you, son?" Daniel Wickman's soft West Country burr echoed down the phone. His voice always caused a sense of peace in Quinn and this time was no exception.

"Daniel! Good to hear from you. I was hoping to catch up with you later but you beat me to it. How's the plan going?"

"That Jeremy is a nasty little bastard. A complete sociopath. It's one thing having the WFG in someone; it's another having it in a psychopathic fifteen-year-old with raging hormones. He took some convincing but I managed to do it."

"Are you tracking him?" Quinn spoke quietly, not wanting to alert Mary.

"We are. He thinks he's working with the real WA now to track down a Warlock. But he's got plans on sorting de Vere out for himself. I told him to watch out for the witch."

Daniel's voice sounded a little uncertain as he continued. "Are you sure about this plan? We could get rid of the little bugger ourselves then go after de Vere without his help. It seems a little risky to sic them both on each other in the hope they'll kill each other."

Quinn closed his eyes and rubbed his hands through his hair. He had to admit he'd been wondering the same thing himself. "Dan, I'm not that strong at the moment. I've had a rough time and I can't take him on one on one now."

"Are you all right? Percy told me about the Unity thing but I thought you were getting over that?"

Daniel's tone was concerned, that of a man for his son and Quinn felt a lump in his throat. Percy had obviously not told Daniel about everything that had happened since the Unity episode. The hex, the undoing of it and the resultant melt down. Not to mention the constant nosebleeds, headaches and ghostly visions.

"I am. I'm just not recovering quickly enough. Dan, you know it would take an army of Warlocks to take down de Vere and he'll see that coming. This is someone we need to be careful with and choose our moment to attack."

Daniel was silent for a moment before speaking quietly. "I know you. You want to do it yourself and you're waiting for the right time to do it, when you're stronger. In the meantime you're trying to weaken him, trying to get him to let his guard down. You have no intention of letting anyone else do it, do you?"

As this *was* Quinn's plan, he couldn't lie to the man who had been a surrogate father to him for all those years and helped him through some very bad times.

"You know there's no one else that can do it. I have to be the one."

"Does Cade know you're planning on taking him down on your own?" Although Daniel and Cade had never met, Quinn had told his uncle about him in numerous conversations.

Quinn's silence gave Daniel the answer he was looking for and he sighed. "Son, you need to be careful. You need backup on this. Please promise me you won't go off half cocked and try and do this alone. Promise me."

Quinn closed his eyes and crossed his fingers. "I promise. But in the meantime, if Jeremy manages to get to him and weakens him, it just makes what we have to do that much easier. He'll be distracted and I need every edge I can get to destroy him. As long as we have eyes on Jeremy, we can take him out anytime. He's not a problem now we've found him and we're controlling him." He chuckled grimly. "He's stepped from the proverbial frying pan into the fire, has our Jeremy. The tables have turned in our favour."

Daniel sighed heavily. "I still think you're holding back. I've known you since you were six years old, my boy. You've never done things the easy way. All I ask is that you be careful. I couldn't bear to lose you too."

Quinn swallowed. "I'll be careful. Scout's honour."

Dan chuckled. "You never it made it through the first year of scouts. I think they said you were too precocious and distracting to the other kids with your magyck tricks. Your aunt had to tell a really good story to cover that all up."

Quinn laughed, remembering the incidents and the look of complete awe on his scout group's face when he'd created a mini thunderstorm in the recreation room, much to the distress of the scoutmaster. He wondered how in hell's name his aunt had managed to explain that one away. He hadn't thought about it in a long time.

"Fine, then. You'll just have to take my word for it."

He glanced into the lounge to see if Cade and Mary were still seated and not tussling on the floor scratching each other's eyes out. He heaved a sigh of relief when he saw they looked fairly civil.

"I need to get back to what I was doing before I have a girl-fight in my lounge. And believe me, this one wouldn't be as much fun as that last one we went to. I'll call you if I hear anything new."

"Fine." Daniel was resigned. "Go stop your girl-fight. Just remember your poor old uncle this side would love to hear all about it later though. He doesn't get much action of his own."

He rang off and Quinn chuckled loudly as he put his mobile back in his pocket. He was better just for hearing his uncle's voice. He went back into the lounge and was surprised to see that the two actually appeared to be chatting amicably.

"Mary was just telling me about a great new restaurant not far from here. We should go sometime." Cade smiled at Mary, who grinned back as she stood up.

"Well, I should be getting off. I'll be in touch as soon as I have any news. Cade, see you soon and perhaps we can do that whole shopping thing together now you're on leave from work." She waved and let herself out the front door.

Quinn stared toward Cade, his jaw virtually dropping to the floor. "Who the hell are you and what have you done with my Cade?" he murmured as he kissed the side of his boyfriend's neck.

Cade chucked. "You're not the only actor in the house, you know. I can hold my own and it's probably a better strategy than wanting to run a sharp sword through her. I think I just made a BFF."

Quinn looked puzzled.

Cade sighed. "Best Friend Forever. God, don't you know anything about women?" He grinned wickedly. "I had no idea playing camp boyfriend could be so much fun." He snapped his fingers in an effeminate gesture. "I gushed on about shopping and coffee and I think she really thinks I like her. Of course she's just tolerating me. Huh. Shows you how stupid some people can be."

Quinn shook his head in amusement. "Hell, Cade, you are trouble. I knew that the minute I saw you in the woods that day." Cade's mouth curved in a sexy smile and Quinn's cock pushed against his zipper.

"That's trouble with a capital T, girlfriend," Cade camped up as he slid a hand over Quinn's crotch and fluttered his eyelashes.

Quinn caught his hand and pressed it harder against his groin. Cade's pupils dilated at the fact he was pinned in place and he took a deep breath. Quinn grinned inwardly.

Time to turn the teasing up a notch.

"I quite like this whole camp thing you have going on," he drawled. "In fact, I think you should model some sexy lingerie for me. Nice satin and lace panties, a camisole or two, high heels. Definitely stilettos." He wanted to laugh out loud at the stunned expression on Cade's face. Quinn kept his face straight, his expression sultry. "Do you think you might be up for that? I can *so* see your cock in silver lace to match your eyes…what do you say?"

Cade's face was a picture of discomfort and desire, trying to tell whether Quinn was being serious. "Really, Quinn, that's one of your fantasies? I didn't think you'd be into that kind of thing and to be honest, I've never thought about dressing in women's clothing before either. Ummm," he stumbled over his words, a deep flush rising on his cheeks. "I guess if you really wanted to, we could maybe think about it." He swallowed.

Quinn increased the pressure of Cade's hand on his cock, then leaned forward and dragged his tongue over the pulse throbbing in his lover's neck. Cade gave a strangled gurgle as Quinn bit him, sucking the skin and then looking into eyes that were both dark with desire and more than a little worry.

"You'd do that for me?" Quinn whispered as he stuck his tongue in Cade's ear causing a squeal. Cade's eyes were closed but he nodded. A surge of love swept through Quinn at the fact Cade would indeed dress in women's clothing for him to fulfil one of Quinn's desires. He pulled Cade closer to him, taking his mouth roughly, feeling Cade's roughness in the thrust of his tongue into Quinn's mouth, the press of a heated groin against his, urgent and all male.

"That's good to know, but I was only joking. I don't honestly have an expectation for you to wear sexy women's underwear." Quinn gasped as Cade's hand gripped his crotch tightly. Quinn's balls contracted in anticipated pain and fear as Cade lifted his head and glared at him dangerously.

"You fucker. You made me agree to dress in lace panties just as a joke, a tease?" Cade squeezed harder and Quinn's eyes nearly popped out of his head. "You're damn lucky I need these, Quinn," Cade squeezed one last time then released Quinn, "otherwise you'd be singing soprano." He moved away from Quinn with a satisfied smile as Quinn took a breath and tried to ease his aching cock and balls. When he'd got the feeling back in his nether regions he moved swiftly after the departing Cade, wrapping his arms around his waist and pushing him against the wall. Quinn pressed his needy groin against Cade's arse, as Cade laughed sexily.

"I know one thing." Quinn growled. "I'm feeling much stronger now and if I remember, I have a standing invitation to tie you up and do what I want to you. And I have some very inventive ideas," he whispered into Cade's ear.

His boyfriend shuddered. "I look forward to that," he murmured as he pressed back against Quinn. "But hold that thought. This morning you have to call Percy. He's been calling every five minutes and he sounds really desperate to talk to you. Consortium business trumps sex, doesn't it?"

Quinn sighed and reluctantly pulled away, his body in turmoil. "Fine. I'll give him a ring now." A thought flashed in his mind. "By the way, what exactly did you do to Mary's coffee?"

Cade's face flushed guiltily and he shook his head. "Nothing gets past you, does it?" he muttered. "God forbid one day I have another man in the cupboard. I won't be able to get away with anything with you."

Quinn watched him, eyebrow raised as he waited for the answer.

"I put a few drops of ipecac in it." Cade muttered.

Quinn looked at him in disbelief. "You laced her coffee with laxative? For God's sake, that was a little juvenile, wasn't it?" A rising surge of laughter rumbled in his chest and as he struggled to compose himself and keep a straight face.

Cade stared at him sulkily. "No more juvenile than you giving me a hickey. It won't do her much harm, just make her uncomfortable. The bitch deserved it after what she did to you. I'm tired of nearly losing you. I'm not sure I can face doing it again."

Quinn heard the catch in Cade's voice and moved over to him, burying his face in his neck. He smelt of something woodsy, smoky with a hint of coffee. "I'm not too fond of it, either. I know I promised you I'll be careful, and I seem to be making a right hash of it. I'll try harder, I promise."

He kissed Cade. "Right. Let me go see what my Marshall has to say and get an update on what's been going on. Are you going home to feed Marco?"

Cade nodded as he picked up his leather jacket and opened the front door. "I'm going swimming on the heath first, and then home. I'll be fine. Magnus is lurking somewhere so I should be safe enough." He waved at Quinn and disappeared out the door. Quinn watched as his lean, confident figure disappeared down the path. He turned and waved at Quinn as he turned onto the street. Quinn saw the huge form of Magnus close behind and felt comforted. He closed the door and went upstairs to his study where he sat down with a sigh.

Time to get back to the real world, the world of renegade Warlocks, Witchhunters, conniving witches and boyfriends who laced said witches drinks with chemicals.

He grinned slightly. *God, I love my life despite all the near-death experiences. It's never boring.*

Chapter 33

Jeremy Payton sat calmly on the dock of the Essex Marina, using one hand to train his binoculars on the yacht known as the *Sept Rois* his other hand clutching a can of tepid Coke. He had his cap pulled down low over his face as he spied on the man who had deceived and tried to make a fool out of him.

His meeting the other night with the man known as Daniel had been useful to say the least, even though he'd wanted nothing more than to rip the messenger's throat out with his bare teeth, so great had been his fury. Jeremy was glad he hadn't done so now. The information and intelligence the man had provided had been invaluable. He knew from his own contacts that Daniel Wickman was a well-known and respected member of the Witches Alliance, and Jeremy would rather have him on his side as not. They were fighting the same common enemy, weren't they?

He could be a valuable ally in tracking down the dirty, vicious witches he'd sworn to kill. Jeremy had actually quite liked the forthright manner and the quiet confidence of the man, not to mention his bravery in coming alone to such a meeting to meet the likes of him. The man was barely five foot five and looked as if a strong wind might blow him down, but his handshake had been strong and his eyes calm. Jeremy liked that.

He could smell the stench of the man he now knew as Andrew de Vere all the way across the water, a stench so foul it made him gag and the Coke taste like urine in his mouth. The witch's scent was powerful, too, and he could see her blond head sitting next to the man's dark one in the cabin. He grinned, his smile feral and anticipatory. He'd take great pleasure in killing her; women always seemed to be much more satisfying in their dying than men. It had been a while since he'd enjoyed himself with a witch. He was looking forward to slitting her throat or piercing her black heart with her own athame.

He raised the glasses again to his eyes and watched with a surge of rage as the blonde woman crawled onto the man's lap and straddled him as his hands reached into her blouse and cupped her braless breasts. His groin tingled and he smiled viciously.

"Enjoy it, you fucking bitch," he muttered darkly, leading two old ladies passing by to tut-tut in consternation and hurry on. "Enjoy the last little screw session you're going to have with that bastard because tomorrow night you're both going to be dead."

Chapter 34

Sophie Mercurio gasped as Andrew de Vere gave one final thrust inside her, groaned loudly and collapsed satiated against the couch. She leaned forward on his lap. He tipped his head back in satisfaction, his hands tightly gripping her hips.

"Not bad my love. I feel less tense than I was before. You always know how to make me feel better."

He motioned to her with an impatient wave to get off him. She moved to the side quietly and he stood up and pulled up the trousers that had been halfway down his legs, zipping them. He made his way over to the cocktail cabinet and poured a large shot of whisky before coming back and sitting down next to her.

"So, what news have you on Quinn Fairmont and the Consortium? He still suspects nothing about you then?"

Sophie shook her head as she fastened her blouse and picked up her underwear and skirt off the floor as she got dressed. "No. I'm still in the clear. He trusts me. His boyfriend even seems to be warming to me more and believe me, that's a feat in itself. He's a suspicious, nosy bastard and I wouldn't mind doing some magyck on him myself when Fairmont is out of the way and you have his Withinner."

Andrew reached out lazily and gripped Sophie's wrist tightly, his fingernails drawing blood. "That man is mine and you will do nothing at all to jeopardise that or I'll kill you myself. I owe myself the pleasure of cutting that snarky son of a bitch into pieces whilst Fairmont watches. I fully intend doing that as soon as I can."

Sophie nodded.

He released her and smiled grimly. "He escaped me once and he won't do it again. I just need to bide my time and surprise them. Fairmont has so much protection around them both it's difficult to get close. And *you* can unfortunately only do so much for me inside their circle." He frowned. "Why did the Fey blood transfusion not work? And the hex?"

Sophie cleared her throat before answering. "He says he's noticed changes since he did Unity with his Withinner. I suppose there could have been some physical difference that renders him less susceptible to the Fey blood now. No one really knows the after-effects of a Unity as hardly anyone has ever done it." She spoke spitefully. "Perhaps you should try it with Algarde, Andrew. See how it works firsthand."

Andrew smiled lazily, drew back his hand and slapped her across the face. She reeled back, blood trickling from her split lip.

He gazed at her flatly. "Pettiness doesn't become you so don't make me privy to it. I don't like it." He turned to look at the twinkling lights of the jetties and yachts beyond then turned back to her. "What about the hex? Could that have been the same thing?"

She nodded as she wiped the blood away from her mouth.

"He did seem a little pale and not quite himself a while ago. He said it was due to the nosebleeds and headaches he'd been having." She shrugged. "I can't say for sure why it didn't work."

Andrew nodded thoughtfully. "It's a little disconcerting having everything I throw at him countermanded by something we'd don't know too much about. Find me a Warlock willing to perform a Unity. Promise them something they need, that they can't refuse. I need to find out more about this process, watch it for myself and see the results. Then perhaps we might be able to understand it and the after-effects."

He turned to her with a faint snarl on his face. "I need to kill him. I want Taliesin for my own, and this time make no mistake, I will take him. The time just has to be right and I can feel that it will be soon. The Witchfinder has agreed to help me."

Sophie's eyes grew darker as she listened to his words. Andrew wondered why her lips thinned and she looked down at the floor, as if she had a secret. For a fleeting moment he entertained getting whatever it was out of her. Then de Vere decided he didn't really care. He was satiated with the afterglow of sex and simply wanted a drink then to retire to bed.

"Everything all right Sophie?" he asked with mock tenderness.

She looked up at him. "How do you know you can trust the Witchfinder? That he's not planning to betray you or hurt you?" There was a note of tension in her voice.

Andrew waved a hand airily. "He can't defeat me, Sophie. He's no threat. Quinn is out looking for him but I doubt he'll find him unless someone tells him where he is. And that's not going to happen is it? No, the Witchfinder will do as he's told."

Sophie looked down at the ground. "What if you're wrong? I don't want anyone to hurt you, Andrew. I couldn't bear if anything happened to you. You know I would protect you—that I truly love you and would do anything to keep you safe no matter what?"

Andrew chuckled throatily. "My darling, I know you would. And I'm never wrong, you know that. Now come on over me and give me a kiss. Then perhaps we can go to bed."

***

Some days later, Quinn got home from a Consortium gathering at one in the morning. He was bone tired, disgruntled, feeling the weight of his Warlock nation on his shoulders. He walked into the drawing room, heading straight for the liquor cabinet and poured a large whisky.

He ran a hand over his eyes, sitting down in the large armchair, closing his eyes in relief at being home. It had been a difficult meeting. Whilst most of his Marshalls and Elects were firmly rooted on his side, there were those who coveted his title and thought they deserved it. James Barton Sinclair was one such man. A Marshall in the West Country, in his fifties, experienced, popular, he was very radical in his views as to how the Consortium should be run. Quinn was not in favour of an all-out war against the Witchhunters, preferring to wield power from within and slowly erode at their ranks. Barton Sinclair thought differently. He wanted to take the war to them, plot their destruction through violence, intimidation and warfare. Unfortunately he'd a lot of followers who felt the same way.

Quinn had to summon every ounce of strength, tact and downright authority to fight James in tonight's meeting. The recent events had made people nervous and they wanted payback for the deaths. More than once Percy had laid a warning hand on his Grand Master's shoulder to try and curb his anger.

Quinn stiffened as he saw a shadow slink across the backlight of the front window cast by the streetlights. He narrowed his eyes at the sight, flexing his fingers ready for action. He almost shouted as the small shadow launched itself at him, landing on his shoulder with a loud purr.

"Jesus Christ, Marco! You almost gave me a fucking heart attack!" Quinn's heart was beating fast as he reached up and grabbed the cat, and placed him on the floor. "What the hell are you doing here anyway?"

"*I* brought him across. He was getting a bit out of sorts on the boat being by himself so much. I didn't think you'd mind." Cade came quietly down the staircase, belting his silk dressing gown. Despite his evening and his sudden scare, Quinn drank in the sight of his man's lean torso and strong, bare, hairy legs as he descended the stairs. "I'm sorry. I forgot to text you and tell you he was here. I'd have hated him to get fire balled or something." Cade smiled and reached up to kiss his cheek, taking in the already half-finished glass of whisky.

"Bit of a rough night then?" He smiled at him sympathetically.

Quinn nodded. "It's one thing fighting an external enemy. It's another thing altogether fighting one inside the organisation. I'm afraid I've got more than a few."

He pulled his lover into his arms, kissing him deeply, feeling taut, hard curves against his own tense body. "I'm glad you're here when I get home. I think we should make it a permanent thing."

Cade stiffened and pulled back, looking at him warily. "What do you mean?"

"I think you should move in with me. You and Marco Polo because I wouldn't think I can have one without the other." Quinn grinned faintly as Cade regarded him with slight trepidation.

"What bought that on? It's only been four months; don't you think it might be a bit soon?"

Quinn's face darkened. He'd thought Cade would have jumped at the chance to give up that slightly leaky old boat and live here with him. "I think we've been through enough in the last four months to make this relationship feel like a couple of years. Of course, it's entirely up to you what you want to do."

He moved away from Cade and topped up his whisky glass. His boyfriend came up behind him and wrapped his arms around his waist. "I love being here with you. I'm just not sure I'm ready to give up Lucky Devil a hundred percent yet. It's a big decision to make, moving in together. You know I like my independence. And to be honest, I think you do too."

Quinn shrugged, moving away from him, knowing he was being churlish but he couldn't help it. "Fine. Forget I mentioned it.

Let's just leave it as it is. I'm sorry I brought the subject up." He sat down, sipping his drink.

Cade sighed. "Quinn, you're tired and irritable. You need a good night's sleep. Then we can talk about this without anything getting in the way."

Quinn regarded his lover broodingly. "Wow, thanks for that quick psychoanalysis. I feel much better now I know how I feel." He frowned.

Cade shook his head impatiently. "God, you can be a miserable git when you're tired. Why don't you finish that," he gestured at his drink, "and come upstairs. Perhaps you'll be less testy when you see what's waiting for you up there."

Cade brushed a hand against the top of his head and disappeared up the stairs. Quinn waited a few minutes, finishing his whisky, his mind already intrigued already by Cade's words. He switched off the lights and made his way up the bedroom. The room was dimly lit, and on walking in, he saw Cade, completely naked on the bed, a huge grin on his face and a green ribbon tied in a bow around his erect cock. The come-hither look in his lover's eyes was an even bigger turn-on. Any ire Quinn had felt disappeared on seeing Cade lying there, sultry eyed and ready for action. Cade beckoned to him with a finger and Quinn grinned, moving across to him, his cock already straining in his pants at its eagerness to be inside his lover, hear his moans as he thrust into him.

"Well, I can't be tetchy seeing this vision of pure sexy maleness, can I?"

"I was counting on it," Cade said drily. "Sometimes I need to appeal to your base nature to bring out the true lion in you and leave the cattiness behind."

Quinn chuckled at that as he started to unbutton his shirt.

Cade shook his head. "Huh-uh. You just get yourself over here. I want to undress you myself."

Quinn obliged, moving over to the bed and laying down beside Cade. Cade got up and knelt beside him, bare chest and nipples tantalisingly close to Quinn's mouth as he slowly unbuttoned Quinn's shirt one by one. Quinn loved the way Cade's tongue moved to the corner of his mouth as he concentrated on undressing him. He slipped his shirt off his shoulders, giving a sigh of satisfaction as Cade ran his hands over Quinn's chest, with its dark covering of hair and the even darker line down to his groin. He leaned forward and kissed Quinn's stomach gently.

"You have got the most incredible body. I never get tired of looking at it and knowing it's all mine." He frowned at him in mock worry. "It is all mine, isn't it? You haven't got anyone else that touches you like I do? Ties you up like I do?"

Quinn shook his head, pulling Cade toward him, feeling his warm body and hardened nipples against his chest as he kissed him, tasting warm, spicy breath in his mouth as his tongue entwined with his. When they drew apart, Quinn got impatient and stood up, removing his trousers and boxers and coming back to the bed to cover Cade's body with his, his hands running through his silky hair, his lips slowly caressing every inch of skin he could find as Cade moaned and caressed him back, touching his hardness with light strokes that made him ache.

Quinn's fingers pulled the end of the ribbon around Cade's erection, untying it and he pulled it gently as Cade hissed with the sensation of the ribbon against his heated flesh.

"Cade, baby, how did you know I love unwrapping presents?" He dangled the ribbon in front of Cade's face then trailed it lightly across his own lips, loving its male musky scent. "I could never have anyone else that makes me feel like you do. You're unique and I wouldn't ever want anyone else. You're mine and I know damned well I'm yours."

"Then shut the hell up and come inside," Cade whispered as his tongue ran itself across Quinn's lips. "I'm all ready; I was practicing before you even got up here."

The thought of Cade getting himself ready, putting his fingers where Quinn's cock so desperately wanted to go made Quinn's heart beat faster, his breath getting deeper. He laid the ribbon beside him on the bed and chuckled as he slid inside Cade. His lover cried out at the sensation and his slow, steady strokes made him rear his hips to meet his. Quinn knew this would be a short but sweet encounter.

"I always do what I'm told," he murmured as their bodies moved together. Cade's mouth claimed his as they made love—slow, passionate movements that seemed to make time stand still. He felt Cade coming in the way Cade dug his nails into his hips, felt his cock throb against his stomach, heard the small moans he made as his body jerked beneath him, his muscles contracting around him as his orgasm took over.

Quinn felt the rising heat in his groin that heralded his own release and he groaned as the feeling took over, his body no longer his to control but slave to this incredible feeling that washed over him and made him cry out as he shuddered and collapsed on top of Cade, as he kissed the sweat from his face.

They were quiet for a while, content to stay as they were until finally Cade shifted uncomfortably. "You're getting a bit heavy. Perhaps you could move over now. Much as I love this position, I'm struggling to breathe a little."

Quinn gave him one last lingering kiss as he rolled off to lie beside him, whilst his breathing returned to normal and his body stopped tingling. "Always a pleasure," he murmured. "I was tired seeing as how it was one o'clock in the morning but you just had to have your way with me, didn't you? Will it be all right if I actually go to sleep now? We don't have to talk?"

Cade laughed softly and tucked himself into Quinn's shoulder. "Yeah, I've had my fill for now. Hopefully you'll sleep better and get up in a better mood in the morning."

"I have to say I like your therapy," Quinn said lazily as he settled down beneath the duvet, his head already on the pillow. "It's a helluva lot better than a cup of Milo to help a person sleep."

Chapter 35

The following morning Quinn was in his study when his desk phone rang. It was Daniel. He put it on speakerphone so he could move around his office as he talked. It always helped him think.

"Daniel? Good to hear from you. What's going on?"

Daniel's voice was terse. "All hell's going to break loose tonight. I managed to find out that the Witchfinder intends taking de Vere on tonight on his yacht. I didn't think he'd make his move this soon."

Taliesin stirred like a dog pricking up his ears. Quinn's eyes narrowed as his mind ran agilely through possible scenarios. "We got another communication from Mary as to where Jeremy would be tonight. It wasn't the yacht that's for sure. He was supposed to be somewhere in the middle of London at some coven gathering. Have you any idea what time this is all going down?"

Daniel grunted. "He'll wait until its dark. He won't make a move in daylight. So anytime after sundown, I imagine, eight thirty onwards. My gut feel is that he'll leave it until fairly late."

"So we wait and see what happens. Perhaps we might get lucky and he'll kill de Vere. One less job for me to do." Quinn's said grimly. "I want to be there tonight when this is all going down. I'll see you at the marina just before sunset. Make sure we have enough men there to keep watch. I don't want either of them getting away no matter what happens. If it all goes pear shaped, I want to be on hand to bring it back on track even if it meets confronting de Vere myself."

"Quinn, you're not strong enough yet, son." Daniel's voice was quiet and Quinn heard the worry in it. But worry wasn't even on the menu tonight.

"I'm not letting him out of my sight. I need to be able to move quickly. Have we got sight of the witch?"

"She's with de Vere. On the yacht. Shall we warn her somehow, get her out of there?"

"No. She made her decision to stand with him, so she can damn well take the consequences." Quinn's voice was hard, his back rigid as he stared out over the heath. "I'm not protecting her, not after what she's done. If we're lucky, she'll be another distraction, the fly in the ointment that might keep de Vere off guard. It could work in our favour having her there."

His Withinner agreed with his strategy.

"Are you sure?" Daniel's voice was soft. "She's just another enchanted woman, a witch, yes, but one that's been blinded by de Vere. Another Adam."

Quinn's fists clenched at his sides at Daniel's words. "I'm well aware of that. No one warns the witch. She nearly got Cade killed." The command in his voice was unmistakeable.

Daniel sighed. "Fine, I just hope you can live with yourself if anything happens to her. I'll see you just before sunset."

He rang off. Quinn stood, gazing out the window.

"Quinn?" He'd sensed Cade's presence even before he heard his voice. He turned to see him standing there. "Did I hear right? Are you going to confront de Vere tonight?" Cade's voice was tight with apprehension.

Quinn nodded. "I'm hoping Payton does the job for me and destroys him. But if he doesn't, or anything goes wrong, I need to be there to step in and finish the job. If he doesn't kill de Vere, then he'll run or disappear again and it'll be the devil to find him. Taliesin and I need to be close by to stop him."

"God." Cade moved over to him swiftly and laid a hand on his arm. "After what you've been through, you're not strong enough, surely. How are you going to defeat de Vere?"

Quinn looked at him in astonishment. "I have no choice, can't you see that? I have to do this. I'll have some help, as much as I can get without him knowing we're there. That's why we can't have too many people going aboard. He'll sense us long before we get there but one at a time, we might have a chance. Percy and Magnus will be there and we'll bring him down together. I won't be alone like I was last time. I was over cocky and thought I could do it by myself."

"Are you sure you don't want to get Mary out of the way first?" Cade said, anxiety in his eyes. "I heard what Daniel said and I tend to agree with him. You might regret it if anything happened to her."

Quinn gazed at Cade flatly. "Give me credit for what I might feel. I know the drill and I need her there to distract de Vere, perhaps give something to Jeremy to focus on, to weaken de Vere."

"Like a goat tethered to a stake with a hungry tiger on the prowl?" Cade's voice was low. "Are you sure that's what you want?"

Quinn looked at his boyfriend in frustration. "Yes, I'm sure. God, when will people stop telling me how to feel? The woman handed you over to de Vere like a joint of meat on a plate, ready to carve! How can I be expected to feel sympathy for her? I nearly lost you!" He paced angrily around the room. "This title I have, Grand Master, isn't just a name. I have decisions to make for a greater good. I'm sorry if you think otherwise but this is my fight, not yours."

"It became my fight when that man decided to slice me open like I was a fucking turkey roast." Cade's voice trembled with anger. "It became my fight when I fell in love with you and watched you almost die twice. Don't you dare tell me this isn't my fight, Quinn Fairmont. Don't you fucking dare, you arrogant bastard."

His eyes glittered with unshed, angry tears. Quinn saw he'd gone too far. He moved over to Cade, gathering him in his arms, his body taut as he held him.

"Christ, I'm sorry. You're right. I'm an arrogant tosser and I shouldn't have said that." He held Cade tightly, willing Cade to embrace him.

Finally Cade relented and wrapped his arms around his waist as he laid his head on his shoulder. "Quinn, I can't lose you again. I just don't have it in me."

Quinn's gut churned. "You won't lose me. I have Taliesin to protect me and Percy and Magnus and Daniel looking out for me. They're all good people and they *will* do their best."

He kissed each of Cade's stormy eyes softly, and then his mouth. Cade held onto him as if he would never let him go. Quinn finally had to disentangle himself from his lover's grasping hands and arms and stand aside.

"I have some plans to make before I go," he said softly. "I need to get organised, there's a lot to still do. Why don't you go for a swim, get that frustration out in the water then I'll see you before I leave."

Cade nodded. "I could do with the water. It always helps me figure things out. Don't you dare go without saying goodbye."

Cade turned and left the study as Quinn watched him go, his heart heavy. He'd hated lying to him but if he knew that Percy and Magnus were not actually going to be with him on the yacht, he'd worry more. There was no way three Warlocks could make to onto that yacht without de Vere getting wise to them and disappearing, God knows where, with his Withinner.

Quinn and Taliesin were the only ones who could get on unseen and face him down if it came to that.

One part of Quinn hoped Jeremy accomplished what he'd set out to do. The other part of him hoped he didn't and that it would be a showdown between him and de Vere, once and for all.

This is going to be hard. Taliesin warned. *We need to be ready. Daniel is right. You are not as strong as you could be. The Unity and the hex have weakened you. It was de Vere's plan all along.*

"I know that," Quinn muttered. "But there isn't a choice. You're just going to have to help me, old friend. I can't do this without your full strength."

You know I would die protecting you. It is the way of things.

"I don't intend either of us dying." Quinn ran a hand over his eyes, feeling extremely wearied. "I need to get some arrangements done. You do what you can to prepare yourself. I have a feeling this battle is not going to be easy."

***

Quinn invoked his Withinner just before sunset and within minutes he was standing with Daniel and Percy on the dock of the Essex Marina, watching the *Sept Rois*. He'd given Magnus orders to remain with Cade, out of sight so he didn't see him, and although the man had been upset at not coming with him, he'd understood that Quinn's first priority was Cade's welfare.

The departure from home had been difficult. He could still see Cade's face, white and drawn, eyes haunted with visions of Quinn not returning to him.

Quinn had tried to console Cade, to tell his boyfriend it was going to be all right, but Cade had been quiet and withdrawn, watching him with eyes that drank him in as if it were the last vision of him he'd ever have.

Quinn had felt the lead weight in his chest as he'd left him, wondering the same thing. But that was a distraction he could ill afford now and he needed to psych himself up for whatever lay ahead tonight.

He looked at Percy. "Has anyone got eyes on the Witchfinder yet?"

Percy shook his head. "No sign of him yet. He'll smell us as soon as he arrives. All we can hope is that his desire to get to de Vere outweighs any desire he has to kill a few Warlocks before he gets to the bigger game."

Quinn shrugged. "Even the Witchfinder General is no match for the two of us, not without his cadmium trick. If we need to destroy him first, so be it. Then we'll just have to finish de Vere ourselves."

"You mean yourself," Daniel said quietly as he stood gazing out over the window. His slight frame was rigid, his dark hair messy and tousled as if he'd been running hands through it. There was no other man Quinn revered or respected more than this man.

Daniel had taken Quinn on when he was just a boy in the worst times of his life and taught him that together they could get through anything. He owed Daniel everything. Daniel turned to him, the crow's-feet in the corner of his eyes crinkling as he frowned. For the first time, Quinn noticed the grey strands at Daniel's temples.

"The two of you will never get near to de Vere before he senses you and disappears. He'll want a one-on-one showdown with you. He has something to prove. So he'll be waiting, have no doubt. With all the dirty tricks he can muster."

Quinn's eyes narrowed. "You sound as if I have a choice not to do this."

"I'm remembering the last time you fought him. You barely made it out with your life. You know the only way to kill him is to either garner enough energy for a full burn or get enough of your blood into his bloodstream. That's going to be a hard one to achieve. He won't let you near him again. And you are weaker than last time thanks to him and his hex."

Quinn waved a hand dismissively. "He's arrogant and cocky. I'll find some way to get him close if the energy burns don't work."

The man has a point. The energy you need to defeat de Vere is going to take everything you have. You cannot afford to draw the battle on too long or you will be too weak. If I was de Vere, that would be my plan. To make the fight last long enough to drain you.

"I agree with you, Taliesin. But he won't give in easily." Quinn paced the dock impatiently.

Percy spoke curiously. "How do you think the Witchfinder plans on killing him then?"

Quinn shook his head. "So far Jeremy has been very successful with his cadmium trick, but you can bet your bottom dollar that the witch has already got de Vere protected against that, the same way she helped us. Payton won't know this, though, so he may try. That might be his undoing. I can't think of any other way he can kill de Vere. If I can't fight de Vere, make him succumb with energy, then my best weapon is to get my blood into de Vere's bloodstream with the spell if I can get close enough. But de Vere's not just any Warlock, so that will be tricky."

Quinn looked out over the dusky setting of the water as it rippled slightly and bobbed against the jetty. He spoke very little about that night, the night he was six and had seen his parents lying dead in front of him, killed by another Warlock using the same blood weapon. It was pure luck he'd gotten away with his life that night and it was all due to another Warlock who was now dead and gone ten years. The death of Edward Mistral and his Withinner,

Adelphi, was another thing that weighed heavily on Quinn's conscience.

You cannot remember such things, now! Taliesin's voice was warning, fierce. *You need all your wits about you. Put those memories back where they belong: deep within.*

"Easier said than done, old friend." Quinn murmured softly.

Percy looked at him in sympathy. "If Taliesin's telling you to suppress any past emotions, I suggest you listen to him. They can do you no service tonight." He frowned as his mobile vibrated in his pocket and he pulled it out, listening to the news and then putting the phone back in his pocket.

"Jeremy Payton's been spotted on the jetty by the yacht," he said quietly. "De Vere and the witch are still on the boat. The fun is about to begin, I think."

Quinn's nostrils flared. "I need to get closer. I need to have a feel for what's going on from a better vantage point." He pulled his suede jacket closer around him as he moved away.

"Be careful, my boy. Don't do anything stupid and no maverick moves." Daniel laid a hand on his nephew's arm as Quinn reached up and grasped it.

"You know I can't promise that. I'll do whatever it takes to get the job done." He smiled faintly at the worried looks on both Dan and Percy's face. "But I don't have a death wish. I have a man who's expecting me home."

He moved swiftly off toward the other side of the jetty, feeling their eyes on him as he walked away. As he got closer to de Vere's yacht, he sensed the presence of the Witchfinder. Jeremy Payton was definitely nearby. Quinn could mask himself from the boy but he didn't want to get too close to de Vere. The Warlock would feel his presence and Quinn needed the advantage.

He found a spot on the jetty about a hundred feet away and hunkered down on his haunches to watch events unfold. He didn't have long to wait. A young man, stocky, with a swaggering gait, approached *Sept Rois* cautiously. Quinn sensed the power emanating from the boy. Despite his youthful size, the Witchfinder General was a force to be reckoned with, a maelstrom of malevolence and determination, his only focus to destroy the likes of Feys like Quinn, de Vere and Mary. Quinn smelt the boy's thirst for bloodshed and Taliesin stirred within, sensing it too.

This is a powerful one. I have not felt the power of such a Witchfinder in many moons. We may have underestimated him.

Quinn nodded and didn't speak his thoughts as he usually preferred to, not wanting to alert the boy. *It can only be good news for us, Taliesin. It will give him a better chance against de Vere.*

Taliesin would hear him either way. It was a strange circumstance that usually made him feel more comfortable actually conversing with his Withinner vocally rather than thinking his thoughts like many other Warlocks did, like some sort of Jedi Knight.

De Vere and Mary sat in the cabin, heads close together. Quinn watched as Jeremy approached the boat, walking diffidently up the gangplank. Quinn frowned. The boy was being very open about his presence, not seeming to care if he was seen or not. This was an unusual manoeuvre. Was it that he was counting on the fact he was a fifteen-year-old boy and de Vere wouldn't take him seriously?

Quinn peered closer in curiosity. A faint sheen emanated from the boy. As he got closer to the lights on the boat, the Witchfinder almost seemed to be glowing. Quinn had never seen such an effect before and he rubbed his eyes. The glow was still there.

Taliesin, the boy has some sort of shining effect all around him—could that be some sort of spell to mask him? Do you know of anything like that being used before by Witchfinders?

There is only one thing that can do that. It is an old wives' tale and I have not heard of it being used before. If a Witchfinder bathes in the blood of a Warlock or a witch, and drinks their blood, it will render him impervious to discovery for a while. This could be what you are seeing.

"Jesus! Bathing and drinking our blood?" Quinn forgot his resolve to converse silently with his Withinner. "That's a bit extreme."

It means he will have a further advantage as de Vere won't sense him until it is too late and he may not even know he is a Witchfinder. It not only masks his presence; it will mask his magyck too.

Quinn went back into silent mode.

Mary knows him, so that might not be to his advantage. He doesn't know Mary knows him though. He's never dealt directly with her. He might not have as much luck as he thinks.

Quinn watched grimly as the boy reached the cabin door and stepped right through it. He braced himself for whatever was coming and he wasn't disappointed. As Mary and de Vere leapt to their feet Quinn felt the sudden violence in the air, smelt the rushing of blood as the opponents faced each other down. A woman's scream and a great flash of light flared brightly in the cabin.

Quinn stood up, watchful, his body tensed for action, every hair on his body upright.

There was a heaviness in the air, a dampening sensation that made his ears pop. He moved his jaw up and down, trying to get rid of the dull feeling in his head. The blood in his veins hissed in his ears, a sound that made him shake his head in frustration, trying to clear it. The sensation of dread was overwhelming. Something was horribly wrong.

He moved swiftly towards the yacht, full intending to board it. There was a shout from across the water, someone telling him to stay put until back up arrived, but he had no time to wait. De Vere could cast a protection spell over the yacht at any time, making it resistant to anyone else getting on board. He had to do it now.

He ran up the gangplank and only just made it into the cabin before the boat shuddered and tilted violently from side to side, as he lost his footing and stumbled against the walls of the cabin.

Quinn knew de Vere had finally sealed the yacht off to anyone else boarding.

Once he had his footing, Quinn looked up to a nightmare tableau in the cabin. It was only a few seconds to evaluate the scene before him. Mary lay blood-soaked against the far wall of the cabin, her eyes still open, her mouth trying to frame words that wouldn't quite come out. Blood rushed from a gaping wound that stretched from her stomach to her chest in great gouts down the front of her blue silk dress. The slippery insides of the woman moved as she clasped the wound.

The witch seemed to be losing mass as Quinn watched, her body closing in on itself.

Jeremy Payton stood, a vision of immense power in the centre of the cabin, his green eyes flaring with disgust and malice, his short, stocky body poised for his next action. In his left hand he held a large black-handled athame, still red with blood and tissue from the witch, dripping onto the thick cream carpets in the cabin.

Andrew de Vere stood with a snarl on his blood-soaked face, looking startled then satisfied at the sudden appearance of Quinn in his cabin. His right arm was covered in blood, hanging loosely at his side and his body was tensed as if ready to launch. He grinned, his teeth stained with blood from a cut on his mouth.

"Quinn Fairmont. Good of you to join us. I was a little busy trying to kill this little witchhunting bastard. Perhaps you'd be so kind to help me then we can resolve our personal differences?" He gestured toward the dying woman in the corner. "As you can see, yet another precious companion has been taken from me. It's so hard to find good help nowadays but she served her purpose."

De Vere grinned wolfishly, his eyebrows rising enquiringly. Quinn's fury ignited at the man's insouciance and blatant disregard for his dying lover.

"Another fucking bastard witch!" Jeremy Payton's voice growled. "Christ, will there ever be an end to your dirty kind? It just gives me two to kill, now, dunnit?"

He moved forward, his athame held out in front of him and de Vere waved his hand, sending the blade spinning out of his hand toward Quinn. Quinn sidestepped sharply, his Withinner's quick reflexes protecting him.

Quinn, try and keep out of his way. Something is very different with him. With both of them.

Quinn had sensed it too, but Taliesin's words still sent an icy shiver down his spine. There *was* something very different about de Vere, not to mention the young teenager.

De Vere shook his head. "Young man, I know you think you have the advantage but I've really just been toying with you. Did you really think I wouldn't be able to defeat you by myself?" His voice was steely. "I needed you to attract Mr. Fairmont in so we can finish what we started all those months ago. He thinks I didn't know he was lurking in the shadows but he underestimates me as usual. That hex I gave him was a little bit more than he thought it was despite him obviously being able to rid himself of most of it. I bet that hurt. But some part still remains so I can sense him. A cover soaked in his blood makes a great talisman."

He smiled at Quinn, who was careful that his face showed no expression. He remembered the night Mary had cut him to test the cadmium defence, his blood falling onto a floor covering she'd laid down.

"I don't give a fuck about your hex or anything else." The Witchfinder moved round the cabin slowly, eying them both out. "I will kill you both and get out of here."

Quinn eyed him out. "You'll have trouble dealing with both of us, Witchfinder. Even you can't deal with those odds." He moved further away from de Vere, trying to put Jeremy between them as a buffer.

De Vere's grin grew larger. "He's right. We will have some sport with you then kill you. You don't stand a chance." He gestured toward Quinn. "My fight is with him. We're old friends. You, boy, are simply the opening act," he said dismissively.

"Don't use the word friend when it comes to what you and I have, de Vere. It's a fucking insult," Quinn snarled as he finally had Jeremy in between them.

The Witchfinder watched him warily. Quinn got the distinct impression he was starting to feel a little out of his depth, both at the fact he had two powerful Warlocks against him and at the distinct animosity between said Warlocks. It was time to bring this to a head. He needed to ignore the Witchfinder and concentrate on de Vere, as he was the more dangerous. The air in the cabin was dense, shimmering like haze coming off a hot pavement.

"Well, lovely as this is getting to know each other, I think it's time we finished it." De Vere's voice was matter of fact but Quinn heard the danger in it. He wasn't sure whom de Vere was going to target first so he readied himself. De Vere hurled a blast of force at Jeremy, who countermanded the attack with one of his own, throwing up some sort of shield that protected him for a moment then shattered into a thousand pieces.

The Witchfinder darted around the room, desperately avoiding de Vere's ongoing assaults, his face growing paler as he must have realised his defences were not proving strong enough against a Warlock of de Vere's calibre.

Quinn tried to stay out of the way, waiting for the right time to make his move against de Vere as Jeremy held his attention.

Jeremy managed to avoid most of de Vere's missiles but one caught him solidly on the left shoulder and the boy staggered slightly, his face thick with pain. From the more hesitant movements he made, Jeremy was obviously starting to get more anxious at his inability to get to de Vere.

One flash of energy surged his way and his face scrunched in pain as it hit his shoulder again. The cabin was awash with the smell of burnt flesh. Jeremy moved painfully to the corner of the cabin. Quinn saw the sudden shift on Jeremy's face as the young man closed his eyes, saw his lips form words that he couldn't quite make out. Then, in an instant, he seemed to dissolve as if being absorbed into the air.

To Quinn's amazement, it seemed Jeremy Payton had left the building.

Quinn could not sense his presence, so it was not a simple masking spell. Quinn hoped Percy and the others would be able to find the Witchfinder again.

Quinn and de Vere were now the only ones left facing each other off. With Jeremy's sudden disappearance, de Vere looked at Quinn in barely concealed surprise of his own. Quinn felt much the same way but he was damned if he was going to show it to the likes of de Vere. He kept his face expressionless as he stared at the other Warlock.

Be careful, Quinn. He is not what he seems. His Withinner's words were soft.

De Vere shook his head. "Well, I confess I didn't see that one coming. Since when have Witchfinder Generals been able to do tricks like that? Even we can't do what he did without a Withinner." De Vere sounded seriously put out and in a more social situation Quinn might have found his astonishment amusing. But now he regarded the other Warlock guardedly.

"Well, so here we stand again, with a dying"—de Vere looked over at Mary—"dead woman on the floor and our only intent to try and kill each other." He smiled lazily and Quinn tensed as de Vere moved closer. "Did you not wonder where I'd been all these months? How I managed to stay alive and come back hale and hearty, albeit a little damaged? You only picked up my scent a while ago and that was when I tried to kill your sarcastic partner. He's quite a screamer by the way; I'm sure he's a great screw in the bedroom."

Quinn's hate and anger rose closer to the surface and he had to fight it back.

He's trying to bait you. Don't let your guard down. Taliesin's voice was fierce.

Quinn stared at de Vere, his eyes flinty. "I promised myself I'd kill you personally after what you did to him, de Vere. You took the coward's way, attacking innocent people. Cade and Jomo had no part in our feud."

De Vere raised his eyebrow in question. "Really? Coming from you I'd say that was a little two-faced. You murdered an innocent when you killed Adam. The only one I'd ever considered a son. I loved him. And you only did that to distract me. So how does that differ from what I did? Then of course there was poor young Honour Whitebrook and her family. A whole family slaughtered because you didn't want to reveal your source in the Witchunters Alliance and thought that killing a whole family would be good cover. It worked but at such a terrible cost."

Quinn clenched his hands and his stomach suddenly had a serious case of turmoil. He tried to shut down the feelings of pain and guilt at de Vere's words.

He is getting to you. Fight it. Your regrets have no place here.

Taliesin's urgent words bought him back to his senses.

"And finally, of course, there were your parents. Of course you were only six years old, but haven't you ever wondered whether you could have stopped their deaths? In fact, you may have even caused them in the first place but you just don't remember. So all in all, I think six innocents dead because of your actions is a fairly serious guilt score."

Quinn couldn't breathe, the emotions inside him starting to well over the container he held inside him like excess dough spilling out of a baking tin. His eyes felt gritty and there was a slow tickle under his nose. He reached up slowly, wiping it, and when he took them away his fingers were stained with blood.

De Vere's eyes were almost hypnotic in their intensity, his voice mesmerising. "The nosebleeds have begun again. You don't seem to be a well man, Fairmont."

He is using psyche against you. You need to shut him out. Your defences are weakening. He is very strong, stronger than he should be. You need to fight him, damn you. Think of Cade, home waiting for you. I will be with you in this. Together we are strong.

Quinn drew a deep breath, clearing away the fogginess in his brain. "Your words hold no sway with me. I swore to kill you. Nothing has changed. I suggest we get on with it."

As he said these words, he flung his hand out, summonsing all the energy he and his Withinner had. He concentrated his energy, willing it to blossom in the air and reach its target.

De Vere, still gloating over his psychic attack on Quinn, was unprepared. The charge struck him centre chest and he was flung back against the cabin wall, landing dazed but not yet done for.

The smell of scorched skin offended the nostrils.

De Vere cursed fiercely as he clambered to his feet, hurling an energy burst Quinn's way.

The edge of the burst seared Quinn's side and he hissed in pain. He'd never felt such power in an energy burst before.

"We're like a couple of fucking teenage Warlocks, hurling these things at each other." De Vere stood, his hand clutching his chest, taunting Quinn. "I suppose your plan is to keep doing it until one of us runs out of energy. Then we'll have to think of another way to kill each other. But I assure you I can last a lot longer than you can."

The two Warlocks circled each other like prize fighters in a boxing ring, each channelling their energy against the other and using whatever moves they had to avoid the debilitating effects of being hit.

Quinn knew he was tiring and even Taliesin was faltering. Quinn gasped, out of breath, his injuries starting to slow him down, his sides scorched, his stomach and legs burnt and his chest feeling as if it was going to burst.

You are running out of energy. Your nosebleeds are getting worse.

Taliesin's anxious voice echoed through Quinn's pounding temples. His nose *was* freely running blood and he hadn't missed de Vere's constant sly looks at him, seeing him faltering. The same elephants he'd felt dancing in his head before were now tap dancing in hob-nailed boots and he was struggling to see clearly.

I know. He's strong, has far more stamina than I remember. I'm not sure how long I can keep this up. Taliesin spoke softly. *If you cannot finish this, you need to invoke me and I will take you away.*

Quinn replied, *He'll never allow that, my friend. As soon as I start invoking, he'll find a way to stop it. That's not an option. I have to win.*

De Vere was breathing heavily as he continued to taunt Quinn. "You can't defeat me this way. I haven't been entirely truthful with you. I'm afraid I have a distinct advantage over your good self."

De Vere's tendency to boast was coming to the fore and Quinn welcomed it. When de Vere was arrogant was the time he let his defences down. Quinn stood, his shoulders heaving, his breaths coming in short gasps as he tried to calm his beating heart.

"You see," de Vere panted, "I have two Withinners, making me even more powerful than before."

Quinn felt a surge of disbelief. *How was that even possible?*

De Vere shook his head in wry amusement. "True, Algarde was not keen on it, but he acquiesced as any good Withinner would do. After our last battle, whilst I was healing, I found myself in Algarde's time recovering. For quite a while he travelled elsewhere. He'd managed to find a really useful incantation that allowed me to acquire another Withinner. As you know, Algarde was a very powerful sorcerer himself; not as good as Taliesin, but then I wasn't a mighty Fairmont. Between us, we managed to entice another one inside. His name is Ajax and he's a little flawed unfortunately, having been a tragic Greek hero who committed suicide, but he has some limited powers that help me. I like to use them when I can. So Quinn, you see, you stand no fucking chance against me."

His face twisted viciously even as he lobbed another energy burst at Quinn, who didn't manage to avoid this one and cried out as it hit his shoulder, causing his flesh to burn and sizzle.

Quinn, I have heard of this chant. It exists. It is not used because of the extreme pain it causes and the high risk of dying. You cannot fight a Warlock with two Withinners. You need to let me take you away.

"No fucking way," Quinn muttered as he twisted in pain. "This ends here."

"How is the wonderful Taliesin? Still holding onto the ideal that you're his perfect Warlock and he'll do anything to protect you? Some Withinners can be so misguided. I look forward to taking him from you with this."

De Vere reached into his pocket and drew out a small item. Quinn drew a breath as he recognised it as a dragon's claw. He imagined that at the tip of that claw was coated with dragon's blood, the only way Taliesin could be forced to serve another Warlock master.

De Vere saw him looking at it. "I didn't get a chance to use it last time. I am looking so forward to seeing you dead on the floor, and then I'll be able to command that imperious bastard Withinner of yours."

Andrew lobbed another burst at Quinn who dived to the floor, hitting his injured shoulder as he did so. A further burst hit him full on the back, causing him to cry out in pain even as he struggled to his feet. His head spun and he felt the room tilt as he got to his feet.

Quinn. Stop being such a stubborn fool and let me take you away. You cannot fight him any longer. It is no defeat for you—he has two Withinners giving him his energy, which is far greater than yours. His surges are incredibly strong. No man, not even you, nor I, can fight that and live.

Taliesin's salty and uncomplimentary muttered curse about Quinn, following on from his words, would normally have made Quinn smile.

Taliesin. Let me be. He's human too, with flaws I know well. That gives me an advantage. He's flawed and arrogant and that I can fight. I just need to get him close enough.

You stubborn human, that dragon's claw is your nemesis. And mine. I would die rather than serve him.

Trust me, sorcerer. I'm human too and I know my kind.

Quinn spied the Witchfinder's athame on the floor and he sidled over to it, grimacing at the pain in his body.

De Vere circled him slowly, gloating. "Feeling the pain a little, are we? You don't look too healthy, old friend. That blood loss from your nose must surely be weakening you. I've never seen such an extreme one before. It reminds me of the time I spent in Yellowstone Park with the geysers." He chuckled nastily.

Quinn watched him closely. He could decide to lob another energy burst at Quinn or try to get closer with the dragon's claw. Luckily for Quinn in the next moment, he apparently decided on the latter as he squinted at the blurred figure of de Vere making his way toward him.

Quinn felt a moment of relief. He thought another surge would have totally disabled him.

Quinn hunched over, unable to see too well, his headache getting worse. It was easy to feign weakness. For what Quinn had planned, he needed de Vere close.

He held the athame he'd picked up close to his chest, wincing at the pain from his burned flesh, waiting for the other Warlock to get nearer still. He knew de Vere would want to be up close and personal when he delivered his final blow but Quinn needed all his remaining energy now to stop that dragon's claw making contact with his skin. He only hoped he had the strength to see it through.

He raised his hand to the blood under his nose and wiped his fingers in it, transferring it to the tip of the blade.

Quinn. Are you all right? I feel you weakening.

His Withinner's anxious voice murmured in his aching head. De Vere drew closer, circling around and coming up behind him and Quinn sensed another energy surge directed his way, hitting him on the back of head. He cried out, hearing the sizzle of his hair and feeling the pain on the back of his neck and scalp. Sick with the pain, he knew he wouldn't survive another one. But he had to get de Vere so confident that he'd move closer. He let his head hang as if defeated. He had to appear weaker than he was.

"I could do this all day," de Vere said conversationally, even as he winced at his own injuries. "But what I really want to do before you die is destroy your face like you did mine. I'd enjoy nothing better than seeing your skin melt like the plastic face of a kewpie doll. And then I'll kill you. And after that, I will pay a visit to your precious Cade and finish the cutting project I started with him, only this time I'll allow time for a little more fun first. I want to hear him scream as I cut him to pieces."

Quinn's fists tightened as he willed himself not to lose control at the man's words. For Cade's sake, he had to win this one. He had no doubt de Vere would do exactly what he said to Cade, and worse. He wouldn't allow that to happen. Cade had suffered enough at his hands.

Relax, don't let him rile you. He repeated his mantra over and over in his head.

Quinn looked down at the floor, his senses on high alert as de Vere came ever closer, his voice sneering. "So, would you like to turn around and I'll fry your face or do I need to get physical and do it for you? Come on man, have some pride. "

De Vere's taunting voice grew closer and Quinn turned slightly, lifting his face towards de Vere's.

The Warlock smiled. "I *see* you," he trilled quietly, the gleam of madness in his eyes. That glimpse fortified Quinn. He knew de Vere's overconfidence was Quinn's one ally.

De Vere came closer yet, so close Quinn smelt the man's sweat and saw the slight spittle on his lips. His madness and his need to defeat Quinn were the weaknesses Quinn intended to exploit.

De Vere raised his hand. "Say goodbye to those good looks. They'll be having no open casket once I've done with you."

In one quick movement, Quinn lunged up and forward with the athame, still covered in Mary's blood mixed with drops of his own, and thrust the sharp blade as hard as he could into de Vere's stomach.

De Vere gasped and staggered back, dropping the claw. Quinn, still holding the athame embedded in de Vere's stomach, fell with him, twisting the dagger viciously to open the wound further. De Vere's face was pale, his eyes wild as he struggled to understand what had just happened. His seemingly weak prey had fought back.

Well done. Now finish it. Taliesin cheered him on.

"Sorry, I like my pin-up boy good looks." Quinn whispered as he leaned forward over the stricken Warlock. "And seeing as how you like the sight of my blood so much, you can have some of it."

He leaned over as the blood from his nose gushed down over his top lip. Quinn watched in satisfied silence as a few drops fell into the open wound on de Vere's stomach.

The other Warlock squirmed, his eyes wide with fear, realising Quinn's intention. He tried to get away, but Quinn held him down in an iron grip as he chanted the spell he needed to fulfil the ritual, summonsing up both his and Taliesin's remaining strength to pin down the already weakening de Vere beneath him.

"How does it feel, de Vere?" Quinn watched with stony eyes as the other man's eyes glazed over, his body starting to weaken. Quinn's blood was coursing through his system, poisoning him, and in time would expel the two Withinners inside. "You're nothing but a bully. You trick women into doing your bidding, seduce them with your magyck charms and then discard them."

"I didn't discard Adam," de Vere gasped, his breathing gone shallow. "You murdered him. You murdered all those other people. Adam was the only man I'd ever loved. You destroyed him. You killed a man you loved, in a heartbeat, to save your own skin. What does that make you?"

"Alive," Quinn said flatly. "To carry on dealing with animals like you to protect this Consortium and our people."

De Vere's face contorted in pain, his body racked with spasms as his organs shut down one by one.

Quinn sat back against the wall, exhausted. He watched, knowing what he had done caused indescribable pain. De Vere lay dying.

"You sliced my boyfriend open, you damaged my friend and you tried to kill me. Twice. You tried to steal my Withinner. Again, twice. Forgive me if I have little sympathy for you in your final moments. The world is a better place without you."

De Vere giggled, despite his agony. Quinn looked at him through narrowed eyes, not seeing any joke.

"You've just killed the one person that could tell you who murdered your parents, Quinn." He heaved a breath, gasping. "I was going to tell you as you lay dying and watch the fury in your eyes at knowing his identity before you left this world altogether but now I'll just die, knowing you'll never know exactly what happened that night."

His voice weakened, his eyes closed at the pain. His chest caved in as his lungs started to constrict. They were always the last thing to go.

Quinn's body went cold and he leaned over de Vere, his voice fierce. "You wouldn't know that, Andrew. You're just trying to rile me."

De Vere gasped, his breath laboured, his eyes gleaming even as the light faded from them. "You tell yourself that. Enjoy the rest of your life. I still won." De Vere's voice faltered, he gave one last choking gurgle and his eyes closed.

Quinn watched as his body stilled.

He lied. He cannot possibly know anything about your parents. He tried to trick you with one final lie before he died.

Taliesin's mutter did little to assuage Quinn's torment that perhaps de Vere *had* known something.

Quinn was still sitting slumped against the wall as de Vere's two Withinners materialised and then disappeared. Quinn watched through half-closed eyes with a mind that felt as if it was shutting down.

The effects of de Vere's protection spell around the yacht dissipated with his death. Daniel ran in, his face grey, Percy hot on his heels.

"Christ, man, you look terrible. I need to get you the clinic." His Marshall helped him up. "Invoke Taliesin. Tell him to get you to the Dorset clinic. Urgently."

Quinn barely had the strength to invoke his Withinner, but he managed and seconds later, Taliesin appeared. His face was drawn, his nostrils rimmed with blood but he looked at Percy steadily.

"I will get Quinn to safety, Marshall. Tell his Cade where he is. He will be mightily worried about him." He swirled his staff around and seconds later they were gone.

Percy looked at the two bodies on the cabin floor. "There are only two bodies here. Where is Jeremy Payton? He should be here too. I don't sense him and if he were on board, this close, I would."

"I have no idea. He must have escaped, but we didn't see him leave. I had eyes everywhere."

"We'll have to hope Quinn can tell us when he recovers. This could be a major problem for us."

Percy looked down at Mary and de Vere and sighed. "The stubborn bastard did it. He finally killed de Vere for good. This man of ours sometimes worries me. He can be a little inhuman."

Daniel's eyes were shadowed. "I know what you mean. He's been like that since he was a boy. He never gives up. I thought his father was bad enough but Quinn? Quinn is something else. He scares me sometimes." He sighed. "I'll take the boat out to sea and sink it with the bodies on board. No one will ever find it out there. I'll get another one to pick me up. You and your team will take care of anyone around that might have seen anything, make them forget?"

Percy nodded. "That's already in motion. I'm going to go see Cade now, tell him Quinn's alive at least and get him down to the clinic. Again. He's not going to be happy with this but at least the daft bugger's still alive."

He turned and looked at the dead witch with sympathy in his eyes. "Poor girl. She got involved with the wrong person when she met de Vere. Look where it got her."

He turned and walked out the door, leaving Daniel standing in the middle of the cabin, a haunted look on his face. He bent down slowly, crouching over de Vere's body, and picked up the dragon claw that lay on the floor. He put it in his pocket thoughtfully. Perhaps this might come in useful sometime. He turned and made his way to the bow of the boat, ready to take her out to sea and hide the evidence of the night's events.

Chapter 36

Quinn's heart lurched at the sight of a pale, red-eyed Cade entering his hospital room, as Dr. Greg Moresmith stood to one side to let him pass. Quinn reflected wryly that perhaps they should move into the hospital with the regularity that he attended it.

He tried to reassure Cade with a smile. He knew the sight of him was enough to make anyone gasp in horror. Quinn's face was bruised, he had bandages on his shoulders and upper body, concealing livid, weeping burns and his hair was singed.

"I'm all right, Cade," Quinn said softly as Cade sat down next to him, hands reaching blindly for Quinn's. The look of anguish on his face when he discovered there was nothing to hold onto other than ointment goo-covered digits broke Quinn's heart.

"Most of them are just burns, caused by the energy bursts we lobbed at each other. I'll heal quickly with Taliesin's help."

Dr. Moresmith's eyes were gentle as he regarded Cade's worried face. "He's been through worse. I heard about the hex spell gone wrong. He had an angel looking after him when he went through that. I've never heard of someone surviving something as deep as that one." He turned to Quinn. "Daniel's on his way down. He said he'd get here as quick as he could." He left the room.

Quinn smiled at him. "See? I do keep my promises and come back to you."

Cade sighed deeply. "Do you want some water?"

Quinn nodded faintly, grimacing at the pain. A hand gently supported his neck as he was lifted up and a straw passed through his lips. He sucked greedily, enjoying the feel of the lukewarm liquid in his parched mouth. The straw was taken away and he fell back gratefully onto his pillow, another one of which seemed to have been magically added, keeping him slightly more upright.

Cade reached out a hand and moved a strand of hair from his forehead. "I'm getting damn tired of asking this but how are you feeling?"

Quinn cleared his throat. "Like I went a hundred rounds with Rocky Marciano. I must look a sight, like something that was left in the oven too long."

"You are a bit of a crispy critter but you're my crispy critter." Cade raised his eyebrows at Quinn's amusement at his words. "The main thing is that you're alive."

"I shall be thankful for small mercies, then," Quinn murmured drily. His eyes narrowed. "Is Percy here?"

Cade stood up, frowning. "Jesus, you've just been through hell and need to rest. What the hell would you want Percy for?"

Quinn looked at Cade gravely. "I need to find out if they have a bead on Jeremy Payton who virtually disappeared before my eyes. If not, it means we have to find him. Is he here?"

Cade scowled. "Of course he's here. He's doing some Warlock-y business somewhere." He stood watching Quinn, not moving.

Quinn sighed in exasperation. "Would you mind asking Percy to come see me? I'd go see him myself but I have a feeling if I try and make a move out of this bed you'll slap me."

"You've got that right," Cade muttered. "And not in that good way you like. Fine, I'll go find Percy but you're not conducting business so soon after waking up from what I've been told was a colossal magyckal battle. I think you deserve a few days of peace. And I for one could do with knowing you're not going to die any time soon—again." With those pointed words, his lover flounced out of the room, still muttering to himself.

Quinn grinned.

Cade would never understand his responsibilities but by God, he loved the man's feisty way of looking after him.

He lay back on his pillows, wincing at the feeling of his skin tightening over his body as it healed. He lifted one hand, noting the rawness, and sighed.

Christ, he was fed up of lying in hospital beds! He'd had his fill of it.

Taliesin spoke in grim amusement.

Quinn, you know this won't be the last time you find yourself in such a situation. You are headstrong and prone to trouble. I would say poor Cade is going to find himself by your hospital bedside many times more.

"Thanks for that," Quinn murmured. "You can be such great bloody comfort." But he smiled, knowing his Withinner was right. He opened his eyes as he heard Percy's cheery voice.

"Welcome back. You're looking better, I must say." Percy sat down by his bedside while Cade loomed protectively in the background. "Are you up to telling me what happened? Where did the Witchfinder disappear to?"

Quinn looked at Percy. "He de-materialised. I saw him muttering something and he just disappeared. I've never seen such a thing before."

Percy's face was a picture. His jaw dropped, his eyes widening. "That's unheard of even for the Witchfinder General. How in hell's name could he have done something like that?"

Quinn shook his head tiredly. "I don't know. We'll have to start tracking him all over again. We've not seen the last of him, by any means, much as I'd like to think otherwise."

Percy nodded. "I'll get someone on that right away. I know you won't want the moss growing under our feet while you're recovering." His face grew more serious. "I saw the aftermath of your battle and it wasn't a very nice sight. That poor woman was cut open like a melon. She died a horrible death. Was she dead when you got on board?"

Cade's jaw dropped in horror at the news. Quinn gazed at Percy, his eyes flat. "No. She wasn't. Why does it matter?"

Percy leaned forward. "Couldn't you have helped her, got her out of there, cast some sort of spell to help the woman die an easier death?"

"I had no time." Quinn's face was implacable. "I had other things on my mind. Like stopping myself from being killed." He frowned. "Why are you and Daniel so hung up on a witch that betrayed us and got herself killed?"

Percy fidgeted slightly. "We're not hung up on the witch, just the fact you didn't seem to care about what happened to her. You seem a little more…*merciless* lately."

Cade drew a deep breath, his eyes shadowing at Percy's words.

Quinn wondered whether Cade was in agreement with that comment. His voice was icy when he replied. "Well, I'm sorry you don't like it. Perhaps next time you and Daniel can take on the super Warlock? I imagine no one's told you that de Vere had two Withinners?" He ignored Percy's gasp of horror. "No? I didn't think so."

Cade leaned forward to lay a placatory hand on his arm. Percy's face was pale.

Quinn's voice was steely, his muscles rigid. "He managed to perform some sort of magyck that allowed him to take on another one. So forgive me if I didn't have time to save the broken witch as I was too busy trying to keep myself alive against an uber-Warlock and make sure only one of us got out—preferably me."

He lay back against the pillows, his face hard. Christ he was so fucking tired.

"Don't shoot your mouth off until you have all the facts, Marshall. Now do you think you could speak to the troops and get me an update on what's being done to find Jeremy Payton? And whether the dragon claw was picked up before the boat was cleaned? I don't want that left around for anyone to find."

Percy nodded. "The boat was sunk, Grand Master. Daniel took it out to sea and sank it with both bodies on board. I'll get right on it. I'm sorry if I overstepped." He got up and walked quietly out of the room.

That was harsh, Quinn. He was only worried about you. You have been more relentless lately. Even I have noticed the change in you.

"Quiet, I'm really not in the mood." Quinn snarled. He became aware Cade was regarding him with some trepidation and frowned. "Have you got something to say too? Some further criticism about the way I do things?"

"No," Cade murmured. "I wouldn't dare, you'd just growl at me. I just think you look tired and need to rest." He stood up and pulled the covers over Quinn as he lay back, exhausted. "Try getting some sleep, perhaps it'll get rid of that prima donna. I'll come back later. Daniel was talking to the doctor so no doubt he'll be in a little while to see how you're doing."

Cade kissed him softly on the lips as Quinn nodded, his eyes already closed. He knew he'd been unfair to Percy but he resented that his motives were being questioned. In his heart he knew he'd become harder, less emotional about what happened to people. He'd put it down to recent events, nearly dying twice and having to make some tough decisions. But a small part of him worried that it may be something more, something deeper in his psyche.

***

He was in a casket, a white, silk-lined coffin, flat on his back, the top of the coffin only inches from his face. He couldn't breathe. His arms were rigid at his side, as if weighted with heavy metal bars. He heard a noise outside the casket, as if someone was trying to get it into it. He tried to shout out that he was there, that they needed to let him out. His voice wouldn't work, no matter how loud he cried out. Suddenly his eyes flooded with light and as he looked up at his rescuer, he saw the blackened face of a little girl staring down at him, her teeth exposed in her small face. She had no gums. Her blue eyes stared down at him, open and bulbous and he wanted to close his own so he didn't have to see her ruined face. But they wouldn't shut. He finally managed to raise his one hand and he reached for his eyes, discovering he had no eyelids.

The ruined face of the child bent toward him, her burnt mouth forming words. "You killed me, Quinn Fairmont. You sacrificed me. Now I'm coming to get you."

Quinn cried out in pain at her words, the pain that comes with grief and guilt. He raised his hand toward his face, to block out the face of the entity staring down at him with revenge in her eyes. He heard someone shout his name even as there was a hand on his shoulder, shaking him awake to a world of dim light and a face peering down at him in distress.

"Quinn! It's Cade. It's only a dream. Jesus, please wake up."

Quinn took in a few deep gulps of air, his heart pounding and his head aching, as he looked around the room wildly, seeing only his hospital room and the faint light drifting in through the far window. He tried to sit up, struggling to get his still-painful arms to support him, only to be pushed down by a pair of firm, hairy hands and instructed by a deep, commanding voice.

"Quinn. Stay put, son. Don't move. Cade and I will get you sitting up as soon as you've calmed down. Take a deep breath. That's it. Relax, son, relax."

As Quinn's heart slowly settled itself, he saw the worried faces of Cade and his uncle Daniel standing over him. Daniel's wiry arms supported him as Cade propped more pillows behind him and he was drawn to a sitting position. Quinn's chest heaved with exertion and he swallowed, the taste of bile in his mouth acrid and sour.

Cade's face was deathly white, his eyes staring at him in horror.

Quinn found his voice. "I'm okay," he croaked, as he lay back against the pillow. "Can I have some water, please?"

Cade reached out and held a beaker of water to his mouth and he drank, trying to get the terrible taste out of his mouth. When he'd finished he reached out a hand to Cade, who took his gingerly.

"I'm sorry I scared you all," Quinn said softly. "I just had a bad dream."

His whole body shivered as he recalled it, wanting to block out all the images that seemed to be burned onto his retinas. He tried a small smile but by their identical expressions neither Dan nor Cade was convinced he was all right. Taliesin's concern smouldered inside too.

Quinn, you have to let this one go. It will destroy you if not.

"You were screaming so loudly that I heard you down the corridor. That must have been one helluva nightmare." Cade's voice trembled.

"I'm sorry," He swallowed. "It just all felt so real and I couldn't get away."

"You were shouting a name in your sleep. You were calling the name Honour over and over again. Who's Honour?" Cade's voice was quiet but determined. "She must have been pretty scary to make you scream like that."

Quinn's eyes caught Daniel's and he winced. The look that passed between the two men did not go unnoticed by Cade.

"This is no time for your Warlock-y secret handshakes and glances," his boyfriend said impatiently. "Who the hell is Honour?"

Quinn raised a still-trembling hand to his eyes as he passed his hand over them. "She was a young girl who was murdered by the Witches Alliance. De Vere talked about her on the boat and I imagine it brought up some memories I had pushed deep down."

Cade didn't look convinced. "Well, they must have been fairly terrible ones to get that reaction from you." He looked at him again worriedly. "Are you sure you're all right now?"

Quinn nodded. "Yes, I feel better. Honest, it was just a bad dream."

Daniel's eyes watched him closely and Quinn was careful not to look in his direction. Daniel ignored his evasion and moved over to Quinn, gently taking his chin in his hand, raising Quinn's face to look deep into his eyes. Cade watched the tender action, his eyes narrowing.

Daniel spoke softly. "Quinn, whatever you have inside you about that event, you need to try and come to peace with it. What happened was not your fault, son, no matter what de Vere said. Let it go, like I did. Please, before it eats away at you completely."

Quinn stared into Daniel's brown eyes and slowly nodded. "I've tried." His voice was full of pain. "I'm still trying."

Daniel nodded. "Try harder before it gets you killed." He softly chucked Quinn on the chin then grinned. "Look at me, treating you like you're still ten years old. I forget you're all grown up sometimes. I love you, son. Remember that."

He turned to Cade. "I'll leave you two lovebirds alone whilst I go help Percy. I'll see you both later."

Daniel turned and left the room. Quinn lay back, closing his eyes, aware of Cade's scrutiny and his curiosity. "I'll tell you about it later. I can't face talking about it now. But I promise I will talk to you about it one day."

"You have so many secrets." Cade's voice sounded sad. "So many people know so much more about you than I do. I just can't ever seem to scratch the surface no matter what I do." He stood up tiredly. "I'm going to go and get something to eat and have a swim. I'll be in later to see you."

He turned to leave and Quinn's heart ached for him, seeing him like this, looking so defeated. "I love you, Cade. I may have things in my past we haven't talked about yet, but that doesn't mean I don't love you."

Cade looked at him, his eyes shadowed. "I know, I just sometimes wonder if that's going to be enough for me." His boyfriend smiled wanly as he left, leaving Quinn frustrated and more than a little scared.

I can't lose Cade. God, I'll die if I lose him.

Chapter 37

Quinn was still feeling anxious when Cade walked in about two hours later, his hair still sleekly wet from his swim. Cade smiled as he saw Quinn sitting up, but it was a forced one. Quinn put down the newspaper he'd been trying to read to distract himself, and he held out his arms.

"Please come over here. I really need to hug you."

Cade sat down beside him carefully on the bed and Quinn winced as his injuries complained. He pulled his lover closer to him, smelling the scent of his hair, feeling his warm body in his arms. "You've only been with me four months. Please be patient with me. It's going to take time to tell you everything you want to know about me and I really need you to give me a chance."

Cade pulled back slightly, looking at him softly. "I know, and I'm sorry I said what I did. You've been through enough and you don't need me getting all insecure. But I get so frustrated knowing you've had these terrible events in your life and I can't help you with them. I just want to be closer to you and sometimes I feel you pulling away. You're a master at keeping secrets."

Quinn nodded. "I know; it's how I've survived as long as I have. It's an occupational hazard. Like nearly dying." He grinned wryly. "But please don't make a comment about leaving again. You'll drive me crazy worrying. And I couldn't face losing you, ever."

Cade kissed him softly on his lips, his mouth sweet. "I'm sorry, I'm not going anywhere, I promise. I was just sounding off." He kissed him again. "I went to see Jomo. He's going home next week. He seems to slowly be regaining some of his memories. He remembered my face. Perhaps he'll remember yours when you're well enough to see him." Quinn's face darkened. "If he knew I was the one responsible for putting him here in the first place, he'd not want to remember me. I wouldn't blame him."

"Stop all that guilt and angst. Daniel's right, it will drive you crazy. You seem to have enough already without adding to it."

Quinn heard the slight edge in Cade's voice and he nodded meekly. "Yes, sir."

His boyfriend grinned and Quinn saw his old Cade lurking beneath the concern in his eyes. "Good man. Now, are you hungry? Do you want me to get you something to eat?"

Quinn grimaced. "I'm starving. I really feel like a juicy steak with those thick-cut chips and mushrooms but I guess that isn't on the cards here?" His voice sounded hopeful.

Cade chuckled. "I believe today's special is roast chicken with peas and mash."

Quinn's face fell. "I guess that'll have to do then," he said gloomily.

Cade smiled as he left the room to organise his meal. "I'll go see if there any leftovers, lunch was over a while ago but I'm sure seeing as how you're the Grand Master, they'll organise something for you." He disappeared out of the room, leaving Quinn sitting moodily in the bed. He heard a noise and looked up to see Percy regarding him warily.

"Grand Master, it's good to see you looking better."

Quinn sighed. "Enough with the title. I know I was a complete arsehole earlier and I'm sorry I took my frustration out on you. I apologise."

Percy moved forward, his expression slightly less wary but still cautious. "I was simply worried about you. I still have my responsibility as Marshall to ensure that you're functioning all right."

Quinn nodded tiredly. "I know. I appreciate the concern but I'm fine, I assure you."

Cade walked in with a covered plate and a wide grin on his face. "One portion of chicken and vegetables coming up." He chuckled at the look of distaste on Quinn's face. "Cheer up; it could have been macaroni cheese."

Quinn hated macaroni cheese with a passion. He sighed heavily and looked at his damaged hands. "I'll try and hold the knife and fork myself, if you don't mind. If I make a mess, you can wipe my chin." He fumbled awkwardly with the utensils. Between the burn ointment making the knife and fork slippery and the bandages he was cursing softly until he managed a firm enough grip to eat his meal.

Cade shook his head in amusement. "Do you want me to cut it up for you and feed it to you?"

Quinn regarded him with a glare that would have turned lesser men to a puddle of ooze. But Cade simply put his hands up in surrender. "Fine, be stubborn, you stupid bastard."

Percy grinned slightly at the exchange but wiped the smile off his face when Quinn glared at him in turn.

Percy spoke swiftly. "I wanted to tell you that we have put all resources on hunting down Jeremy Payton. No leads yet but it's still early days. Daniel had the dragon claw. He's passed it over to the Reponosium where it'll stay until we have need of it."

Quinn nodded as he ate. "One day I'll have to get down to that storeroom and see exactly what's in there. I heard a rumour that we had the Book of Kells down there and that the one in the Trinity Library in Dublin was a fake?"

Percy smiled. "I've heard that rumour too. I think it's more a myth propagated by the librarians down there to raise their profile a little, make them feel a little bit more important."

Quinn knew Cade was watching him eat but he ignored the look and struggled valiantly along on his own, feeling a sense of frustration at being so useless. The sly smile on Cade's face was annoying as Quinn struggled, taking his time just getting one piece of chicken onto his fork.

"I suppose then we are forced to simply wait and see what happens with finding the Witchfinder." Quinn frowned, his tone ominous. "I don't like the fact that he simply disappeared. That means very powerful magyck is at play and I don't know where he'd have gotten that. Unless someone was helping him—another Warlock perhaps?" He scowled fiercely. "I can't abide another traitor. Perhaps I haven't been making as many examples as I should have. I'm getting soft."

He didn't miss Percy and Cade's sideways glance at his words. But he meant them all as he considered Jimmy Christie, de Vere, and Sophie Mercurio—all working against their own kind for their own ends. He had to stop the insidious flow of betrayal in the Warlock and witch populace. It was out of hand.

Perhaps he should consult with Valensia, leader of the witches, and see if they could form an alliance again. The last Alliance had been disbanded almost a century ago when the two powerful organisations couldn't arrive at a mutual agreement to manage their enemies. Perhaps now was the time to revisit that. Although a meeting with the infamous Valensia would not be something he'd look forward to. He had a history with her and her temper and propensity to destroy anything that offended or anyone who disagreed with her was well known.

He pushed his plate away, tired of having to struggle. He'd rather stay hungry. He saw Cade's exasperated look at him and grinned at him slightly, hoping he looked like a little boy who knew he'd done something wrong but was too cute to be scolded. It had the desired effect as he saw Cade shake his head at him affectionately.

"Honestly," he murmured. "I don't know why I put up with you. You're so damned stubborn."

Percy chuckled. "I think it's time for me to be on my way, leave you two alone. Don't overdo it and try and stay out of trouble." He waved a hand and left.

Quinn lay back, glad that all the activity was over. He'd noticed a marked improvement in his injuries but he still felt fairly tired and his body was starting to itch as the burns healed. Cade sat down at his bedside and reached out a hand to caress his face.

Quinn smiled at him as he took his lover's hands in his bandaged ones gingerly. "Another few days or so and I'll be back to normal." His eyes scanned Cade's face tenderly. "I need to be because I have an overwhelming desire to drag you into this bed and ravage you. It's been far too long."

"It's been a couple of days, Quinn." Cade's face was alight with amusement.

"Really?" Quinn said in mock surprise. "It feels a lot longer since I made love to you. Now, you could close the door and crawl in here with me. My face is okay and my lips are all right. As long as you're gentle with me, I think I could stand it if you at least kissed me properly whilst I have your body in here with me. And perhaps you can think of something else you can do for me."

Cade drew back the bed covers, raising his eyebrows at the sight of all the wrappings and various plasters doctoring Quinn's body.

"You look like a mummy," he muttered as he lay down carefully beside Quinn and drew the covers over them both. "I've never been in bed with a mummy before."

"I think I might have been." Quinn drawled, his eyes mischievous. "At least I think she said she had a child, I couldn't quite hear properly because she had her mouth around my—"

His words were cut off suddenly as Cade covered his mouth with his, kissing him deeply, his lips bruising Quinn's as he took his mouth with an urgency he knew was born of both relief and passion for him. Cade's slick tongue slid into his mouth and he met it, hearing his small moans of pleasure as they kissed. Cade's hands moved down to Quinn's groin, caressing him gently, and he groaned in satisfaction at his touch.

"At least there's one thing at wasn't injured," Cade whispered as he stroked him gently. "But I think I'd better make sure it works properly after all the trauma it's been through."

Quinn chuckled softly. "It? I'll have you know that *it* has a name. It's called Cade's." His body tensed as Cade's hands moved up and down around his erection, causing him to close his eyes and give way to the sensations flooding his lower body.

"I'm glad to hear it," Cade's mouth found his in another kiss and Quinn thought he was going to explode there and then as his hands increased their activity. "At least this might relieve some of that tension in your body and stop you being such a bitch to everyone. They should reward me for doing this. It's my civic duty to the Consortium."

Cade's throaty laugh caused Quinn's groin to grow even more aroused and he was starting to lose control. He gasped. "I just hope no one comes in and finds us doing this. I'll never live it down."

"Do you want me to stop then?" Cade whispered as he thrust his tongue in Quinn's ear.

"Don't you dare stop. Just keep going. I can promise you it'll be all over fairly soon. You're just too good at this."

Cade bit him gently on the side of the neck where he found undamaged skin, nipping him and making Quinn wince in both pain and ecstasy as his boyfriend's nimble hands continued their slow movements. Quinn's groin once again swelled with heat and the familiar feeling of pins and needles in the tops of his thighs that heralded his orgasm. He buried his mouth in Cade's neck as he came, his body shuddering in release. He could feel Cade grind his mouth against his, still holding him in his hands as Quinn's body finally relaxed from its spasming. He lay back, spent.

"Well, I think we can safely say that worked just fine." Cad drawled huskily. "I look forward to a time when you can return the favour."

He kissed the side of Quinn's neck and clambered out of the bed to wash his hands in the corner basin. Quinn watched him, satiated now and not wanting to move right at that moment.

"I will be getting up just now and taking a shower, bandages be damned," he murmured. "I can't have Matron coming in to check on me and finding me in a pool of semen, that wouldn't be a good idea. God knows what stories would be told at the next Nurse's Annual Dinner."

Cade chuckled and leaned down to kiss him again. "The Great Grand Master, jerking off in his hospital bed. That'd go down a treat at the next Consortium Round Table meeting." He raised an enquiring eyebrow. "Do you have round-table meetings, like King Arthur?"

"No, there's no round table. It's just an ordinary room, with ordinary tables and chairs, much like a corporate boardroom." Quinn shook his head in amusement. "First you think witches go poof and disappear into thin air, now you think I hold court like some medieval king. You read too many fantasy books."

Cade shrugged. "I'm just an anthropologist." He looked at Quinn glumly. "An anthropologist who probably doesn't have a job after all the time I've taken off. I really think I might have to make another plan. The Institute will only take so much and I think their patience is wearing thin with me. I've got half a dozen texts and missed calls from Ambrose asking me when I'm coming back from my 'sabbatical.'"

"I know you've had a lot to put up with me because of me," Quinn said quietly. "Now that de Vere's gone I hope we can get back to some semblance of normality when we get home."

"You've still got a missing Witchfinder General." Cade looked at him grimly. "Until you find him, nothing is going to be normal."

"We'll find him." Quinn's voice portrayed more confidence than he felt. "And when we do, we'll deal with it and get that last threat out of the way. I'm hoping he'll lie low for a while, give us a chance to reconvene our efforts to find him."

Cade didn't look convinced. "And each time he kills a Warlock, you'll feel it and have that awful reaction."

Quinn couldn't argue with that. "We're more prepared against him, now. I'd like to think we can hold our own."

"I hope so, I really do. Because the last thing I want to is to end up back at this hospital with you in that bed, looking all 'at death's door.' I've had enough of that to last me a lifetime."

Chapter 38

A week later Cade was sitting on his houseboat waiting once again for Quinn to arrive. He'd recovered well from his ordeal. Cade thought wryly that in Quinn's usual autocratic fashion, he'd dared his body to defy his request to heal and he'd landed, once again, like a cat on his feet. Cade stroked Marco Polo's back softly as he sat on the deck, his bare feet propped up on the rail, enjoying the feel of the early September sunshine and sipping a glass of red wine.

"He's such a bossy boots, isn't he, Marco? Like a big ogre, just giving orders and expecting people to jump when he does. It is very sexy as long as you're not the one he's giving orders to."

An amused voice broke into his conversation with the cat. "Whilst I'm glad you find me sexy, I'm not sure I like being compared to Shrek."

Quinn leaned down and kissed the top of Cade's head as he grinned.

"Eavesdroppers hear no good of themselves." Cade shooed the cat off his lap and stood up to kiss him properly. They stood entwined for a moment then pulled apart.

Cade looked at him appraisingly. "You clean up nicely. To say only that a week ago you looked like you'd had an argument with a sun bed." He nodded approvingly at Quinn's cream linen chinos, his deep blue open-necked shirt and the expanse of chest he could see beneath.

Quinn grinned. "I had a great nurse. Said nurse even climbed into bed with me occasionally and I found that really helped the healing process. I might use him again some time."

Cade smiled, remembering the last time they'd made love just before Quinn left the clinic. The hospital bed was fairly narrow and the acrobatics and callisthenics required making things work had been quite challenging. He was glad to say that both of them seemed more limber then they'd thought.

Quinn sat down in the other deck chair and as ever, Marco Polo jumped on his lap. He regarded the cat suspiciously as Cade sat back down.

"I really don't know why you think you're my new best friend, cat. Heaven knows I try not to encourage you."

Cade smiled. "He knows you're like him, a Leo. A big, strong, proud and noble beast."

Quinn raised an eyebrow. "An ogre and now a beast? God, the compliments just get better. Now, is there any way I can get a drink, boyfriend, or do I have to do it myself?"

Cade was about to retort indignantly when he saw the twinkle in his eyes and he sighed. "I'll get you a beer. I imagine that's what you want?"

Quinn nodded and leaned back on the deck chair, raising his face to the sun. Cade saw the faint scars on his face in the light. The scar on his chin he was used to now but there were marks from previous battles that he could only see now.

Cade brought him a beer and sat back down next to him.

Quinn looked at him tenderly. "How was work today? Is everything going all right—you still have a job?"

Cade nodded resignedly. "Yes, I'm back in the thick of things. They're taking their pound of flesh though. I had three classes today and the rest of next week is going to be one of the busiest

I've had. Professor Tickler-Brown is certainly making me pay for my unplanned sabbatical." He wrinkled his nose in distaste.

He was damn lucky to still have a job indeed.

Quinn reached over and took his hand, rubbing a thumb down it idly. "You'll get back into the swing of it. I told you things would quieten down."

"Has anything happened on finding Jeremy Payton yet?"

Quinn shook his head. "No leads, no news. But no deaths either, so I'm thankful for small mercies. We'll get him." He sounded grim and Cade thought this was good time to get serious.

"Quinn, does your offer of moving in with you still stand?" he asked quietly, watching his lover's face.

Quinn stilled slightly and looked at him out of hopeful eyes. "Of course it does. Why, are you thinking of considering it?"

Cade stood up and went to sit in his lap, chasing the cat away and wrapping his arms around his neck. "I've watched you nearly die three times in four months. There are so many things I need to find out about you still and I can't do that without having a lot more time with you. So I thought at least living with you, I'd get to be there when you get home and see you in the morning when we wake up and if you can put up with me being there all the time—"

"Cade, shut up." Quinn kissed him fiercely, his mouth passionate and warm, his hands circling his waist and pulling him closer to him. Cade gave into Quinn's embrace and it was some hot and heavy minutes later when they finally drew apart, both breathing deeply, wanting to take it further.

"I'd like nothing better than having you there with me," Quinn whispered in his ear. "I miss you when you're not there and I love coming home and finding you in my bed."

Cade nuzzled his ear. "There's someone at the Institute who'd love to rent this place, because I wouldn't give it up. Just in case I got tired of you when you get all prima donna and I wanted to move out. But you'd have to take on Marco because I won't move in without him."

"It's a small price to pay, having the fleabag at home, if I get you." Quinn chuckled at Cade's frown.

"He's not a fleabag, Close your ears, Marco, he's being mean." He punched Quinn lightly on the shoulder and Quinn stood up quickly, arms and muscles tensing as he picked Cade up in strong arms and walked swiftly over to the side of the boat. Quinn held him over the water, a wicked glint in his eyes as Cade shouted.

"Jesus, put me down, you Neanderthal! Don't you dare throw me in that water. I've just got changed."

"You're a Sprite; you'll love it." Quinn saw the owner of the houseboat next to Cade's grinning widely and giving him the thumbs up. "Your neighbour seems to think it's a good idea," he murmured.

Cade glared over at the other houseboat. "Freddy would find anything funny. He's a stand-up comic in the city, for God's sake. Put me down, you bastard!"

Quinn laughed huskily. "I have a better idea, actually."

Cade saw where this was going as Quinn carried him inside the bedroom and laid him down on the bed, a grin on his face. Cade shook his head at Quinn's forwardness even though he wanted nothing more than to undress him and get on top of him himself.

"You are really something, you know that? So damned arrogant," he said, watching as Quinn unbuttoned his shirt lazily.

His groin throbbed as Quinn took off his shirt and laid it on the bed. Cade loved the sight of his lover's muscled chest, his taut stomach and the scar he loved to run his tongue along, an action he knew drove Quinn crazy. Quinn smiled, reaching down to him as he sat on the bed. His hands reached out to slowly lift Cade's tee shirt over his stomach and kiss the firm skin beneath as he pushed him back onto the bed.

"I'm not feeling your resistance, despite your words of protest," Quinn murmured as his lips travelled across his stomach and he lifted the tee shirt higher to suck Cade's nipples, his tongue circling them languorously, paying special attention to Cade's piercing.

Cade's stomach muscles tightened at the movement of his mouth as Quinn's hands moved down to his jeans to unzip them. Cade's hands buried themselves in Quinn's thick hair as he pulled him up toward him. Both of them were breathing deeply. Quinn stood up and dropped his chinos to the floor. Cade watched lazily.

"I know I've said it before," he whispered, eyes greedy at the sight before him, the proud erection already glistening and rock hard. "But you do have really big feet and I love every inch of them. I'm really a very lucky man."

Quinn's eyes darkened and as he lowered himself on top of Cade's eager and oh-so willing body, Cade closed his eyes and prepared to be on the receiving end of Quinn's big feet.

***

Two hours later they lay entwined together, drowsy and satiated after their energetic lovemaking. Cade was a boneless jellyfish, feeling as if he'd melted into the bed. Finally, when he'd recovered enough, Cade leaned over and kissed Quinn's chin. "Quinn, are you sure about this whole moving in together thing? I don't want us to be getting on each other's nerves and starting to fight. You know you can be a bossy boots and I can be a stubborn arse."

Quinn chuckled. "I know too well what you're like. But I still want you around more. You're my sanity, the place I come to when everything seems crazy. You see the real me and treat me like the person I am inside. That's what I love so much about you, apart from the obvious attributes of course."

Cade harrumphed. "Well, I'm not sure about knowing the person inside as you're the most complicated man I've ever met, with so many secrets and hidden compartments. You're a regular Chinese puzzle. But I do know that what I can see I love dearly and I want to get to. But there is one condition—a serious one."

Quinn stirred. "What's that?"

"Now all the excitement is over—at least for now—I want to know everything about being a Sprite, and I mean everything. I want to check out my trunk and try finding out who I am. It's time."

Quinn took a sharp breath.

Not for the first time Cade wondered why it bothered him so much. "You have to promise me faithfully that you'll tell me everything I need to know, about the whole healer thing and find some way that I can learn about what and who I am. I know you have the resources to do that. I also know you've been holding back on it. I don't know why." Quinn's silence confirmed his suspicion. "And that's a non-negotiable condition. If I'm going to be living with you, learning about you, I want to be learning about me too."

Quinn remained silent and Cade waited impatiently for his reply. When Quinn spoke, his voice was quiet, almost resigned. "Fine. I suppose it's a fair condition. I can tell you what I know." He frowned suddenly. "Shut up, Taliesin," he growled. "Stay out of this conversation, go find a milkmaid to ravage."

Cade smiled at the conversation that in other circumstances would have appeared quite bizarre and had him calling the men with white coats.

"I take it he agrees and you don't like that? Why are you so scared to tell me about it all?" he asked in puzzlement. "I would have thought you would have been eager to tell me all about other

Feys, and what they can do, their beginnings. Why are you so reluctant to tell me about mine?"

"It's complicated. It's not quite as simple as you think, trying to find out about someone's origins and their powers. But I promise you I'll do my best."

Cade nodded, not quite sure Quinn was telling the truth but deciding not to push it yet.

"Maybe we can look in the trunk tonight?" Cade said yearningly.

Quinn's eyes shadowed but he nodded and smiled—a little forced, Cade thought. "Tonight is good if that's what you want."

A surge of excitement ran through Cade. "This is going to be great. Maybe you'll see something we missed. And when I move over to your place, I'll have those great pools to swim in on the heath every day, weather permitting. Perhaps I'll even meet another Sprite in there," he murmured jokingly. Quinn started slightly but thought it might have been because Cade had caressed the inside of his thigh.

Cade lay there, content in the knowledge that he might find answers and would soon be living with Quinn. He was excited about it, despite his earlier misgivings. It would feel good to have him close and learn as much as he could about this man he was in love with. He had a feeling that with Quinn, he needed all the time he could get.

Chapter 39

Cade sat on the floor in the lounge on his boat gazing at the large brown trunk in front of him. He stared at it as if he expected something to jump out. It held painful memories and had been sitting in a spare space on his houseboat, covered with a cloth and used as a table for many years. But now with Quinn by his side, Cade really needed to figure out exactly who and what he was, and to do that he had to face the trunk and its contents. He looked up as Quinn came in with two glasses of wine and set them down on the side table. His lover sank to the floor gracefully, catlike, sitting cross legged next to him and raising an enquiring eyebrow in his direction.

"Well…I thought you were going to open it?" he said quietly. "What's the matter? Are you worried about what you might find?"

Cade nodded. "This has everything from my life in it, anything that was passed onto Sally when she took me in. She tried to put everything she could find at my father's house into that trunk." He smiled. "She said it was my inheritance and one day I'd be rich."

Quinn nodded. "She sounds like a wise woman." He peered short-sightedly at the lock. "Do you have a key for it?"

Cade held up a small brass key. "It's been in my desk drawer for years. I've only opened this trunk once, when Sally died. There were too many memories in it and I closed it. Since then, I've never opened it."

Quinn reached over and placed his hand on Cade's. "Then open it. Let's see what's inside."

Cade heard a faint note of apprehension in Quinn's voice and he wondered why. He reached over and fitted the key into the rusty lock. It clicked open easily considering it hadn't been unlocked in so long. Cade looked at Quinn and slowly raised the top of the trunk.

A musty smell seeped out and Quinn twitched his nose in distaste. "That's pretty yuck. Smells like an ogre's armpit."

Cade stared at him. "Please tell me you haven't actually ever smelt an ogre's armpit?"

Quinn chuckled. "That's for me to know and you to find out." He peered inside the trunk and reached a hand inside, a hand that Cade slapped smartly. He looked up, an injured expression on his face.

"What? I was just trying to help."

"Hold your horses, mister. It's my trunk. I get to go first."

Quinn shook his head and waved a hand, inviting his boyfriend to go ahead. Cade leaned over the box, wrinkling his nose at the smell. Quinn peered myopically inside, squinting his eyes, and Cade looked at him in exasperation.

"For goodness sake, put on your damn glasses. You'll be no use to me without them and you'll just end up with sore eyes."

Quinn frowned and stood up to go to his chair and pick up his glasses from the jacket slung over the back. He put them on and regarded him frostily. "Better?"

Cade grinned. "I love it when you wear those. You look like some sexy geek guy, a professor." He stroked Quinn's cheek suggestively. "I think you should wear those to bed tonight. I think I'd like to shag a teacher."

Quinn grinned. "I think I might manage that. Remind me to put them on later. Although I think they may tend to steam up during said activity."

Cade chuckled. He rummaged through the papers and documents in the trunk and pulled out a handful, placing them on the floor between them. "Maybe we can just take a look at these for a start, see what we have?" he suggested. "We can have a pile for different things as we find them and that might help."

Quinn nodded. "Good idea." He picked up a document. "Let's start with this. School certificate, it looks like. This one is Year 10 school results for you. A for English, A+ for History, A+ for Maths, A+ for Geography…"

He looked at Cade in amusement. "You were quite a nerd, Cade. Those results aren't half bad."

He picked up another one and whistled, looking at him again over his glasses.

"I didn't realise you went to Cambridge to study. That's quite an achievement. I thought they had some of the highest entry-level requirements in the country?"

Cade flushed. "I managed to get into Residence there. It was one of the best times of my life. I loved it there."

Quinn was staring at him admiringly and Cade became quite self-conscious.

"So I'm bonking a very clever nerd," Quinn murmured, his eyes focusing on Cade's lips. "I like that." He grinned and placed the document on a pile.

"The education pile," he proclaimed as he picked up another document. Cade shook his head at him and returned to the document he was holding.

"I think we'll call this one 'medical.' This is my history of vaccinations and such."

Quinn held up another one. "Boyfriends," he remarked slyly. "This is a picture of you with a very tall young man who looks like Lurch. It looks like some sort of prom photo. Even back then you were seriously hot. What did you see in a lumbering giant like this chap?"

Cade frowned as he plucked the photo from his hands. "Luke was a very nice young boy, one of the basketball players in secondary school, and very sought after by all the ladies." He smiled. "As was I. So we made quite a statement going as a couple. I was tired of being endlessly harassed by young ladies wanting me to take off their knickers and Luke felt the same. We decided to come out together that night. But we had to get it passed through the damn PTA first." He frowned. "They were worried we'd cause a riot. We told them that whether they said yes or not, we were going together." He grinned. "We threatened to kiss and grope each other on the floor anyway if they said no. So they sanctioned us going as a couple. It was quite a night, statement-wise. Luckily there were very few repercussions. Both of us had tempers and could hold our own in a fight once college started again." Cade shrugged. "It only took a few good punches from us both to knock down a couple of bullies and we were left alone. There was some harassment but it could have been much worse." He looked at the picture. "Luke had quite a thing for me. Such a thing that I let him be my very first."

Quinn's mouth fell open. "You lost your virginity to that bloke?" He looked aggrieved at the fact and Cade laughed softly.

"He wasn't a bad lover. At least he had some experience and he did his best to make it as comfortable as possible for me. We went to the after-party at one of the girls' houses, and one thing led to another and we found ourselves in the bedroom, and"—he shrugged, noticing Quinn's look of jealousy—"we did it. It was all right, nothing earth shattering. I had my anal cherry popped at sweet sixteen."

"Hell, that's a bit raw." Quinn frowned as he picked up the photo again from the pile and looked at it fiercely. "I still say he looks like Lurch." He placed the photo face down on the pile and picked up another document. Cade watched him in amusement. He leaned over and kissed the corner of Quinn's mouth softly.

"He couldn't hold a candle to you; no man could. I bet even at that age you had the girls and guys crawling all over you. I bet they all wanted you to take them to the prom." He drew back and looked at Quinn curiously. "Who was your first? How old were you? Was it with a man or a woman?"

"I'm not talking about this now." Quinn's face flushed. "Let's just get on with the matter in hand."

He picked up another document. Cade stared at him, his curiosity unsated.

"Why don't you want to talk about it? I've told you mine. You need to tell me yours."

Quinn sighed in exasperation. "You have this annoying tendency to worry at things like someone picking at a scab. What does it matter when my first time was?"

"Because you don't want to talk about it. That makes it very mysterious and I love a good mystery. You know I'll nag you until you tell me so best tell me now."

Cade leaned in and kissed Quinn's ear, his tongue darting inside, causing him to start, and Cade increased the pressure, hearing him draw in a deep breath as he turned to glare at him.

"Fine, but don't say I didn't warn you. The first time I had sex, I was thirteen. It was with a woman. I wasn't as sure then as I am now."

Cade gazed at him open mouthed and Quinn watched his face with what appeared to be satisfaction. "Shocked? I know that's underage legally but when you're a Warlock and the woman is a Fey, that doesn't really matter to you. She was sixteen, and believe me, she knew exactly what she was doing. Her name was Sylvia and she sort of initiated me into sex. It was a pretty good initiation, I have to say."

He grinned at the memories. "I suppose I grew up a lot more mature than most young boys, having the background I did. It didn't help having Taliesin egging me on, being ancient and all that and getting fed up being celibate on the Warlock side."

Cade stared at him. "That's pretty young to be having sex."

Quinn shrugged. "From the age of six, I was old enough to see my parents die, to be taught magyck and how to kill Witchunters. What makes sex so taboo?"

"I suppose it's just not the normal course of events. It's not the usual thing. None of that is for a young boy."

Quinn's voice hardened. "I'm a Warlock. I killed my first man when I was just twelve. Surely after that, sex is less of an issue?" He laughed cynically. "Christ, in the U.S. you can go to war and kill men when you're seventeen, but you can't take a drink till you're twenty-one. What kind of a system puts those ridiculous rules in place? Well, it's the same with Warlocks and sex. I was pretty much ready at thirteen, I can assure you."

"You were twelve and you killed someone?" Cade's voice was horrified. "Who did you kill at such a young age?"

Quinn took off his glasses and rubbed his eyes tiredly. "It was a rogue Warlock. He'd been feeding the Witchunters information that led to seven Warlock deaths. Daniel caught him and asked me what we should do with him. Even then, I was being groomed for the Grand Master. My father had died, I had no brother or other male blood heir and I was all that was left. I had to decide what to do. I decided he should pay for his crime."

He shook his head angrily. "Hell, how the hell did we get onto the subject of me? This evening was supposed to be about you, not me. I don't know what trick you have of getting me to talk about myself, but you're pretty good at drawing me in." He stood up abruptly. "I'm going to get more wine."

He disappeared toward the kitchen, leaving Cade looking after his retreating figure with a sick feeling in his stomach. He'd known Quinn had had a fairly unusual childhood but being given the responsibility at twelve years old to decide whether someone should live or die seemed pretty dire. He got up and went in search of his lover. Quinn was in the kitchen, hands placed firmly on the sink top, staring out across the river, his body rigid, his face blank.

Cade came up behind him and touched his shoulder gently. "I'm sorry. I didn't mean to pry like that. All I wanted to know was the first time you had sex; I'd no idea it would open up such memories for you. It was supposed to be an innocent question."

Quinn turned to him, running a hand through his already mussed-up hair. "With me there are no such things as innocent questions. I told you I have too many secrets, too many memories. Sometimes it's just best not to ask anything. Then I don't have to answer."

"That's a very sad thing to say," Cade said quietly. "And not something I can do. I told you I wanted to get to know you better. It's the reason I want to move in with you, so we can spend more time together. If you're going to just shut me out every time I ask something about your past, this relationship will go nowhere." He turned to leave. "And I don't have tricks to get you to talk; I just care about you. I want to share things with you and I expect the same back. I'm sorry you don't see it that way."

Quinn simply shrugged and continued staring out of the window, his body taut.

Cade shook his head and moved swiftly into the lounge, packing the piles of documents and pictures on the lounge floor back into the trunk and locking it. He pushed the trunk into the corner of the room, wishing now that he'd never opened it. Then he went into the bedroom and climbed into bed with a heavy heart as he tried to fall asleep.

When he woke up the following morning, Quinn wasn't in bed. In fact, it looked as if he hadn't come to bed at all. Cade got up to change. Perhaps he'd left and gone home. Cade needed a swim to relax him. As he walked into his lounge, Quinn was stretched out on the sofa, his arms flung above his head, his legs, too long to fit properly, propped up on the chair arm. Cade walked over quietly, watching him sleeping, noticing the empty whisky glass beside him and an opened bottle of Jameson on the table next to him, three-quarters full. It had been a full bottle the night before. Cade's pang of guilt at having driven him to this soon faded as he then almost immediately experienced a sense of anger that he felt that way at all. It wasn't his fault that Quinn was so closed about his past and got a bug up his arse every time he tried to get close.

Cade glanced at his watch. Nine a.m. Time for Quinn to get up anyway and face the day. He walked over to heavy curtains across the small windows, pulling them back swiftly. Early morning sunlight streamed into the room. Sunlight glinted off the water, casting mirrored shadows on the walls. Cade enjoyed a mean sense of satisfaction when the rays of sunlight hit Quinn full in the face, causing him to groan loudly and open his eyes, wincing as he did so.

"Hell, close the curtains! My head's splitting." He peered up at Cade from bloodshot eyes. "What time is it?"

Groaning, he swung his legs down from where they'd been, his face twisting as muscles obviously protested at the change of posture. He ran his hands through his tawny hair which was spiky and untidy.

Cade's nose twitched slightly. "It's nine o'clock. I thought you'd probably want to wake up and have a shower. It smells a little rank down here." He sniffed. "I see you had yourself a little party."

Quinn looked up with a scowl. "I couldn't sleep. I needed something to help me."

"Then perhaps you should have come to bed," Cade said sweetly. "It would have been a lot more comfortable." He turned and wandered over to the kitchen. "Do you want anything to eat?"

Quinn shook his head and winced at the movement, his face paling. "God, no. I'm going to go shower. Maybe that will make me feel better." Quinn looked at Cade hopefully. He ignored him, not wanting to appear sympathetic. The man had brought his condition on himself by being stubborn, arrogant and a downright pain the arse. Quinn frowned when he saw he was getting no words of sympathy and stood up, stretching as he did so. "I guess I need that shower," Quinn muttered, his nose wrinkling in distaste.

"I think that would be a good idea," Cade remarked dryly. "I'm going to go swimming at the pool. I'll be back later."

Quinn nodded at him as he walked upstairs. "I'll see you later then." He disappeared up the stairs. Cade shook his head and picked up his swim bag. He had a feeling he'd need the solitude and the solace the water brought for whatever conversation he'd be having with Quinn when he got back. Because there most definitely would be some sort of conversation whether his boyfriend liked it or not.

Chapter 40

Quinn sighed in satisfaction as the hot waters of the narrow shower drenched him, easing his aching muscles and the pain in his head from over-imbibing a good bottle of whisky. He stood with his hands flat against the shower wall, eyes closed, letting the aches and pain drain away through the shower plug. He knew he'd been a complete prick last night. The easy banter of the evening and Cade's innocent question about his past had led him to once again get overemotional. He was guilty of being a complete prat.

Quinn owed Cade a lot more than he'd ever asked about. He'd been right—it was the reason Cade was moving in with him. His lover had made it abundantly clear that he expected to get to know Quinn better, good and bad. And he'd agreed—even though reluctantly—because he knew if he didn't, he'd lose him. But if he was going to get mouthy every time Cade asked him about something, he was going to drive him away. He leaned his forehead against the cool tiles, feeling the ache in his head abate a little. He'd talk to Cade when he got back from the pond, tell him he was sorry and perhaps they could start again.

When Cade came in from his swim an hour later, his hair was wet, stuck to his forehead and his face pink with the exertion of his swim. Cade looked wary as Quinn approached him, pulling him closer in a fierce hug, burying his face in wet hair.

"I was an idiot last night. I'm sorry I got so riled. I deserve the hangover, I deserve your anger and I deserve to be punished. That last bit can wait till later though when we're in bed."

Quinn smiled down at Cade and he saw amusement in his eyes at his words, even as he pulled away firmly.

"I'm glad you feel that way but this isn't the first time we've had this conversation." Cade put his holdall on the floor, and turned to face him, his grey eyes questioning. "I can't have this reaction from you every time I ask you something personal. Can you honestly say things will be any different?"

Quinn regarded Cade sombrely. "I promise to try; that's all I can do. You took me on knowing what I'm like. I can't change overnight; it's going to take time."

Quinn reached over and took Cade's hands, still cold from the cold water. "I can't lose you. And I know I will if I continue to hide everything and overreact every time you try and find out something about me. So I have to change a little. To keep you around because I honestly couldn't face a life without you in it."

Quinn pulled Cade to him, finding his cool lips, Quinn's own warm against them. His lover's lips parted and he kissed him back, his hands encircling his neck, twining themselves in the curls of his hair. Finally they parted and Cade looked at him softly with eyes that were both desirous and smoky. "I think that apology will keep me going for now. And I think I'll take you up on that punishment later on. That behind of yours had better be ready for a good slapping."

Quinn laughed loudly, glad that Cade was no longer mad with him. "Slap away. I look forward to it." His face became serious. "Now, get yourself into dry clothes and come back into to the lounge. We're going to continue what we started last night and look through that trunk of yours. I made you a promise to try and find out more about you and your family and that's a good place to start." He grinned wryly. "Hopefully this time without the prima donna in the room."

Cade reached up and kissed him gently on the cheek then scooted off to change. Quinn had the trunk out of the corner when Cade came in and gave him the little key, now worn on a silver chain around his neck. They sat with steaming cups of coffee, working through the documents as they sorted everything into piles.

They'd been working about half an hour when Cade triumphantly held up a sepia-coloured piece of paper, with lines and squiggles, waving it around with the air of someone who was about to shout *Eureka!*

Quinn raised an eyebrow. "Found something good then, have we?"

He nodded, his eyes shining. "It's a family tree chart, Quinn. It has generations of my family on it. It was rolled up in this little tube. I don't remember seeing it before." He looked puzzled. "In fact I'm sure it wasn't in here."

Quinn took the old piece of paper from him, feeling the energy in the document as he touched it. He imagined it had been in the trunk all the time, but Cade hadn't been able to see it until now. Whether it was Quinn's presence or simply the fact that Cade was closer to his Fey side now through his involvement and close physical contact with Quinn, he wasn't sure. He scrutinised the parchment with the practised air of one who was used to making sense out of old documents. His face paled as he looked at the family tree. There was no way he could keep this from Cade, even though it might mean trouble.

Cade looked at him anxiously. "Quinn, you look strange. What is it?"

"I don't believe it. Your great-great-great-grandmother was Hester Vickers. It says here she lived in the 1700s which tallies in with what I know about her."

Taliesin moved in interest. Despite his concern at Cade's parentage, Quinn felt a frisson of excitement as such a monumental discovery.

Cade gazed at Quinn in amazement. "How do you know anything about that?"

Quinn smiled despite his apprehension. "Because Hester Vickers was a very well-known Fey of that time. A Sprite healer and spokeswoman of note who lived a very long time, and when she died in the early 1800s she was finally buried in the Lakeland District, somewhere around Windermere Lake. She seemed to be the last in that line, there's not much mention of anyone after her in the same line. There's your link, that's who you're descended from. It's incredible, I can't believe it. I've done research on her before but had no idea of this connection!"

Your Cade could have incredible powers. Now will you listen to me and show him what he's capable of?

Quinn ignored his Withinner's comment, flapping the paper around with abandon. "Hester Vickers was an amazing woman. Using her leadership abilities she single-handedly stopped a couple of insurrections between two factions that sprung up in the ranks. With her foresight and wisdom, the ruling body was able to stop the rebel one from causing absolute havoc in the waters around the North of England. They planned on sinking ships, drowning mortals and generally creating mayhem against the human race. She forced them to mediate and negotiate."

Cade watched him with stunned eyes.

"She mediated on the Council for over fifty years, guiding them, advising them and using her powers keeping peace in a time when the Sprite nation was actually undergoing a lot of turmoil. At the time—"

"Quinn!" Cade finally shouted and Quinn looked at him in surprise. "Please—can I get a word in?"

He nodded guiltily. "Sorry, I was going off at a tangent. What do you want to ask me?"

"You said she was the last of that line. Do you mean that after she died, there were no more references found?"

Quinn nodded. "Hester had three daughters, Celeste, Bronwen and Elsa. All of them would have the Sprite bloodline passed down to them. Bronwen died very young, she was about eleven. Elsa disappeared when she was in her twenties and no one ever heard from her again. The rumours say she ran away with a mortal and left her Fey life behind. Celeste"—he looked at the family tree, squinting over his glasses—"She married a mortal man called Jacob Summers and had a child called Chloe. There's nothing mentioned at all after that birth. It's as if the bloodline was hidden or even just forgotten about."

He looked at Cade. "Chloe was your great-grandmother. Chloe had a daughter called Sarah, who was your grandmother, who had your mother, Anna." He waved the paper again. "This confirms everything for you, Cade. We know where you come from. We just don't know why the Sprite teachings died out with Celeste or Chloe, whether your mother even knew about any of this. It's probably something we'll never know. They may have chosen to take a different path and not wanted to be burdened by what they felt was something beyond their control. I think your mother, and probably your grandmother as well, had no idea who or what she was, which is why the Fey echo was so faint in you when we first met."

He sat back as Cade looked blankly at him, clearly stunned by the news.

Quinn sat down beside him. "I know you're pretty shocked at all this." He took a deep breath. "But it's good news for you. You can trace your roots back to a famous healer, one of the most powerful women in your race. Isn't that what you wanted? To know where this Fey inheritance came from and why nobody told you about it? I can't believe we waited so long to open this damn box."

Is it what you wanted? I think in hindsight this news disturbs you mightily.

Quinn frowned at Taliesin's words as Cade nodded uncertainly.

"I suppose so. But what does it all mean? It still doesn't tell me what powers I have or how to use them."

"We'll figure that out." Within reason, Quinn told himself silently. "Now we know who your ancestors are, I can do some more research, find out what they did and knew and see if we can help you find yours."

And pigs will fly, Quinn.

"Taliesin, shut the fuck up," Quinn muttered angrily, seeing Cade start at his words. He shrugged. "He's being a little irritating. He can be a right know-it-all."

Cade nodded, still unsure. "Can Taliesin tell you anything about how to find out what I can do?"

Quinn squirmed uneasily. He didn't want to tell Cade an outright lie and tell him Taliesin would be unable to help, knowing his Withinner's views on the subject. He decided to be evasive instead. "He'll help any way he can. He knows something of Sprites and he's always looking for information."

He winced at his Withinner's furious explosion.

Another bare-faced lie! I am one of the most knowledgeable about Cade's people and you are nothing but a charlatan! One of these days I am going to see Cade again and I will tell him of your duplicity in keeping him in the dark.

Bite me. Quinn snarled at his Withinner as he smiled at Cade's bemused face. "Is there anything else in this box of tricks of yours that I should know about?" He waved the paper in his hand in front of Cade's face. "Would you mind if I took this back to my place and made a copy? I'd like to add it to my archives on Hester. It'll give me a lot of new leads to follow on the family tree angle."

Cade nodded. "Sure, knock yourself out." He peered in the box again. "I can't see anything else like that. Some letters, some old maps, a few photos of me with other boys which we won't talk about lest it lead to an argument." He smiled wryly.

Quinn's ears pricked up at the mention of old letters and maps. "Would you mind if I took a look?"

He pushed Cade out the way in his haste to retrieve the documents and sat down cross legged on the floor, his attention span focused directly on what was in front of him.

***

Cade watched him in amusement. Quinn was like a kid in a sweet shop not knowing which one to eat first. His lover was entranced in the contents of the treasure chest, muttering to himself as he trawled through must-smelling papers. He shook his head and went into the kitchen to make more coffee, his mind still racing with what he'd discovered about his heritage. He couldn't believe that the woman Quinn seemed to know so well was actually related to him.

"What are the odds of that, Marco?" he murmured to the Persian, who was curled up on the kitchen stool in the late-morning sunlight streaming through the window. "I imagine Quinn would know. It's meant to be, kitty, me and Quinn. It has to be, surely, given what we know now. Who the hell plans all this stuff anyway?"

He frowned as he poured boiling water into cups and then took the coffee through to the lounge where Quinn still sat, poring over the contents of the trunk. He nodded absentmindedly at Cade as he passed him his steaming cup.

"Thanks. These maps in the chest are actually documented waterways of Britain, all the known rivers, lakes, streams and seas of the whole island. It's quite an incredible find. I'll take a better look later when I go home in a minute."

Cade raised an eyebrow. "Are you going to disappear that soon? I thought we might go for a walk, get some fresh air. You can work that headache off."

Quinn looked nonplussed. "I guess we could do that." He glanced longingly at the trunk.

Cade wasn't going to let him off the hook. "That can wait," he said firmly. "It's been in there over twenty years; it'll wait a little bit longer. We've done well for a first pass." He was still a little gobsmacked about finding his descendents but had no doubt there was more to come.

Quinn sighed. "Fine, a walk it is then." He looked over with a smile. "I truly am glad we found out the link to your past. And that you're not mad with me anymore."

Cade grinned. "And don't forget I get to slap your butt later when we go to bed, just to keep you in line."

Quinn chuckled. "I get the feeling you're really looking forward to that bit. It's slightly scary." He stood up and beckoned to his boyfriend. "Come on then, let's go for that walk if you're so hell bent on it. The exercise will do me good."

They grabbed coats and jerseys and left the house, heading down the river.

Chapter 41

Quinn sat opposite Jomo in their office, as he dealt with a mountain of paperwork on his desk. It was Saturday afternoon and the two were working some overtime to catch up on a sudden rush of grant applications. He peered at Jomo over the top of his glasses.

"Have you got that proposal for HGF with you? I know I had it here somewhere but I can't find the damned thing now."

Jomo grinned as he rifled through a pile of files on his desk and passed it over to Quinn. "You gave it to me yesterday. Your memory is going, my friend. Unlike mine, which is coming back bit by bit every day."

He beamed a large flashing of white teeth and sparkling eyes. He was right. Every day he was retrieving memories as Quinn worked with him to regain them. Under the guise of an exercise proposed by Jomo's psychologist, Quinn was quietly performing a series of his own magyck on the man's brain to help him even further. Jomo had no idea it was going on. It was carefully orchestrated and part of the workout he was expected to do. But magyck could be subtle as well as overpowering and Quinn was a master at it. And he had no doubt that his Withinner's power was contributing to the success as well. Together they were a force to be reckoned with and Quinn would have it no other way.

The Warlock's biggest triumph had been unlocking part of the memory in which Jomo remembered who Quinn was. Slowly, memories were coming flooding back of their friendship as boys and their deep commitment to each other as grown men and Quinn would forever be grateful for that victory. It was something he held very dear.

He took the file that Jomo held out with a smile. "I *had* forgotten. Perhaps I need some of those brain exercises you're doing too."

The two men grinned comfortably at each other. They'd settled back into a work routine very easily and Quinn was glad Jomo was back. The strain of trying to run his business alone for the past two months had certainly detracted from his other, more secret, responsibilities. There had still been no news about the whereabouts of Jeremy Payton. He hadn't made contact with his buddy Kyle, Daniel had not been able to track him down via the Witchhunters Alliance and Percy and his team had seen no particular magyckal activity related to the Witchfinder General. It was as if he had literally disappeared into thin air when he performed his dissipating trick on the yacht over a month ago.

Quinn was thankful for the lack of activity but frustrated that he was not in control of the situation as he would have liked. The Consortium was pleased with the result, thinking it was over. Quinn knew better, that this was simply a hiatus before the storm which he felt in his bones was coming.

But other than what he was doing—having everyone and anyone in the land looking for the boy and drawing on his considerable influence in the magyckal world—he knew he could do no more but simply wait for the next actions in the drama to play out. He had no doubt he'd find the boy; it was simply a question of when.

The two men worked in companionable silence until a knock on the door disturbed them. They looked up to see Cade standing there with a smile.

"Lunch is ready in the kitchen, chaps. Chicken cacciatore, French bread and a good glass of Chianti waiting for you." He disappeared down the staircase, the two men hot on his heels, stomachs grumbling. They all sat around the kitchen dining table and tucked into Cade's signature dish as they conversed about business, Cade's work and the general state of the nation.

Finally Jomo sat back with a satisfied smile. "That was wonderful. You are indeed a great cook. I shall need to give Ulinda that recipe and she can cook it for me."

Ulinda was Jomo's new girlfriend, whom he'd known for around three weeks. She was a tall, slim and very lovely professor of literature at Cambridge University and he was totally smitten with her.

Quinn grinned. "Knowing Ulinda, she'll tell you to cook it yourself. She's a very independent-minded individual."

Jomo chuckled, a deep belly laugh that made the walls reverberate. "You are probably right. But I know the way to her heart, so I think she might make an exception for me."

"What's the way to her heart then?" Cade asked curiously. Quinn laughed out loudly and Jomo regarded him loftily.

"Ignore him. He is a peasant in the ways of romance. I sing to her. She enjoys the sound of my lovely baritone voice as I belt out tunes from the past. It always puts her in the mood."

"God, Quinn can hardly hold a tune in the shower, let alone belt one out to me!" Cade sounded envious. "I think that's a wonderful story."

Jomo laughed as he stood up. "I am glad you appreciate it. When I told Quinn here about it, he laughed so hard he nearly fell off his chair."

Quinn snorted into his wine but when Cade looked over, he gazed at him innocently, amusement in his eyes. Jomo waved at them both with a hand that looked like a garden spade.

"Thank you for lunch. I am going to get back to the files upstairs so I can get out of here before my date with Ulinda. Your man is such a hard taskmaster. He has no idea how to relax on a weekend."

Jomo left the kitchen and Cade looked over at Quinn.

"I'm so glad he's back. He's almost like the old Jomo now. You're doing a good job with him."

Quinn nodded. "It's the least I can do." He smiled at Cade as he drew him closer. "That was a great meal. I'm glad you're living here now. I love having you around."

Cade kissed his neck. "I'm enjoying being here with you too. I'm also enjoying finding out more about my origins. It's fascinating. You and Taliesin are a font of knowledge."

True to his word, Quinn had been helping Cade discover more about himself. Not as much as his Withinner would have liked, but Quinn was determined to take it slowly. He looked at Cade. "Any plans for swimming today? I know the heath pools are too cold but I wondered if you were going to the swimming pool. If you are, would you post a letter for me on your way?"

Cade nodded. "I'm going later, and yes, I'll post your letter. Pop it in my jacket pocket when you bring it down." He started to clear up the dishes and Quinn stood up to help.

Cade waved him away. "You get back to work so Jomo can get off. I'll sort this out."

Quinn nodded. "I just need to get something out of the library. I'll be up there in a minute." He walked out of the kitchen.

Cade watched him go curiously. Quinn seemed to be spending a lot of time in his library lately, being very cagey about what he was doing in there. He'd told Cade he was busy cataloguing a very rare collection he'd recently purchased, but he had a sneaky feeling that was just a cover story. He laid the dishcloth down on the side of the sink and quietly followed him down to the basement. He watched as Quinn did his retinal scan, thinking not for the first time that it was a very extreme security measure. Cade knew

Quinn wanted to preserve his identity as a Warlock from outsiders but it seemed overkill to him.

As Quinn entered the room, he waited for him to disappear and then quietly followed him in, slipping through the open door just as it closed behind him. The library was an enormous room, close to ninety square feet, set on two levels, with gleaming cherry-wood bookcases and shelves running the whole surround of the room. A set of spiral stairs led up to the upper half. The floors were also cherry wood, with scattered tapestry rugs laid across and a magnificent wooden desk in the corner with a leather chair, where Quinn did most of his reading. It was a truly impressive sight and Cade had never seen such a luxurious collection of golden-edged tomes, old parchments and truly awe-inspiring books.

Because of the lack of natural lighting, the room was fitted with what looked like old-fashioned oil lamps, set at about two metre intervals along one wall where there was no bookcase. Instead below the lamps, at waist level, ran a cherry-wood shelf, about forty centimetres in depth, which held a variety of strange artefacts, sculptures and what Cade thought looked like treasure chests, due to their old and weather-beaten nature. Cade thought this room was incredibly atmospheric, and it suited his man with his traditional outlook, his love of old and beautiful things and his mystery. This was indeed the inner sanctum of a Warlock king.

Cade looked around puzzled, not seeing Quinn and started as he heard a low throat clearing from behind him. He turned guiltily to see Quinn standing behind him, a quizzical expression on his face.

"Was there something I could do for you?" he murmured. "Did you need a clean dishcloth perhaps?"

Cade scowled. "Don't be snarky. I was just wondering what you do in here all the time. Lately you spend a lot of time here."

"So you sneak in behind me like Marco Polo? I sensed you the minute you crossed the threshold." He moved toward Cade, eyes narrowed. "So, you want to see what I do down here." Quinn waved a hand around. "I buy them, keep them here, catalogue them, sell them at auctions, buy another one, and just generally absorb myself in the world of books. It's my other passion besides you."

"Did you ever find that rare volume you were looking for of the *Malleus Maleficarum?* I read in a newspaper article that you were looking for it." Cade wandered around, touching various things, picking them up and looking at them closely.

Quinn gazed at him in a way he hadn't before—watchful, careful and almost predatory. He shivered, thinking once again with resignation this was yet another side to his lover he hadn't met.

"I'm still hunting it. I'm close." He came over to him and drew Cade closer, his mouth taking his in a kiss that was hungry, proprietary and very sensuous. When he finally released him, Cade's body was craving to do more and he wondered for a moment whether he'd ever made love to anyone down here before, even Adam.

"I've never made love to anyone down here," Quinn murmured quietly and Cade felt a sense of unease that he'd garnered his thoughts so accurately. "This is a sanctuary, not a bedroom. It's where I come when I need to escape some of the madness I have in here." He tapped his temple gently. "And there's a fair amount of it. I'm trying to share some of it with you but there are some things I'll never be able to tell you."

Cade watched his face, the expression of both love and regret plainly etched on it and he reached up and kissed him again.

"I do understand. Everyone has to have secrets. You more than most. As long as you share some of them with me so I can get to know you better, it's okay."

Cade moved away from him and idly walked over the desk, on which a huge book sat, opened on a page with what looked like a giant gold curtain tassel marking the place. He just had time to make out the rather intricately engraved words on the page before Quinn moved over quickly, almost guiltily and stood in front of the book as if he didn't want Cade to see what was in it.

A sudden wash of apprehension cascaded through his body. "Quinn? Why does that page say 'Sprite Binding Chant?' What exactly is that?"

Quinn looked at him carefully, his face expressionless. "It's just some research I'm doing to find out more about you. You asked me to tell you more about yourself and that's what I'm doing."

"I may not be a witch or a Warlock but I've watched *Charmed* and *Buffy* and I know a binding spell is normally when you want to stop someone using their powers."

Quinn shook his head in amusement. "God, you watch too many dodgy TV programmes. I promise you I've been reading up on everything I can find out about your kind. That just happens to be one page of many. I was interested to find out whether perhaps you've been bound before and that's why you can't remember anything. You said your mother died in childbirth. She must have had the Sprite blood in order to pass it down because it can only be done through females. I thought perhaps the binding chant might give me a clue where to start looking."

Cade's face cleared. "I see. And was there? Anything in the book about unbinding?"

Quinn shook his head. "I haven't found it yet. But I'll keep looking, I promise."

Cade nodded, satisfied. "Good. I really want to know all I can about me." He brushed his lips across Quinn's stubbled cheek. "Now I shall go see what Jomo's up to and let you get back to whatever it was you were so secretly doing."

Quinn watched as his boyfriend disappeared and breathed a sigh of relief.

I cannot believe you told such lies to Cade.

Taliesin's aggrieved voice echoed loudly through his mind and Quinn winced. His Withinner was very upset.

I have heard you talking to yourself about binding Cade and his powers. I stayed quiet as you have made it very clear it was not my place to get involved. I truly do not understand why you fear it so, Cade being able to find his true self. It is ungracious of you to even think of binding him. Then to lie like that, with such ease, it is truly not noble and does not befit your station as either a Fairmont or the Grand Master.

Quinn spoke angrily. "You said it. It's not your place to get involved. I have my own reasons for looking at that binding chant and not telling Cade everything too quickly. Please do me the courtesy of keeping your opinion to your self."

I have given you my thoughts, unwanted as they are. I still believe your intentions are selfish and do not have Cade's interests at heart.

"Then it's a pity you're the one that's not here, isn't it?" Quinn said silkily, his voice dangerous. "Now leave me be, so I can finish what I was doing."

Quinn sat quietly, looking through his ancient book of mystical chants and spells, a book he'd been bequeathed by his father. The words of his Withinner still smarted, not least because he'd asked himself a thousand times whether he was doing the right thing.

All Quinn wanted to do was protect Cade from the dangers he'd face if his true powers became known. It was why he'd really wanted him to move in.

As a Sprite healer, his powers would be in great demand and would be a draw for every crazy magyckal being out there to either steal them from him or steal Cade away from Quinn. He wouldn't risk either of those scenarios happening. The first one would mean Cade's death and the second would mean Quinn's. It might be a spiritual death if his lover disappeared but it was a death nonetheless. Not to mention the fact that he could be taken by force and he might never be able to find him. He'd done that once and had no expectations he'd be able to do it again easily. Cade had no idea just how vulnerable he'd become if he did begin to use the power he had inside.

What Quinn was, a Warlock and Grand Master, was a danger enough to Cade and recent events had borne that out. Quinn wasn't going to have double the trouble for them both. The binding spell was simply an idea, and he wasn't even sure he could do it himself. But he wanted the option in case things got out of hand. He sighed as he ran a hand through his hair.

Life had gotten more complicated since meeting Cade. He'd have it no other way but it gave him something and someone else to think about. He loved him deeply and wasn't prepared to even contemplate a world without him in it.

Quinn knew things would not remain the same as they were now, quiet and fairly angst free. He knew the storm clouds were building and that with the Witchfinder General being out there, with powers Quinn had never envisaged, he was going to prove a dark and dangerous enemy when he did resurface. At least with Cade close to him, under his protection where he could keep an eye on him, he would be safer than on the houseboat where it had already been proven people could get to him no matter what Quinn did to protect him.

Marcus Aurelius had said, "Accept the things to which fate binds you and love the people with whom fate brings you together but do so with all your heart."

Quinn fully intended carrying out his responsibility to his man, a man whom fate had seen fit to throw his way, and nothing would stand in his way. He had no idea what the future held but whatever it was, he'd be watching for it.

THE END

AUTHOR'S NOTE

I am lucky enough to live in a beautiful part of Essex where I have access to many scenic parts of the country. One of them is Mistley, which is mentioned in the book and is the supposed burial place of the Witchfinder General Matthew Hopkins. I visited the area on a day trip and fell in love with the solitude and quaintness of the place. Of course, the fact that it was an epicentre for witch hunting during the seventeenth century had its appeal as well. As a Wiccan myself, this is a fascinating—albeit bloody—part of history. I wondered what would happen if this rather famous and feared figure appeared in a contemporary setting and played havoc with modern men. Thus was the plot for *Double Alchemy* inspired, so if you are ever in this part of the country, this village is well worth a visit.

http://en.wikipedia.org/wiki/Mistley

ABOUT THE AUTHOR

Sue Mac Nicol was born in Leeds, Yorkshire, in the United Kingdom. At the age of eight she moved with her family to Johannesburg, South Africa, where she stayed for nearly thirty years before arriving back in the UK in December 2000. The first year Sue was back in the UK, it snowed on her birthday, as it did the day she was born in 19—*cough*—and she swears this was England welcoming her back.

Sue's career has mostly been in the financial services area, and she specialises in what she calls "boring" compliance and regulatory work. That's why she escapes into the world of writing and fantasy where she chats to her characters ad nauseum and is overjoyed when they reply. It beats the monotony of legalese, contracts and legislation; and let's face it, writing hot scenes between men can only be rewarding.

Sue's M/M Romance books, *Stripped Bare*, *Saving Alexander*, *Worth Keeping* and *Waiting for Rain* have all hit various bestseller lists, a fact that continues to awe and humble her. Sue is a PAN member of Romance Writers of America and a member of the Romantic Novelists Association in the UK. She lives in the quaint village of Bocking in Essex, set in the countryside and not far from the sea should she get the yen to eat oysters.

Did you enjoy this book? Drop us a line and say so! We love to hear from readers, and so do our authors. To connect, visit www.boroughspublishinggroup.com online, send comments directly to info@boroughspublishinggroup.com, or friend us on Facebook and Twitter. And be sure to check back regularly for contests and new releases in your favorite subgenres of romance!

Are you an aspiring writer? Check out www.boroughspublishinggroup.com/submit and see if we can help you make your dreams come true.

Made in the USA
San Bernardino, CA
01 May 2014